SPHINXES

A Novel By

James Patterson

ISBN: 1-4140-2475-4 (e-book)
ISBN: 1-4140-2474-6 (Paperback)

This book is printed on acid free paper.

1stBooks – rev. 01/08/04

Dedicated to Betty, my loving and patient wife for her encouragement
and inspiration
of a novelist who got started way past his time.

Thanks to Norman and Jo Anne Haddad for their editing and help
in improving the manuscript.

Thanks to Leah Odden for her help with my
French translations.

September 2003

The Sphinx:

Keeper of Ancient Egypt's secrets.

The symbol of the secretive Counterintelligence Corps of the United States Army.

A gold and purple sphinx adorned the campus of the CIC's training school at Fort Holabird, Maryland, in the 1950s and 60's.

Prologue

Little would prepare Five Lowrey for his arrival as a freshman at Ohio University. Armed with undeveloped talent, unbridled enthusiasm, and uncovered naïveté, Thomsen Lowrey V blunders through his first semester to gain notoriety on the Athens campus.

With only one hometown friend on campus, Five is thrown into university life without a clue of a goal. That changes rapidly as his penchant for drawing brings him early campus recognition, rare for a freshman.

He discovers drinking beer, eating pizza, a unique moneymaking scheme and above all, a wonderful variety of girls.

His love affair with Darcy Robinette leads to even greater recognition and leads to his first conflict between life and love. When fraternity rush rolls around, Five goes along with the crowd and finds himself a member of The Thirteen, the pledge class of Alpha Chi Epsilon.

The ACE pledge class moves from early euphoria to depths of despair as their pledgeship reveals some of the harsher aspects of brotherhood.

Five's role in this story of changing college life in the Fifties brings him into the realms of Korean War veterans, secret society intrigue, modern art and ultimately, vengeance for a murder that he and his pledge brothers seemingly cannot prove.

From *The Thirteen* by James Patterson <www.1stbooks.com>

And now, life continues for Five Lowrey in the pages of

Sphinxes

1: Welcome Home Sailor

1958 wasn't such a hot year. My four years at Ohio University seemed to have fluttered by like a drunken hummingbird. After a chaotic first two years, I settled into the average student's routine of trying to make classes, make grades, make out and make myself occasionally drunk. My painting partner and muse, Culden Ellis, graduated in my junior year, went off to grad school in the northeast, and took my intensity for work with her.

Indifference toward my fraternity, classes and university routine was relieved only during vacations when I crewed on Ohio River towboats. Before our senior year, my girlfriend and pinmate Andy Logan tearfully told me of her decision to transfer to the University of Florida so that "we could find ourselves." I wandered through that last year with a steadily falling GPA and had to scramble to finish a desultory painting that was accepted as a required graduation project.

As graduation neared, I interviewed for several high school teaching jobs, then ignored the offers that came in. My late applications to graduate schools were unanswered on that June morning when I marched under the elms to graduate with the Class of 1958.

And so I find myself on the Texas deck of the *Aspinwall Victory*, a barge hand again and wondering if I should've ever gone to college in the first place. But the power of the Ohio River to revitalize me was working and once more I had my sketchbook out, capturing the scenes along the river between Pittsburgh and Cincinnati.

One September afternoon, the *Victory* eased into Lock 19 and I waved good-bye to Captain Lowell Manders in the pilothouse, off for a

1

week's furlough. To my surprise, it wasn't Mom at the top of the embankment but Sissy Eileen, looking grown up and very womanly with a Chi O pledge pin on her maturing bosom.

"Hey Five, welcome home," she cried with a big hug. "There's so much news. I don't know where to start."

"Start by taking me home and telling me that Mom baked an apple pie," I said, returning her hug.

"Pie's waiting and the Bear got drafted by the New York Giants and Darcy's on the cover of *Harper's Bazaar* and I, er, we got a letter from Andy and she's going to Europe to teach and I pledged Chi O and you've got a letter from the draft board," all in one breath, "and Jack Gestner's home on leave and I'm going to the movies with him and the Captain'll be in tonight and we've got a new car."

Indeed, a shiny white on red '58 Chevy hardtop waited in the parking lot. As I slung my duffel into the back seat, I noticed OU, Chi O and ACE decals on its rear window.

"Mom lets you drive this?" I asked Eileen as she slid behind the wheel.

"Oh, yeah, isn't it cool? Won't I be hot shit when I get to take it up to Athens?" I was impressed as she eased the new car out of the parking lot instead of burning rubber as I would have as a college freshman. "I wish it were a convertible," she chortled.

Eileen chattered on as she drove us home to Hockingport. "Wait'll you see Darcy's cover. And she's on four pages inside."

My heart flopped as I thought about Darcy Robinette, my first love from OU four years ago, and her rise to the top as a fashion model. Just about the time the memory of her would almost fade away, her face would appear in some magazine (usually Mom's or Eileen's) and memories of those sweet months would coming roaring back.

"And you should see Gestner. He's got a tattoo and a mustache and a body. God, he's got a body. He says he's a 'lifer' in the Navy and he's been to so many neat places."

She didn't shut up until Mom came out the door and gave me a big hug, shushing her daughter with a wave.

"Five, look how brown you are. And you've gained a couple pounds," Mom exclaimed. "Are you drinking too much beer or is the food on the *Victory* that good?"

2

Over warm pie, I listened to the continued chatter of the two Lowrey women. My Dad, Thomsen Lowrey IV, would be home tonight when the *Triangle Queen*, his new boat, docks in Pomeroy for a two-day off-loading. We call him The Captain and he is, now senior captain of the entire Valley Barge Line.

Girl talk is interrupted by loud footsteps on the porch, then insistent knocking, then the door bursting open to reveal my high school buddy Joe Gestner. "Five, I'll be damned," he laughs, "now we're both sailors!" Gestner gives me a knuckle-crushing handshake and a hearty punch on the shoulder. "Hi, Sissy, how ya doin?"

"It's Eileen, Joe," she says coldly.

Talk turns to the Navy and Joe's travels. Hong Kong. Yokohama. Singapore. Hawaii. Hating to be shut out, Eileen chirps, "Five, my big sister is the neatest girl. Susie Lampson. Do you remember her?"

Before I can reply, Mom reappears with two envelopes and the copy of *Harper's* with a cover photo of Darcy in a black gown getting out of a yellow taxi. "Here's your mail, Five," she says softly. "The magazine's mine but…"

"And the letter from Andy was inside the one she sent me," Eileen adds. "As you can see, I didn't open it."

I peel open the small envelope and remove the folded sheet of note paper.

Dear Five,

Well, that's it for college. Got my BFA and a whole bunch of job offers to teach art down here. Florida really needs teachers but they pay absolute crap. Even Athens High would be better.

So I've signed up with American Field Service and will be part of their Exchange Teacher Program — somewhere in Europe, I hope. I'd like to see some of the works of those great masters in person rather than from Dad's slide show. I'll be home for about a week in early October, then on to Washington for training. Then who knows?

Gainesville has been a pretty neat experience. UF's a lot bigger than OU but their football team is just about as bad. Plus it's so terribly hot and everyone dresses to the nines for the games. How silly (and sweaty)!

3

Don't think I haven't spent plenty of nights wondering whether I made the right decision when I transferred down here. Time will tell, I guess. Sigh!

Please come and see me while I'm in Athens, if you can. And at least stop by to say hi to Mom and Dad. Take care of yourself.

Love, Andy

P.S. I heard from the grapevine that Sissy went Chi O. That's great news. The Chi O's down here don't match up to our chapter in Athens. Tell Sissy to watch out for the Aces.

I folded the note and thought to myself about Andy's decision. Was it the right one? Time will tell? Then my eye caught the next envelope in my tiny pile, the ugliest envelope I'd ever seen... from the Athens County Draft Board.

Greetings From Your Neighbors... it began and went on to tell me the deadline for extending my student deferment was long past.

I groaned. "I've got to report for pre-induction on November 2."

Gestner's reaction was immediate. "God Five, join the Navy. See the world." Eileen elbowed him in the ribs after one glance at my stricken expression.

Welcome home, sailor!

The weekend blurred by with a rattle of unending conversation. I can't remember the Lowreys ever having so much to say to each other.

"I sympathize with your predicament, son," the Captain said. "You've gotta choice to make and it looks like going back to school is not one of 'em. And you'd rather be a barge hand than teach art... where was it, Middleport High?"

"If you can't do, teach!" I responded. "And it's been pretty clear in the past two years that my ability to do hasn't been growing," I moaned.

"Five, it's not like you to feel self-pity," Mom chimed in. "I know you were blue about breaking up with Andy but you *did* date some nice girls last year. And your senior project painting *was* really quite good."

"I don't want to hurt your feelings but, as an art critic, you're still my mother. Also… I think Doctor Logan would've accepted that piece of crap just because he was sorry for me."

While Eileen and Gestner made eyes at each other all weekend, I spent my time studying the *Harper's* with Darcy's photos and thinking of her… rereading Andy's short note and thinking of her… and staring at the homely draft board envelope and thinking of nothing useful.

On Monday morning, our family group piled into the new Chevy and headed for the lock to let Captain meet his boat. We then dropped Mom off at her job at the paper and just out of Hockingport, I slid over to let Eileen take the wheel and drive us to Athens.

Car and mouth both going fifty five, she continues her breathless monologue — classes, parties, rush, Chi Os, dates, on and on. I am near to drowsing when she says, "I got a letter from Darcy." I respond with silence.

"She heard about you and Andy breaking up. She wondered why you never answered any of her letters?"

"Darcy's ancient history, Sissy." For once she doesn't correct me for our childhood nickname.

"Oh, Five, aren't you just the big man of mystery? Darcy. Andy. Everyone I've talked to at the ACE house. What's with you? You're too damn young for, for… menopause!" She giggles although I can see she's sore at me.

"I don't know, Eileen… Sissy. After The Thirteen affair, I thought everything would pull back together. And it did, the rest of that year, sort of." I paused and she kept her eyes on the road.

"What happened your junior year?" she asked. "You and Andy seemed like such a great couple."

"Nothing happened. Nothing at all. And I guess that's part of it. Andy and I had a great time together. We were comfortable with each other… maybe too comfortable. Perhaps that's part of the problem.

"And with Culden gone, the studio seemed so empty. So did my brain. I just couldn't get into painting anything that interested me. And classes and Homecoming, J-Prom, all that stuff, just seemed like a repeat of the year before."

Eileen exhaled, "Whew, why does it take four years to get a degree? Didn't you feel like you were learning anything new?"

"Oh, yeah, electives were interesting. I liked art history. The journalism course I took. I even took a photography course in my senior year and really liked that. It just seemed as if... every blank piece of paper or canvas and the first pencil stroke was 'here we go again'.

"Then with Andy gone last year, I decided to really go out in a blaze. But a few dates with different girls and that feeling of repetition set in again. It was easier to just go to the library and look at magazines or hang around my empty studio."

What had started out as a festive ride had turned into a gloomy entrance to Athens. Still, Sissy Eileen's spirits picked up as we turned onto College Avenue. Headed toward the College Green, she honked the horn and waved to friends.

"I've got to stop by the Chi O house before we go to Scott," she said, pulling up to the curb across from the radio building. She honked again and waved at a group of girls on the Chi O steps. "Hey Five, come on and meet my big sister. She and her boyfriend just broke up and she's a great gal. You'll really like her."

So the little sister and her alumnus ghost brother trudged across the street. I said hi to some of the girls I knew, shook hands with Susie Lampson who really *was* cute and I *really knew* I'd like her. Then, her mission accomplished, Eileen headed back to the Chevy and we left for her dorm.

2: The Art Of Going Home

Dropping my sister and her laundry box at Scott Quadrangle, I circled the campus several times looking for a parking spot. Even though I'd been gone less than five months, OU and Athens seemed strangely different, diminished in scale. Students strolling or sitting on the warm afternoon grass looked younger and fresher.

I lucked out by Chubb Library and eased into a just vacated spot. As I walked by Studio Row, I noticed the door to my old studio was open and caught a glimpse of a pretty girl standing at an easel. I resisted the urge to drop in for a visit.

The Fine Arts Department seemed gloomier and also smaller. I caught a startled look from Jan Dabny as I walked by her office and entered the main office suite. The familiar odor of Gordon Logan's pipe smoke indicated the professor was in. I knocked gently.

"Five Lowrey, for God's sake, come in!" Logan was leaning back in his chair with a sheaf of loose drawings in his hand. "How are you son?" He leaned over and extended his hand. My mentor and good friend gave me a smile that was genuine, perhaps thinking he might have been my father-in-law as well.

"Hi, Professor Logan, it's good to see you."

"What brings you here?" he asked. "I thought by now you'd be off the boats and in a classroom somewhere… or maybe foxed some grad school into accepting you." There was a long pause. "I won't mince words Five. I didn't think you had much of a shot at grad school with your GPA. What was it? A 2.8?"

"Almost that, professor. I just couldn't see myself teaching a bunch of high school kids when my enthusiasm for art is what it is. And I did apply to a couple of graduate schools but too late. Carnegie said they'd put my application on their provisional list for next semester but that'll be too late."

"Too late for what, Five? It's never too late to continue learning."

"My student deferment's run out. I've got a date with the draft board in November."

"Oh, my, what are you going to do?"

"Not sure yet. My next stop's the draft board office. Maybe a couple of years in the Army might be the change I need."

"I can't entirely disagree with that. My time in the Army was the most exciting part of my life, except perhaps when Andy was born. Listen, I've got to make a quick phone call and then let's go over to Quick's for a cup of coffee. Smoke's gettin' too thick in here." I nodded OK and he continued, "I'll meet you in the hall."

In the hallway, I lit a Pall Mall and glanced into the Life Study classroom, which was empty except for Jan Dabny straightening easel benches. I could see the wall behind her, which held a charcoal drawing of Darcy when she had been a figure drawing model for Dabny. It was my drawing.

"Admiring your work, Five?" Dabny said, startling me. "Or something else? Come in here and look what I've got."

"Hi, Jan, it's great to see you." I stepped into the studio, dusty with conté crayon and charcoal. She gestured toward another wall and there was a giant poster of Darcy, nude, hands folded across her breasts and cropped just below her navel. A discrete logo was printed on the bottom. *Vogue.*

"Darcy sent it to me. It's her first *Vogue* assignment. I thought it would be an inspiration to students and to our models. Do you hear from her much?"

"Nope! Our paths have definitely parted." I stared at the photo in awe. "That's a terrific photo."

"It should be. It was shot by Richard Avedon. God, that angelic face," Jan said with an equal amount of awe. "That terrific little body. She's one of the great ones now… and to think she started right here."

A grunt from the door indicated that Professor Logan was ready. I made my good-byes to my old figure drawing teacher, took one last glance at Avedon's Darcy and we left the building.

The walk to Quick's Drugs was a short one, filled with small talk about Andy, her experiences in Florida and her future with American Field Service. As we walked up the three steps to Quick's front door, I saw Sergeant Bernie Kostic in the window booth. He gave me a small wave and Doctor Logan led me to the circular booth.

"Hey Sarge," I greeted him, "it's great to see you."

He grinned and pointed to his fatigue blouse. "Hi, Five, how are 'ya? And it's "sir" these days. I'm an officer again, even though it's only a First John."

"Geeze, a lieutenant. That's great. They re-commissioned you?"

"Yep. The ROTC Department's in good hands again. And I guess the Army needs some extra leadership with things heating up in Indochina. But enough about me. The professor tells me you have a problem." So that was the professor's telephone call.

I explained my draft board situation and my lack of a deferment-qualifying job.

"Well, this is a biased opinion but I'll give you the same advice as I gave Joe." Benjamin Josefus "Benjo" Kostic was my fraternity pledge brother and the strategic brains of our embattled pledge class.

Lieutenant Kostic continued. "The Army's not a bad place... if you're not an infantryman. And three years may seem like an eternity from this vantage, but it's not really a very big chunk of your life."

"Three years?" I exclaimed. "I thought the draft was for two years."

"So it is. And it's the direct route to a bunker on the DMZ or somewhere even more unpleasant. An enlistment is for three years and you can enlist for the specific branch or duty of your choice. That's what Joe did."

"Benjo's in the Army? No shit?" Both men grinned.

"Yessiree. He's Private Benjamin Kostic right this moment, with three weeks to go of Basic Training at Fort Campbell."

"And then what?"

"Well, that's what I wanted to tell you about. The Army has a mission that you're tailor-made for. It's called the Counterintelligence

9

Corps or CIC. And it's a good deal. As a CIC agent, you'd in all likelihood work in civilian clothes and be called 'mister,' or at least wear an officer's uniform.

"Agents do investigative work and other, er, secret stuff and the Army only accepts college graduates who enlist for the duty."

"And that's guaranteed?"

"Sure is! Today's Army can't afford to break its promises. Talent is too hard to come by and the draft takes care of the other branches' basic needs. Unless you fuck up somehow," an embarrassed nod to Doctor Logan, "go AWOL or get thrown in the stockade for some crime, you'd go to the Army Intelligence School and then get assigned... chances are to some college town to run investigations out of a local office."

"So I'd be like a spy for the Army?"

"We joke about 'em as spooks but yes, in a nutshell, that's what you'd be."

"It sounds like it'd be exciting."

"It's the Army, Five. It's 90 percent boredom and the ten percent of excitement happens infrequently. At least in the CIC, the excitement wouldn't be in a fighting hole with shrapnel flying overhead."

Two cups of coffee and five cigarettes later, I left Quick's, my mind aswirl with new ideas and headed down for a visit with the ladies at the draft board office.

Later, as I drove out of Athens, I realized I'd forgotten to stop in the Begorra for a burger and visit with Duff and hardly glanced at the window in the ACE house tower where my room had been just five months before.

3: Meeting Running Bear

Mom and the Captain wore skeptical frowns that evening as I told them about my day, my thoughts about enlisting in the Army and the new excitement that had come into my life.

"I just don't know about enlisting, Five," Captain said. "I was just a young ensign driving newly-launched LST's down the river from Sewickley to Cairo on the Mississippi during World War II but I can tell you being an officer beats hell out of enlisted life."

"Yeah, but Captain, if I enlisted for OCS, I'd just end up as an infantry lieutenant or something, leading a bunch of scared guys. I'm not ready to be a leader. I could've gone into teaching to do that."

"You're a grown man and of legal age, Five," Mom said with tears glistening. "And I think it might be good for you. But I'm glad I don't have to sign approval for you to do this." Captain nodded his agreement.

I smiled and added, "Lieutenant Kostic said he'd call down to Fort Campbell and arrange for Benjo to get out of training Saturday. I can ride the train down to Cincinnati and get down to Fort Campbell to hear what he has to say. I called Captain Manders and he said the *Victory'll* be a day out of Cincinnati Sunday morning. I can join them there.

"How about I do that before I make a decision?"

They both smiled weak agreement.

The B&O's National Limited arrived in Athens at midnight and gave me barely two minutes to shake hands with Lieutenant Kostic, take a box from him for Benjo and hop on my coach. Then the train glided westward through the night past Chillicothe, Midland City and finally Ivorydale before pausing, then backing up into Cincinnati Union Terminal. Walking out of the concourse, I gave the blue and gray observation car a last look and entered the mammoth vaulted cave of the terminal.

After a cleanup and quick breakfast, I found my gate and boarded the Louisville & Nashville with a round-trip fare to Fort Campbell. It was fun to look out the window at still-dark Cincinnati as the blue train took a broad curve and then followed the Ohio until it eased over the bridge into Kentucky.

Towboat searchlights pierced the glistening water below, which reflected the bridge's warning lights. I knew the bridge only as the "L&N Span" and had been under it several times.

The L&N train was neither as fast nor comfortable as the B&O's and we made endless long stops at tiny stations along the rolling Kentucky right-of-way. After a dry tuna sandwich and a warm Coke, I drifted off to the rocking motion and awoke to daylight only when the vestibule door opened and the conductor called "Clarksville. Clarksville, Tennesseeeee. Next stop."

The Clarksville station was bustling with soldiers in dress uniforms and what I would later learn were called fatigues. I headed for the street, pausing at a small stall that said *military transportation.*

"Goin' to the main post, young troop?" a soldier asked as he passed by with a monster duffel bag on his shoulder. Without waiting for my answer, he strode off with a "follow me" order. I dutifully followed through the crowd to a bus stop.

"Never been here before?" he asked, dropping the duffel to the sidewalk where a sign read "Dime Bus: Main Post." He nodded at the sign and said, "Well, this old school bus beats hell out of the six bucks a cab'll cost you."

When the decrepit bus, indeed an olive drab painted school bus, pulled up, I followed the GI into the line and up the bus steps. Painted over the door was "Fare 10¢" and I had my dime in my hand. When I reached the driver, he indicated to drop my dime in the fare box and asked, "Where's your ID, soldier?"

I whipped out my driver's license. "No, no. Your military identification."

Dumbly, I nodded comprehension. "I don't have one. I'm not in the Army."

"Well, what in hell are you getting on this thing for?" he responded.

"I'm just visiting, er… Fort Campbell."

The crowd of GIs in seats and behind me in line roared with laughter.

"Aw, shit!" the driver said with a grin, "get on. No one's going to stop us at the main gate. Just visiting. I'll be goddammed."

Clarksville's main street was lined with tailor shops, pawnshops, bars, strip joints and populated with jeeps with "MP" painted on them. The bus wound through some scrubby countryside. At first glance, Fort Campbell was a pretty shoddy looking place. Sure enough, the guards at the gate waved us through and we passed beneath an arch reading "101st Airborne. Home of the Screaming Eagles." I was on my first Army post.

The driver let me out at the Main Post Exchange to a chorus of jeers from the rest of his passengers. "Come and visit again! Would you like to see where I live?"

I walked toward the doors of the big PX and was once again confronted by the question of ID, this time a sign informing me I *must* have military identification to enter. At a loss, I loitered outside the door as soldiers, women, little kids and teenagers went in and out. I almost jumped out of my skin when an iron grip froze my bicep.

"You look like your poor civilian ass is lost, old buddy."

I whirled and there stood Benjo Kostic, dressed in olive drab fatigues and wearing one of the flat-topped hats that was obviously part of the uniform. We pounded each other in delight, then stepped back to examine the other.

"Lookin' pretty fit, Five. And your suntan and that shirt sure as hell didn't come from a PX." Benjo grinned, took off his hat and wiped his hand across a nearly bald head.

"Christ, Benjo. What've they done to your hair?"

"Standard issue GI haircut, Five. Takes two minutes and costs a buck a minute. C'mon, let's go over to the beer garden and get a cold one. It'll be the second beer I've had in six weeks."

The beer garden turned out to be a big barn of an Army building, full of smoke and soldiers. Two jukeboxes, each playing Johnny Preston's "Running Bear," competed with each other out of synch. The place was filled with an uproar of soldiers singing and clanking their beer

13

cans to the chorus, *"Running Bear loved Little White Dove... with a love as big as the sky... "*

"Not quite The Keep is it, Five?" Benjo screamed above the cacophony as he barged into the crowd at the bar. Indeed, it was a scene that could've never been imagined at the Alpha Chi Epsilon house. Soldiers celebrated finishing a beer by mashing the empty cans against their foreheads.

We found a pair of seats at a table as far from a jukebox as possible. "What the hell is that song?" I screamed.

"Number one on the Fort Campbell hit parade. That sonofabitch'll play all day unless someone plunks in a nickel for 'Alley Oop.' If we stick around long enough, someone will break in with some shit by Peggy Lee and then there'll be a fight."

Before we'd finished our first beer, one of the jukeboxes did indeed play 'Alley Oop' and half the room echoed with hoots of *"Oop, oop, oop"* against the chorus of *"umpha, umpha, umpha"* of the Running Bear crowd. Talk was impossible. We drained our beers and Benjo led the way out.

We walked through the immaculate grounds of the main post and sat on a bench beneath a statue of a soldier in parachute gear. Benjo accepted a Pall Mall from my pack and we lit up.

"So... you're gone for a soldier, eh Five?"

"Might be if you can tell me something about it... and this CIC stuff."

"The Army's not a bad life, I guess. At least basic hasn't been that tough. The ACE house helped get me ready for all the bullshit in basic. If you just think of it as a 56-day hell week, it's even kind of fun."

"Fun? You mean push-ups and harassment?"

"Oh, yeah. But it's a lot of great kid stuff, too. Firing rifles... never a gun, Five... with live ammunition. And throwing grenades, real grenades that blow the shit out of stuff. Crawlin' through the mud and under barbed wire on the combat range," he paused. "Scary but fun too, if you keep your cool and a sense of humor. Just like being a pledge again."

I wanted to get to the point of my trip. "What about the CIC, though?"

"Aw, that comes later. Basic is simple, just like pledging ACE. It's designed to teach you the lore... in this case general orders... and military customs... saluting and all that. And their goal is to break down your ability to think independently... blind obedience to orders, that's it.

"It's all to get a soldier ready to go to school. In the case of eight out of ten of these poor ignorant fuckers, that'll be Advanced Infantry School. That's where the kid stuff, shooting and bayonets and grenades, becomes pretty serious business.

"For me, it'll be Fort Holabird in Baltimore and I'll say good-bye to all this chickenshit."

I flipped my cigarette butt into the grass and Benjo leaped up in alarm. "Christ Five, don't you know anything?" He retrieved the butt and ground it out on the sole of his shiny boot, then carefully tore the remaining paper and made a tiny ball, scattering the tobacco to the wind.

"If you don't field-strip a smoke, you'll get KP for a week." He grinned, "I don't know what they'd do to a civilian, probably the firing squad." And so I learned my first customs of the United States Army: field stripping cigarettes and mashing empty beer cans on my forehead to the tune of "Running Bear."

4: A Through M Left Line And Drop Your Drawers

Back in Cincinnati after a train ride that seemed twice as long, I rode the bus down to the Valley Barge Line offices on the river and sacked out in the transient quarters for a restless night's sleep.

The next morning, I boarded the *Victory* and became a bargehand again. Short hauls for the *Victory* between Cincinnati and Ashland, Kentucky, meant it was nearly three weeks before we got upriver as far as Hockingport.

By that time, I had bored the entire crew with my constant talk about the Army and the CIC. It all seemed so exciting compared to the slogging life of a barge hand and I'm sure Captain Manders was glad to see me step off the deck for the last time.

My trip to Athens to see the Army recruiter was uneventful except for a worrisome moment when he couldn't seem to find the Counterintelligence Corps mentioned in any of a huge stack of loose-leaf career notebooks. After discovering the pertinent records and reading it, he exclaimed, "Man, Lowrey, that sounds like a good deal."

The recruiter seemed amazed when I finished the 150-question eligibility test. And even more so when he graded it and found I'd only missed two questions. I signed the necessary papers and three days later was on a bus for Columbus and the Army Induction Center. I was truly *gone for a soldier.*

16

After a half-day's indignity of the pre-induction physical, I began to appreciate Lieutenant Kostic's statement about 90 percent boredom. There was a lot of humor in the scene. Guys with ducktail haircuts standing naked didn't look half so tough as they did in their Cleveland hood clothes. A skinny, short little guy got a lot of notice because of the inordinate size of his organ.

A mean looking older man, with tattoos on his arms, chest and calves turned out to be a 12-year Navy vet who was trying the Army "because I couldn't make it on the outside."

Finally our motley group stood in five loose rows, raised our right hands and swore our oath to "protect the Constitution." With the final "so help me God" uttered, we were soldiers and I had a strong feeling that God's help might be needed in the weeks to come.

The rest of the day was more boredom, sitting around as each of us was called to be given a big manila envelope and a copy of our orders. Then we were herded downstairs to the sidewalk, where names were called and groups were made up. An Army bus pulled up and the biggest chunk of our group boarded and trundled off.

I had assumed I would be going through basic training with this bunch of recruits, but in short order, I was alone on the sidewalk in the company of a tired-looking Specialist 4.

"Well shit," he muttered. "Which bus were you supposed to be on, asshole?"

"No one called my name, sir."

"Spec 4 Hooly, shitbird. Not sir. Let's see your orders."

Spec 4 Hooly compared my orders with his clipboard, cursed some more and headed for the front door of the induction center. "Stay right here, Lowrey. Do not move! If you're gone when I get back, you're AWOL. Understand?"

A half hour passed with no sign of Hooly. Then a cab pulled up and the cabby yelled, "You the guy for Port Columbus?"

"I don't know, sir. I'm supposed to wait here for the Spec 4 to return."

"Well hell. If you wait here you're going to miss your plane. I'll wait here two minutes while you go find this spec guy."

I raced up the stairs to the now empty induction center. A girl sat at a desk in the lobby area, looking startled when I burst in. "Where's Specialist Hooly?" I gasped.

"Oh... Hooly went home. What's your problem?" Then she glanced at the big manila envelope on her desk. "Are you Recruit Lowrey?" I nodded. "Hooly called a cab and then left you standing down there? What a numbnuts!"

She thrust the envelope at me. "Hurry! American Airlines to Columbia, South Carolina. God, it leaves in 30 minutes."

Another fact learned about the Army. Hurry up and wait or wait and hurry up.

I'll gloss over the 90 percent of the next three weeks. You've got it: boredom.

My first airliner ride introduced me to the barf bag as the American DC-3 lurched its way over the Appalachians. Landing in Columbia, I was herded into an olive drab bus with a group of guys just like the ones I left at the induction center and we were driven through some piney woods to Fort Jackson.

There, we were met by a trio of NCOs with clipboards and very loud voices. "Fall in you shitbirds," the guy with the stripes screamed. Some of us looked around for something to fall into but two specialists rapidly formed us up into two lines.

Thanks to Benjo's advice, my personal possessions were toiletries, cigarettes and a paperback copy of "From Here To Eternity," all in a small cloth ditty bag. Some of my companions were ordered to turn over their suitcases, footlockers, guitars and other gear to one of the Spec 4s and get a receipt. The whole cadre broke up at the sight of one guy lugging his bowling ball.

We were given a 'left face,' a maneuver that caused the sergeant near apoplexy and then marched in a fearful shuffle into the maw of the Army.

A week later, I had been paid eleven dollars for two official days in the Army, shorn for two bucks, issued a half-ton of gear which I had to sign for and marched off to a PX and ordered to buy Brasso and a Blitz cloth, shoe polish, safety razor, bowl of shaving soap and a brush and some other crap. With my remaining 45 cents, I bought three packs of Pall Malls.

Our group was then marched to a barracks area where another NCO called names from a clipboard and sent each recruit to a squad. 'Lowrey' was not one of the names called and I was ordered to find the *repple depple* and settle in. I asked a kindly looking specialist what a *repple depple* is.

"Replacement depot, dumbass," he growled.

Two other recruits occupied bunks in a 24-bed barracks that must've been built in World War I. They sat dejectedly on footlockers in front of their beds. I selected a cot, dropped my duffel and began to sit on an empty bunk.

"Hey, don't sit on the bed," one guy yelled at me. "There's a little cocksucker lurking around who'll make us sweep and mop this joint... again."

Shortly the aforementioned cocksucker appeared, a PFC France, who demanded my orders. "OK, Lowrey. Go to the quartermaster shed and draw your bedding. You'll be here for awhile since you missed your training cycle."

Benjo's admonition to not ask, just obey, worked until France screamed at me, "I didn't say *walk* to the quartermaster shed asshole. Double time it." I ran out of the barracks into a misty gloom and realized I didn't have the slightest idea where the QM shed was.

Once I found it, I was sent back to get a requisition chit from PFC France, who yelled at me for taking so long. Finally, I staggered in with a pillow and case, two sheets, an OD blanket and two towels.

France gave the *repple depple* trio a brief lesson in how to make a tight bunk, how to fold our gear in the footlocker, how to build a footlocker tray display and a couple of dozen other things I didn't remember the next morning.

And that was the excitement part!

5: Welcome To The Queen Of Battle

The excitement quota for the next twenty days ran about two percent. That included a train ride down to Atlanta. Coffee and donuts at Atlanta station with a flirty USO girl. An even slower train ride from Atlanta to Columbus, Georgia. The PFC driving the bus from the station to Fort Benning points and says, "See that chick there? That's Brenda Lee. She lives here."

And we arrive at another Army post, this one's sign declaring "Fort Benning: Queen Of Battle," meaning the infantry obviously as there's a big statue of a doughboy titled "Follow Me."

At the reception center, I handed over my envelope and join a hundred or so other new recruits who, as it turns out, are members of my basic training company. At long last, the Army has found someone who could read my orders and got me to where I was supposed to be.

We fall in on the sidewalk outside the reception center and watch while a jeep followed by four OD trucks roll up. A big, graying sergeant steps out of the jeep. His stripes are many and there's a diamond over his rockers.

"I am First Sergeant Gornochek of Infantry Training Company B, 21st Engineering Battle Group, Second Infantry Division. Welcome to Fort Benning and the Infantry... Queen of Battle. One of these four sergeants here will be your platoon leader. As your name is called, step forward and fall in." He surveys our group with a slow turn of the head,

20

his expression is one of having just been served a plate of bad oysters. "Sergeant Teasdale, call the First Platoon."

A very tall, very thin black sergeant steps forward and stares at us with hooded eyes. His voice rumbles deeply. "Blessing, Glen. Cantrell, John. Dubois, Alvin." Someone titters and Teasdale rumbles, "Quiet in the ranks."

He continues down his list. "Moran, Charles. Nelson, Dewildus." A pause. "Dewildus?" A chubby little black soldier squeaks, "Yessir. Dewildus."

Teasdale continues his list and then, "Lowrey, Thomsen."

I step forward and say, "That's Lo-ree, Sergeant."

Teasdale's eyes seem to spark as he glares at me. "Did I ask you, Recruit Lowrey?" pronouncing my name correctly.

"No."

"No, Sergeant." He corrects me, spins and salutes the first sergeant and says, "First Platoon, presented and accounted for."

The first sergeant replies, "Mount 'em up, Sergeant." We board a truck which we'll soon learn is a deuce and a half and roll off to Sand Hill.

We stack our duffels and fall in before a wooden barracks, not unlike several others I've occupied in the past weeks. But this one isn't a repple depple. It's the home of First Platoon, Company B, 21st of the Second… whatever that means.

Sgt. Teasdale looks us over and then unleashes his bass drum voice. "How many of you young soldiers have graduated from high school?" About two-thirds of the group raise their hands, including me of course. Teasdale frowns.

"Any of you gone to college?" One of Benjo's pearls of wisdom was 'never volunteer' but this is a direct question, so I raise my hand… along with three others. Teasdale slowly glides along our ranks, making tick marks on his clipboard as he reads our name tapes.

"Blessing, Dubois, Cantrell and Lowrey. Follow me into the barracks. At ease in the ranks. Smoke 'em if you've got 'em." We hurry along in the sergeant's long strides and into our home at the Mother of Battle.

"All right, troops. Let's see what we have here. Blessing! Where you go to college... and how long?"

"Kentucky Wesleyan, Sergeant. I, ah, attended for two years."

Teasdale nods to Dubois. "Tulane, Sergeant. To be honest, I flunked out after my second semester."

"To be honest is a good thing," Teasdale intones. "A very good thing. And you?" he looks at his clipboard. "Cantrell?"

"University of Florida! I, ah, did not matriculate, also," he says with a shy grin.

"How long did you last, Cantrell? That's a fine old military name."

"I, er, did not return for my second semester... freshman year."

Teasdale's eyes roll up 'til he looks like a zombie. He lets out a long sigh. "OK, and you recruit, Lowrey. Tell me you lasted more than a month."

"Well, yes Sergeant. Ohio University. I, er, graduated."

"You got a degree? What major?"

"A Bachelor of Fine Arts, Sergeant Teasdale."

This was followed by the zombie look again.

"Well troops, you are my leadership cadre, like it or not. Lowrey, you're obviously senior so you'll be the First Squad Leader and acting Recruit Platoon Leader until you screw up or I decide otherwise. Dubois, you'll take Second Squad. Cantrell, Third Squad, and Blessing, Fourth Squad.

"First and third squads will bunk on this floor. Second and fourth on the upper floor. Keep your squads separated by the aisles. You squad leaders will bunk in this little room at the end of the bay. As we say, rank has its privileges."

He pointed out a door opposite our little room. "This is my office. I'll sleep here some nights. Other nights, I'll go home to my family. That'll be when your butts are on the line. You'll be in charge."

With those long cat-like strides, he started down the empty barracks. "Follow me. Let's get this platoon organized."

Teasdale calls "Ten'hut!" and the First Platoon snaps to some semblance of upright posture, many of the recruits dropping smoldering cigarettes to the ground. Teasdale doesn't seem to take notice.

"Count off by fours," he orders and the basic training begins. "All you soldiers who're ones, grab your gear and follow First Squad Leader Lowrey into the barracks."

I lead my new squad into the barracks and tell them to pick a bunk and drop their duffels. I can hear my fellow squad leaders directing their troops up the stairs, then Cantrell brings his third squad in. They drop their gear and mill around for a few seconds when a whistle blows outside. "Fall in! Fall in!" Teasdale's voice booms.

We pour out of the barracks and line up in four rows, me on the left of the front row with my squad beside me. The last guy out of the barracks is Dewildus Nelson who falls flat as he tumbles down the stairs.

"While you're down there, troop, give me twenty," Teasdale calls out. Nelson looks up with a puzzled expression. "Twenty push-ups, recruit. Right now!" And Dewildus Nelson begins the process of losing 25 pounds.

Next we get the lecture and demonstration on field stripping cigarettes and littering.

"Now that we all understand," Teasdale says, "we shall now police the area. This means lining up in a long row and picking up every bit of unnatural material in your path. He double-times us to the wall of the next barracks and we start to police.

I don't immediately appreciate the fact that policing an area is one of the few times in basic training when we can enjoy the luxury of moving slowly and out of step.

6: Happy As The Day

When the Army gets its pay, according to the old song, is a time for celebration and wild ruckus. Not on Sand Hill where First Platoon, Company B, is finishing its fifth week of basic. I have 64 silver dollars and change and not a damn place to spend it other than the company's tiny shoe polish PX.

"I ask you, Acting Platoon Sergeant Five, what has Damballah told you about getting a pass out of this shithole?" The question comes from Bebop Moran, one of my First Squad troops. As everyone in the company does, he calls Teasdale "Damballah" after Dubois compared the sergeant with the voodoo god for his habit of silently appearing from nowhere.

"Bebop, we'll get to Main Post when the Army decides it wants us to go there." Moran's the squad's main bitcher, but as he's been in four different military schools as a "bad kid," he's a first-rate soldier.

"Man, I'd sure like a taste of a cold frosty one," John "Mad Jack" Cantrell tossed in. "Marching by that beer garden this morning almost made me go AWOL."

Our squads had been detailed to escort the paymaster up from Battle Group headquarters and marched off Sand Hill past the Company B beer garden where, of course, the sounds of "Running Bear" and clanking cans reached the road.

Now we're on our footlockers shining boots, polishing brass, smoking and bullshitting, another typical waste of Saturday afternoon "free time."

24

"Somethin' happened to me the other night, set me thinkin'," Dewildus Nelson said.

"Dewildus, everything happens to you sets you thinkin'," mimicked Bebop Moran without having to change his Mississippi delta accent. "What be de thought dis time?"

Everyone had taken to the shy, friendly Dewildus, now on his fourth pair of glasses in five weeks. It began when he related how he got his name. "My Daddy looked at me, dis' lil' ole bitty baby and says to my mamma, 'Ain't dat de wildus thing you ever see?' and my mamma say, 'Thas beautiful. We be namin' him Dewildus."

Barely able to reach the chin-up bar at the mess hall entrance, he had developed to the point where he could crack off a dozen chin-ups and go directly into the chow hall, not back to the end of the line to try again.

Dewildus brought his high school band skills to the Army and had started the First Platoon's "for fun" drill team and, we'd become so good we were ordered to perform at the graduation review for the training cycle ahead of us.

"Well, you know how I lost my glasses on guard duty at the motor pool 'n Porky Dubois marched the detail home widdout me?" We nodded at the memory. "Well, I got my black ass off the road before the MPs got me, snuck through the woods, and there I found de most amazin' thing."

At 2300 hours, the barracks was filled with snores, dream groans and flatulence. Cantrell and I walked silently through the bay and slipped into the latrine, where Bebop, Dewildus and Porky Dubois waited. To our best knowledge and highest hopes, Teasdale was home with his family.

We slipped down the steps into the silent platoon area. "Halt, who goes there?" was whispered at us by Glen Blessing, the platoon's fireguard for the night.

"Good friends," I whispered back. "Very good friends."

"Pass good friends. And bring me a cold one."

We slow-walked between our barracks and the one behind us, then through the light brush that bordered the ridge road above our area. The post has very little traffic three hours after lights out. Wearing my Platoon Leader brassard, I formed up my detail of four and we set off up the ridge road, me calling a quiet cadence.

As we neared the one intersection, I called "road guards out" and Dewildus and Bebop ran ahead to block the road. We "hup, two, ree, fo'd" through the intersection and I retrieved my road guards. One hundred yards later I called, *"columnnn right, harch"* and my four man detail performed a snappy right turn onto a path in dense woods.

The path led us to a clearing with a building from which came the smells and sounds of our mission. *"Detaillllll... halt."* Perfect halt and click of heels. "Fall out and let's dig in."

The smoky building, about half the size of a barracks, had a bar and a grill tended by a young soldier in fatigues and a GI chef's cap. He greeted us with a grin. "Welcome troops. You look hungry and thirsty and it's payday." A few soldiers at tables in the far end of the room paid us no attention.

"Is it OK?" I asked. "I mean... what is this place anyway?"

"We call it the Dark Angel Club. It's the EM club of the 22nd Antiaircraft Company... you know those mobile Nike missiles you see along Sand Hill Road? That's us, and I trust you guys are from next door. So long as you don't get drunk, don't start fights and don't get caught, your money's welcome." He paused and grinned again. "Cold beer?"

Specialist Herman handed over five icy Budweisers and took our orders for cheeseburgers with the works. The beer cost 30 cents a can instead of the usual quarter and cheeseburgers were 60 cents which, in my book, made the Dark Angel a pretty ritzy place.

Herman laughed as Dewildus described his journey through the 22nd's area and discovering the club. He laughed even more when he heard how we'd formed "The 2300 Drill Team" to look as legitimate as possible on our journey.

"I swear, you can get away with any kind of shit in this Army, so long's you look like you know what you're doin' and some silly asshole gave you the order to do it," he said, sliding steaming burgers across the counter.

Closing time was 2345 hours so we ordered a cheeseburger and a beer to go for Blessing. "Beer's against regs," he said with a grin, "but I guess everything you guys are doing is against regs. Don't get caught and ruin a good thing."

We formed up in front of the Dark Angel and my drill team did a snappy right face. I saluted Specialist Herman and we marched smartly into the woods. At the intersection, my road guards halted an MP jeep which dipped its light. I threw them a salute and we marched on undisturbed.

7: A Spooky Experience At Benning

Basic training at Sand Hill was almost exactly as if Benjo had written the script. The exciting things — firing live ammo, tossing live grenades, choking on live tear gas, a 20-mile forced night march, crawling under a hail of machine gun bullets on the combat obstacle course — were a kid's dream come true.

The other 90 percent of the time was plain old soldiering. Crappy details. Emptying butt cans. Early morning PT and two-mile runs. Trying to stay awake as nearly illiterate instructors read verbatim from their printed display boards in stuffy classrooms. Close order drill and rifle inspections. The blessed solitude of "smoke 'em if you got 'em" breaks.

The 2300 Drill Team visited the Dark Angel three more times without detection, although Sergeant Teasdale hinted on graduation day that he was aware of our "unauthorized nocturnal missions" and he "admired our display of initiative."

At the end of our seventh week, I was helping Dewildus put the finishing touches on our "fighting hole" in some swampy woods where we were on bivouac. Dewildus was at the bottom of the five-foot deep pit, enlarging the grenade sump. I lay on the edge of the hole dangling my helmet for him to fill with dirt, which I then had to scatter in the woods.

"Private Lowrey," a voice behind me said, "you're wanted at the CO's tent right now. Bring your gear." I grabbed my pack and rifle and followed the CQ through the woods.

"Private Lowrey reporting as ordered, sir," I rattled as I snapped my best salute to Captain Gale Gaston, the company commander.

"At ease, Private." I snapped to *at ease.* "I received a call that you're to report to the CID office at the main post. Any idea what this is about?"

"No sir. No idea at all, sir."

"Well, leave your gear in the CQ tent. They said you'd be back today. There's a jeep waiting for you at the road." He looked me over. "And brush yourself off a little. You don't look too bad for having been in the field. Dismissed."

I snapped to attention, threw another salute, did a very smart about face on the dirt floor of the tent and marched out.

A group of HQ loiterers stared as I climbed aboard the MP jeep and drove down the road with an MP specialist at the wheel.

"What's going on, Spec? Am I in trouble."

"Reckon so, troop. Got a couple of civilians waiting for you." We rode on in silence and my mind worked over the possibilities. *Something had happened to the Captain, Mom or Sissie? Who knows?*

Two guys in civvies stood up as I was led to a small room with a field table and three chairs. "Private Lowrey? I am Special Agent Frink and this is Special Agent Sartorious, Military Intelligence." He snapped open a leather case, flashed a set of credentials in my face, then snapped them back quickly. "Have a seat, Private."

Frink opened a file folder and withdrew a folded sheet of paper and handed it to me. "Is this your SPH, Private Lowrey."

I examined the sheet and recognized the *Statement of Personal History* form I had filled out and signed when I enlisted. "Yessir, that's mine."

"When you filled out this form, you signed it as a written oath that it was a truthful document. Is that correct... and do you understand?" I nodded yes. Agent Sartorious made a note in his pad.

"We are here as a part of the investigation of your background in order for you to be cleared for classified information. Some questions have arisen in the course of this investigation. Questions which must be answered by you. Truthfully! Do you understand?" I am dumbstruck. Again, I nod affirmatively. Sartorious scribbles.

"Private Lowrey, why did you fail to disclose your arrest in Athens County, Ohio, on 4 November 1956?" My jaw dropped. My mind went blank.

"Because... er, sir. I have never been arrested. Then. Or any time."
He looks into the folder and extracts another sheet and reads.

"Do you deny that you and twelve other people were detained on 4
November of '56 by the Athens County Sheriff's Department?" My mind
races back. *Of course.* The day we turned Galen Curtis over the to law
instead of leaving him to burn in the Sharpsburg Hell. The twelve
surviving members of our ACE pledge class... and Culden Ellis... spent
the rest of the day being questioned.

"No sir. I can't deny being detained. But I do not believe any of us
were arrested, except for Galen Curtis."

"And who is Galen Curtis?"

And so I spent the next two hours telling these two guys the story of
Galen Curtis, his attempted rape of Culden, his probable murder of Joe
Ransom. They kept asking questions about details. I was being
interrogated.

"Who is Asa Benquist?" *Asa Benquist? Who in hell is Asa Benquist?*
I shrug my shoulders.

"I don't know, Agent Frink."

"Do you deny that Asa Benquist called the Athens County Sheriff's
Department on the morning of 24 October, 1956, after you attempted to
break into his house?"

"Ohmygod, of course." And so I had to detail the night of our ill-
fated pledge ride again, identifying the farmer whose door we knocked
on to call an ambulance for Ransom.

"Why did you deny knowing who Mr. Benquist is?"

"I forgot his name. I'm sorry." *What a lame response that was.*

Some more scribbling by both. Frink shuffles through the file — *my
file* — again. Frink looked up and frowned. "Who is Darcy Robinette?"

"My girlfriend, er... my ex-girlfriend. In my freshman year."

"During what period of time did you know Miss Robinette?"

"Ah... from October of '54 to Easter of 1955."

"What was the nature of your relationship with Miss Robinette?"

"We dated. We kind of went steady. She moved to Cincinnati to
work."

"Did you have sexual relations with Miss Robinette?"

30

My temper and composure are going out the window. *What gives them the right? And why are they interested in Darcy?*

"Yes. We loved each other. We fucked like minks. Every chance we got. Does that satisfy you?"

"Why didn't you disclose in your earlier statement that you saw Miss Robinette again? To be exact, in September 1956?"

My God. These guys know everything. One night in Cincinnati. One magical night and now it's all turning to shit! Lamely I respond, "I forgot."

"To your best knowledge, Private Lowrey, is Miss Robinette a member of the Communist Party, or any other organization which advocates the overthrow of the lawful government of the United States?"

"She wasn't when I knew her. She was just a sweet little girl who loved me. What's this all about?"

"Remember, you are under oath, Private. Are you... or have you ever been... a member of the Communist Party, or any other organization which advocates the overthrow of the lawful government of the United States?"

"No! Come on, Agent Frink. No! What in hell is this all about?"

"I'm sorry Private but I'm not at liberty to disclose any information to you. I can tell you that the answers you have given us will have a great effect upon your future in the U.S. Army." He gave me a J. Edgar Hoover stare. "I believe we are finished. You may go now."

We got back to the bivouac area after dark. Chow was done. Dewildus was in our fighting hole, his M1 pointed at the perimeter. The training cadre would no doubt be attacking our position that night.

Fuck 'em. I gathered my sleeping bag, went deep into the swampy woods, curled up in some brush and spent a night of bad dreams, undisturbed by the training firefight only a hundred yards away.

8: Ruffles And Flourishes

The parade ground at Sand Hill was washed with sunlight and a chilly breeze. The four platoons of Company B, plus the troops of two other training companies, stood in formation facing the reviewing stand and a small crowd across the field.

The Second Division band formed behind us and played patriotic tunes, then paused and broke into *Ruffles And Flourishes* as the Commanding General and his party arrived and mounted the reviewing stand. On order, we presented arms.

A lump formed in my chest and tears came to my eyes as the band played *The Star Spangled Banner*. Then silence ruled the field until a voice called out, "Order" and was echoed, "order, order, order" pause, "Hahms." The butts and bolts of a thousand rifles clattered in unison.

Then came "Right shoulder, right shoulder, right shoulder," pause, "hahms." Again, that awesome clatter. Finally, the order echoed across the field, "Passss in review."

More echoing orders. "Right face." The band struck up *Colonel Bogey March.* "Foooraaard... harch." And we passed in review, no longer recruits but soldiers, infantrymen, and one solitary me whose future lay in an envelope back at Company headquarters.

Our packed duffels waited in the spotless, empty barracks. Our pristine rifles were racked and locked in the armory. Buses idled in the company road. We formed up in our platoon area and Sergeant Teasdale made a brief, moving speech. Then he produced the thick stack of envelopes within which our futures were written.

As he called each name, he handed the envelope and returned the salute with some low words to the new soldier. "Here you are, Private Lowrey. You turned out to be a good soldier. Good luck. I was stationed at Fort Meade once. That's pretty good country." He grinned, returned my salute and did his zombie eye roll one more time.

"Stand at ease, troops," Teasdale ordered. "You may open your orders now. As you probably appreciate, most of you won't be making a very long trip. For those with orders to Advanced Infantry School, these buses will take you to the Main Post.

"Those with other orders should check with the company clerk regarding transportation. Once you leave the company area, you're on your own to make your next assignment on time."

With trepidation, I opened the flap of my envelope and extracted my orders. The words on the mimeographed form swam before my eyes until I focused on "Fort Holabird, Baltimore, Maryland."

Up yours, Agents Frink and Sartorious!

As the buses loaded and the platoon area cleared, I sat on the barracks steps and read my orders carefully. My God! The Army was showing compassion. With Christmas only six days away, I was ordered to report to Baltimore no later than 1200 hours, 2 January, 1959.

And… in its arcane language, the paper in my hand authorized, "travel via home of record by most direct route." I had Christmas leave!

I stood in the short line at the company area phone booth and in turn, called Mom collect.

"Hello Five darling. Are you in trouble?"

"No mom. I'm a real soldier now and I'm comin' home. For Christmas."

"Oh, my word. Just like in the movies. When will you get here?"

"I don't know yet. We just got our orders and I have to go to the transportation office to get travel orders cut. But it's six days 'til Christmas and even if it's by bus, I should be home well before that."

"Oh, that'll be so grand. We'll have a terrific time. You call me as soon as you know anything, OK?"

I promised and hung up, as I could see the line growing outside the company clerk's office.

The wait in line seemed endless. After all, I was operating on my own time. Finally, it was my turn and I passed my orders to the bored looking specialist at a field table piled high with timetables and schedules.

"Ordinarily, I'd ask you where the nearest airport is to... er," he glanced at my orders, "Hockingport." The clerk looked up. "If you were going on directly to your next assignment, I could write you a flight. But this time of year, I wouldn't even book you 'space available' and let you take your chances. All the airlines are full."

He paused and looked at a fat book. "Your hometown near a railroad?"

"Yep. It's near the B&O halfway between Athens, Ohio and Parkersburg, West Virginia."

"Trains OK with you, then?" he asked.

"Yeah. I like trains."

"Well, I can get you out of Columbus to Atlanta in about two hours. Southern leaves Atlanta at 1700 and gets to Cincinnati at 0800.

"B&O connection to, let's see, Parkersburg at 1000 hours in Cincinnati, gets in Parkersburg at 1430. That sound OK?"

"Spec, it sounds great. Let's do it."

"OK Private. I'll write you a through ticket, Cincinnati to Baltimore, Maryland, but you're responsible for booking that ticket out of Parkersburg."

Travel orders in hand, I hoisted my duffel bag and staggered aboard a bus bound for the Southern station. *Good-bye, Sand Hill. Good-bye, Queen of Battle. Good-bye, Columbus. Good-bye, Brenda Lee.*

9: Holiday Interludes

Thick snow blew a white screen across the landscape of Belpre, the little town across the Ohio River from Parkersburg, as B&O's number 22 rumbled toward the bridge. Street lights glowed through the storm even though it was mid-afternoon as the train eased into the Sixth Street Station.

I wrestled the duffel bag down the aisle and off the steps of the coach onto the snow-slicked brick platform. Sissy Eileen squealed and threw her arms around my neck, causing the duffel to tumble off my shoulder, and we went down on top of it.

"Oh, Five, look at you! The big soldier," she said, kissing my cheeks. People on the platform grinned and laughed as I picked her up and we brushed snow off our coats.

"Hi, Sissy, you look terrific. It's so great to be here. Let's go home."

We got to the Chevy and I dumped the duffel in the trunk. Eileen held out the keys. "Mom said for you to drive if it was still snowing."

"No way. I haven't driven in 12 weeks and don't want to start now. We'll just take it slow." And so we did, crossing the big Belpre suspension bridge and heading down Route 7.

"Hang a right up here at the Blue Moon," I ordered. "I've been dreaming about their cheeseburgers for months." We went inside the nearly empty drive-in and took a booth. Eileen had a cherry coke and peppered me with questions while I devoured two cheeseburgers with the works.

35

"Mom'll kill you for spoiling your dinner," she said with a grin. "Captain's due in any time and we're having a huge feast. All your favorites."

Except for the dark green Class A uniform and the chilly wind blowing on my nearly bare scalp, I felt like a civilian again.

Eileen's prediction of a huge feast was accurate. Dressed in worn corduroy pants and an OU sweatshirt, I dug into spaghetti with Mom's great sauce, toasted garlic bread, shrimp cocktails and homemade angel food cake for dessert. Captain built a fire in the fireplace and our family reunion was warm and cozy, even with the wind howling off the river and icy snow rattling against the windows.

Around the fireplace, we sipped our coffee and I told war stories. Lots of laughter met my depictions of Dewildus Nelson and how he got his name and the ghostly Sergeant Teasdale and what a cool guy he was.

I left out *some* details of my strange interview with Agents Frink and Sartorious but the mood got somber as I described it.

"That's why I asked if you were in trouble when you called," Mom said. "FBI agents were at the high school asking about you and everyone in town was all excited."

Eileen chimed in, "Yeah. And F.X. Costellano called me from the ACE house. Said the FBI had been there asking questions and he said the brothers all wondered what you'd done."

"I think it's just part of my background investigation... and they weren't FBI." I tried to calm them. "But I'm really puzzled why they'd ask if Darcy is a member of the Communist party. Or me!"

"I'm sure the ACE house hasn't been identified as a subversive organization," Eileen contributed. "Their goals don't seem to extend beyond booze and pussy."

"Eileen!" Mom screeched. "Where did you pick up such talk?"

"At the ACE house."

"That does it," Mom shouted. "I won't have you associating with them. It may be Five's fraternity but I don't want it to hurt the lives of both my children..."

"Let's change the subject," Captain interjected. "Right now."

I broke the pall of gloom with a big yawn. "OK, maybe Darcy's a Commie but it's not going to keep me awake. I've been riding trains for nearly two days and it's time to hit the sack." I hugged each of my family and went off to bed.

Bright sunshine beamed through the window of my little room... Sissy Eileen's room until I went off to OU. Out the window was a Christmas card scene, snow covering the ground and trees, although the streets were already clear and wet.

Eileen sat at the kitchen table wearing a baggy sweater and sweat pants. Smoke from a cigarette hung in tendrils through her tangled hair.

"Lookin' good this mornin', kid. Where's everyone else?"

"Shithouse mouse, Five. I'm really in it with Mom for my pussy comment," she grinned, pouring another cup of coffee. "Captain took his car down to Pomeroy to check on the crew. He let Mom off at work." She looked at me morosely. "She said you could take the Chevy if you want to but I can't leave the house. Shit!"

"Well, Eileen, I learned pretty quickly not to bring all my bad old college habits home with me. I guess you're learning, too."

I poured some coffee and lit up a Pall Mall. "I was planning to run up to Parkersburg and do some Christmas shopping. If you want, I'll stop by the paper and see if I can talk Mom into letting you come along."

"Naw. Let her think she's teaching me some discipline. Besides, you may want to go up to Athens instead, and alone."

"How come?"

"I got a call yesterday morning from Andy. She's home for Christmas." Eileen gave me her sly smile. "She didn't come right out and say it... but I got the feeling she wouldn't mind seeing you."

Mom didn't exactly let on that she didn't believe my story about spending the night in Athens with some buddies at the ACE house who didn't go home for Christmas. But as I started out the door of the paper, she said, "Five, in case your sister didn't tell you, Andy called her yesterday. If you should see her, give her our love."

Athens looked festive with its street decorations and banks of melting snow. But Court Street was empty of students, just locals doing last-minute shopping. Not wanting to stretch the truth too much, I stopped by Alpha Chi Epsilon but found only two pledges, strangers to me, watching the house for vacation.

I pick out a scarf for Mom and a sweater for Eileen. My present for the Captain is a Zippo lighter with Fort Benning PX "Queen of Battle" in an enameled seal on its side. In the College Book Store, I buy myself a new sketch book and a Kho-I-Noor drafting pen.

Then, having put it off as long as I can, I drive out to Sunnyside Drive and the Logan's house. As I reach for the bell button, the door swings open and there stands Andy in jeans and a sweatshirt with "Gators" on the chest, a big smile on her face.

"Oh, Five," she says, enveloping me in a huge hug, "I hoped I would see you today. Welcome home."

Holding her tightly, I kiss her softly on the neck. "Andy, Andy. God it's good to see you. I've missed you... terribly."

Andy spins away, kicks the door shut and leads me by the hand into the living room. We land on the couch in a tight embrace. "It's good to be missed, Five. And I've missed you, too. So much."

"Where are your folks?" By this time, the Professor and Mrs. Logan should've been shaking my hand and giving me a warm Logan welcome.

"Big Christmas concert at Mem Aud," she mumbles, smothering me with soft little kisses. "They just left half hour ago. Oh, Five! You feel so good."

She wiggles and maneuvers me into a leaning position on the couch, snuggling against my chest. I put my arms around her and slide my hands beneath her sweatshirt, feeling her bare back!

Andy suddenly sits upright. "Your hands are cold, really cold, Five." She leans back and the motion naturally slides my hands around to her chest. I can feel her nipples growing beneath my fingertips. She leans forward and whispers in my ear, "We need to warm those hands, Five. But not here."

And she leads me down the hall to her door with the Chi O paddle hanging on it.

"Did you bring me a Christmas present, Five? I'll bet you did."

Later, back on the sofa and fully dressed, I admire Andy's curves hidden beneath a long, soft green robe. "Ah... shouldn't you maybe put something else on? I mean... won't your folks be back soon?"

"Nope," she chirps as she hands me my cup of hot chocolate. The robe falls open revealing all her curves. "After the concert, they're going to dinner with the Shivelys and then to a party at the Faculty Club."

It's all I can do to keep from spilling my cup as she snuggles up. "You're so lean and hard, Five. The Army's changed you."

"You're different, too," I respond. "So tan... all over."

"The Chi O house in Gainesville had a neat terrace on the roof. Big wall around it. No one could see us sunbathing. No one at all," she laughed. "So we got great tans."

"So... did you like Florida?""It was great, in its way," she says solemnly. "I missed you. And I didn't meet anyone as neat as you. But I still feel I did the right thing by getting away from here."

"How so?"

"It was nice being in a school where I wasn't a faculty brat. And it gave me lots of time to think about us. Were we in love, Five? Are we in love?"

The question catches me off guard and I ponder before trying to answer. She answers for me.

"We weren't, were we? I mean, really in love."

"Andy, our junior year was so great. And I love every memory I have of us being together.

"When you left last year, I thought my heart was broken. Nothing here was the same. But as time went by, I began to wonder what you just asked. Were we in love with each other... or just in love with being in love?"

She takes the cup from me and walks to the kitchen. Returning, she plops onto the sofa and throws a mock right cross to my jaw. "Five! That's exactly what I wondered. Making out seemed... just... sort of routine after awhile. I wonder if that's what it's like to be married?"

Reaching into her robe, I cup her breast. "This hasn't been routine. I know that. And I know that my senior year was really a loser. But where we go from here..."

"Where we go from here, mister, is back down the hall. We'll let the future take care of itself."

The rest of the Christmas holiday was a great whirl. I returned to Hockingport that night and the next day, Mom called Mrs. Logan and invited them down for Christmas dinner. Andy and I found very few intimate opportunities, but made the most of them when we could.

As December drew to a close, Andy and I made plans to take the train east together. Andy to Washington. Me to Baltimore.

At the B&O station in Athens, I drag my duffel into the ticket agent's office and check it, hand over my orders and get my ticket from Athens instead of Parkersburg. Then I have a brainstorm and step back into the station.

As I return to the platform, the Logans arrive with Andy. Everyone admires my uniform and as the headlight for the National Limited appears in the distance, last-minute hugs and kisses are exchanged. Mom and Sissie Eileen have tears in their eyes. The Captain gives me a firm hug and a handshake. Then Andy and I climb aboard the blue and gray coach, me carrying my little Gladstone bag of civilian clothes.

Christmas in Ohio is over.

10: On To Crabtown

Once in the nearly empty coach, Andy started toward the center of the car, but I caught her arm and indicated a seat near the vestibule.

"But it'll be so noisy and cold, every time someone opens the door," she complained. "And we'll never get any sleep with the wheels clacking like they do."

"Ah c'mon, just sit. We can change later," I said, waving to the expanse of empty seats. "I like it here."

Reluctantly, she took a window seat and I sat facing her, both with our faces against the glass to wave good-bye. A muted diesel horn sounded and slowly the faces of our loved ones seemed to move away. We were off.

As the National Limited picked up speed toward the outskirts of Athens, I stood and grabbed our bags from the overhead rack. "Here's something I learned in the infantry," I grinned at her. "Follow me!"

With a bewildered look, Andy rose and followed me into the vestibule and through the next coach. Then another vestibule and halfway down the car where I produced my ticket and checked the door number.

"Here we are, miss," I said, opening the door. "My little New Year's surprise."

"My gosh, Five! A roomette?"

"Yep, I didn't save all that bargehand money to ride to Washington with you snoring on my shoulder putting my arm to sleep. And take note. It's right in the middle of the car so you won't hear those awful wheels clacking."

41

I opened the tiny closet door and hung my uniform topcoat and blouse. "Let me get into some civilized clothes and we'll go to the club car for a drink."

We walked the aisle past the Pullman compartments of the *Genesee River* and into the observation lounge, which was empty except for the porter at the bar and a sleeping salesman type.

"Anywhere you'd like folks," the porter said with a smile. "As you can see, we're not exactly crowded. The little couch at the end is very popular."

We could see why. The horseshoe-shaped couch looked directly out the car's curved rear window and the track, illuminated by the drumhead, vanished into the night as we rolled along.

As the porter brought us our ordered rum-and-Cokes, Andy said, "Look Five, it's the Hocking! You're nearly home."

Half an hour later, the train stormed past the stock pens and out onto the elevated fill that carried the tracks through Belpre. The rumble of the short bridge, followed seconds later by the longer Ohio River Bridge, told me we were arriving in Parkersburg.

It seemed weird not to be getting off the train in this familiar station. As we peered out the window back at the long black bridge, snowflakes began to come down in the drumhead light. As the train rolled through the Parkersburg yards, we looked at each other and faked giant yawns. And headed back to our little rolling room.

Sometime past midnight, I awoke and watched the snowy scenery roll by under a full moon. Grade crossing bells would clatter briefly as we sped by and an occasional farmhouse showed a window light. Snuggled next to me, Andy made soft snoring noises. With the rattle of wheels on rail joints as a lullaby, I drifted back into sleep.

Later... "What time is it, Five?" Andy's face showed from the flashes of lights we passed as she leaned on her elbow and peered at me.

I groaned and looked at my watch. "0420 hours. Why?"

"Well, we've only got three more hours before we get to Washington"

I groaned again and rolled over. Andy scooted against my back and threw her arm over my chest. "Five... are you going to waste those three hours sleeping? I'm disappointed in you," she murmured. "After all, it is

New Year's Eve." Her tongue flicked on the back of my neck. I rolled back over.

The National Limited followed the tracks across the Potomac at Harper's Ferry and we sat propped up against our pillows to watch the Allegheny Mountains give way to the broad river valley.

"Gee, Five. I've dreamed for months of spending New Year's Eve with you. Now we've done it." She stretched her arms wide. "I just wish it could go on all day."

"And why can't it? You have a date tonight?"

"Well no. But you have to catch your train for Baltimore."

"Ah, Andy. That's part two of my New Year's surprise. My train for Baltimore leaves *tomorrow.*"

"You're kiddin' me. Really?" Andy gave me a huge hug. "But you can't stay at my apartment. It's tiny and I've got two roommates! I even share a bedroom with one of them."

"No worries. I've got a bed at a place the USO runs for enlisted men on E Street... the Army-Navy Club."

"But I can't stay there!"

"Andy, I'm spending New Year's Eve with you. So we can't sleep together? At least we'll *be* together."

"That's wonderful. It really is," she whispered, stripping off her pajama top. "But we'd better make up for tonight's lost opportunities."

With me back in uniform, we took a cab from Union Station to the Army-Navy Club with my promise to meet Andy at her apartment in a couple hours. I checked in, claimed one of a dozen bunks in a big room and hit the shower. Cleaned up and in civvies again, I walked the dozen blocks to Andy's apartment house.

"Hey Five, that's not two hours. My hair's still wet," she greeted me at the door. "Welcome to AFS transient quarters." The apartment was tiny, decorated with travel posters and equipped with worn, overstuffed furniture and a brick and board bookcase. Two doors led from the living room. I raised my eyes in question and nodded toward the doors.

"My roomies have gone to breakfast," she said. "They'll be back any minute. And the answer to what you're thinking... what I'm thinking... is no!"

43

31 December, 1959, was a glorious day. We stood on the Memorial's chilly steps and looked into the brooding eyes of Abraham Lincoln. We walked hand-in-hand on The Mall and wiled away the rest of the afternoon in the halls of the National Gallery.

We kept company with the best of them — our favorites — Vermeer, Renoir, Monet, Van Gogh.

"Just think, Andy. I first saw these paintings on a screen in Mem Aud five years ago. And you were there, right beside me. Isn't this great?"

"Maybe someday your work'll be hanging here, Five."

"Well... a year ago, I would've said there probably wouldn't be any more painting. But now I'm enthusiastic to get back at it. But... I'm scheduled now to learn to be a counterspy."

"Oh. That's just for a little while. You'll find time to get some work done, I'm sure."

That night, we ate shrimp at a place called The Boathouse, watching the lights shimmer across the surface of the Tidal Basin from the Jefferson Memorial. The American Field Service New Year's party would be in the upstairs room of The Boathouse.

Two more couples, Andy's roommates Denise and Barbara and their dates, joined us. Denise was a large, jolly girl with pigtails that hung down her back. Barbara was a tall, slinky, chocolate-colored woman in a shiny green dress. Their dates looked like college guys in khakis and tweed sport coats.

We climbed the stairs and found a closed deck with a jukebox and about 50 people standing around. "No bar for AFS," Barbara muttered, "but Jackson came prepared. Her date, Jackson, opened his sport coat to reveal a flask. Denise's date did the same.

We bopped to *Stagger Lee* and Rusty Bryant's *Night Train* and slow-danced to Paul Anka's *Put Your Head On My Shoulder.* Examining the jukebox, I was delighted to find a couple of favorites and plunked nickels in for *Running Bear* and *Alley Oop.* Andy shook her head ruefully as I demonstrated the Army technique of mashing a 7Up can on my forehead and "oop, ooping."

Someone contributed more nickels and the group lined up for *The Stroll* through several repetitions.

The Penguins' *Earth Angel* started up with its mournful chorus and Andy slid into my arms. "It's nearly 1959, Five," she murmured into my ear. "The last part of 1958 has been really terrific."

We dipped at the end of the song and then went out to the open deck with the rest of the crowd. Somewhere along the Tidal Basin, a band played *Til' We Meet Again.* Then an aerial salute boomed, followed quickly by another and another. The crowd chanted the countdown to midnight. The band struck up *Auld Lang Syne,* and Andy and I shared a long, lingering kiss, washed by the glare of fireworks over the Tidal Basin.

"We're a good pair, aren't we Five?" Andy asked as we walked across The Mall, arms around each other's waist.

"Yep, we are. No doubt about it."

"But we're not quite a set, yet, are we?"

"Nooo? But maybe someday?"

She gives me a squeeze, "That's what I'm thinking too." We pause for a sweet kiss.

"You said in your letter when I got home, 'time will tell.' I guess we should give it time, some more time. Huh?"

"I guess.

We catch a bus and ride to Andy's apartment building. A dim light illuminates their living room where Denise and Barbara have occupied the available furniture, necking with their dates. Andy leads me back to the hall by the hand and puts her arms around my neck. "I don't want to end it like that, Five... making out in public."

"And we can't go to the bedroom," she giggles.

And so we start 1960 in the dim hallway, hugging tightly and whispering goodnight. I walk back to the Army-Navy Club and flop on my bunk, surrounded by snoring soldiers and sailors.

As agreed, Andy is waiting at Union Station's Concourse Restaurant for a last breakfast together.

"Oh, my," you're a soldier again." She brushes imaginary lint from my uniform blouse. "And a handsome one at that."

45

Our breakfast is a quiet affair. "I've only got two more weeks of training," she said, squeezing my hand across the table. "It's so exciting to know that in less than a month I'll be in Europe."

"And I've got at least twelve weeks to go," I respond, "probably more, the way the Army works. And then, who knows? You're absolutely right, Andy. It *is* exciting."

"Gee. Five, we may not see each other again for months and months, years maybe. We should be sad, huh? You don't look sad." Andy paused and her face broke into a big smile. "And I don't feel sad. Isn't that weird?"

"All I know is I'm gonna' be doing something different. I'm gonna' miss you terribly, Andy, just as I have for the past year. But I feel like this CIC thing is going to be good, and if it's not good, it's not for the rest of my life."

With promises to write each other, we walk down to the concourse. I try my best to look like I've got my duffel bag under control. Thank God Andy carries my Gladstone.

At the train, the conductor flashes a grin. "Give her one last smooch, soldier. I've got to get this train out of Washington." Good soldier that I am, I follow orders. And once more, the face of a loved one glides away from my train window.

11. Under The Gaze Of The Sphinx

Camden Station's military transportation desk is crowded with soldiers but I'm the only one who receives a taxi chit for Fort Holabird. What I see on the long ride is a gray city accented with banks of dirty snow. A city the cabby refers to as 'Bal'mer.'

Even on New Year's Day, housewives are out with mops and steaming buckets to clean the white marble steps of houses stuck all together for a solid block. The driver tells me they're called row houses.

We pull into the main gate of Fort Holabird where a guard checks my orders and directs the cabby to a three-story brick building. I dig in my pocket and come up with three quarters for a tip. "Thanks a lot, young spook," he says genuinely, "and Happy New Year."

Lugging my gear up some concrete steps, I enter a door marked *Support Company* with a paper sign that reads *Reception Office*. A Spec 4 looks up from his newspaper.

"Happy New Year, Spec. Got the duty, eh?"

"Yeah, Happy New Year, Private." He shrugs, "Luck of the calendar, I guess. Least I don't have much of a hangover. Let's see your orders."

He checks my orders envelope and consults a clipboard, ticking off my name. "Lowrey, Thomsen. That's you? Can I see your ID?"

I dig my military ID from my billfold and hand it over.

Satisfied that I'm me, he hands back the card. "Well, you're 18 hours early but that's better than being AWOL. You're assigned to Class A59-1, up the stairs one flight and to the right in Bay 2E. Dump your gear by any rack and come back down here. I'll take you to the supply room and issue your bedding and towels."

Bay 2E is just like all my other barracks spaces except for a *pair* of upright lockers behind each single bunk. A wide aisle separates eight bunks on each side. Rolled mattresses sit on each bunk except for one by the door, where a man in strange-looking fatigues is curled up and asleep on the made-up bed.

Quietly, I go to the far end of the bay and put down my bags near the bunk by the windows of the end wall. Then I return to the reception office where Spec 4 Legget is back reading his *Baltimore Sun*.

"Find it OK, Lowrey?" I nod yes. "Did you meet Gaffney?"

"There's a guy up there asleep, wearing green fatigues."

"That's Gaffney. Gunnery Sergeant Emmit Gaffney, U.S. Marine Corps." Legget motions for me to follow him down a hallway. "He's a lifer, I guess. Probably a RIF'ed officer. We get a couple of 'em each class reduced in force from officer to GI."

"A Marine on an Army post?"

"Oh, yeah. You'll find out the 'Bird' is kind of a different place," he said, opening the Dutch door to the supply room. "Here's two blankets, sheets, pillow and case, towels, washcloth. Not sure when laundry call will be for you but your class leader will know soon enough.

"Today bein' a holiday, mess hall's only open until 1600 hours." Legget looks at his watch. "So you've got a few hours. I think you'll like the food.

"Post uniform of the day is civvies or fatigues for the rest of the weekend since Friday's an off day too.

"But your class is due in by 1200 hours tomorrow so I'd reckon your class leader'll have some kind of loose formation by 1300 hours. You'll have an orientation briefing in the Support Company day room at 1400 hours. The Top's a little pissed about having to conduct a briefing on a holiday weekend but he's a good guy and will get over it."

As we reach the reception office door, another GI struggles up with his gear... a Chinese-looking guy with a strange unit patch on his shoulder. I give him a nod and head up the stairs for Bay 2E.

Bouncing a quarter on my newly-made bunk, I'm startled when a soft voice behind me says "Pretty good job, GI. They taught you well in basic."

I turn to find the once sleeping marine standing in the aisle, hands on his hips, observing me with hooded eyes of the palest blue.

"Hey Sarge, Private Thomsen Lowrey," I extend my hand.

His grip is crushing. "Gunnery Sergeant Emmit Gaffney, USMC. But my friends and shipmates call me 'Gunny' or worse, Tom."

"Actually, er, Gunny. It's Thomsen Lowrey V. No one calls me Tom. My friends call me Five or sometimes 'shithead.'"

"OK. Five it is. Welcome aboard. I'm glad to have some company." He looks up and sees the Chinese soldier staggering through the door. "Looks like we've got some more company."

"Where do I dump this crap?" he asks, dragging the duffel bag across the highly-waxed floor. Without waiting for an answer, he lets the duffel fall and walks forward with his hand extended. "Hey guys, I'm Luther Chan. San Francisco. And lately of Fort Ord."

We all shake hands and introduce ourselves. "That's my rack down there by the door," Gaffney points out "and we've got another NCO due in so we'll save the one across from me for him. I think one or the other of us'll be class leader and we should be near the door.

"Until then, pick any rack you want."

Chan surveyed the room, saw my made up bunk and said, "I like having two windows. Don't know why. But is it OK if I bunk across from you, Lowrey?"

The three of us entered the big mess hall on the ground floor of the building. Round tables with eight chairs each sat under low lights, giving the place the look of a civilian restaurant. The place was empty except for a huge black man behind the serving counter. He grinned as we approached the counter.

"Good evening Sergeant, troopers. Welcome to my establishment." A big grin from Gaffney. "I'm Adolphus Melville, Master Sergeant and, with the aid of my able supply officer, I run this joint."

We introduced ourselves. Melville held up a huge hand and showed a huge expanse of white teeth in a monster grin. "For the life of me I can't imagine why, but I'm known as Big Spook. Maybe because I'm so much bigger than all the little spooks that run around here.

"When you're on KP, I'll be addressed as Sergeant. Otherwise, you can call me Big Spook or Sergeant Big Spook but... always with a smile on your face." He paused and surveyed the steam table.

"Sorry our menu is kinda small tonight but we're on Sunday schedule all weekend and I've got little help and no KP's. So you'll wash your own silver and glasses and we're using paper plates.

"Now, we've got lasagna, ribs, fried chicken and some vegetables. Coffee, tea, milk and water at the end... bone appeteete."

"Damndest mess hall I've ever been in," Gaffney mumbles through a mouthful of chicken. "This chow is delicious."

Chan and I nod our agreement. My plate is piled high with lasagna and ribs, baked beans in thick molasses, incredible coleslaw.

A pair of lieutenants enters the mess hall, make small talk with Big Spook and take their trays to a nearby table.

Gaffney looks puzzled. "No section for the brass? That's amazing." He nods a greeting, "Afternoon Sirs."

Big Spook walks up to our table. "How's the food, gentlemen?"

"Incredible," Chan enthuses, "er... Sergeant... er Spook." The giant chef smiles his approval. Gaffney and I shake our heads enthusiastically.

"I try to run the best mess in the U.S. Army. Got a good crew and KPs are always gung ho. KP isn't a punishment here at the 'Bird.

"Anyone told you about our hours?"

We all nod no.

"Duty days, three meals a day. Saturdays, breakfast from 0900 to 1200 hours. Dinner from 1600 to 1800 hours. On Sundays... *your* day of rest... we serve one meal from 1000 hours to 1400 hours. Omelets custom-made, if I'm in a good mood, and all sorts of other specialties. So sleep in, if you can, next three days and we'll eat like royalty."

The nearby lieutenants smile at this speech and one gives us a thumbs-up sign.

Melville turns to leave, then adds "I've got some apple cobbler about ready to come out of the oven. Soldiers like it on Sundays cold with whipped cream. I think it's even better hot. Any takers?"

We return to the bay where another NCO is making up his bunk. Tall, thin and sporting a flattop head of almost silver hair, Master Sergeant Daniel Clankus must be nearly 40 years old. He finishes his bunk and walks with Gunny Gaffney over to the day room.

Shortly they return and walk to the end of the bay occupied by Chan and me.

"Well, Sergeant Clankus and I have compared pedigrees and he's the ranking NCO and will be the class leader. We agree that bunks are taken on a first-come basis so you guys can go ahead and stow your gear."

Clankus introduces himself with a voice that echoes a million cigarettes. "From everything I've been told, this is going to be a pretty casual operation. There'll be no barracks inspections except for what Gunny and I conduct… if and when we feel the need.

"Therefore, I can't see any need for you to build a footlocker display. Just keep your footlocker tray clean and neat and I think we'll get by. We'll get a briefing tomorrow afternoon about post regulations but 'til then, I'd go ahead and hang uniforms in one locker, civvies in the other.

"Barracks lights out at *Taps*. Gunny and I are going over to the NCO Club and scope the place out. No formation in the morning. We'll sleep in 'til we have to get up.

To my delight, I discover a dozen wire coat hangers stuffed into my Gladstone. Also stamped envelopes. Good ole' Mom. After getting everything put away, I take my sketchbook and pen into the day room to make a list of stuff I'll need. And to write notes to Mom and Andy.

Long before the recorded notes of *Taps* sound outside, I'm in my bunk and almost asleep. Across the aisle I can hear my very first Chinese snores.

I wake to rain rattling on the bay windows. Chan continues to snore. Dim morning light reveals the figures of five more classmates, most rolled under their blankets on bare mattresses. Grabbing my Dopp kit, I head for the latrine. On the hallway bulletin board, I find a typed roster of Class A59-1.

√ MSgt Daniel Clankus, Squad Leader

√ Gunnery Sgt Emmit Gaffney,
   USMC, Asst. Squad Leader

Private Jeffrey Adamich

√ Private Luther Chan

Private David Clay

Private James L. Desmond, III
√ Private Tomas Escobar
Private John Linscombe
√ Private Thomsen Lowrey, V
Private Lindbergh Luck
Private Vladivic Mennosovich
√ Private Calvin Moon
Private Samuel Ploughman
√ Private Ray Stein,
Private Richard Wheeler
√ Private Henry Zigafoos:

Beneath is a handwritten message:

No formation. Breakfast/lunch/dinner served from 1000 hours. Non-compulsory breakfast formation at 1030 hours. Be there. Uniform of the day: civvies if you have them. Fatigues otherwise.

Clankus / Gaffney

Dressed in chinos, a crew neck sweater and loafers, I wander around the building and find a *Baltimore Sun* newspaper kiosk. Dutifully, I deposit a dime and take a paper. I notice the mess hall door is open and peer in.

"Coffee machine's on, young solider," calls Big Spook. "Come in and make yourself to home... and be sure to police your butt tray and cups."

"Thanks Sarge and TGIF to you."

Over my usual breakfast of coffee and a Pall Mall, I read the day's news. Most startling is the story of the Russians sending a 3,000 pound rocket into orbit around the sun, "creating the world's first man-made planet." Senator John Kennedy of Massachusetts is strident in his call for the Eisenhower administration to do something to get America back into the race for outer space. Chinese soldiers are fighting skirmishes on the Tibet and Indian borders and an invasion is threatened. Iowa beat California 38-12 in the Rose Bowl.

"May I join you Private Lowrey?" Sgt. Clankus asked.

"Actually, it's pronounced Lo-Ree, Sergeant. But it's not a big deal. Sure, have a seat!" I slide over the front sections of the *Sun* to him.

"Damn!" he exclaimed. "Look what the Commies have done now. If they can put one of those mothers around the sun, they can sure as hell send a tactical rocket onto a battlefield."

"And thanks to the Rosenbergs," I contributed, "it could be a nuke, too."

His eyebrows arch and those ice blue eyes get bigger. He smiles and says, "Wow. I'd forgotten I'd be working with college grads at this school." Pause. "I'm not used to having soldiers in my command who read newspapers and understand them."

"In your command, Sarge?"

"Oh, yeah, Private Lowrey. My NCO rank is fairly new. I was a major in artillery until I got caught in the RIF a few years ago."

"Oh, God, should I call you 'sir?'"

"Nope! Sergeant'll do just fine. Or Dan will do just fine also, unless we're into a military protocol situation."

"OK, Dan... sir. Ah, where did you serve."

"Oh. War stories? Shipped out of OCS to Okinawa in '45, just before Hiroshima. Was on McArthur's staff during the occupation of Japan. Battlefield promotions to Captain and Major in Korea. RIF'ed in '55."

Chan and a little olive-skinned guy peer through the door, then enter the mess hall when I wave them in.

"Mornin' Sarge. Lowrey. This is Tomas Escobar."

"Hey Luther," I reply. "You sure you don't want to take a rack further down the bay?"

"Shit! Did I snore?"

"Snore!" Clankus laughs, "Was that you? Damned but I thought the railroad parked a switch engine in there."

Chan grins and turns to Escobar. "See. I told you he seemed to have a sense of humor... for an old fart sergeant."

Over coffee and smokes, we find out Escobar is from Tampa where it doesn't usually get so cold. One by one, the others drift in and by 1030 hours, half of the class is present and chowing down. Pancakes, waffles, omelets, lots of milk and coffee.

Calvin Moon is a stocky, well-muscled guy from Steubenville, Ohio, with a shy smile and deep voice. He looked familiar, then it dawned on me. "Hey, I know you. You played football at Ohio State." He grins and nods yes.

Ray Stein introduces himself in a broad southern accent. "Ah'm from Savannah, a UGA Bulldog, and we could'a kicked Ohio State's ass." Moon arches one eyebrow in question.

We all scoff when Henry Zigafoos tells us he's from Mars. "Mars, Pennsylvania. My Dad's the undertaker there."

Stein has a question, "What's he do with the bodies? Bury 'em or just let 'em float out into space?"

12: The Making Of A Spook Begins

"Welcome to Fort Holabird, home of the Army Intelligence Center and the Army Intelligence School. I'm First Sergeant Dottreau of the AIC Support Company and this is your post orientation." Dottreau is thin and tall with thick dark hair in a widow's peak that nearly reaches his eyebrows, shadowing a set of flinty eyes.

He calls the roll and checks our names. "One not accounted for, Sergeant Clankus?"

"Yep, Top. Private Lindburgh Luck."

"Well, let's hope he gets here. He's not AWOL for 12 more hours." Pause. *"Dai jobi.* Let's get to it.

"Fourteen, or at least 13 of you soldiers, are fresh out of Basic Combat Training. You'll find Holabird a bit more casual than those posts where you experienced Basic. You *will* observe military protocol and courtesies... on post... when in uniform.

"But due to the nature of our mission, you'll find very little chickenshit and no one doing pushups unless he feels like getting the exercise."

Our group grins and emits an audible sigh.

"Uniform of the day will be posted by your Class Leaders and will depend upon your schedule. Some days you'll even wear civvies. No one leaves the post in uniform unless on an assigned duty.

"You already know the mess hall schedule. This weekend is kind of special due to the holidays but tomorrow we get back on a regular schedule. Support Company pulls KP on class days. Student troopers will

55

pull KP on weekends but for those of you in this Agent class, that'll probably be no more than two days during your 12-week school.

"Reveille is at 0600 hours and class formation is at 0745 hours. Taps and lights out is 2230 hours but the day room is open for study all night long. The day room TV goes off at lights out.

"You'll march to and from instruction in your class group. Route step is permissible once you leave the area of this building... depending upon the will of your class leaders."

The day room door cracks open and an officer steps through. "Ten hut!" Dottreau calls and we snap to.

"At ease," the young captain says. "Seats men." We sit.

"Captain Smith, do you have anything to say to the men?" Dottreau asks.

"I'll just repeat the welcome I'm sure Sergeant Dottreau has already extended to you, men. I'm Captain Alvin Smith, commanding officer of the AIC Support Company. Our cadre and men have the mission of making your duty at Fort Holabird as comfortable as possible, within Army regs."

The top sergeant continues his indoctrination and I find it hard to remember everything. The post library and recreation center. The post rathskeller, open every night and selling only 3.2 beer. Off-limits places in the Dundalk area. Our flagging attention perks up.

Monday's breakfast was standard mess hall fare. Scrambled eggs. Incredible SOS. Fat, buttery biscuits. Fresh fruit, pancakes. Right! Standard mess hall fare.

Dan Clankus calls us to attention and reports "All present or accounted for, Sergeant." Indeed, we're all accounted for since Lindburgh Luck arrived from Duluth about 0300 hours, proclaiming to a sleeping bay "Shit. I thought I'd never get out of Minnesota."

We perform a left turn and march off to school, falling into route step (smartly) as we pass beyond the vision of First Sergeant Dottreau. Across the main road and past the statue of the sphinx we shamble, falling back into step as we near the main classroom building.

With actual coat hooks to hang our field jackets and flattop caps on, we settle into a small auditorium. A swarthy, short man in a strangely cut suit moves to the podium.

"Good morning, men. I am John Scarletti, an adjunct instructor at the Army Intelligence School and you're class A59-1, the first class of the year in the Intelligence Analysis course, commonly known as the Agent course. At the successful completion of this 12-week course, you will be qualified to serve as a Special Agent in the Counter Intelligence Corps.

"The history of intelligence, or spying if you will, goes back to Biblical times. And the history of the CIC dates back to 1917 when the Corps of Intelligence Police was formed to protect the American Expeditionary Force from enemy spies. This force was composed of 40 non-commissioned officers, mostly linguists, and was the beginning of the CIC's strong reliance upon college educated enlisted men."

Scarletti pauses and sweeps his gaze around the room, as if to assess the wakefulness of his new class.

"I'll condense the events between the world wars except to say that by the end of World War II, more than 7,500 trained agents made up the CIC forces. It was during World War II that the mission of the CIC evolved into one of investigative duties while military intelligence remained the responsibility of combat units.

It occurred to me that Scarletti's presentation was the first lecture that had held my attention in the last three years. My classmates appeared equally rapt.

"In 1945, training in counterintelligence resumed and was located here at Fort Holabird, an old quartermaster depot and vehicle proving ground. Ten years later, the Combat Intelligence School was merged here to become the Army Intelligence School.

"That's about it for history in this orientation." Wry grin from Scarletti. "You'll get a much stronger dose during the course from one of my less interesting colleagues." Our class laughed uneasily.

We huddled in an open hallway for our first smoke break. Through the door, we could see crews demolishing a set of two story First War barracks beyond a strange, steep hill.

"This seems a lot like that deja vu thing," Chan muttered to me, clinching his filtered Old Gold between thin lips. "Did'ja hear that little Italian cutting on his fellow faculty?'

"I tink dis be a lot like collidge," chimed in Vlad Mennosovich, a New York City boy who sounded as if he'd just arrived from Budapest. "My professors vas alvays bad-mouthing each udder."

"Where'd you go to college?" Ray Stein asked, "Dracula U.?"

Vlad shoots him a bird and grins. "CCNY, mushmouth."

"Wasn't anyone like him at my school," Lindburgh Luck chimed in. "At St. Olaf, all our professors were nice."

"I somehow don't think Scarletti attended the University of Nice," Gunny Gaffney said. "Maybe more like the University of Sicily. He looks like a Mafioso to me."

Back in the small auditorium, Scarletti continued. "Your course, I think you'll discover, is going to be very intense but very interesting. The major portion will be involved in learning the techniques of investigative interviewing and report writing. How many of you can type?"

Nearly all hands go up. I'm surprised to see the two sergeants raise theirs.

"Well, you'll learn to type... all over again." He flashes us an evil grin.

"In addition, you'll have introductory courses in intelligence photography, surveillance technique, what is called 'days' or DAES, defense against electronic surveillance, and DAME, defense against mechanical entry, a little bit of weapons training, a small glimpse into countersabotage and, before you know it, you'll be counterintelligence agents. If... you, make it!"

We peer at each other quizzically. Scarletti holds up a thick book. "This is FM 30-5, the Field Manual for Counterintelligence and it'll be your bible. It is a classified document... classified *Confidential*... for which each of you has provisional clearance.

"At the end of each class day, you will store your 30 dash fives and other classified materials in your class security safe. Sergeant Clankus and Sergeant Gaffney will serve as your class security officers. If you choose to have a night study session, you can do so in this building as long as one of the security officers accompanies you to open the safe and sign the log. Is that clear?"

After a long day of lectures and dinner, our classmates go their various ways. Several head for the rathskeller. I stay in my fatigues and walk over to the post library with Stein and Chan. It's already dark at 1900 hours and a chill wind blows across the flat grounds of the post.

"Wonder what that dago meant this morning when he said 'if you make it'?" Chan muttered aloud.

"I reckon a guy could flunk out of this place," Stein said, "but I think it'd take some serious goofin' off."

My thoughts were in another direction. "Perhaps it has to do with security clearances. Remember he said we had 'provisional clearances for Confidential'? Did you guys have some CIC agents pull you in during basic?"

Chan shrugs no but Stein speaks up. "Sheeit, yeah. Two hard characters got me out of CBW training and grilled mah ass about why I didn't put down my place of residence in my junior year. They went on and on... wouldn't believe my excuse that I couldn't remember the address of some damn Athens, Georgia, roomin' house."

"Yep, that could be it," I confirmed, deciding to keep my own experience to myself.

Andrew Carnegie obviously didn't know about the Holabird post library. The one-story barracks structure had a small reading room, a couple racks of magazines and two library stacks of books. Grim as it was, it was brightened by the pretty young woman who looked up from behind the donut-shaped counter as we entered.

"Evenin' troops," she smiled. "Welcome to the number two cultural center west of Holabird Avenue. The rathskeller being number one, of course."

Suddenly, this was looking like the best part of the day. We introduced ourselves enthusiastically.

"I'm Peggy Muldoon, post librarian, and when I face that side of the counter," she pointed behind her, "I'm director of the post crafts and recreation center." A low room with tables and lockers stretched behind her.

"We have all kinds of therapeutic crafts, and painting and drawing, even classes sometime.

"And," her smile got even bigger, "if General Muldoon would permit, we would have coed mixers every night. As the commanding general is sort of close-minded, we have to open the gates to girls from Goucher, Towson or Hood just twice a month. Those girls *just love* you spooks in training." She looks Chan directly in the eye. "You're Chinese, aren't you?"

The open-mouthed Luther nods yes.

"I know the cutest little girl from Goucher that you'll really go for. Her Dad 's a diplomat but I don't think she's a security risk."

Chan and Stein practically melt into the counter, drooling at the librarian with her big smile, huge green eyes and fluttery lashes, and dark curly hair. I note that her body doesn't look too bad, either, as I coolly saunter toward the magazine rack where I spot Darcy in some slinky purple thing on the cover of *Cosmopolitan.*

"I'm in love. I'm in love." Stein chants as we trudge back to the bay. Dust and grit blow at our backs from the pile of destroyed barracks.

"I'm in love, too," Chan adds, "with the cutest little Chinese Goucher coed who I haven't even met. What's Goucher?"

It's 1145 hours, 15 minutes after the gorgeous librarian has closed her doors behind us, as we climb the steps to the bay. We can hear raucous laughter coming from our sleeping quarters so the rathskeller is obviously closed as well.

Linscombe, a lanky farmer from Missouri, Zigafoos the mortician and a guy named Adamich are sitting on their bunks, butt cans drawn close.

"Where you guys been?" Adamich yells. "You missed some great lookin' chicks at the beer hall."

"Ohhhh, right!" Zigafoos slurs, "that great lookin' babe you were buyin' beer for had a face like a rusted radiator."

"Chicks in an Army beer hall? Are you guys shitfaced on 3.2 beer?" I ask.

"There's a WAC detachment, right in ole' Fort Holybird," Linscombe drawls. "Real women soldiers. The cutest one beat my ass at arm rasslin', beat me chuggin' and then tried to beat my meat under the table." His face splits exactly in half with the widest smile I've ever seen.

"I think she was almost purty," he sighed, flopping back onto his bunk "Where'd you guys say you went?"

"Oh," Stein replies casually, "nowhere special. Just the library."

13: We Meet The World Champion

Imogene Klecko looks like someone's gussied-up grandma. Silver blonde hair radiates out in big perm curls. A very un-January print dress is splashed with flowers. And from her thin, creped neck, half a dozen strands of fat beads dangle nearly to her waist, their colors doing battle with the flower pattern of her dress.

"How many of you men have taken a typing class before?" she asks in a high, thin voice. "Come on, don't be shy. Let's see those hands."

All but three of us timidly raise our hands.

"And can some of you type very, very rapidly?"

No one volunteers. Why she looks at me, I'll never know. "How about you, soldier. Lowrey, is it?"

"Lo-ree, ma'am. I, uh, can type about 30 words per minute, I guess."

"And why did you take typing, Private Lo-ree?"

"Ah, my mom said it would be valuable in college. And in my high school, it was a good place to meet girls." The class roars and Mrs. Klecko responds with a thin smile. "I like to cook, too, but I would've had to wear an apron in home ec." My colleagues love my humor.

Mrs. Klecko swings her glance to the other side of the room, her beads in a clacking orbit. "Anyone else here can beat 30 words per minute?"

Jim Desmond, the guy we've already nicknamed "Harvard," raises his hand. "I can hit about 60 words a minute. I used to type reports for my roommates."

61

"Ahhh, 60 words a minute," Klecko looks sagely at Desmond. "Very impressive."

She pauses, then whirls with beads a split-second behind, and aims a long pointer at the huge keyboard chart in the front of the room. "And you, Sergeant? How fast do you type?" Gunny Gaffney turns scarlet and hangs his head.

"Well, ma'am, ah... I'd say about five words a minute. Two fingers. If I move my mouth."

"OK then," she drags out in a long breath. "We'll take a little timed test. Open your book to page three and when my bell rings, we'll type the exercise there. If you finish the three paragraphs, begin at the top again. Three minutes on the bell."

"Ding!" and 16 shiny new Olympus typewriters begin to chatter in unsyncopated effort. I'm on the last line of the third paragraph when the bell sounds again, no more than 30 seconds from the start, it seems.

"All right. You there, Private," she points her stick at Desmond. "Bring your work forward."

Desmond rises and with a big shit-eating grin, strides to the front of the room brandishing three pages of typed material. He hands the pages over and Mrs. Klecko sits at her desk. She motions Desmond back to his desk and her pencil flies over the papers, making check mark after check mark.

She then looks at the ceiling, making a mental calculation, then writes on the paper.

"Eleven words a minute, Private Desmond. Not bad." Desmond looks astonished. Klecko points to his papers. "Here we have 21 typographical errors... or typos. And we have, by rough count, 44 strikeovers. And we have at least 300 understrikes... Private Desmond, you have very weak index fingers. Unusual. It's usually the pinkie that is weak."

Then the thin woman sits to her own Olympus, identical to ours, and motions for silence. She resets her clock to a timer mode, pushes the button and begins flying her fingers over the keyboard. The line-ending bell sounds nearly like a telephone ringing and her hand is a blur as she pushes the carriage return. She finishes the last line of the three paragraphs and pushes the timer.

"Hmmm. Forty-one seconds. Not very good but it *is* a chilly afternoon. Come forward gentlemen and compare my effort with Private Desmond's." Mrs. Klecko's three paragraphs are a flawless field of black characters on a pristine white sheet. Desmond's are double black, gray and filled with tiny check marks where the teacher has caught his errors.

We return to our seats and Mrs. Klecko assumes parade rest, her stick behind her skinny butt. She gives us a great General Patton frown... a drill instructor in drag.

"Gentlemen. Three of you were honest in admitting you do not type. The rest of you were a teensy bit dishonest but... you do not type.

"Speed *is* important. But accuracy... more so.

"In 1936, I was the *World Champion Typist* in Zurich, Switzerland with 176 words per minute. When we are finished, you will all be typists capable of 30 words per minute for you have thousands of pages of reports in your future. And they must be typed accurately.

"We have work to do. Let us begin with the home row."

14: The First Weekend

Back from our second day of class, we find the weekend KP roster posted with Adamich and Chan the only two from our class. After dinner, I stroll over the tiny PX, buy a pack of Pall Malls and get a couple dollars worth of quarters. At the pay phone booth, I deposit my quarters and dial Andy's number in Washington.

I check my billfold as the call goes through. $24. Enough to get me through a weekend if I don't do anything extravagant.

"Hello!"

"Hi, this is Five Lowrey. Is Andy in?"

"Oh, hi, Five. This is Denise. How are you?"

"Fine. Just great. Is Andy there?"

"Aw, Five, she's already gone. We have a seminar in Williamsburg for the rest of the week and she drove down early. Just left a little while ago." Pause. "And I can't talk long 'cause we've got to leave to catch the bus."

"Ah... Denise. That's a shame. I've got the weekend off and was calling to see if I could come down. Nothing fancy but..."

"I think she already has plans for the weekend, Five. Staying with her, er... friend's parents in Alexandria. Is there somewhere she can call you?"

"Naw. Just a pay phone booth. Maybe I'll call her next week."

"OK, Five. I'll tell her you called. I know she'll hate that she missed you. Ooops, gotta go. Bye!"

"Bye!"

64

Somewhat dejected, I walk back to the bay. $24. That'll buy nearly a hundred beers. Changing into civvies, I pick up my sketchpad and leave the bay by myself, heading for the library.

The lights in the craft room are on and I can see Peggy Muldoon standing by a table talking with some soldiers. It looks as if they're working on some sort of leather work. I go to the periodical rack and pick up the copy of *Cosmopolitan* with Darcy on the cover.

Opening my sketch book, I begin to make a quick pencil sketch of her face. It's not like the old days when Darcy was a living, warm, loving model but her heart-shaped face and big eyes quickly take form beneath my pencil. Finishing the sketch, I leaf through the magazine and find an article with some more fashion photos of Darcy.

A shadow falls over the pages. "Hi, soldier. Just a snoopy librarian seeing what you're reading. *Cosmo?* I would've picked you more for the *Sports Illustrated* type."

"Hi, Peggy. Five Lowrey. We met the other night."

"Sure, I remember you, Five. With the drooling Georgia cracker and the Chinese guy. You like *Cosmo?*"

"Aww, I just spotted it and the cover. An old friend of mine."

"You know Darcy? My God!" She steps back with a look of mock awe, then her eyes fall to the open sketch pad. "Did you do this? It's terrific."

"It's just a quick sketch," I say modestly. "Yeah, I majored in art and Darcy was, er, a life studies model and... ah, my friend."

"Oh my God, that's unbelievable." She glances toward the craft room. "Listen, don't go away. I'm almost finished with this leatherworking class. If I'm not around, they'll bug out for the rathskeller and leave me to clean the mess."

As she scoots away, I take a last look at Darcy's photo spread and trade the magazine for a copy of *Sports Illustrated.* Then I scan through the meager stacks, finding two or three books on painting masterpieces and several how-to books on painting and sketching.

A few minutes later Peggy returns and beckons for me to sit on the plastic couch beside her. "Five, I've got a proposition for you."

Hot damn!

"My last art instructor graduated in December and I'd love to have another class. They're our most popular, which surprises me. Would you be interested in teaching it?"

"Geeze Peggy, I don't know. I mean... I've just been here a few days. I don't know if I'd have enough time."

"Oh, pooh, enough time. It only meets two nights a week and I'll bet you're no different than the rest of the guys who go through here. You won't be over at that classroom studying at night. I'll bet you right now."

She gives me an appraising look. "And there's a budget. Not much but I could pay you five bucks a class. How does $40 a month extra sound?"

Frankly, it sounds terrific. And it'll put me in the company of this great looking librarian. But I decide to negotiate a little harder. "Tell you what. Let me buy you a beer at the rathskeller and we'll talk about it."

Peggy frowned just as the library door opened for a couple of WACs and a soldier. "I can't close for another hour and only if there's no one here. Hang around and it's a deal... only I can't go to the Rat."

I settled in on the couch with a fat book called *The Post-Impressionists* and renewed my friendship with Degas, Van Gogh, Renoir and that gang.

A heavy-set WAC picked up the copy of *Cosmo* and waved it to her companion, a Spec 4 with short-cropped blonde hair.

"Look at this dress, Fiona. Isn't that something?"

The blonde made a face. "Dress nothing. Look at that girl. Shit! I'd give anything to look like Darcy."

Peggy glanced up from the counter where she was checking out books for a GI. "See that guy over there, Sammy? He *knows* Darcy."

The stocky WAC spun around and stared at me. "No shit? You know Darcy? I don't believe it."

Peggy's smile broadened and her eyes had a mischievous glint. "Believe it. He used to sleep with her!"

Both WACs stared at me with little "o's" for mouths. I kept a straight face, which I buried deep into *The Post-Impressionists.*

Peggy slipped her arm into mine as we walked away from the darkened library.

"Man, Peggy, that was a mean thing to say. Besides, you don't know anything about me and Darcy."

"Aw Five, I'm sorry but I couldn't resist. Either of those two dykes would give anything to crawl in the rack with Darcy."

"Dykes? You mean lesbians?"

"Yeah, they're always slippin' into the library when I'm alone and saying suggestive things. I think they'd love for me to be part of a threesome." She giggled. "Now they'll be on your case to get all the details about their fantasy goddess."

As I started to turn toward the rathskeller, I felt the pressure of her arm as she headed straight ahead. "Remember, I can't go to the Rat. We'll go across to Semenkov's."

"I guess it's OK," I said, trying to remember the off-limits places from our indoctrination lecture. "But why can't you to the Rat."

"Oh, the general doesn't like for me to be seen in there."

"The general? You mean Brigadier General, ah, whatisname, Muldoon? Peggy Muldoon? Is he your father?"

"Lord, no," she chuckled. "My uncle. And he's a very, very nice man."

"Oh, thank God *for that.*"

We settle into the last empty booth in Semenkov's, a long room with a crowded bar and a hazy cloud of cigarette smoke mixed with steam roiling up from the grill. The place smelled of burgers, onions and bratwurst.

Peggy pulled off her coat and signaled for a very pretty waitress who gave us a big smile as she approached. "Hi, Simmy Two. How about two National Bo's and a brat... or do I want a burger?"

"Hey Peggy," the waitress smiled and glanced at me. "You *surely* don't want grilled onions with your brat... or burger." She winked at Peggy.

"Oh, yeah? Whatta you think this is, a date? Five Lowrey, meet Simmy Two. You'll never know her first name. That's classified by her Daddy."

I shook the waitress' graceful hand. "Pleased to meet you. Do your good friends call you 'Two' for short? Mine call me Five."

We settled on burgers with grilled onion and Cheeze-Whiz, a specialty of the house Peggy assured me. "There's Simmy One at the end of the bar. Their old man is a mystery, opened this place about five years ago. Lay a finger on either of those two girls and you'll get a hot, greasy spatula along side your head.

"But it's a friendly place and the girls are great kids. Never a fight in here. Lots of loud arguments but never a fight."

"OK, Peggy. I like Semenkov's. Now what's this about the general being your uncle."

She reached over and gave my hand a squeeze. "You're a nice guy, Five. And I want you for a friend and... more importantly, I want you for an art instructor. So I'll tell you what's what.

"I'm the baby girl of a big family. My Da's a homicide captain in the Baltimore Police Department and three of my four brothers are on the force. Two detectives. One a forensic technician.

"My other brother — he's the youngest before me so he's called 'Little Al' — is an open hearth foreman at Sparrow's Point Works. I grew up in Dundalk. Wanted to be a cop too but Da and the brothers wouldn't hear of it.

"So I graduated from the University of Maryland in library science and Da called upon the brand new commanding general of Fort Holabird to find me a safe place to work."

I held up a hand. "But don't you have to take a Civil Service exam and all that stuff?"

"Why sure! But the Army has its ways, especially when you're dealing with a bunch of big protective Irishmen. And now the rest..." she looked me squarely in the eye. "I am well-connected. And well-protected, as you can imagine. And I've made a lot of friends in this job... people scattered all over the world.

"Having guys think I'm the CG's daughter is a good way of keeping the more aggressive ones from trompin' on my shadow. I like to have a good time." She paused, then "other than Darcy, do you have a girlfriend, Five?"

I shrugged. "Well, there is this girl down in Washington for a little while. And until I called her tonight, I thought maybe..."

"But she's not available this weekend, right?"

"Right. She's away for the week... with a... friend."

"That's great, then. We've got a social with Hood College Friday night and you'll come. You do like to dance, don't you?"

"Sure do. Do we dress up?"

"Slacks and a sweater'll be fine. Hood's a really neat girls' school in Frederick… maybe not as classy as Goucher… but those girls will ride a bus for four hours just to come over here and mingle with the spies. Bring your classmates, too."

Peggy looked up as a gust of cold air blew down the bar. Through the door came Escobar, Linscombe, Mennosovich and Ray Stein. All waved and headed for our booth, except for Stein who sidled into a space at the bar and glared at us.

"Hi, guys," Peggy said, "you must be Five's buddies. Have a seat and meet my new art instructor."

15: Mysteries Of The SPH Revealed

Marching route step to class after Assembly, I hear Stein muttering behind me.

"Sheeit, Five. I cannot believe you. Cutting me out with my girl. Some buddy you are!"

"Sheeit, yourself, Ray. Your girl? Where were you last night when I went to the library."

"Bastard! Sneaked off to the library, you mean. Bet your ass I'da been there if I'd know you were going sniffin' around."

"Knock it off, you guys," Gaffney called from the rear of the column. "This ain't no picnic detail."

A blue *Classification: Confidential* placard hung from the podium of our classroom.

"Good morning, gentlemen. I'm Walter Blevins and this is the first class in investigative technique. You will want to make notes, but observe that the materials are classified 'Confidential' and handle them accordingly.

"The basic mission of the counterintelligence agent is to conduct investigations leading to the award or denial of a security clearance for military personnel. For conscripts, no background investigation is conducted until the soldier moves to an advanced course."

"What's a conscript?" Sam Ploughman whispers to anyone in general.

"Soldier, stand if you have a question. And state your name," Blevins admonishes. "Next time." He peers at Ploughman's nametag. "Private Ploughman, a conscript is a citizen who has been drafted into the United States Army.

"For volunteers, Regular Army soldiers such as yourselves who have enlisted for a particular branch or duty, such as the CIC, a routine background investigation is initiated when the volunteer is inducted to active duty. The routine BI is based upon the document that each of you filled out upon induction — the Statement of Personal History or SPH.

"If you will recall, you filled out this form with a list of all your addresses, schooling, employment and personal and professional references. The special agent will begin the investigation by contacting the references given and interviewing them.

"I'm sure that some of you, during Basic training, heard from concerned parents or friends that 'the FBI is asking around about you.' This is a source of confusion among the civilian population. And, at times, it is not an unhelpful factor in the course of an investigation."

"When a conscript, or draftee if you will, Mister Ploughman," Blevins says with a wry smile, "is assigned to an organizational duty where security clearance is required... say to operate a classified weapons system... a background investigation is also initiated."

Blevins picks up a chalk and draws a series of boxes on the blackboard. "As you conduct each investigation, you will do your utmost to gain an additional reference from each interview from the SPH. This is generally termed 'a throwoff'.

"There is a specific format to the interview which we'll go through and practice in the days ahead. But each interview must end with this question: 'Would you recommend that the Subject... that's the name of the person being investigated... should be considered favorably for a position of responsibility and trust within the United States Government?'

"Gentlemen... if the answer to that question is 'no,' then the investigation goes 'negative' and it becomes a whole new ballgame.

"After the smoke break, we'll watch a prototype investigation interview being conducted. Fifteen minutes, gentlemen."

In the bright winter sunlight, our breath and our cigarette smoke mingle in the clear air.

"What're you sayin' Five? They're gonna bring in a whole busload of pussy Friday night?" For a Harvard man, Desmond has a way with words.

"I think it's more like a college mixer, Des," I reply. "These are girls from Hood College. Peggy says they're really classy."

"Peggy!" Stein snorts. *"My Peggy* tells *you* about a busload of quiff?"

"Stein!" Clankus says in his authoritative low voice, "shut the fuck up about *your* Peggy. I don't think she's Five's Peggy either... not in three days. But your mushmouth whining is getting a bit tiresome."

Stein grins and drawls, "Sorry Sarge. I'm just funnin' ole Five, here. If he's man enough to take her away from me... and keep her... more power to him."

"Still, do you think there's a chance, ah..." Zigafoos hesitantly asks, "that one of us might get laid?"

I decide to play a high card. "I doubt that General Muldoon would approve of Peggy installing beds in the Rec Center."

"Who's General Muldoon?" Stein looks puzzled.

"The Commanding General, US Army Intelligence Center," Clankus responds.

"General Muldoon? Peggy Muldoon?" Stein looks at me with arched eyebrows. "Oh, shit!"

After the break, we find the paneled front wall of the classroom opened to a broad window.

"This is our interview room, jokingly called 'the fishbowl,' and in the weeks to come, each of you will be the fish," Blevins explains.

A middle-aged woman enters the room and takes a seat at a plain table. "The fishbowl is soundproofed and this window is a one-way mirror so that the participants won't be distracted." Blevins turns to look at the woman. "This lady is the person whose name was given as a reference."

A young man in a suit enters. "And this is our investigative agent. Now pay careful attention and let's see how this plays out."

The young man smiles and produces a small folder from his inside coat pocket.

"Good morning, are you Mrs. Annabelle Mims?"

"Miss Annabelle Mims, young man."

"I am Special Agent Dan Hollister with Military Intelligence." He opens and holds the small leather case before her eyes for a few seconds. "As I told you on the phone, your name has been given as a reference by James L. Johnson, who is being considered for a position of responsibility within the United States Government."

"Little Jimmy Johnson!" Miss Mims retorts. "Why that little rascal."

"What is the nature of your acquaintance with Mr. Johnson, Miss Mims?"

"Why, he used to cut my lawn. And when he got bigger, he used to peek into my bedroom as I undressed for bed. Of course," she smiled sweetly, "I had a lot better body back then."

Gales of laughter outside the soundproofed room.

After about 20 minutes during which the sweet Miss Mims tied Agent Hollister into embarrassing knots, he asked the key question and got this answer, "Why, certainly not. I'd trust little Jimmy with anything, even the atomic bomb."

The interview was followed by another smoke break and then Walt Blevins began his wrap-up.

"First, let me tell you that Agent Hollister and Miss Mims are professional actors. Agent Hollister followed the interview protocol. Miss Mims made up her answers as she went along and, as you can see, she's a pretty salty lady.

"You'll meet both of these people and their fellow thespians in the weeks to come. And you'll never know what role they're playing." He slammed his fist onto the podium. "Do not! I repeat, do not, take these people lightly. This is deadly serious business and these folks are employed to help you learn."

In a milder tone, "Now. Let's examine a few of the points where Agent Hollister got into difficulty."

16: The Bus Arrives

It's Friday afternoon and we seem to be getting the hang of the Agent Class after a short week.

"Let's recap the last interview one more time," Blevins says. "What mistakes did Agent Korum make?"

"He asked about six 'either-or' questions," Calvin Moon volunteers. "Mr. Scanlon really screwed him up with those answers."

"Right, Mr. Moon," Blevins responds. "Keep in mind those five types of questions you must try to ask."

The class chants, "Who, what, why, where and when."

"How about 'H' Mr. Blevins?" I ask, standing behind my desk. "How?"

"How can be helpful, Mister Lowrey, but the *how* of something calls for supposition on the part of the interviewer. It's best left up to the analyst who handles your agent report. Any other questions?"

"Well, that's it for the week. Next week we'll start our first practice interviews. To be fair, and for fun, we'll draw straws Monday morning to see who goes first. Dismissed!"

We file our class folders, lock up and log out, then form up outside the classroom to march home.

"Let's look snappy now. We're running late. Ten' hut!" Clankus orders. "Forrrrd' harch." No route step on Friday afternoon. As Clankus pulls his road guards beyond the Post Road, the Retreat cannon booms. We come to a halt, snap to attention and face the direction of the post flagpole. As the recorded bugle sounds the first notes of *Retreat,* we salute without command.

Out of the corner of my eye, I see Peggy Muldoon standing beside her idling car, hand over her heart and facing the flag. At the last note, she gives us a little wave and we march off for the free weekend.

Dinner is steaks and fries with a huge tossed salad. Everyone chows down quickly and we run up to the bay to "shit, shower and shave" for the big Hood College mixer.

At 1830 hours, about 45 guys are milling around outside the Rec Center. Stein, Chan, Ziggy and I had gone over right after dinner to help Peggy mop the floor and stow craft materials, fold the tables and generally try to make the Spartan hall into a place of romance. Or at least flirtation.

I'm wearing my coolest outfit. Khakis, penny loafers, a gray turtleneck and my faithful blue blazer. Its patch pocket has a dark spot where my *once cool* ACE medallion was worn.

Finally, a big gray and red bus pulls down Post Road, its headlights flashing. A rousing cheer goes up from the troops and then, the Hood girls come down the steps. I'm standing by Peggy as we watch the coeds and their hosts file into the Rec Hall, now lighted with blue and red gels over the basket lights.

"The first half hour is always fun," Peggy says. "Watching all the pussy hounds trip over themselves trying to sort the winners."

Suddenly I'm shocked by the appearance of a familiar face in the bus door. I duck behind Peggy and speak softly into her ear. "Whoa! You think this is going to be fun. You ain't seen nothin' yet."

She turns and gives me a quizzical look.

"Just let me stay out of the way for five minutes or so, then watch."

I slink into the Rec Hall behind Peggy and sidle into a dark corner, keeping my eye on the familiar figure, now more familiar as she removes her long coat. Peggy's low-bidder 45rpm player drops the first platter on the stack and the party is on.

Couples get into the dance with the first song, gyrating on the floor to *Shake, Rattle & Roll* and I use the commotion to walk quietly behind her. In a low voice, I ask softly, "Can I have this dance, ma'am?"

"I'm not dancing, thank you," she answers and turns her head slowly, just in case I might turn out to be Ray Milland.

"Five? Five Lowrey?" Culden Ellis shrieks, startling even the rockin' dancers on the floor. She flings her arms around my neck, still making a shrill, banshee-like noise. "Goddamn sonofabitch, Five! It's really you?"

I squeeze my old studio partner tightly and give her a smashing kiss, right on the lips. "It's really me, Culden, but what in hell are you doing here?" Peggy has a strange look on her face.

"I'm the chaperone," she says loudly, then hugging me to her she whispers, "to these prissy little bitches. Hormones on the hoof. God, what did I ever get myself into?" she laughs.

Peggy appears at our side. "Peggy, this demure thing is Culden Ellis, my old studio partner at OU."

Peggy also gives Culden a hug. "Hi, Culden, we've talked on the phone. I'm Peggy Muldoon. You should've seen the look on your face."

"Did you know Five was going to pull this shit?" Culden asks her.

"Nope! Not 'til you stepped off the bus. What a surprise, uh?"

"God, I'll say. I was lookin' forward to this like a case of crabs but now it's going to be a ball. Peggy, can you help watch this crowd with Miss Hemorrhoid Face over there... Donna Alexander... so Five and I can talk?"

Peggy nods enthusiastically and starts around the dancers. Culden calls out, "Keep a sharp eye. I don't think half of these hussies wore any underwear."

"So now I'm a fucking art instructor at fucking Hood College in fucking Frederick, Maryland," Culden says with a huge grin. We're scrunched up on the library's plastic couch. "And you're in the Army here? Goddamn, but all these girls have talked about is the secret agents at Holabird. And you're one of 'em."

"That's us, Culden, fucking secret agents. I'm glad to hear you've cleaned up your vocabulary now you're on the faculty of a fancy girls' school."

"Well, tell me everything Five. How'd you get here? How's Andy? Have you seen her? And Darcy? I see her repulsive little face in every dorm lounge I go into. Have you heard from Dicky Reb? Is Doc Logan OK? About Trish Bitch? God, I miss her stares of disapproval!"

Punctuated with Culden's expletives, I tell her everything. Well, almost everything. Peggy appears with three paper cups of punch and joins us.

"I added a little something from my private stock," she grins. The Hawaiian Punch is definitely improved by a generous dollop of vodka.

"Peggy, let me tell you," Culden waves her arm toward me, "this guy is the best fucking artist that Ohio University ever turned out. Except maybe for Jim Dine. And me!" She squeezes my arm. "And he's one of the smartest, bravest, sneakingest, low-down nice guys I've ever met. He's a fucking hero."

Peggy looks at me. "Five, did you give Culden as a reference on your SPH? You should be on Uncle Dick's staff by now if you did."

"Or in the stockade at Fort Meade," I grin. "But Culden does tend to exaggerate."

The two seem delighted when I excuse myself for the head. "Take your time, Five, I've got a lot to tell Peggy here."

Culden's fellow chaperone looks frazzled, and not just a little put out at us, as the evening comes to an end. The lights come up and the couples rush out the door for some passionate good-byes before the bus loads.

"We're missing one, Culden," Miss Hemorrhoid Face hisses, "but I haven't been around the building yet."

"We'll take a look, Donna," Peggy grins. "You just keep an eye on the bus and don't let any of my GI's sneak on. It's a long walk back from Frederick."

"I'll tell the world it is," Culden mutters as the three of us start around the library building. "Two and a half hours of oversexed girl talk and it'll be worse going back."

In the lee of the library door, we find the missing couple, wrapped in her coat and a deep embrace.

"OK lovebirds, party's over," Culden shouts. The people spring apart and Ray Stein's face, covered with lipstick, shines under the security light. They scurry past us to the front of the building.

"Nice to see you, Private Stein," Peggy calls in their wake.

Hoots, squeals and screams come out of the loaded bus as Culden and I put on a real Hollywood farewell hug and kiss. Someone screams from the vehicle, "Miss Ellis, you're *Frenching* him!"

"Come and see me, Five," she gasps. "Frederick's really the sticks but I feel better about it now that I know you're here. And I didn't even get to tell you about Dicky Reb. He's now Richard West and a contract photographer for *Look*.

"But you're a better kisser," she whispers as she boards the bus.

As the big bus moves off to the accompaniment of shrill whistles and cheers, Peggy takes my arm.

"Wow, what a night." She looks up, "and you really did sleep with Darcy, huh? And you'll have to tell me about this Andy, too."

"Some other time, perhaps. Can I help you clean up?"

"Naw. Jeannie Best, she's my weekend staff, will be here in the morning and we'll police the place then. I'm beat and want to get home."

She stood on tiptoes and gave me a light peck on the cheek. "Thanks for your help. It was one of the best mixers we've ever had, thanks to you and Culden."

17: Crabtown Weekend

Saturday morning, bright and clear with an incredible breakfast. Chan, in fatigues and a white apron, plops down at our table. "Sorry about the homemade donuts, guys, but Chef Spook said only two to a customer."

The donuts were wonderful, fat and fluffy with a thick, crackly glaze. "Of course, we kitchen slaves get to eat all we want," Chan grins, "of those that weren't perfect. You'd be amazed at how many don't get an exact coating of glaze."

We sit around, having one more cup of coffee and one last smoke. Ray Stein has said little during breakfast, either eating or sitting with his chin on his chest. Finally he speaks, "Guess I screwed the moose with Peggy last night, huh Five?"

"Oh, I don't know. She didn't seem too shocked. What was that babe's name, anyway?"

"Damned if I know. But if you guys would've showed up just five minutes later…"

I bus my tray and pull on my coat. "Well, if you want, I'm going over to the library and help clean up. You can come along and see how Peggy reacts."

Peggy's reaction was a cheerful hello to the pair of us. She was dressed in jeans, her Maryland sweatshirt and a ski cap, a push broom in one hand.

"Hi, Ray," she chirped at Stein, "here's something you might want to return to your little friend." She reached behind the counter and handed Stein a big lumpy mailing envelope.

He reached in and pulled out a pink brassiere. His face quickly matched the bra in color.

"I found it out by the back door this morning. B cup. Not much but she may need it to keep warm." Peggy's grin was evil.

I couldn't resist. "Or I could mail it to Culden if you didn't catch her... ah, address, Ray." He looks chagrined. "Culden could just ask around Hood for the girl with the bare B-cup boobs."

A young woman with a little kid in a snowsuit came up to us. "C'mon you guys. Let's get to it. I've got a book discussion group coming at 1000 hours." Peggy introduced us to Jean Best and her two year old daughter, Blossom.

"Jean used to have this job before Blossom came along," Peggy explained. "Now she works part-time during the week and runs the center on weekends."

"I think most of the soldiers who come in on weekends do so because they want to play with Blossom," Jeannie explains. "She loves to have 'big soldjahs' read books to her. It's hilarious."

In short order, the Rec Center looks as if the Hood invasion had never occurred. Zigafoos and Escobar arrived to man the push brooms and triumphantly displayed several other pieces of undergarments.

"We put 'em in a box and I take them to the Little Sisters. We've got some charity cases running around Dundalk in pretty racy underwear," Peggy cracked.

"Say, Five. I've got to run into Baltimore to pick up some books at the library... and some art supplies for *your* class. Want to ride along and see the city?" Peggy glances at Zig and Escobar, playing with the baby. "Think your buddies would want a ride downtown?"

I ask and they accept effusively.

"I'll pick you up at the barracks circle in about a half hour. Don't forget to sign off post at the CQ's desk."

We pile into Peggy's little yellow sedan, me riding shotgun as befits the art instructor.

"What kind of car is this, Peggy? One of those new Japanese jobs?" Escobar asks.

"Oh, no. It's American. Count on that. It's a Studebaker Lark, just been out a few months."

"It's really neat," Zigafoos exclaims. "And the color... it's ah, really, subtle!"

Peggy laughs. "My Dad picked it up for me. He claims this was the only color they had available. I think maybe he just wanted me driving something he'd recognize. Keep me on the straight and narrow.'

I recall her description of her family and their protective nature, grin at Peggy and nod. "All girls name their cars! Does this one have a name yet?"

"Oh, yeah! I call it *Meadowlark Lemon."*

We hoot at the idea of the Harlem Globetrotters' ball-handling wizard tooling around Baltimore in this yellow machine.

We're rolling along Eastern Avenue when a short bleat of a siren gets our attention.

"Uh oh, Peg," Escobar exclaims, looking out the back window. "A cop's flashing his light and I think, for us."

"Oh, crap," Peggy sighs and hits her turn signal to pull into the curb. The car with its flashing red light pulls in behind us and an enormous guy in civilian clothes gets out and approaches.

"Good morning, miss," he booms and leans in the open window. "And how are we today?" He gives Peggy a big kiss on the cheek.

"Officer, don't you have anything better to do than molest young drivers on Eastern Avenue?"

"Aw Pegeen. I just wanted to see what bunch of orphan sojur boys you'd be luggin' downtown today." He leers at each of us, as if memorizing our faces.

"Police harassment," Peggy mutters but smiles. "Next it'll be police brutality, right?"

"If they don't mind their step with me little sis, that could very well be," the giant growls but with a smile on his face.

"Detective Sergeant Seamus Muldoon. Meet Privates Escobar and Zigafoos. And Private Thomsen Lowrey V, my new art instructor. He's called Five." The giant cop reaches in and shakes each of our hands.

81

"And this clown is my brother," Peggy says. "Friends and relatives call him 'Little Sham' and wrongdoers call him 'that big Mick sonofabitch'."

"Is there a 'Big Sham?' Escobar asks.

"Oh, that would be my Da," Peggy responds in her quaint accent, one we've heard very little before now. "Maybe some day you'll get the opportunity to get the joke."

"Now Pegeen, you should show the lads The Block and make sure they know where all the bad places are," Little Sham instructs. With another kiss to Peggy's cheek, Little Sham gives us a wave and returns to his car. With a light hoot on the siren, he pulls out and waves again.

Peggy says to us as we pull out, "Now you know why my Da picked a yellow Lark."

We drive into downtown past bustling docks and turn right onto Baltimore Street. Playing tour guide, Peggy drives us into a canyon of bars and strip joints.

"This, gents, is The Block... East Baltimore Street. And that," pointing to a huge gray building at the end of the strip, "is where my Da and brothers work... Bal'mer's conveniently located police headquarters." She pulled into the cop shop parking lot and reversed our course through The Block.

"This is literally the roughest place in town, maybe the world," she said as we cruised past open strip clubs and saloons although it was early afternoon. "You can, for sure, get screwed, blewed and tattooed... as they say... 24 hours a day. And you can get picked up by whores, homos or cops or pick up some really nifty diseases.

"I'm not speaking from experience... just what the two Shams tell me," she laughed. "And they say if you wanna go to The Block, stick to the Two O'clock Club. I *have* been there and that's where Blaze Starr works. What a show and it's relatively safe!"

She turned right and we headed up Charles Street. "Culturally, things pick up a little bit. That's the Peabody Bookstore over there where H.L. Mencken used to hang out. It's a good little coffee house where you can loiter all day without spending much.

"And this is the *real* Washington Monument," as we approached a park topped by a tall, round tower. "The one down in D.C. is a johnny-come-lately. Mount Vernon Place runs east-west, and this is Charles Place. We're in the heart of old Bal'mer."

"And this is Cathedral Street and there's our destination, the Enoch Pratt Free Library."

A tweed-suited librarian greeted Peggy enthusiastically and led us to a storeroom where we hauled six cartons of books to the car. The little Studebaker squatted like a chopped and lowered hot rod.

"Now for a real treat," Peggy announced as we headed south again. We pulled into a crowded parking lot and she led us into a giant, low shed of a building. "Lexington Market's one of the neatest places in Bal'mer."

Indeed, the market was a wonder. Row after row of stalls filled with wonderful smelling sausages and meats, wheels of cheese, fresh produce, oysters, fish and writhing blue crabs waiting for the steamer. We wandered the stalls in amazement.

"Peggy, who possibly could eat all those oysters?" I asked as we stood before a mound of glistening bivalves that extended above our heads.

"You should see the Muldoon family on a Friday night," she responded. "These're just an appetizer to a crab feed."

Peggy and I left my buddies in the market with instructions from her on which buses to catch for Dundalk, another motherly warning about The Block, and ensuring they had enough money to eat and ride home.

"I feel kinda bad dumping them like that but I get the feeling they'd rather check out the strippers than go to an art supply store."

I nodded agreement, privately thinking that checking out the strippers wouldn't be a bad way to spend the afternoon.

Kastner's Art Supplies made the College Book Store look like a roadside stand. Peggy whirled through, picking up contè crayons, newsprint pads, charcoal sticks and inexpensive watercolors, never once consulting me, the new instructor.

"Your sketch pad looked nearly filled," she said surveying the assortment of sketch books. "How 'bout a new one?"

"OK, but something a little smaller. Easier to carry around."

She wrote a check for more than $200 for two huge boxes of supplies. "I'll get most of this back with the $5 fee for each student. We're not supposed to make a profit."

Since the trunk was full, I piled the supplies into the Lark's back seat and we headed east again, turning north on Charles.

"One more stop," she grinned. "But this one's for pleasure. And GI's can get in the BMA for free. I've got an annual membership."

The Baltimore Museum of Art resembled the capital of a small country. After eating hot pretzels from a vendor on the broad front steps, we wandered the halls through amazing displays.

"The Cone sisters amassed this collection. Etta just died ten years ago but before that, they were constantly loaning the BMA works from their apartment." Peggy looked up at the row of Matisse masterpieces lining one wall. "How I would've loved to see that apartment."

It's dusk by the time we arrive back at the 'Bird and get the supplies and book cartons unloaded. Blossom Best is sacked out on the couch as her mother starts sorting the book boxes.

"Five, it's been a good day. Be sure to thank your friends for their help... and thank you, too."

"It *was* fun, Peggy... Pegeen. Thanks for taking me to the museum." Digging deep for courage, I pause... "Ah, I've missed dinner and... ah, I wonder if you'd like to get a burger or pizza or something?"

My courage plummets with the look on Peggy's face. "Oh, Five. I'm sorry but I've already made plans for tonight." The look on my face must tell her how I'm feeling. "It's not a date! I've got to go home and clean up for mass and then after, I'm going home... their home, not mine... to have dinner with Da and the family. 'Cause I missed our regular Friday night."

Her face screws up and she stamps her foot. "Damn! Why am I telling you this? It's none of your... I mean, I don't have to explain..."

"It's OK, Peg. I understand. No big deal."

"Yes it is, and I feel bad. I'm going to mass tonight so I can go up to Gettysburg tomorrow... to see my old roommate." She takes a deep breath. "Ever been to Gettysburg, Five?"

I nod no.

"If you don't have anything else to do, why not ride up with me? It's a beautiful place and you can make some good sketches."

"Can I ride home, too?"

18. To The High Water Mark Of The Confederacy

Hungry and with nothing better to do, I wander back to the barracks and find it empty, except for a snoring Chan curled on his bunk.

So I decide to visit the rathskeller for the first time, discovering there most of my class well into a Saturday night celebration. I order an iced mug of National Bo and pull up a chair at a table occupied by Jeff Adamich, Calvin Moon and Escobar, whose head is dangerously close to the table.

At the next table, Ploughman, Linscombe and Luck are playing *Cardinal Puff* with a trio of women. I recognize the pair of WACs from the library among them.

Tomas raises his head and slurs, "Damn Five, but you should see the babes in that Two O'clock Club. Shit, man! They run around naked as babies. Tit city."

"Where's Zig?" I ask.

"I ran outta money. Zig didn't. He's still down on The Block, I guess. He had some ole' naked gal sittin' on his lap when I pulled outta there."

A hip bumps me nearly off the chair. The tall WAC with short blonde hair has left Cardinal Puff and joined me. "Hey! You're the guy who knows Darcy. I'm Fiona Briscoe. Remember me from the library?"

"Hey Fiona, make yourself comfortable."

"All right, I will." And she squirms her hip tighter to mine. Into my ear she whispers, "Did you really sleep with Darcy?"

"For me to know and you to find out... it'll never happen."

Fiona is kind of cute to begin with and after a bag of pretzels and five or six mugs, she's downright alluring. The tables get pushed together and a couple more WACs join the crowd for a chugging tournament.

Calling up all my athletic reserves, I make it to the semifinals and whip Fiona's butt. She promptly wobbles and falls off the chair. Then I'm facing the WAC they call Sammy, Fiona's heavy-set friend.

"All right you college boy puke. Five bucks side bet says I win the pot," she growls at me as two fresh mugs are placed before us.

"You're on, Specialist," I growl, digging into my pocket for my rapidly diminishing funds. "What *is* your *specialty,* anyway?"

The crowd chants the countdown and we lift our mugs. I can feel icy National Bo running down my chin but can see the bottom of the mug coming up fast. I slam the mug down just an instant before Sammy. The agent crowd cheers and the WACs look glum.

I scoop up the bills in the pot and Sammy's fiver and in a single, smooth motion, head off to the latrine to barf.

As I scurry away from the table, I hear Fiona's muffled voice from the floor. "Did you kick his ass, Sammy?"

Someone's trying to shake my head off. I snap from sleep into an earthquake of violent proportions but as my eyes open, I discover it's only the CQ shaking my shoulder.

"C'mon troop, rise and shine," he says, giving my shoulder one more brutal snap. "Uppy, uppy."

"Whas'up?" I mumble. "It's Sunday. Quit shakin' me. Go 'way."

"Nope! You Lowrey?" I nod affirmative.

"General Muldoon's office just called. You got one hour to shit, shine and shave and if you're lucky, get a bite of chow." He surveys me. "Wheew. You stink."

"General Muldoon?" I'm alarmed. Why would the CG want to see me? On Sunday morning?

"Yep, at least it was his secretary. She said a car'd pick you up at 0930. It's 0830 now."

87

Dragging my dying body down the cold barracks floor to the latrine, my mind suddenly snaps into gear. "General Muldoon? Muldoon?"

I'm first into the mess hall where two cups of black coffee and a big pile of buckwheat cakes breathe some life back into my soul. Into the latrine for a third tooth brushing of the morning and back to my locker for my jacket. I spot my khakis from the night before lying in the bottom of the locker.

With a slowly-returning memory, I rifle the pockets and come up with two $5 bills and a double handful of singles. I count out $34 and all of a sudden, my hangover isn't as acute.

"Good morning, General Muldoon, sir!" I snap off a salute as I climb into Meadowlark Lemon.

"C'mon, Five. Don't give me that stuff. I saw you headed for the rat when I left post last night. I figured it would take some authority to get you going this morning." Peg leans over and sniffs, "Whew, you could stand a day of airing out."

"I showered and stuff."

"Yeah, that much beer will come out of your pores for days."

Driving up Route 30 through northern Maryland, we talked over soft music from the Lark's radio.

"My big mouthed brother told the whole family about his 'suspect stop' on Eastern Avenue yesterday," she dropped into our small talk. "He took special pains to describe you to the rest of the family."

"Why me? Wasn't he interested in you riding around with a Cuban revolutionary in the back seat?"

"My brothers have *The Sense*. They can recognize the threat at first glance."

"Me? A threat? To what? What's your mom have to say about all this?"

"My mother died in childbirth," Peg says quietly. "I'm the youngest child." She gave me a firm look. "I'm also the mother now. Or so it seems."

"God, Peg. I'm sorry."

"So am I, but there's never been any blame. It was God's will that I would grow up to be Mam to five hulking Irishmen."

As we crossed the Pennsylvania line, the first fluffy snowflakes begin to splat against the windshield.

"Snow! I can't think of any place prettier than Gettysburg in the snow." She seemed happy although visibility was rapidly vanishing as the flakes grew thicker. I was thinking maybe we should turn back.

We drove in thoughtful silence, broken only by the swish of the wipers. Little walls of snow began to build at the edge of their sweep.

"Who's this roomie we're going to see?" I asked. "Can I buy lunch? I'm richer than I was yesterday."

"Oh, you'll find out. It's just an old friend."

"Ahhh! So I'll just wait 'n find out."

"Yup."

Although I'd teased Peggy about the roommate possibly being a guy, I was sure I hadn't angered her. The snow had stopped before we reached Gettysburg and a bright sun was blinding across the battlefield, casting thick black shadows from dozens of monuments.

In town, Peggy stopped the car. "Out you go, boyo! The museum is up that way a couple hundred yards. Cemetery's up the hill there behind that wall." She looked at her watch.

"There's a cafe downtown, over there. It's got a yellow front. I'll meet you there in, oh, no more than two hours."

"But I don't understand."

Peggy's lower lip puffed out and quivered. "Oh, Five, I'm going to see Mary Frances Calabahn. She's in a convent. She's now Sister Joseph." Giving my hand a squeeze, she pulled my door closed. "I'll explain later."

I wandered among the markers of the National Cemetery, their tops pillowed with snow. Bright sunlight made the white markers glisten in uniform ranks. Also uniform was the date of death on the stones in the older section. 1863.

From my vantage point on Cemetery Hill, I could look down the length of the battlefield, its orchards bare of leaves, its once bloodied fields now a soft blanket of white. Monuments and statues, large and small, decorated the landscape, punctuated by a few dark, lonely figures

89

walking and a single photographer, setting up his view camera and vanishing beneath the black folds of the focusing hood.

I dusted snow from a stone wall and sat to sketch the photographer at work. What appeared on my paper might've been a scene of Matthew Brady, recording the fields where more than 50,000 bodies lay less than a century ago.

To be in this hallowed place brought on a range of emotions. Sadness and awe, mixed with admiration for those who fought here. The memory of last week's lecture on this history of espionage came back. How General Lee's success on this field was thwarted by the delivery of his lost marching orders to the Union Army staff.

I walked slowly toward the little town, sketching buildings pocked with the scars of Minie balls from 1863, and a group of children sledding on the lower slopes of Cemetery Hill. When I saw the cafe with its pale yellow front, I also saw the brighter hues of Meadowlark Lemon. Looking at my watch, I realized I had been lost in the Civil War for more than three hours!

Peggy's smile was faint as I entered the restaurant and joined her at the only occupied table. She reached out to hold my hand as I sat, squeezing gently. I could see a potential tear glistening in the corner of her eye.

"What do you think of the battlefield?" she asked softly.

"It's tremendous. Hard to find words to describe how I feel. I'm sorry I'm late but I just lost track… How is your friend?"

"Oh, Five. I just love to come visit Mary Frances. And then… I'm always so sad. And she seems… so, well happy and content. I always end up imagining myself in a habit and I don't think I could be happy and content."

"You said she was your roommate?"

"Yeah! We roomed together for two years at U of M. And were greatest friends. Two girls from Catholic schools having the time of our lives.

"Mary Frances is little and gorgeous. She lit up every room she entered. She became a cheerleader. And she met this great guy."

"And?"

"And got pregnant. They were in love but the guy's goal was med school and he wouldn't marry her. She would not get an abortion. Neither would I in her place. So she had the baby, put it out for adoption, quit the university and entered the convent."

Peggy swiped the back of her hand across her eyes. "She took her vows last year and now she's Sister Joseph."

I drank my coffee and lit a Pall Mall. Peggy reached over and popped a cigarette out of the pack for herself. "I didn't know you smoked."

"I don't, ordinarily," she said and blew a practiced smoke ring. "But it reminds me of the old days of plaid skirts and knee socks at St. Brendan. We'd smoke behind the boiler room and confess impure thoughts to each other.

"It reminds me of how many times I've had a near-miss with the opportunity to become a nun."

Peggy drove us down the winding road of the battlefield, past the Copse and High Water Mark of the Confederacy, past the Round Tops. We strolled through the boulders of Devil's Den and tried to imagine the scene as sweltering July, not a snowy January afternoon.

I made my first sketch of her, perched on a rock with her scarf thrown over her shoulders and curls glistening in the afternoon sun.

"Oh, wow, that's good, Five. Really flatters me," she said, peering at the sketch pad. She leafed through my other sketches. "This one would make a great painting. Almost chiaroscuro with a light touch of gold on the snow. The photographer looks just like the Civil War."

I resolved to make the painting.

19. Would You Recommend...

Dave Clay draws the shortest straw, and Calvin Moon the second shortest, to begin the day's first interviews. Walt Blevins hands them each an SPH to study and gives us a small briefing.

"When you're on permanent assignment and in the field, you'll be issued a set of credentials. These are two identity cards commonly referred to as 'boxtops' but believe me gentlemen, lose your credentials and I can't measure how deep the shit you'll be in. The word is that the Russians will pay $10,000 on the street for an authentic set of CIC credentials.

"The credential will be laminated among twelve sheets of thin plastic. A luminescent thread and some translucent material are embedded in the finished credentials to make it difficult to photocopy them.

"You'll also be issued a badge to go with the credentials. Most agents don't bother to carry the badge. Others do, finding it a good quick ID to bluff their way into a situation. There's no specific protocol to follow."

"For our practice interviews, we'll use a credential case with blank cards. Don't worry, the actors won't give you a rough time about the contents of the blank cards... though they might incorporate your presentation of the credentials into the interview."

Blevins leads Clay out of the classroom and our lights go down as the interview room lights up. A man of about 40 enters the room and takes a seat in one of two chairs. Blevins returns and takes a seat with us and the interview begins as Clay enters hesitantly.

"Mr. Casey. I'm David Clay of the U.S. Government..."

To everyone's amazement, Clay gets through the interview with very few stumbles and no really awkward moments. Mr. Casey turns out to be the Subject's high school speech teacher and has nothing negative to say about him.

Walt Blevins' critique is kindly. "Well done, Mr. Clay. My only criticism would be your introduction. You're not really 'of the U.S. Government' but 'Special Agent Clay of U.S. Army Intelligence.' The idea of the U.S. Government coming calling will scare the shit out of many people.

"Our purpose with the introduction is to establish a friendly rapport with just the least bit of intimidation. In the long run, you'll do better with most interviewees by following that procedure."

When the lights signal readiness for the second interview, we discover in the Fishbowl our friend Miss Mims from last week's demo interview. But this is a vastly different Miss Mims... her hair in an attractive roll on the top of her head, a tight purple dress that reveals a lot of thigh when she crosses her shapely legs. She smokes a cigarette in a long holder that matches the dress.

Moon's jaw drops when he enters the Fishbowl and sees the interviewee. But he starts smoothly.

"Hello Mrs. Dragle. I'm Special Agent Calvin Moon of U.S. Army Intelligence. I'm here regarding Frank Sampson who is being considered for a position of trust within the military. He provided your name as a reference."

"Frank Sampson? I'm not sure I recall the name... Agent... is it Loon?"

"Moon, ma'am. Franklin Joseph Sampson?"

"Oh, you mean Joey. Oh, sure, Joey's a wonderful person."

"When did you first meet Mr. Sampson?"

She cocks her head and flicks a long ash from her cigarette in the direction of Moon's shoes. "Oh, my God. Let's see... must be 13 years ago. He was just a little guy when he first started coming to me."

"And when did you last see him?"

"Oh, I can tell you that. It was my birthday, my 35th birthday, just four months ago."

"That would be September?" She nods yes.

"And what was the nature of your relationship with Mr. Sampson."

"Well agent, I'm surprised at you. Did you read the sign by my door? I'm a piano teacher."

"So he was your student?"

"I should say so, and a very accomplished one at that." She gives Moon an arch leer. "His accomplishments were truly magnificent. He has the tools to be one of the greats."

Moon hesitates, looks down at the tiny cheat sheet concealed in his hand. "Well, that's fine. Now... who were his associates? Who did he run around with?"

"Oh, I don't know. He had some friends but he never brought them here. When he came to me, he was dedicated to his practice and performances." Moon starts to speak again but she cuts him off. "I taught him the beauties of a well-performed fellatio and in later years, he became a true master of cunninglingus."

Our room is filled with gasps and giggles but in the soundproofed Fishbowl, Moon soldiers on, even getting a throwoff reference and a positive recommendation for the musician.

As he makes his exit, Mrs. Dragle rises and rubs his shoulder. "My but you're a big man," she murmurs. "You're, ah, colored, aren't you?"

Moon's complexion turns from beige to nearly purple. "Both my parents were, ma'am," he growls. "Good-bye."

"Good-bye, Special Agent Coon."

Both Calvin Moon and Walt Blevins are flushed and sweating. Blevins produces a handkerchief and wipes his brow. "Good job, Calvin. Very cool," he says, patting Moon on the shoulder.

"Well, gentlemen. You've now met Mrs. Dragle. Ain't she a peach? And you can thank your stars that you won't meet *her* again during the course.

"But in real life, gentlemen, you will probably encounter men or women who are vulgar, bigots, exhibitionists and seducers. Now Calvin, I know it was rough but you did let a few important things get by you. Anyone have any ideas?"

"Moon... you obviously ain't too *experienced,*" Harvard Desmond chimes in.

"Correct, Mr. Desmond. Her mention of *fellatio* should have led you to a new line of questioning," Blevins says.

Calvin looks puzzled. "What's fellatio?"

Gunny adds to the discussion. "A blow job, Calvin."

"Shit!" Moon growls. "I thought it was some damn musical term like *largo* or *cappricio.* And that other one, that cunning…?"

"Cunninglingus," Clankus contributes, "is what's commonly known as *muff diving."*

Convened again after the smoke break, Ray Stein has a question. "What's this sex business have to do with a security clearance, Mr. Blevins? I thought what people do in their own…"

"Blackmail, Mr. Stein. Normal, healthy sexual relationships are the business of those who take part. But abnormal, or illicit, sex can lead to blackmail by the opposition and blackmail is a powerful tool of espionage.

"We don't know a lot of facts about Calvin's interview. But if Mrs. Dragle is married. Or the Subject is married. Or either is a member in good standing in the society of their community… well, you get the point. And the acts that Mrs. Dragle alluded to would definitely be considered abnormal by the community and the U.S. Army." He paused. "Calvin, your interview's line of questioning should certainly have been expanded along those lines."

Moon stood and shrugged. "OK. But what about that racial shit she pulled? Do I have to stand for that?"

Blevins looked Moon straight in the eye. "Calvin. Just 25 years ago, our country was full of bigotry and intolerance. Common terms like… nigger, spic, kike, chink… were used in everyday conversation. Many appeared in newspapers. There is much intolerance and bigotry still, even though World War II taught us some powerful lessons.

"You handled that situation quite well and I'm proud of you. Class dismissed."

As we started filing our manuals and notes, Blevins called for our attention.

"One other thing, guys. Remember Mrs. Dragle doesn't exist except in that room. The actress who plays her role is a very nice person and, I think you'll admit, quite good at her job.

"So Calvin, if you see her in the street, don't go poppin' her one in the jaw."

20. Days Turning Into Weeks

Our classes become a Mixmaster blur of counterintelligence skills. Mrs. Klecko continues to torture our afternoons with the home row and endless exercises but even the two-fingered Gaffney is using all his digits and is up to a respectable 12 words a minute.

My turn in the Fishbowl hasn't come but watching the interviews of others builds confidence in all of us. The Bird's troupe of thespians confounds us with an array of characters and personality traits.

Among their favorite tricks *is the either or question.*

"Did you accompany him on this trip or stay at home?"

"Yes!"

Report writing is painfully dull. Desmond, the would-be journalist, keeps getting gigged for striking over typing errors in his reports. Mennosovich can't get the hang of writing the word 'Subject' and the dozens of times the word appears in each report comes out as 'Subjet.'"

New aspects of the course begin to appear in small doses. We get an intro lecture to *tradecraft* and terms such as *surreptitious, dead-letter drop,* and *microdot* fall into our everyday conversation. Slowly we're being enveloped in the cloak of the clandestine world... or at least we like to think so. Next week we start on surveillance technique!

"Peg, you should know that I've never actually taught an art class before."

We're sorting through materials, laying out newsprint pads and charcoal sticks. In less than 30 minutes, my nine students will be taking their place in the Rec Center. It's the first time we've seen each other since the Gettysburg trip and Peggy seems a lot more cheerful.

"Oh, I don't care. I doubt if any of these folks have ever had a *real* art teacher and you know your stuff. You'll be fine." She picks up my sketch pads. "Mind if I show them your work? Sort of establish your credentials?"

I take my older pad and leaf through it. "A couple here I'd just as soon not show around…" Specifically, I'm looking at two drawings of Andy in our railroad roomette. In one, she's looking out the window in her pajamas. The other shows her smiling at me… not in her pajamas."

"Can I see?" she asks? I pull the pad away and carefully remove the Andy sketches and the one I made of Darcy from the *Cosmo* cover. I tuck them into my portfolio. "Aw, you're a poop."

"Maybe sometime," I respond, trying my shy smile. "But who's in the class?"

"Well, let's see," Peg responds, holding up a clipboard. "We've got three WACs, Sammy, the Fiend and someone named Shandra."

"The Fiend?"

"Yeah, Fiona The Sex Fiend. You remember the dishwater blonde that was here last week. She and Sammy take a lot of classes."

I remember Fiona The Fiend from Saturday night. *"Did you kick his ass Sammy?"*

She continues, "And a couple of guys from the Agent class that graduates at the end of the February. I've seen them around. And two guys, one from the Analyst class and the other from Photo Interp.

"And one officer, Second Lieutenant Glen Buckner. He's the CG's junior aide."

"Oh! And how do I address him?"

"Just Glen is OK. He takes every course we offer. He kind of fancies himself my beau… and likes to keep an eye on me."

"Well… another *Sham* in your life?"

Peg introduces the group and passes around my sketchpads. They all make appreciative noises. Fiona arches an eyebrow at the sketch of Peggy in the Devil's Den. Since she's sitting next to me at our big table, it's easy to hear her whisper, "All right. Takin' a little trip with Pretty Peggy, already?"

I ignore her and place a fat pear from the mess hall in the middle of the table, then position a gooseneck study lamp to its side to illuminate the subject.

"OK guys, we're going to take five minutes and I want each of you to sketch this pear. Don't worry about technique. Just let your hand guide the charcoal to paper and let your mind tell your hand what to do."

The time trial is a direct steal from Imogene Klecko's technique, but what the hell do I know about teaching art?

"What's this pear shit?" the black WAC says in a whining tone. "I thought we was gonna be drawin' people. Nekkid people. I want to be a model."

"Shandra. Shandra, is it?" I try to be earnest. "This pear is as sensual as most naked people you'll ever see." Shandra has a gorgeous thin face and long slim nose flanked by enormous eyes. "Just draw."

To my surprise, a couple of the students show some flare, especially Fiona. Her sketch is a bundle of thin lines that, in viewing, make up the essence of the pear's rounded contours. Shandra's is two continuous lines, one limning the outline of the pear, the other swashing out its stem.

Lt. Buckner's resembles a sketch on an officer's club napkin for a new bascule bridge. Each of them still holds his new charcoal stick like an expensive fountain pen.

"OK, let's start by talking about the medium." I snap off about two inches of a charcoal stick and rub it flat on my newsprint pad. "Charcoal is a cheap, very porous medium. And it's hard to draw with if you hold it like a pencil. So try what I just did."

They all snap off small chunks of charcoal and rub a flat side on them.

"Now watch this." With the nub of charcoal, I run broad strokes onto the rough surface of the newsprint, creating the outline of the pear. "You each saw the pear with different lighting. From where I'm sitting, the pear looks kind of like this."

I shade in the shadowed bottom of the pear and with my thumb, erase the highlights. Compared to their efforts, my pear fills the whole newsprint sheet.

"This newsprint is cheap, too. Don't treat it like a clean shirt. Don't be afraid to draw a big ole' image. Add more charcoal for shadows, Erase some with a finger to create highlights." Their eyes express interest. "Now trade seats and let's do another one."

Their second effort is better, except for Buckner's, which is nearly an exact duplicate of his first constrained drawing.

I move them through several more exercises and then, drawing upon memories of Jan Dabney's classes, decide to try perspective.

"All right, Shandra. You want to be a model. Roll up your sleeve and plonk your arm down here." Shandra rolls up her sleeve with the restrained enthusiasm of a junkie.

"Now, everyone stand up and move over here." They obey. "Look at Shandra's arm. Take in the light and how it falls on her black skin."

"Watch yourself, white boy," Shandra mutters.

"Shandra. You've got beautiful skin. I meant no offense so don't you go be takin' any." Shandra preens without moving her beautiful arm and long fingers.

"All right. Now, one by one, move over here where I am and squat down to table level and look at her arm from here." One by one, they follow instructions. Fiona takes great pains not to squat but to bend over, presenting her fine bottom to me.

"Notice how long her fingers look from this point of view. And how her arm seems to get smaller as it moves away from your eye." They all murmur recognition of my wisdom. "This is the effect of perspective and it's called foreshortening."

As they pack away their gear and put on coats, Shandra comes up to me. "Hey Mister Five. You think I could be a model? I mean, I got tits out to there and everyone say I got a fine body."

"Shandra, I'm sure you could. But I'm not sure post regs will let you pose in the nude."

She pouts. "Well shit. Maybe I try the mothafuckin' camera club, then. You don't know what you're missin."

After they're gone, Peggy grins at me. "Fun. I mean, really fun. You're a naturally good teacher. That was the first art class I've ever *really* enjoyed."

"Thanks a lot, boss. But what can I say about your Lieutenant? Everything he did looked remedial."

"Oh, don't worry about Glen. I don't think he expects anything out of these classes but looking at me... and after tonight, at Shandra's tits 'way out to there.'"

"Oww, Shandra. There's a real piece of work."

"Yeah, but she *does* have a great body. I could see ole' Sammy shaking her head in agreement. Nite, Five."

21. How To Describe A Spook

Walt Blevins begins A59-1's segment on surveillance with a short lecture. "Not all reports you'll write will be the result of subject interviews. Surveillance is the art of surreptitiously observing the actions and activities of a subject and then writing a report based upon your observations.

"One of the important aspects of surveillance is being able to describe in great detail persons the subject might contact, especially if your team is too small to switch an agent to the contact.

"So we'll start today with description techniques. We have with us Lt. Jack Barrone, of the Baltimore Police Department. Jack, it's all yours."

Lt. Barrone produces a flip chart and begins describing body types, facial characteristics, and the like, all in terms which can be read and understood by an agent reading a report in another location.

He goes on for more than half an hour then is suddenly interrupted the lights going down. The lights go up in the Fishbowl to reveal people we've never seen before. Two men seem to be in an argument, although the sound system isn't turned on. Then a woman joins them and enters the conversation.

I sense that watching carefully may be very important. Like my classmates, I take notes of their appearance.

After about three minutes, the Fishbowl goes black and our classroom lights pop back on.

"All right, gentlemen. You've just watched an encounter simulating what might be seen during a surveillance... except you had a much closer view than would likely be normal."

Blevins wrinkles his lips into a smile. "I'll give you four minutes to write a description, based upon what Lt. Barrone has just outlined, of the... woman!"

Our pencils fly. I feel confident of my notes and set to work. At the end of four minutes, Blevins calls a halt.

"OK, write your names on top of your descriptions. But first, some questions. What was her estimated age," he asks.

Answers range from 18 to 50. As he continues, we offer even more contradictory observations. Gray coat, blue coat. Long coat, car coat. Short straight hair. Blonde curly hair. Glasses. No glasses. We are in a fit of giggles as the observations continue.

"Now, Lt. Barrone, if you'll take up the written descriptions, we'll see who maybe even came close." I hand in my two pages and am relieved to see him put them on the bottom of the pile. "Officer Rangely, will you please join us?"

The woman comes into the room. Her medium length auburn hair curls over the collar of her gray coat. She has wide-set eyes, which we can now see are blue, and a wide mouth with well-applied lipstick. She lets the coat fall open to reveal a red dress, which matches her high-heeled shoes. In between is an unbelievable body!

Barrone reads the descriptions aloud, not announcing the identity of the writer. The laughter gets louder with each description and the policewoman wears a big grin. A couple of the descriptions come fairly close.

Then the lieutenant starts another description, pauses and looks up. "Mr. Lowrey?" Am I about to get my ass kicked or...

"This isn't a description son. Just some scribbled notes and numbers."

"Sorry, lieutenant. There is a second page," I respond.

As he looks at the page, his eyes grow wider. He holds up my drawing and compares it with the policewoman. "Well, holy shit," he exclaims.

While the rest of the class files out for a smoke break, I'm detained by the cops and Walt Blevins.

"You've never worked as an ID artist?" Barrone asks.

"No sir. I've just had a lot of figure drawing... and I can work kind of fast."

They nod agreement. I go on, "I'm sorry but there wasn't time to do a second face to cover when she put her glasses on. I think I could've done better with more than four minutes, too."

The lieutenant begins to put my drawing in his briefcase. Blevins puts his hand on Barrone's arm. "Sorry Jack but that's a classified document. You can't take it with you." He grin is evil and triumphant.

"Lowrey." Blevins gives me a look. "What you did is rather unorthodox but it beats any written description I've ever seen. It's not exactly the Army way but..."

22. My Pencil Gets A Promotion

Quarters jingle into the pay phone by the Rec Center and once more I dial Andy's number in D.C. This time she answers.

"Andy? It's Five. Glad I caught you in."

"Hey Five, how are you anyway? I'm so sorry you missed me last week."

"No more so than me. Listen, I don't have much change so I'll make it quick. Are you free this weekend?"

"This weekend. Well... Friday night's our graduation dinner. I'd ask you to come down but... well, guests aren't invited. I mean, parents and relatives... you know."

"But not boyfriends."

"Five, there are just so many seats. Ah, friends... well, there's no room for friends."

Not boyfriends. Just 'friends.'

I won't give up. "Well, what if I come down Saturday morning. Friday's payday and we can do something that costs money, sort of."

"Oh, Five. I leave for Europe Saturday. I'll fly to Paris and then get my assignment there. Isn't that exciting?"

"Yeah... that's *really* exciting."

There's a long pause, then "Five. I know you're disappointed. And so am I. But I'll be qualified for home leave in five months. We'll see each other then."

"Andy! In five months, I could be on the DMZ. Don't forget I'm in the Army."

"Five..." a hint of exasperation is in her voice. "We *will* work it out. Some day."

"Andy, I've got a question. Is there someone else?"

"Of course not." She's getting pissed. "I've been going out with a guy in my class... but..."

"Have a wonderful time in Europe, Andy. Write to me when you can. My time's running out." And the operator breaks in.

"Please deposit 75 cents more, caller."

My pockets are empty and I replace the handset.

"Why so glum, chum?" Peggy's cheer makes me even more blue. "I hear you really made an impression on Jim Barrone yesterday afternoon."

"Jim Barrone? You mean that cop that was in our class? How do you know about that?"

"He was over at Da's house drinkin' Harps with the boys last night. They all got a huge laugh when he told about your *description*. He said Laurel Rose wanted the drawing for herself."

"Who's Laurel Rose? That policewoman?"

Peggy whoops. "Policewoman! That's Laurel Rose Swinney. She's one of Jack's little buddies from The Block. Her working name's *Thunder Rose*. He introduced her as a policewoman? Oh, shit." Peggy holds her sides, she's laughing so hard.

"You mean she's a whore?"

"God no, Five. She's the number two stripper at the Two O'clock Club. They say she may be as great as Blaze Starr someday."

I return to the bay after an uneventful and unenthusiastic — on my part — art class. When Dave Clay asks if anyone will trade him KP this weekend, I take him up.

"Great Five. You're a terrific guy. I'm invited out to Hood for some dance by that Kathy chick from the mixer. Want me to say hi to your girlfriend? What's her name again?"

"Culden. Culden Ellis. Sure, tell her hello for me but don't cross her. She's liable to snap your head off and shit down your neck."

It's cold and rainy for Friday morning's formation. Clankus counts heads and calls us to attention and we salute as *To The Colors* begins to sound. As we go to parade rest, Sgt. Dottreau walks up to Clankus.

"Sergeant. I believe you've got a Private Lowrey?"

"It's Lo-ree, First Sergeant. Yes we do."

"Have him see me. He won't be going to class this morning."

Clankus marches A59-1 off to class, leaving me standing in place. "Private Lowrey? You're ordered to report to Colonel Stendall at AIC at 800 hours. You know where that is?"

"No Sergeant."

The top gives me directions and a final admonition. "You haven't forgotten how to report, have you?"

The freedom of walking, not marching, in uniform, is tempered by the anxiety of being ordered to report to a bird colonel at headquarters. I throw snappy salutes at a couple of cars bearing officers plates then with a sense of dread, I enter the Army Intelligence Center.

The clerk at the reception desk directs me to Col. Stendall's office and his receptionist calls him on the intercom then directs me to enter his office.

I knock on the door, stride forward and click my heels to attention. "Private Thomsen Lowrey reporting as ordered, suh!" I throw a snappy salute.

Stendall looks up. He's in his shirtsleeves and his uniform tie is pulled down from an unbuttoned collar. His sandy buzz cut is turning gray. "At ease, Private. Take a seat."

As I sit in one of the chairs before his desk, my spine is a ramrod.

"I said *at ease,* Private Lowrey." I relax slightly.

Stendall leans back in his swivel chair and picks up a form from his desk. "I see your BI is still underway. Hasn't been completed. Have you been in trouble son? With the law?"

As succinctly as I can, I related the Galen Curtis incident at Ohio University, maintaining that I was neither arrested nor under suspicion of a crime.

"Hmmm. That must be it. As you should know by now, once a BI goes negative, it takes a lot longer to complete. I'm sure it'll be cleared up in short order."

He leans forward and replaces my file with another piece of paper, which I recognize.

"Is this your work, Private?"

"Yessir," I reply. "I realize I shouldn't have…" but the colonel holds up his hand.

"Mr. Blevins brought this to my attention. Is he correct that you did this drawing and annotated the colors in less than five minutes?

Weakly. "Yes sir."

"And is he correct in saying, er… 'it's the goddamned spitting image of the subject'?"

"Well sir, it could've been better if I'd had more time. But yes sir, I believe it's a pretty good likeness."

"Had you seen this woman before, Private?"

"No sir, I had not."

The colonel smiled. "Well, I have. On several occasions. And as chief of instruction, I know for a fact that she is *not* one of *our* actresses. And it is a pretty good likeness! A damned good likeness." His smile turns into a grin. "You'll have to see her without all those clothes on sometime."

I'm lost for an answer. Where in hell is this going?

"Private Lowrey, after you successfully complete the agent course, I would like to assign you to an advanced course, investigative photography, and some special training. If… you successfully complete the agent course.

"Do you have any objections, Private?" *My God, do privates have a choice, or a right to object?*

"No sir. Would it mean staying here at Fort Holabird?"

He leans back again and stares at the ceiling as if the answer to my question is dangling up there among the tiles. "Ah, temporarily… at least during the course of your training. But I'm sure we could arrange it so you start earning time in grade, which you're not doing now."

Without pause I respond, "Sir! I have no objection. It sounds, ah, *interesting.*"

"Very well. It's not *that* often that the Army employs the special skills of an individual. I'll try to keep an eye on your progress and keep G1 from assigning you to Iceland. That'll be all, Private Lowrey."

Snapping to attention, I give the Colonel my sharpest salute and on his "dismissed," I do a smart about face and march from the office.

Smoke break has just begun as I reach the classroom. I'm peppered with questions but keep my revelations to myself, except for the colonel's comment about time in grade.

"You mean we don't get credit for the time we're here?" Luck asks querulously.

"Sgt. Clankus, what's this TDY shit all about anyway?" Moon asks.

"Well troops, it's a sad fact. I'm here on TDY from my permanent assignment so I keep my days in grade on the record books. But you guys are fresh from basic and don't have a permanent assignment."

"Yeah," Gaffney adds, "you'll get promoted to PFC as soon as you report to your permanent assignment. Right now, you're just E-2s in limbo, kind of."

"Limbo, my ass," Escobar says. "I'm Catholic and this ain't no iimbo. This is the Army!"

109

23. Grounds For Article 15

Saturday doesn't dawn. It just begins with the CQ shaking me for KP to the background of howling rain, thunder and lightning. Fortunately, I don't have to go outside and make it to the mess hall at 0629.

"A minute early, Lowrey. You're still a greenhorn," Fiona Briscoe says to me from behind the entrance desk.

"Mornin' Fiona. I thought permanent personnel didn't have to pull weekend KP.'

"Right. But we do pull CK — clerk of kitchen — and I'm it this weekend. Now get your ass in the kitchen and report to Chef Spook." I throw her a mock salute and hurry away as she mutters "shitbird."

"Good morning, Sgt. Melville. I'm Private Lowrey."

"Morning, Private. S'what I like, enthusiastic KPs. But I don't got a Lowrey on the roster."

"I'm standing in for Private Clay."

"OK but make sure Clay's ass is here when your name comes up. I ain't keepin' no track of all you sojurs tradin' off so you can go sniffin' around tail.

"Now, since you're first one in, you get the goodest job. Check with the CK, she's got all the ingredient lists and then tend the coffeepots. We'll use all four of 'em since it's such a foul morning. Little pot back here's already done and it's for kitchen staff only so you can help yourself."

Back to Fiona who's now harassing later arriving KPs. I sip my black coffee and recall I never had such good coffee in basic.

"OK Lowrey. I bet Spook assigned you to coffee. Right?"

"Right. And can I get you a cup right now?"

Her frown brightens to a wee smile. "Why thank you, Private. Maybe you're not such a shitbird after all. Cream and *lots* of sugar."

When I bring Fiona her coffee, she smiles and mouths a thank you, then hands me a clipboard. "Don't lose this. It's got to last all next week. And ignore the instructions about turning the pots on. As soon as you get the first one filled, turn it on so anyone who comes in early can get a cup."

She directs me to the dry stores room where I start searching for coffee in cloth ten-pound bags. I've never made 500 cups of coffee before and find it surprisingly laborious, filling each huge pot and then dumping the grounds into the giant perk containers. The recipe sheet also calls for two eggs in each pot after the coffee is brewed and the grounds removed.

My first pot is chugging along pretty good and I start to fill the second pot when the lights flicker and fade to darkness. After a few seconds, a generator kicks in somewhere and my coffee pot resumes its steamy chuffing.

Standing on a two-step ladder, I'm carefully pouring coffee into the second pot when Fiona screeches… "Ten 'hut!"

My reflexes take over, even though I'm three feet above the floor. The lip of the coffee bag catches the edge of the urn and as I totter off the ladder, about eight pounds of dry coffee shower down with me.

"As you were, men," General Muldoon commands, shaking rain off a black poncho. "Except for you, son," he says with a chuckle, looking at my brown, grainy form on the floor.

Big Spook comes forward with a big mug of coffee with stars painted on it. "Mornin' General. Good day not to have a parade, don't you think."

"I certainly think so, Adolphus. What's for breakfast?"

"First batch of sticky buns due out in about six minutes, sir. Please have a seat."

"All right, Sergeant. And by the way, please don't dock that young soldier's pay for the coffee. He'll learn not to snap to from a ladder."

Rank has its privileges, and its kindnesses, too.

111

Soggy patrons began filing into the mess hall right at 0930 hours and Big Spook and his crew scrambled to keep the line moving. Sticky buns, eggs how you like, home fries, tiny link sausages, crisp bacon, fresh fruit. I scrambled right with them, hauling bags of grapefruit from the reefer, shiny peeled potatoes, crates of eggs and other heavy commodities. Thankfully, I had use of a four-wheel dolly.

By 1100, the rush had subsided and Spook told us to take 15 minute smoke breaks in small groups. "The hangover crowd'll be comin' in pretty soon and we'll be at it again," he said in his deep voice.

Even on the sheltered loading dock, the rain slashed in and forced us to huddle against the rear wall. A relaxing Pall Mall wasn't the same on a day like this.

"Smokin' light's off," Fiona screeched from the doorway. "Main gate just called and we've got a delivery truck comin' in. You guys are the unloading detail and get the stuff off as quick as possible to keep it from getting soaked."

The driver eased his big truck back against the loading dock and we swung open the doors to a wall of bags: rice, beans, flour. We slammed the doors quickly to keep the swirling rain from wetting down the cargo.

Fiona and a couple of GIs arrived with tarps and we rigged one over the half opened doors. Then, two of us would grab one of the 50-pound bags and sheltered by two people holding a tarp, lug it directly into the hallway and stack it on the floor.

Forty minutes later, the truck was empty, an unholy mess of bags cluttered the hallway and all of us were soaked.

Sgt. Melville gave us all 15 minutes to go change. When I returned, he assigned me to sorting and loading bags for the dry storage room. With my faithful four-wheel dolly, I set about the task thankful they weren't 100-pound bags.

Flour was fairly simple for the cloth bags were packed tightly and easy to get a grip on. The bags of rice and beans were another story and I labored to get them stacked five high with still some extras left over. Near exhaustion, I was leaning against the stack of bags when a giggle alerted me to a sudden attack of blindness.

I grabbed at the thing over my face and ripped it away. An olive drab brassiere.

"Betcha never saw one of those before," Fiona said, grabbing for the bra. "GI issue. All I had left that was clean and scratches like a bitch." She stood before me, hands on hips in fatigue pants and boots and an OD tee-shirt on.

"What in hell are you doin', Fiona?" I growled, handing the bra back. "Put that thing on."

"I'm just playin', Lowrey. Don't you want to play a little? Things are quiet out front 'til the 1500 rush." She grabbed my arm and dragged me into the aisle between rice and beans and pulled her tee shirt over her head. Nice little breasts with erect brown nipples stared at me between the rice and beans.

Fiona advanced and made a grab at my crotch. "I just wanna' see what you got that got Darcy in the sack," she said in a husky voice. I pushed away and came in contact with a soft breast, which she took as encouragement.

"C'mon Lowrey. Just a quickie." She punched a quivering rice bag. "These bags are nice and soft," she whispered, fingers working at the buckle of my GI belt. "And so are these," as she wriggled her boobs under my grasp.

I have an idea what I was saved from by the blast of a whistle from inside the mess hall.

"Sonofabitch," Fiona gasped. "Sonfabitchin' bitch." She whipped her tee shirt over her head, tucked it into her fatigue pants and vanished into the hall. I picked up her abandoned brassiere and tucked it deeply between two rice bags, then stiffly went back to my chores.

24. Honey Traps And Jambalaya

Sunday's KP wasn't such an ordeal. At least it was only drizzling, not performing a cyclone. After an extra five minutes' sleep, I was the last to report and got assigned to slicing and dicing stuff for custom omelets. Onions. Peppers green and red. Cheddar and provolone. Ham. Sausage, some kind of Louisiana sausage with big chunks of fat.

Delivering another huge pan of diced omelet ingredients, I encountered Fiona across the steam table. She leaned forward, hissing "Where is it? Tell me. Right now!"

With a shrug of feigned disinterest, I turned and retreated to the kitchen.

Other than that encounter, the KP was uneventful save the sniffling and sneezing that began around noon. By 1600 hours quitting time, I felt like shit.

And still do. Itching eyes, a runny nose and the scratchy tickle in the throat, the vanguards of a cold coming on. It's a hateful, familiar experience to snap your head back to wakefulness just before it comes in contact with the smooth, warm, soft, comforting surface of a classroom desk.

"Sexual favor has always been a currency of espionage, since Biblical times," Walt Blevins intones. While our brains are filled with the exploits of Richard Sorge, that marvelous caucasian Russian genius who spied against the Japanese in Tokyo for nearly a decade, the history of espionage has basically been a dry subject. Until now.

114

"Certainly, the most famous of the female spies was Margie Zelle, better known as Mata Hari, a young German dancer whose career as an exotic dancer and an agent came to an end in 1918 before a French firing squad.

"Her ineptitude and her dramatic cover made her both a very dead World War I double agent and the synonym for the sexy espionage agent."

Despite the miasma of colds or potential flu, the class perked up. History was warming up. Blevins continued.

"The Soviets and Germans have improved their sexual techniques since Mata Hari's day. Today, the *honey trap* is as effective an espionage technique as electronic listening devices." We're all ears now.

"Simply put, the honey trap is a gorgeous young woman who seems uncommonly willing to disrobe and dispense sexual favor to the lonely businessman, diplomat or young Marine embassy guard." Walt smiled. "They take advantage of our common failing... that men are horny as hell when it comes to a strange piece of tail.

"Once the liaison is accomplished, it is recorded in sound and on film, which is stored until the appropriate moment when the trap is sprung. Then what happens?"

We resound in unison, "Blackmail."

My mind goes back to Saturday in the dry storage locker. Could Fiona be a honey trap?

By the dim light cast by the Fishbowl, I study the SPH of one Axel Bergdorf, the subject for my first interview exercise. My interviewee is a Mr. Daniel Gracy, a blessing since I had been fearing an embarrassing encounter with one of the female actresses.

Occupying the Fishbowl as I read is Gunny Gaffney, who's having a rough time with a wisecracking, gorgeous redhead. She crosses her legs dramatically with each of his questions and leans forward earnestly to answer. The leaning forward business reveals a great deal of elaborate bosom and Gaffney struggles to keep his composure.

The class cracks up as the interview nears its end. "Oh, I don't know if I'd recommend him for a position of trust, Mr. Gaffney. I've seen him in a lot of positions that I'd recommend. But trust him? Never!"

With one last blow of my nose, I knock on the Fishbowl door and enter. The room seems very bright and the wall to my right is a shiny black mirror. The Fishbowl set alternates among a desk, a kitchen table or two easy chairs. I get the desk.

Behind it is Mr. Gracy, his compressed face a mass of deep wrinkles hiding behind half-moon glasses perched on the tip of a button nose. This elf of a man is dressed in a white shirt and an archaic bow tie, a suit vest and arm bands on his sleeves. I feel like I've stepped back into the Depression.

"Mr. Daniel Gracy?" He nods affirmatively. "I'm Special Agent Thomsen Lowrey with Military Intelligence."

Gracy dismisses my proffered boxtops with a wave.

"Your name has been given as a reference by Axel Bergdorf who is being considered for a position of trust and responsibility within the United States Government."

Gracy just stares at me without emotion. "Are you familiar with Axel Bergdorf, Mr. Gracy?" He nods yes. I begin to worry that I'm being tested by a mute subject but recall that I've only asked a *yes-no* question.

"What is your relationship with Mr. Bergdorf, sir?"

He speaks! "I was his employer."

"When did you first become acquainted with him?" Gracy pulls a paper to him and reads for a second. "October 21, 1955, when I hired him as a part-time reporter. He was a student at the college, then."

"And when did you last see him?"

"Oh, I saw him all the time, but our *relationship,* as you put it, ended in late 1957. When I fired him."

The SPH clearly shows me Bergdorf's stated reason for leaving the small daily newspaper was to "pursue better opportunities."

"For what reason did you fire him, Mr. Gracy?"

"He was a damned Red, that's why!" Gracy shouted, pounding the desk violently and making me jump. "Just like his old man, damned Wobbly... worthless Commie. The whole bunch of 'em."

"Wobbly?" From reading Steinbeck I had a suspicion, but needed confirmation.

"IWW! International Workers of the World. Jerome Bergdorf was just a goddamned German Jew Commie union organizer. He damned near got run out of town when he tried to organize the thread mill."

"But we're discussing Axel Bergdorf, Mr. Gracy. What was the nature of his activities that made you think he's a Communist?"

"Always reading that Red filth. Nazi subversion. Marx. Lenin. Hitler's *Mein Kampf.* Claimed it was for political science when he was at the college. Kept reading it after he graduated and I put him on full-time."

Control of our practice interviews was in the hands of the actors and, through their answers, could bring it to an end almost any time. But Gracy threw himself into it and the vituperation kept pouring out for nearly an hour.

"He was a homo, too!" he ranted. "Never went out with girls. Not even my daughter and every young stud in town has tried to get into her pants."

And, "I know he was trying to organize my back shop. Always hangin' around the linotype operators."

And, "He was an agitator. Always writing funny heads for the obits. And slipping dirty words into his copy to try to catch the proofreaders off guard."

Finally, my notebook nearly full, I popped the question. "Mr. Gracy? Would you recommend Axel Bergdorf to be considered for a position of trust and responsibility within the United States Government."

"Why sure, son. He's a hell of a writer!"

25. Laid Low On Colgate Creek

"Come on, Mr. Blevins. There's no way this case shouldn't go negative," Zigafoos argued vehemently. "Gracy said Bergdorf's a homo and a Communist. If that isn't negative, what is?"

"Cool down, Mr. Zigafoos," the instructor responded. "Think back to your own SPH, the people you gave as references. What about your neighbor whose outhouse you turned over back in '52? I'll bet you think he's your best buddy and all these years he's hated your butt.

"Mr. Lowrey covered the situation very handsomely… asking Gracy if 'to his knowledge, Bergdorf is a member of the Communist party or any other subversive organization.' When Gracy admitted he had no specific knowledge of Bergdorf's political activities, the case remained clean.

"And," he continued, "Bergdorf did turn out to be a political science major."

The warm feeling of praise and accomplishment was rapidly being washed away by the miasma of flu symptoms. With a runny nose, watery eyes and the overwhelming urge to sleep, I cranked through my report on the Gracy interview and asked to go to Sick Call.

A friendly medic on duty at the infirmary confirmed a fever, gave me a bottle of terpenhydrochlorate — 'in case you cough' — and wrote a *no duty* chit for me. On the way back to the barracks, I stopped by the library to tell Peggy I would miss that night's art class and suggested an exercise to keep them busy.

Bundled in my blankets shivering with chills or the effects of the bottle of *GI gin*, I was barely aware of noise and activity in the bay. I must have slept though Retreat and dinner, waking to dark windows and a nearly empty bay.

Padding off to the latrine, I nearly stumbled across Dick Wheeler, the quiet kid from Santa Fe, who was silently packing his duffel bag.

"Hey, Wheeler, what's going on?" I muttered, making bladder-filled conversation.

"Hey, Five," he snuffled. "I'm gone."

"Gone?"

"Gone!"

And when I returned from the latrine, he was indeed gone.

Gaffney's bark of "rise and shine" stirred the bay and I awoke feeling better. Returning from the latrine, I noticed Wheeler's bunk had its mattress rolled up and blankets folded on top of his footlocker.

"Where's Wheeler, Five?" Chan asked as he tied his boots.

"Damned if I know. He was packing his gear last night, last time I saw him."

At Reveille we formed up and Clankus saluted and reported "A59-1. All present or accounted for." Top Dottreau returned his salute and ticked his clipboard.

Breakfast was somber and muted, everyone asking the same question, no one getting an answer. Clankus and Gaffney sat off to a table by themselves, heads together.

As we fell in for class formation, Clankus spoke softly. "Private Wheeler is no longer within our ranks, as you may have noticed. Now you know as much as I do."

Luther Chan was in the Fishbowl, interviewing a throwoff from my Gracy interview. I had missed yesterday afternoon's session and from the tenor of the interview, it sounded as if Subject Bergdorf was cruising along in good shape, despite the rantings of the bigoted editor.

In real life, I might've missed the throwoff interview had it been conducted by another agent in a different location. As Walt Blevins kept emphasizing, our role was to collect information, not analyze and judge it.

119

The standard report format was so cut and dried and Chan's interview so uneventful that writing my report was a matter of 30 minutes and I finished early. Peggy's orange pennant was flying above the library, indicating it was open, so I walked over there to see how last night's class had gone.

"Hey! If you've got the flu, don't come closer," Peggy grinned, making a vampire cross sign.

"Just sniffles, I hope. Felt like crap last night. Better today."

"I hear you guys lost one yesterday," she said, stacking new magazines on the shelves.

"How in hell did you hear that? For a top secret installation, word sure gets around fast."

"It's a nest of spies, Five. Don't know his name but Glen told me this morning that one of the A59's had busted out on his BI."

"Busted out?"

"You know, negative investigation. Security risk. Surely you guys have covered that stuff? I mean, it happens at least once with every class."

"It does?"

"Sure does, bub. Say, you haven't got any skeletons dancing in your closet, do you?"

At lunch, I exchanged Peggy's tidbit of information with my classmates.

"Wheeler? What in hell did that quiet cat ever do to be a security risk," Stein asked. "I never heard him say ten words, much less advocate the overthrow or whatever."

Mennosovich contributed, "Man, we all got some kind of crap in our past. But a lot of guys get through this place. So if you get jerked out, you must be a real jerkoff. Shit, my grandfather was a soldier in the White Russian Army. Does that make me a security risk?"

Returning to the classroom, we found Walt Blevins and a stranger spooling a reel of 16mm film into a projector. Blevins stepped to the podium.

"Just as you started to believe your future was all BIs and dull reports, we begin a new unit in your training. It's affectionately termed Tradecraft and will cover a variety of interesting subjects.

"This afternoon, we have Bob Reese on hand to introduce you to the first aspect of tradecraft — surveillance."

Reese stepped up, cleared his throat, and brushed invisible lint from the sleeve of his blue Colts jacket.

"Surveillance is the business of observing the activities and actions of a suspect without being detected. Each surveillance is completed with the creation of a dull report." Nervous chuckle from the class.

"A surveillance is conducted when the subject of an investigation is judged to be acting in a manner that is detrimental to the security of the United States. In plain language, he is suspected of being an espionage agent... a spy.

"By nature of his business, a spy is paranoid and aware that he... or she... could be watched at all times. It is this paranoia that makes surveillance such a difficult challenge."

Reese motioned to Blevins who hit the dimmer switch. "What we're about to watch is a couple of films of actual surveillances. Please observe closely and we'll discuss later what you think you saw."

We watched two films in black and white. Each in a different setting. As the room lights came up, a *Confidential* warning appeared on the screen, signifying the end of the presentation.

"OK, let's talk about the first clip. As you could see, Fat Boy was a very difficult subject to tail. He should be, since he was a KGB agent under cover as a cultural attaché in the Russian U.N. Mission in New York. He was very good at his tradecraft... until he was expelled from this country.

"Could any of you identify a member of the surveillance team?"

We all shake our heads no. Reeves continues, "That's because there was no surveillance team. The camera did all of the following. But Fat Boy's actions demonstrate that he thought he was being watched. The constant stopping to window shop. Throwing away the newspaper. The abrupt change of direction and pace."

"Now, what did you notice about the second film?"

Desmond stands. "The surveillance team was obvious. They all wore dark, heavy looking suits on what was obviously a hot day."

121

"Correct. Absolutely correct." Reeves nodded. "That's because the FBI has a dress policy that puts its agents in the field that way, even if it is inappropriate. This was, by the way, an FBI field exercise... and not a very good one."

"Does this mean we shouldn't wear suits on a surveillance?" Ploughman asked.

"Not necessarily. You should be as inconspicuous as possible. In a busy city such as New York, a suit would be appropriate. In downtown Dundalk, people will make you for a spook, an undertaker, or a preacher."

Reeves pulled off his shiny blue Colts jacket, revealing a blue shirt and dark blue tie beneath. He quickly turned the jacket inside out, revealing a dull black second surface.

"This is a good surveillance outfit," he said. "Especially for Bal'mer. And with the jacket off, I could look like a businessman on a hot day...if it's a hot day. And the black side of the jacket gives me a third look.

"These," he said as he donned a pair of horn-rimmed glasses, "give me still another look."

"A couple of you would not be appropriate for surveillance in many places," he grinned. "With all respect, you mister..."

"Chan, sir."

"Mr. Chan, because of your ethnic characteristics, would not be inconspicuous in many locations. But... in Chinatown."

He pointed to Moon. "And you, because of your dark skin, would stand out and even be unwelcome in many places."

"Yassuh," Moon drawled with a grin, "but a honky like you would look like birdshit on a chocolate cake in Harlem."

"No offense, son. But you're exactly right and I think we all get the point."

Reeves' class on surveillance got more interesting as he progressed through the makeup of a team, hand signals, points, trails and cutouts. It was fascinating stuff and we didn't even notice the classroom clock moving through the afternoon.

Blevins went to the door to answer a quiet knock. He turned from talking to someone in the hall, looked over the class and beckoned to me with a finger, indicating to stow my notes in the secure file cabinet.

Waiting at the door was Specialist 4 Fiona Briscoe, natty looking in her Class A uniform.

"You're wanted in CI, Mr. Lowrey," Blevins said in a low voice. "Please go with this soldier."

As we walked down the hall, Fiona said quietly, "Second one in two days, Lowrey. Hope this one turns out better for you."

"What's up, Fiona? What's CI?"

"Counterintelligence. Haven't you learned anything? You sound like you've got a cold."

"Yeah."

"That'll teach you to play in the rain."

26. My Skeletons Do The Boogie

Fiona deposited me in an obvious interview room furnished like the Fishbowl but with no one-way mirror. That I could see.

After five solitary minutes, the door burst open and two guys entered.

"Agent Clive and this is Agent Gilroy," the shorter of the two growled, flipping his credential case in my face.

"May I see those, please?" I extended my hand and Clive reluctantly handed me his credential folder. I looked carefully at the first set of authentic CIC *boxtops* I had seen.

Both men sat and Clive leaned forward. "Lowrey, this is a continuation of your background investigation concerning certain discrepancies in statements you have made."

I nodded but said nothing.

Without consulting a file, Clive demanded, "Why did you not disclose your relationship with Darcy Robinette?"

"Why should I have? She was a girlfriend. I don't recall a place for girlfriends on the SPH form."

"Don't be a wiseass, Lowrey. Why did you deny knowledge of her political activities?"

"I have no knowledge of her political activities. She never expressed any opinions about politics to me."

"Why did you state that you have not seen her since... ah, 1955."

"Because I haven't. I haven't talked to her on the phone. Not even a letter. She hasn't written. She hasn't called."

"That's your story, Lowrey?" he said sardonically.

"That's the truth Agent Clive," I snapped.

The silent Agent Gilroy stepped forward and put his hand on Clive's shoulder. "Ah, Pete. Why don't you get us some coffee and let me talk with Private Lowrey?"

"Well shit," Clive leaned back in his chair, "you gonna hold his little hand, Sampson?" Without another word, Clive left the room and Gilroy took his seat. The blond agent appeared at least a year older than me.

"Son? Why don't you square with us about this Robinette woman?" he asked with a friendly smile.

I suddenly recognized this as a "sugar-vinegar" interrogation. "What's to square? I've told you the truth."

"OK." Gilroy reached into a file folder. "Do you recognize this?"

I stared incredulously at the pencil sketch of Darcy I'd done in the library two weeks before from the *Cosmopolitan* cover. "Of course. I drew it."

"When?"

"Two weeks ago. It was in my sketch pad. In my footlocker. How did you get it?"

"So you saw her two weeks ago?"

"No. I made the sketch from a magazine cover in the post library. Peggy Muldoon was there. Ask her." I was outraged that these guys had searched my locker but decided to stay cool.

Gilroy scribbled in his notebook, then looked up. "We already have. That checks.

"Let me ask you about some other things. See if any of these ring a bell."

"Go ahead."

"Students For A Democratic Society?"

"Never heard of them."

"Jerome Dukas?"

"The director? I've seen one of his boring movies. That's it."

"Riverside Acting Guild?"

"Nope."

125

"Lowrey, would you be willing to take a polygraph test?"

"Bring it on, Agent Gilroy."

27. Passing With Sinking Colors

Perhaps my enthusiasm for a lie detector test did it, but whatever, my interview with Clive and Gilroy came to a sudden end. Fiona escorted me back to the class building with a lighter attitude, giving my arm a squeeze as she left me to return to work.

Reese was still talking as I returned to my seat. Blevins went to the secure file cabinet and retrieved my note folder for me.

"The Russians are very infatuated with tradecraft… and they're well trained and quite often very good.

"However, they tend to take for granted the superiority of their training and that's often a mistake. For instance, they love the recognition technique of carrying an American publication… a magazine… a folded newspaper. Not understanding cultural differences can make for sloppy tradecraft," he slowed and grinned.

"For instance, if you ever see a guy in a shiny blue suit, a black fedora and a copy of the *Junior Miss* under his arm, you can bet he's a Russian agent."

Reese darkened the room and showed us a fascinating series of slides. A hollow quarter for concealing messages. Messages written on the back of postage stamps. A fake peanut for the same purpose.

"This one is a classic," Reese pointed to the peanut. "The agent left this device in a bag of peanuts on a Central Park bench. His cutout was supposed to pick up the bag and retrieve the information from the peanut. Central Park squirrels got to it first and the exchange was never made."

When my art class takes a smoke break that night, Fiona clutches my arm and drags me to an empty corner of the studio.

"C'mon Fiona. I don't know where your brassiere is."

"Screw the bra, Lowrey. You didn't hear this from me. Promise?" she whispered.

"I guess."

"My boss got his ass reamed this afternoon," she said softly into my ear. "By none other than Colonel Stendall himself. And those two assholes, Clive and Gilroy, were ordered to wrap up your BI double-time.

"Looks like you're in the clear. I have to type their final report tomorrow."

"I was never *not* in the clear. Don't even understand what all this is about. What about the polygraph test?"

"Oh, those two dickheads beat everybody up with the polygraph threat," she chuckled. "Like it's some final litmus test. It's a terrible interrogation technique."

"But what's all this crap about Darcy? I haven't seen her in years."

"Aw, your little model girlfriend's been hanging around with the wrong folks, I guess. I wouldn't worry about her," Fiona shrugged. "And if you get horny, well... you know where to look."

Peggy walks through the building flipping off lights as I wipe up charcoal dust from the table.

"So why was Miss Fiend cornering you during the break, Five? Volunteering to *model* for you or slipping you the latest poop on your BI?"

"Peggy, for a civilian, you seem to know a whole lot. Is my BI post gossip?"

"Nest of spies, Five, remember?" She grins wickedly. "Guess I've got a need to know since I'm your second employer. At least Glen thinks so."

"Man! You mean the general's staff knows about... cares about my background investigation?"

"You betcha! You're Colonel Stendall's pet project. Besides... I think Glen doesn't like the idea of me hanging around with a possible subversive like you."

28. I Get To Try On A Cloak

A week later, I'm called out of class again. As I stow my materials, my classmates exchange knowing glances.

In the hallway, a bespectacled man in civvies is waiting. "Lowrey? I'm Agent John Glisson. We're going over to CI."

As we walk out of the building, my curiosity overwhelms me. "Is this about my polygraph?"

"Hell no, Lowrey. That shit's over. This is work."

We enter Colonel Stendall's office without ceremony, where three other men are sitting in civvies in front of the colonel's desk.

"Hello, Lowrey. How's school going?" Stendall asks.

"Fine sir, thank you sir."

"You're well into the surveillance phase, I believe. Do you think you're ready for a little field exercise?"

"I guess so, colonel." *A field exercise? Without the rest of my class?*

"You've met Agent Glisson. This is Cowdrey. Franklin. Simmons. Gentlemen, this is Private Thomsen Lowrey, the young man I've told you about." The other three nod hello. "John, it's all yours."

Glisson beckons me to a chair, looks me over carefully, and says, "Lowrey. Do you have some civilian clothes that aren't too PX?"

"I have some flannel slacks and a blue blazer. Couple of dress shirts."

"Civilian shoes?"

"A pair of penny loafers."

129

"OK, that'll do. How about a small sketchpad? Something that'll fit into a jacket pocket?" I nod yes.

"All right then. Cowdrey and I will drive Lowrey to the barracks to change. You guys will proceed. We'll brief Lowrey on the way downtown."

We get up to leave the office. I'm wondering whether to salute the colonel but he just waves me off with a smile. "Hope you like crabs, Private Lowrey."

Cowdrey drives the dark blue '51 Chevrolet. Glisson is turned halfway in the front seat, talking to me in the back. I'm in my blazer, a blue oxford shirt and no tie.

"We're from a field office in Washington, Lowrey. Can I call you Thom?"

"Five is what I answer to best. Thom's OK, though."

"Five it is. I want you to wear these," he says, handing me a pair of horn-rimmed glasses. "They're plain glass but they may come in handy. Our subject's name is Behrens, a captain at Aberdeen. He's a one-man shop, translating eastern bloc, German and Russian technical documents. Our field office is in charge of the case. He has been suspected of security violations for quite a while. Then, AIC Records informed us that he's requested access to classified agent report files… files he's not cleared for.

"We have information that he's meeting someone for dinner in Fell's Point. Your job will be to draw as accurate a sketch of that person as you can.

"After the dinner, if they split up, Simmons and Franklin will take the cutout and we'll come home for you to go to work… if everything goes well. Understand that?"

I nod yes. "What can go wrong?"

"Not much, I would think." Glisson smiled at the driving Cowdrey. "By the way, this is a classified mission. Secret. And you're cleared.

We drive through the crowded mix of bars and warehouses that make up the waterfront at Fell's Point. Parking on East Pratt, we walk about a block and enter a dim place on the corner with a sign that says

Obrycki's Olde Crab House. From the outside, I can't see in due to the steamy windows.

The place is crowded and filled with wonderful aromas... beer, pepper, spices. It's noisy too, with the sound of mallets cracking huge piles of steamed crabs. We spot Simmons and Franklin seated at a table on the far side of the room, a pitcher of beer and frosty mugs between them.

A waiter in a floor-length white apron leads us to a table near a window opposite Simmons and Franklin and removes a small *Reserved* sign. Only one empty table remains in the room and it also sports a *Reserved* table tent.

Glisson points for me to take a chair with my back to the window facing the empty table about twenty feet away. "Treat's on Uncle Sam," he mutters. "At least our boy didn't pick some rat hole to meet at."

A giant platter of steamed crabs arrives, along with a pitcher of National Bo and three mugs. Sheets of the *Baltimore Sun* are spread out on the bare wooden table. I watch as Cowdrey and Glisson each select a crab and begin tapping its shell.

The crabs are red and gray brown, covered with a thick coating of grainy stuff... pepper and spices.

"These are the lungs and guts, Five," Cowdrey speaks for the first time. "They call 'em Dead Man's Fingers. All the good stuff's in this part of the shell." He pulls off a leg and a huge piece of white meat comes out of the shell with it. With a dainty swipe of the meat across the back of the shell to pick up the seasonings, he pops the meat into his mouth.

"Mmmm, man!" Glisson says, "this beats bowling at the Pentagon any time."

I imitate their actions, discarding the slimy mess in the carapace and discover one of the greatest flavors of my life.

We're on our second platter of crabs. Glisson leans over and whispers, "Heads up. Here's our boy now."

Behrens looks just like the small photo I'd been shown. He's dressed in a windbreaker over a gray crewneck sweater. He's led to the empty table and takes a seat, talking to the waiter, who shortly brings a pitcher of beer and three mugs.

"Uh oh, two people coming," Glisson whispers. He takes his napkin and wipes his brow back and forth. Across the room, Simmons gives an imperceptible nod.

We continue eating crabs. Behrens sips his beer and continually looks up toward the door, ignoring several people who enter and wait for a spare table.

Then a tall, thin man with a long face enters, accompanied by a small, very pretty woman. He's dressed all in black, a black turtleneck under a black leather coat that almost touches the floor. A brassed Leica camera hangs on his chest. The woman has a dark blue trench coat on with a matching scarf tied over her head. She wears dark glasses, but even so, she looks familiar.

Behrens lifts his mug and gestures toward the couple. They make their way across the room. Behrens shakes hands and motions to the empty chairs. The man sits facing me, the woman with her back to me. The tall man helps her drape her coat across the chair and as she removes her scarf, I glimpse her profile.

My stomach lurches and my mind reels as I recognize her. I would recognize her anywhere.

"You OK, Five?" Glisson looks at my stricken expression. I nod yes.

"Can you do a sketch of the woman, too… if you get a better look at her? I'd like to get a better look at her. Much better. She's something else."

"Oh, yeah. Don't worry about that," I reply.

When the tall man signals for a check, Simmons puts on his coat and leaves with Franklin. Glisson gets up and walks to the cashier's desk to pay our bill.

The girl's wonderful breasts swell against her blouse as she shrugs into her coat held by Behrens. Once more she glances in our direction, her gaze hidden by the dark glasses.

I move to the window, rub a small clear place and watch as the tall guy hands Darcy into the cab, then gets in. The cab moves off and I hurry out the door to the sidewalk. Glisson is still at the cashier's and there's no sign of Simmons and Franklin. The cab reaches the next intersection and its taillights go on as it stops.

From the shadows, a shorter, stocky figure approaches the cab and gets in as the door swings open. I barely get a glimpse of the newcomer but make a couple of quick annotations in my notebook.

We're in the car and headed for our rendezvous diner. "OK Agent Glisson! What is this shit?" I growl.

"What shit's that, Five? Seemed like a pretty simple meet to me."

"Don't you know who that was?"

"The guy with the camera? He was obviously Behrens's contact."

"No, damn it. The girl?"

Simmons leans over the seat and stares directly at me.

"No, Five, I don't know who either of them is. Do you?"

"I know the girl. Her name's Robinette. Darcy Robinette." I pause. "And, someone else got in the cab at the last minute. Did anyone else see him?"

29. Debrief And Be Brief

We're in a diner where, under the greenish fluorescents, the image of the tall thin man takes shape on my pad.

"OK! Let me get this straight. This woman, this Darcy girl, is an old girlfriend and she didn't even look at you?" Glisson has an incredulous expression.

"I had my head down and had the glasses on. I don't think she made me. But we'll never know 'cause of her sunglasses."

"And she's a famous model? How in hell did a guy like you get hooked up with a famous model?"

"She wasn't famous... or a model, sort of... four years ago. She was just my girlfriend and she waitressed in a hamburger joint."

"Why'd you let her go?"

"She just went. To Cincinnati for a summer. And stayed. Next thing I know, she's on magazine covers."

I rotate my pad to show Glisson the finished sketch.

"Damn, Five. That is excellent. Hope you like Baltimore... I think you'll have a hard time getting out of Colonel Stendall's sight. Wonder what kind of camera that is?"

"It's a Leica M3. Very expensive but well used. Say Mr. Glisson what do you think this is all about? Why was Darcy with this guy?"

"Don't know for sure. The girl may just have been along for the ride... giving him cover. Or... her coat may have been a dead drop. The photographer helped her out of it; Behrens helped her put it on."

"Her name came up during my background investigation," I said hesitantly. "I got two heavy interrogations about her."

"Well, whatever it was, it didn't affect your clearance. Otherwise, you wouldn't have been along tonight."

Simmons and Franklin come into the diner and slide into our booth.

"Cab took 'em to the Lord Baltimore," Simmons said.

"I followed them in," Franklin added. "The tall guy took the girl into the cocktail lounge and they met two more babes. Great lookers. Then the guy left the hotel and went back to the cab. There was another guy in the cab."

"Where the hell did he come from?" Simmons asked.

I responded, "When you guys went for the car, Mister Glisson was paying the bill. I went outside as soon as the cab moved out. It stopped at the corner and this little squatty guy hustles out of the shadows and jumped into the cab."

Simmons continued, "We followed it to Penn Station where they bought tickets to New York separately. I think the second guy was another part of the drop," Simmons contributed. "We couldn't get close enough to catch a better look at the him."

Glisson finished his cold coffee and said, "All right. Let's saddle up. We've got some creative writing to do tonight."

Everyone seems amazed to see me when reveille sounds in the morning.

"Thought you were gone for sure," Vlad Mennosovich says, speaking for the others.

"Naw. Just a little job to do. Did I miss anything exciting?"

"Just more of the same surveillance stuff. We learned what a dead drop is," Escobar comments. "Here I thought it was what all my dates do to me."

"And how spies will sometimes take a gal long so they don't look suspicious," Zig chimes in. "Ain't that some shit?"

"Sure is," I responded. "That's a good thing to know."

At breakfast, Gaffney follows his usual practice of eating with one hand and holding a folded newspaper with the other. "Hey Five, looky here," he mumbles with a mouth full of biscuit and gravy. "Here's your old girlfriend, right in the *Baltimore Sun.*"

He hands me the paper and sure enough, there's a picture of Darcy and two other models at Fort McHenry. They're standing arm in arm with the tall man from last night.

Paris Match shoots feature in Baltimore. Famed photographer Luc Roituer of the French magazine Paris Match relaxes after shooting super models Lynette Stevens, Annie Tressor and Darcy. The magazine has spent the last three days shooting on location at famous sites around Baltimore, including Fort McHenry, Poe's House, and the Fell's Point waterfront.

When we enter the classroom, I ask Walt Blevins quietly if I can be excused for a short period.

"It's important, Mr. Blevins. I've got to go to Colonel Stendall's office."

"Make it quick Lowrey. You've already missed some important segments on surveillance."

Fiona's at the CI reception desk and rings Stendall's office. "Go on back, Five. You should know the way by now." Big smile.

I report and salute. Colonel Stendall returns the salute and orders me to a seat.

"Sir! I didn't know how to get hold of Agent Glisson so I came right here. I think I have an ID on last night's subject."

"Agent Glisson has already reported in, Private Lowrey. He says your sketch is first-rate. And he told me about your acquaintance with the woman. We've heard her name before, haven't we?"

"Yessir. And this morning's *Sun* gives us a positive identification. It's on page four."

"Clermont," Stendall yells. "Bring me this morning's paper. On the double!"

The colonel's clerk comes running with the *Sun*. Stendall opens it and peers at the picture. "Luc Roituer, uh? A Frenchman. Supermodels. And there's your old flame. You have good taste, Lowrey. And your likeness of the Frenchman is excellent."

"Thank you sir. I'd better get back to class."

"Yes, you had. Dismissed."

My classmates are in a line, waiting their turns to look through a tripod-mounted camera with an enormous lens. The camera is aimed out the window.

"As you can see, we can make out figures walking along Holabird Avenue. It's nearly a quarter mile from here.

"But even with this 600 millimeter lens, you can't make a positive identification of anyone."

When my turn comes, I see a great view of Semenkov's and passing cars. As I watch, Simmy Two comes out the door and heads up the sidewalk.

"Mr. Blevins. I can make a positive identification. That's one of the Semenkov sisters."

"All right, Lowrey. But she's not a stranger and there wouldn't be enough detail to make an ID of a stranger.

"This points out the difficulty of surveillance photography. From fifty feet, we could get an excellent head and shoulders shot with this equipment. But it would have to be hidden."

Back in our seats, we see some silly slides of surreptitious photography set-ups. A bakery truck with the lens pointing through a hole in its side. A parked car with tinted windows and the shiny front element of this same long lens poking out the window. A guy holding a tiny little camera — a Minox — that has been the star of many spy movies.

"My point here, regardless of what you'll hear when we get to the photography sequence, is that nothing can take the place of personal observation or close-up photos."

30. Peg 'O My Heart And Other Irish Favorites

Even with earplugs, the noise of Fort Meade's pistol range is incredible. Two agent classes have been bussed down to the sprawling post for a day of instruction in the S&W .38 caliber Chief's Special, the official firearm of the CIC.

"Now you men aren't going to be able to hit shit past five meters with these two-inch barrels," the instructor announces, eye hidden behind his yellow shooter's glasses.

Indeed he was right. At three meters, I was able to hit the standard bullseye target three out of my five rounds. The foot-wide black circle became a tiny dot at five meters and only one of my five shots was in the black.

"I see a few of you people think you're at the Oh-lympic games," the instructor boomed through his bullhorn. "That side stance with hand on hip shit is for dueling... in the last century.

"Now let's unlearn a few bad lessons."

We learned the combat stance, arms forward with both hands on the grip, aiming with our arms and not the revolver's sight. This technique slowly improved my shooting until I got four out of five in the five meter target.

Then for laughs, I guess, we blasted away five rounds at the 10 meter target and I was amazed to hit the black three times, including a bullseye.

Chilled and filthy with powder residue, we rode back to the 'Bird,' our basic firearms initial training complete.

"C'mon Five, it'll be fun. I *know* you'll have a good time," Peggy pleaded.

"I'm not sure I'll feel welcome, Peg. I mean, all those cops and all. I've never even met your Dad and the rest of your brothers."

"But they want to meet you," she said, squeezing my arm tightly. "Little Sham and Jim Barrone have told 'em all about you."

"What about Glen? Why don't you take him?"

"Glen's not exactly welcome... by my brothers. Besides, I'll ask who I want. It will be leap year, you know. And it's my Da's fourteenth birthday."

"Fourteenth? I don't understand."

"February 29th. It's leap year. He's actually going to be 56 but he's only had 13 birthdays. C'mon. Pleeeze? I need someone to keep me company besides a bunch of weeping, singing, drunken Irishmen."

"Why weeping? I thought a birthday, especially when you have so few, would be a happy thing."

"Oh, it's happy alright. But you see, my mum died twenty-two years ago on February 28th. So every time Da has a birthday, it reminds him of Mum."

"And your mom died in childbirth... so that means the 28th is..."

"Yep, but never mind that. It's Da's that's important."

"OK. I'll go... on one condition. That you don't ask me to marry you."

"What!" Peggy shrieked.

"It is leap year, you remember?"

As the weeks go by, our proficiency at interviewing and report writing grows and even the slowest of typists can get out of the report writing class before the two-hour time limit. Mrs. Klecko becomes almost motherly although she continues to count weak keystrokes as errors. Calvin Moon, whose fingers are bent and gnarled from football injuries, still scores below 20 words per minute by Imogene's stern measure.

Henry Zigafoos is the only class member who can't get the hang of interview technique. "Did the subject drink to excess or was he a moderate drinker?"

Answer: "Yes."

My biggest weakness appeared during our introduction to DAME — Defense Against Mechanical Entry. After three frustrating days, I decided that locksmithing, or burglary, was not a viable career choice.

Each of us was issued a small case of weirdly shaped tools. Some were obviously handcrafted while others looked like refugees from a dentist's junk pile.

"The simplest way to gain surreptitious entry," the instructor intoned, "is to turn the doorknob first. There's no need to bust your ass trying to pick a lock if the door isn't locked in the first place.

Describing our tools, "This is a simple set of rakes, picks and tension wrenches. For some locks, a paper clip could do the job. You will not remove these tools from the lab... not a single one.

"Under Maryland law, these are burglary tools and their possession is a felony."

After demonstrations and diagrams, we tackled a wall of simple pin-and-tumbler locks. The exercise was met with grunts and groans of frustration. Trying a rake and inserting a tension wrench, I yearned for a third, then a fourth hand to manipulate the slender tools. I felt like a gynecologist for a brass hamster.

Following an all-too-short smoke break, we resumed our labors. A few minutes later, Ray Stein let out a squeal of glee and success. Escobar and Clay soon had their locks open. Within twenty minutes, I was the only one locked out.

I spent my evenings at the library, either teaching my art class or working on a couple of personal projects.

"You're a bastard for not letting me see," Peggy groused at me. I was locking my work in a private locker, now suspicious that even Peggy might be a better lock picker than I was.

"Go ahead, nosy. Look. Ruin the surprise. See if I care."

"Secretive bastard."

Two days of lectures and demos on murder, mayhem, theft, surreptitious entry and sabotage were followed by field trips. We broke into teams of five and accompanied our instructors in plain sedans to various industrial sites. My group went just down the road to Bethlehem Steel's huge Sparrow's Point Works.

Walt Blevins introduced us to a round, balding man in an inexpensive suit who led us to a small conference room.

"I'm Jack Windross, chief of security for Sparrow's Point Works. We're always glad to host you young gentlemen and, during your visit, if you notice any security faults, I'll appreciate you telling me. But first, let's talk a little bit about steelmaking."

He showed us a short film on basic steelmaking: melting iron ore, limestone and coke to make pig iron, refining it to molten steel in open hearth and Bessemer converter furnaces, pouring ingots and rolling them in mills into sheets or huge coils.

"One of our biggest concerns about sabotage is *plastique* explosive, which I know you've just been introduced to," Windross said. He produced several lumps of material. Holding up a handful of little reddish pellets, he said, "This is Taconite. Iron ore that has been crushed and refined to make the concentrate we use in our blast furnaces.

"And this is limestone," he continued, producing a baseball-sized rock.

"As you can imagine, it would be pretty simple to create a couple of pounds of explosive to resemble either of these raw materials. Dump them into the ore pile or limestone field and blow a blast furnace to kingdom come.

"Now we'll take a walk through the works and I'll show you some of the opportunities a saboteur might find."

We moved on to a huge building where a dozen huge furnaces stood in a row with glowing light casting shadows across the floor. The noise was deafening and a chilly wind howled through the building, open at the back.

"This is Open Hearth Number Five, where the molten pig iron is refined with more fluorspar, sometimes scrap steel, and additives to make steel. The temperature in these furnaces reaches 3000 degrees to burn off impurities and lower the carbon content of the steel.

Sirens and flash strobe lights drew our attention to a giant ladle being trundled down the building by a huge crane. Slowly the ladle was lowered and tipped before the mouth of a furnace and a steady flow of molten iron was poured into the furnace.

Finally, we reconvened in the conference room where Windross offered coffee and answered questions.

On our way out, we shook hands with the security chief. At his turn, Chan reached into his jacket and produced a handful of plastic Bethlehem identity tags.

"Where in hell did you get these?" Windross asked incredulously.

"They were laying in a box over there," he pointed. "I think I helped you find a security risk."

31. Big Sham Becomes A Teenager

February drew to a close with Peggy celebrating her birthday by escorting a busload of soldiers to a Friday night mixer at Towson State Teacher's College. I stayed behind to finish off my projects. Tomorrow, the 29th, was my big day.

After locking my work and saying goodnight to Jeannie Best, I wandered over to the rathskeller. Fiona, her friend Sammy, and Shandra DeWitt beckoned me to join them at a table.

I bought a pitcher at the bar, which made them delighted for my company.

"Hey Five. Isn't that good news?"

"What's that, Shandra?"

"Miss Peggy says I can pose for y'all next week. But I gotta wear a bathing suit. I've got a great one, though."

"I can't imagine who'd want to see your skinny black ass," Sammy laughed.

"I'll put my tits up against your tits any day," Shandra challenged.

"There's a deal," Sammy hooted. "I'll see you in the barracks tonight, baby."

"Now girls…" Fiona said in a calming tone, "and boys… whatever you want to be. Play nice now." She smiled at me. "This poor soldier embarrasses easily."

Peggy's smile lit up when I returned from my library locker with two big wrapped packages. I was dressed in my gray flannels and a crewneck sweater, casually according to her instructions. She wore a gray flannel skirt and a white sweater set with saddle oxfords.

"Promise me you won't arm-wrestle with any of my brothers," she laughed as she drove Meadowlark Lemon toward Patterson Park. "They love to show off, especially when they've been drinking."

"Oh? Will there be drinking tonight?"

"And singing. And drinking. And weeping. And drinking. And eating. I hope you like crabs. It *is* Lent you know. The Muldoon clan always gives up red meat for Lent. Makes it easier to eat crabs and oysters seven days a week."

The home of Seamus Muldoon the Elder was a huge brick pile set into a small hillside near a big park. The door swung open and I was confronted by a giant Irishman, bigger even than Detective Little Sham.

"Pegeen, my darlin'. You're right on time." He picked Peggy up in a huge hug and swung her around. "And you brought your new fella?"

"Five, this is my littlest big brother, Alyn. Little Al, this is Five Lowrey."

I shook hands with the giant who gave me a surprisingly soft grip. "Lo-Ree is it? And would that be Chinese or Hindoo?" he grinned.

"Can the blarney bullshit," Peggy growled. "We'll have enough of it as soon as the poteen is poured."

"My Dad says it's Irish," I replied. "My mom argues that it's English."

"Well then, if it's Irish, you're more than welcome." He clapped my shoulder and nearly floored me. "If it's English, I'll just wring your neck right here and save the trouble later on."

We followed Little Al through the big house, past rooms of furniture decorated with lace doilies, down some stairs and into a vast basement room that opened onto a porch overlooking the park.

In short order, I reacquainted myself with Little Sham and met Sean the Detective and Patrolman Michael. Except for a slight graying of Little Sham's hair, the four brothers might have been quadruplets.

"And here's the Da!" Michael cried. "The birthday boy himself."

Captain Seamus Muldoon was fireplug short compared to his sons. His broad face was the map of Ireland, framed by receding white hair and accented by a bright red nose, many times broken.

"Happy birthday, Captain," I said as he pumped my hand. "I understand you're finally a teenager. Those were some of my best years."

"Thank you, young man. I think our Pegeen has picked a fine lookin' lad this time. Do you drink, man?"

Before I could speak, Sean Muldoon had filled my hand with a glass of brown liquor. "A toast to the teenager Da," he boomed. "Don't be afraid Five. It's only Jameson's."

Peggy and I raised our glasses to the birthday boy, who chugged his Jameson's in a single gulp. I sipped at mine.

"Go on, Five. Bottoms up. The Jameson's is the good stuff. Wait'll they break out the poteen."

Quickly I was provided another Irish whiskey and introduced to my first oyster. Not bad but oysters wash down better with whiskey.

"Well, well. 'Tis' Rembrandt himself!"

"Hi, Jack!" Peggy said. "Five, you've met Lieutenant Barrone, haven't you?"

"Oh, yeah, what say, lieutenant?"

"I say if you can do that trick again, you can have a job with the Bal'mer PD anytime you can get out of this Salvation Army."

Peggy smiled and replied, "I think he can, Jack. As a matter of fact, he has a little *surprise* and this seems as good a time as any." She picked up my packages. "Which one, Five?"

I took the smaller of the two packages and turned to Captain Muldoon. "Sir, seeing's how I've never met a fourteen-year-old with gray hair before, I brought this little token in honor of you."

Muldoon's thick black eyebrows rose like fighting caterpillars. He unwrapped the package and stared at my watercolor of Peggy. Tears came to his eyes.

"My God, man. It's beautiful," he sobbed. "It's my very own Margaret, herself." He clutched the painting and bawled.

"Good lord, Englishman. You've made the Da cry already and him only havin' had five Jameson's." Little Sham was grinning broadly. "It's a beautiful likeness, Five. Of my Little Sis and *my* Ma."

As all the Muldoons stood around in tears, Peggy leaned up and planted a big kiss on my cheek. "It's gorgeous, Five. Thank you so much."

Then the weeping Captain of Homicide planted a wet smack on my other cheek. "You're a fine lad. Now, let's break out the poteen."

Poteen is Irish moonshine of some kind and we could almost see the fumes rise from the neck of the thick pottery jug.

"This beauty was under the barn in County Clare just a month ago," Sean Muldoon proclaimed. "Glasses everybody. It's time to celebrate." He poured just a little into each glass, then raised his. "To the Da, everybody."

Muldoon raised his glass. "And to me own sweet Margaret. May God rest her soul."

Tears came to my eyes, proving to all present that Lowrey is indeed Irish.

The crowd continued to grow. More cops. Cops' wives and girlfriends. A priest and a monsignor. Cousins and uncles.

"Hi, Uncle Dick. Glad you could make it," Peggy pecked the cheek of Fort Holabird's commanding general. "I don't think you've met my friend, Five Lowrey."

"Ah now, Peggy," *Uncle Dick* said and shaking my hand, "but you do look familiar. Have we met?"

Trying to look casually at attention, I returned his handshake. "Not exactly, sir. I'm the dunce who did the nose-dive in the mess hall last month."

He smiled. "Oh, yes. Now I remember. Threw yourself upon your coffee canister, as I recall. I hope Spook didn't mistreat you because of that." I shook my head no.

My second and third oysters were better and they didn't have to be washed down with poteen. The fourth and fifth were *very* good and by the time I'd finished a dozen, oysters were among my favorite foods.

Except for steamed crabs, of course. The back porch, with a roaring fireplace, held a large round table with a hole in its middle over a garbage can. Pages of the *Sun* covered the table and then piles of crabs covered them.

Those at the table made satisfied animal noises, picking, sucking legs and shells, and reveling in that most primitive of dining experiences.

Surely, Indians along the Chesapeake Bay made the same sounds 400 years ago?

The singing had begun. I swayed arm in arm with my new best buddy, Dick Muldoon, commanding general, to an awful rendition of *I'll Take You Home Again, Kathleen,* and then a truly maudlin version of *Danny Boy* which left everyone in tears again.

On the couch, I tried to focus on the bleary activity of the room. Peggy snuggled into my shoulder, making small noises that sounded a lot like snores. I think my watch said 1 a.m. — 0100 hours in Army talk — and my head felt like it would tumble off my shoulders.

Light was a weak rinse of less darkness through the windows of the porch. Peggy was definitely snoring and two huge Muldoon brothers joined the chorus, flat on their backs before the smoldering fireplace.

Several urges moved me. Barf? Or pee? Ease the cramp in my arm? The birthday boy was opened-mouthed and sound asleep in a big leather chair, my painting of Peggy clutched to his chest. The swarm of other guests seemed to have gone someplace else.

Gingerly, I slipped off the couch, allowing Peggy to slide into a recumbent position, and searched for a latrine — *bog* in Irish-American cop talk.

Upstairs, I found the john then followed my nose to the kitchen where one of the wives or girlfriends was cooking sausage.

"Hi, early riser," she said. "I'm Melissa, Alyn's wife and you're Peggy's friend Five, right?"

"H'lo Melissa. I thought this gang swore off meat for Lent?"

"Not me! I swore off flavored lipstick. I converted to marry Alyn but not very far. Want some eggs and sausage?"

"Thanks, but coffee'll be fine. I don't think my stomach's ready for food yet."

With black coffee and the first smoke of the day, I began to feel almost human. Peggy's arm snaked over my shoulder and intercepted my coffee cup.

"Mmm. A lifesaver, Five. Mornin' Mel. You let me sleep, Five. That was thoughtful."

"All of ten minutes more. I couldn't stand the Muldoon snoring chorus."

147

Still draped over me, Peggy whispered, "Five, we brought two surprises last night. I've only seen one. What's the other?"

"I'll go get it. It's in the hall."

"No it's not, it's right here. Is it for me?"

"Yeah, it's a belated birthday present. I'm sorry I didn't give it to you last night."

"Oh, it would've spoiled Da's present," she cried, ripping off the brown paper. "Ohhh. It's just wonderful. Oh, my, oh. Thank you." Peggy circled my chair and clasped me in a giant hug, a big kiss right on the lips.

"It *is* really pretty," Melissa said from an art critic's perspective. "I didn't even know you liked photography, Peggy."

Peggy held the painting at arm's length. I had given the photographer a long coat and cast him in a dramatic backlight beneath the Copse of Trees. "It's a special moment, Mel. The High Watermark of the Confederacy... at Gettysburg."

She hugged me and kissed me hard again. Perhaps I was on the comeback trail as a painter.

The morning fog turned to mist as Peggy drove us toward Dundalk.

"Aww. I feel like crap," Peggy groaned. "But not as bad as if I'd not received a fine birthday present." She leaned over and squeezed my arm. "Thanks again, Five."

"C'mon Peg, it's not that big a deal."

"Do you have to get back to post in a hurry? I never thought to ask."

"Nope, I've got a weekend pass and it's Sunday. I'd be sleeping in right now."

"OK. Do you mind if we stop by my place? I want to clean up and hang my new painting."

"I don't mind at all. Do you have a coffee pot?"

Peggy's place was an upstairs apartment overlooking an alley somewhere in Patterson Park. We parked the Lemon in her garage off the alley and I followed her up the stairs in the mist.

"Neat place," I observed. A big living room looking out onto a porch over the garage with an alley landscape below. "I like the couch," plopping onto the overstuffed furniture.

"Thanks. One of the brothers found the place. It's on Alyn's beat and they liked the garage and upstairs, for safety." She bustled in the kitchen and as my eyes grew heavy, I could hear the gurgle of a percolator. "I'm going to take a quick shower. Coffee'll be done in about ten minutes, so help yourself."

Against a chorus of perking coffee, dripping mist from the porch roof and a shower somewhere, I must have drifted off. The aroma of coffee dragged me back to consciousness.

"No fair. I'm clean and sweet and you're just snoring away. Here. Sit up and have some coffee."

Peggy's hair was swept back into a wet ponytail and she was swathed in a big red terry cloth robe. As I sat up, she eased onto the couch beside me.

"See! While you were sleeping away, I put up the painting. It needs a frame but I just swung it from the nail already in the wall."

My Gettysburg painting did look good, hanging against the moss-colored wall of Peggy's living room. The coffee, scalding hot, erased the memories of oysters and crabs from the night before. Peggy put her legs up onto the coffee table. Her bare feet and mine in socks contrasted against the magazine covered table.

"That was so fun, Peggy. Thanks for inviting me."

"Oh, good. Don't forget, you acted like I'd asked you to the guillotine. And I think Da and the brothers liked you." She snuggled into my shoulder again. "Do you realize we've spent the last five, what? six hours, like this?

"I put a cloth and towel out for you. Go take a shower and I'll make some breakfast."

"Nah. I'll shower when I get back to the post."

"No way. You've got the whole day. Go clean up. I'll make some stuff to eat and we'll just laze the day away."

Still steamy from Peggy's shower, the bathroom revealed a huge, claw-footed bathtub.

"Hey! Do I have to shower? Can I take a bath instead?"

"Sure," she called back, "just clean up the tub. I've got some bath oil there you can use if you want."

While the tub was filling, I decided against using Peggy's razor to do a rough shave. The nicks in the blade convinced me it would be a very rough shave, indeed.

Then I eased into the nearly scalding tub, alarmed as my body displaced the water nearly to the top. Peggy's bath oil was in a squeeze bottle and I squeezed it, the entire cap popped off. Instantly a mound of bubbles began to form. "Oh, shit!" I screamed.

From beyond the door comes Peggy's alarmed "Five, are you all right?"

As the bubbles climbed to my chin, "Yeah. I'm OK. But you'll want to see this."

"Five, I'm not coming in there. What're you up to?"

"No Peg. It's pretty funny. And I'm decent... sort of."

Hesitantly, she cracks the door open and peeks around. Only my eyes and the top of my head are still visible.

"I think I owe you a bottle of bath oil."

"You boob!" Peggy screams in a fit of giggles. "That wasn't bath oil! It was bubble bath. Oh, God. I've always wanted to do that."

Forty-five minutes later, I've finally beaten the bubbles down with cold water. Shivering, I stand under the hot shower to try to rinse the slimy stuff off.

Dried and dressed, I emerge from the bathroom and am confronted by a giggling Peggy. "My, you sure do smell sweet. How do you like your eggs?"

After breakfast, we settle into her cozy living room and leaf through the Sunday *Sun*. Outside, the mist has turned to a steady drizzle.

"How did you do that portrait of me, Five?" Peggy looks up from the sports section. "I mean, it looked as I'd posed... and you never had me pose."

"I just watched you. You're easy to watch, you know."

"But the bare shoulders? I could've been naked. When they sober up, my brothers will think we've got something goin' on," she murmured, sliding closer on the couch.

"Well, you'll just have to tell them we don't."

"Oh! I could *never* lie to my brothers," she whispered as she nibbled at my neck. "You wouldn't want me to lie to my brothers, would you?"

I turned my head toward her and suddenly we were locked in a big kiss. Her arms went around my neck and I held her tight, running my hands across her back. We leaned back on the couch and watched in silence as the raindrops turned to fat, wet snowflakes. They landed on the porch with a soft *plop* sound.

Peggy squirmed around so she was leaning with her back on my chest. I nuzzled her neck beneath the ponytail. I eased my hands up to cup beneath her breasts and she didn't move them away.

"Peggy. I'm sorry my painting of you made your Dad so sad," I whispered.

"Oh, he loved the painting. For someone who lives with dead bodies all the time, he's a terribly sentimental guy. We hardly ever get together without him looking at me, seeing my mom, and weeping."

My hands moved higher and I could feel her taut nipples beneath her soft bra. She turned again and kissed me fiercely. Then, she leaned back and looked directly into my eyes.

"That's enough smoochin' for one day, Five. Look, the snow's beginning to stick."

Indeed, little mounds of snow were forming on the railing of the porch.

"So?"

"I'd better get you back to the post. I don't have snow tires on the Lemon and the city will declare a snow emergency within the hour." She grinned. "Bal'mer doesn't cope with slick streets very well."

Reluctantly, I pulled a mock frown and asked, "OK. And what are you going to tell your brothers? If they ask?"

"The truth, Five. The truth."

32. The Irish Go To Pot

The bleakness of Baltimore winter begins to change as the weeks of March go by. Warm breezes off the bay melt the frozen ground, creating muddy slicks where crocuses try to pop up. By nightfall, the ground is frozen again.

Instruction all day, art classes at night, and the light routine of soldiering at Fort Holabird are punctuated by interludes with Peggy. I would help her close the library at night and we'd stay behind to neck in her dark little office.

Our romance is discreet, we thought, but her watchdog Glen Buckner must have noticed something for he's quit appearing at the library. Our dates are simple. Burgers at Semenkov's. A couple of movies in Dundalk. Weekend excursions in the Lemon to Fort McHenry, down to Annapolis and D.C.

Returning from class on a Tuesday afternoon, I find in my mailbox a note from Peggy.

No dinner. No art class. Nice clothes. Be at the library by 6 p.m. Peg

I hurried to follow orders, taking a quick shower and changing into my blazer and slacks outfit. I grabbed a knit tie and hurried to the library to a background of jeers from my mess hall-bound classmates.

"Ah, you got my note," Peg smiled. She wore a pleated white blouse beneath an embroidered black jacket and a pleated black skirt with a dark plaid pair of knee socks. Her hair was in a ponytail held by a long green ribbon. "Put that tie away. I've got one for you." She handed me a kelly green tie which hardly went with my blue blazer but matched Peggy's ribbon. "Hurry up. We'll be late for mass. It *is* St. Patrick's Day, you know."

St. Matthews was crowded when we arrived and squeezed into the last pew. When the mass began, I was lost in a swirl of Latin and Catholic confusion. I stood when everybody else did. I kneeled when Peggy elbowed me in the ribs. I muttered *amen* when I thought it appropriate.

Peggy put a hand on my thigh as she rose to walk down the aisle for Holy Communion. Like a faithful puppy, I remained kneeling.

After mass, we waited on the sidewalk until Alyn and Melissa Muldoon joined us. We crowded into Peggy's Lark and drove down Dundalk Avenue to a place called Finn's. The sidewalk was crowded with people holding mugs and glasses.

Alyn instructed, "Take your blazer off, Five."

"But it's colder'n hell, Alyn."

"Yeah, and your shirt is cheaper to clean than your blazer. It'll be warm inside."

Entering Finn's, I was immediately grabbed by an old duffer in a leprechaun costume who said something unintelligible and with a finger covered with some charcoal mixture, inscribed a cross on my sleeve. Seeing Peggy, Alyn and Melissa submit to the same kept me from punching him.

Somewhere in the smoky back of the tavern, a group played lively music and bobbing heads above the crowd showed that a dance was going on.

Alyn came back from the bar with four glasses. "Jameson's," he said, handing us each a glass.

Peggy held her glass and started, "Ordain a statute to be drunk…"

"And burn tobacco free as spunk…" Melissa intoned, holding her glass high.

Alyn boomed, "And fat shall never be forgot…" and in unison, they all three shouted.

"In Usquebah, St. Patrick's Pot."

The crowd around us cheered as we clinked glasses and chugged the Jameson's.

Oh, God, Tuesday night. Will I make it to class tomorrow?

"Did you enjoy the mass, Five?" Melissa asked.

153

"And did you pray to the Holy Fahtha, Five?" Alyn asked.

I nodded but Peggy spoke for me. "Aye, he did. Many times."

Alyn signaled the bartender who reached for the Jameson's bottle. "You see, Five, it's a tradition that many acts of devotion must be followed by an equal number of copious libations. St. Patrick's Pot."

"So we're glad you were so righteous," Melissa giggled.

"Ah, we'll switch to beer after this one," Peggy said. "I've got to work tomorrow and Five has class."

Alyn saluted with his fresh glass. "Aye. And I'll probably fall into the maw of the bloody open hearth tomorrow."

They greeted old friends and I was introduced to countless people who were assured that I, too, was Irish despite my English-sounding name. We drank and smoked and watched the dancers. Little kids in costumes. Old folks who did a lively shuffle.

Something was called out and the band struck a loud chord. The crowd roared and quickly opened a path that led directly to us. Alyn took Peggy's hand and they walked quickly through the aisle of people. Melissa grabbed me and we tagged behind.

"Watch this," Melissa screamed in my ear. "You're about to see something wonderful." We stood at the edge of the dance floor.

Alyn and Peggy moved to the center of the floor as the guy at the mic shouted "Alyn and Pegeen Muldoon. Dundalk's finest. Ireland's finest." The crowd noise grew. The band struck another chord and Alyn and Peg swept into a deep bow, still holding hands.

Then Alyn lifted Peggy's arm and she swept up on her toes like a ballet dancer and began quick little steps around him to the tapping beat of a drum. The other instruments joined in and Peggy leaped across the floor, dancing back toward Alyn on her tiptoes, her arms straight at her side. Alyn responded with similar steps and the pair gracefully stepped around the floor to the ever-faster music.

Alyn danced up behind Peg and lifted her by the waist, dancing forward while she continued her staccato steps six inches off the floor. Melissa squeezed my arm.

Their performance went on for nearly ten minutes. Peggy's ponytail flew back and forth and then, with a flick of the ribbon, her dark hair fell out of the ponytail and swirled wildly around her head. The pleated skirt flared up and again, I noticed what great legs she had.

With a crash of drums and a wild banshee wail from a flute, the dance ended with the Muldoons in a deep bow. The front windows of Finn's vibrated with the cheers.

"Now we'll really start drinking," Melissa yelled as she lit up a pair of Pall Malls. She handed the cigarettes to a dripping Alyn and his sister as they left the floor.

After the ruckus died, we settled at a table cluttered with mugs of beer brought by admiring Irishmen.

"Aw, she's been dancing since she was a wee girl," Alyn grinned. "When did you first dance here at Finn's, Peg?"

"Oh, I think it was five or six," Peggy gasped. "That's when I had my first Patrick's Pot. Don't look shocked, Five. It was just a wee one... for a wee lass."

Huge earphones sent a steady hum to my brain, fighting with a buzz of a slightly different octave already there. I was suffering with what I'd heard described as "the Irish ailment," a raging hangover. As I strolled the room of the DAES lab, I slowly moved the detection wand up and down, hoping to hear the music playing on a small portable radio sitting in the windowsill.

DAES, or Defense Against Electronic Surveillance, was more fascinating to me than lockpicking but it still smacked of drudgery. Installing or detecting hidden listening devices, or bugs, was a challenging but boring game of electronic chess.

I was using a Scan-Lok device, which scanned for a signal from a hidden microphone-transmitter and indicated its presence with an oscilloscope and the earphones. As I neared a shelf of books, I could hear a lessening of the hum and the beginnings of a Fats Domino song.

Getting closer, the signal of the transmitting bug grew louder until it sounded as if I were tuned to the radio itself. The scope needle pointed straight up as I pointed the wand at a copy of *Tom Sawyer.*

"Good job, Lowrey," the instructor said encouragingly. "Now you know what the signal from a good Scan-Lok search sounds like. Where would you think the device is?"

"In the book? It's a hollowed-out book?"

The instructor removed the book and leafed through its pages. They appeared to be intact.

"Good guess. Activate the Scan-Lok again and follow me." He carried the book away from the shelf and I pursued him with the wand. The signal remained at its original strength.

"It's the book all right... I think."

"Right you are. If I just pull this little tab up..." He did so and out slid a long board from the spine of the book. "This is a temporary bug," he pointed out the row of round discs, "with these hearing aid batteries giving it about nine hours of life. I'll disable this one for the next victim. He'll have a different live bug to detect. And you can go to the next station."

Even with the penny whistle hangover, I managed through the rest of the DAES lab stations, removing receptacle faceplates to peer for hidden bugs. Unscrewing the mouthpieces and earpieces of telephones. Peering into empty lightbulb sockets. Crawling along baseboards in search of hair-width wires.

The mixture of Jameson's and Harp Lager threatened to leave my stomach the wrong way as I studied a pair of glossy stripes in the paint of a baseboard.

"Sir? I don't know exactly what I'm looking at but this looks suspicious."

"Terrific, Private. You're the first one in this class to discover a metallic paint stripe. They're thin strips of dense copper paint, applied before the room is painted. These guys run to the power source and supply juice to any number of bugs in this room... although there aren't any."

"Gee sir, that's wonderful... ingenious."

"Let's see," consulting his clipboard, "Lowrey. Hmm, do you have any electrical... electronic background?"

"Well, I managed to burn down my Dad's toolshed once. Too many devices on an extension cord. Does that count?"

"I kind of like that bugging crap," Jeff Adamich drawled during the smoke break.

"Wouldn't say that out loud, troop," Clankus whispered. "They may have this hallway bugged and you'll end up at DAES school."

"Might not be bad duty," Adamich answered. "It'd beat hell out of running interviews and writing reports."

Although we'd been repeatedly told that the CIC's technical schools were highly prized assignments and very competitive, the general consensus was that if a student showed any inclination, his future was assured. For me, DAME and DAES seemed too much like locksmithing and television repair.

"How you feelin', Five?" my buddy Chan asked. "You look like shit."

"Oh, sure and I want to celebrate St. Patrick's Day every twenty years," I gasped. "What do you guys drink for Chinese New Year?"

"I just *loved* the little toe dance you did in the bay last night, Lowrey," Desmond cracked. "Especially the part where you tripped over the footlocker and passed out on your bed."

"Hope Miz Peggy looks better than you do today, Five," Stein chimed in.

Miss Peggy was AWOL when I stopped by the library after an early out from report writing. No note, no lights, no nothing. Just a locked door.

I dug out a dime and called her apartment from the pay phone.

"H'lo?"

"Peg, is that you? You OK?"

"No, I'm not OK. I'm asleep... or was. Now I'm sick... or gonna be. Who is this?"

"It's Five. Who else? I was worried when I found the library closed."

"I'm never gonna dance again. I'm never gonna drink again."

"I thought you were wonderful. I still do even though my head says St. Patrick's Pot is a murder weapon."

"That's nice of you to say, Five. And now I think I'll go barf. There's a death in the Muldoon family... any minute now."

Click!

33. And We Do The Rest

A metallic clatter is followed by a scream of anguish. "Sonofabitch. I dropped the motherfucker. And it's goddamned dark in here."

"Turn the light on," laughed another voice.

"I can't, damnit. I've got the film out of the fuckin' cartridge and the reel is somewhere on the floor."

I can sympathize with Gaffney's plight. Even though we've practiced spooling the 35mm film on the little wire Nikor reels for a half hour in the light, my fingers seem to have swelled to sausage size in the dark. And it is a darkroom!

Finally, the tongue of film slips beneath the wire clasp and I can feel as the film begins to curl onto the spiral reel. Winding with my left hand, guiding with my right. Corporal Ashmore, our instructor in the photography sequence, assured us that an experienced photographer can load a Nikor reel in 20 seconds. *I've been in this damned darkroom for twenty days.*

Finally, I can feel the film snug in its wire cage. I drop the reel into the little stainless steel container, then try to get the lid onto the developing tank. I try again. And again.

"Sonofabitch!" I scream. "I can't get the motherless lid on the tank."

Laughter echoes up and down the hallway of darkrooms.

Intelligence Photography is the first of the technical schools I've really enjoyed. With a couple of fine arts photo classes behind me, I'm familiar with development and enlargement and the sequence doesn't seem so alien as lockpicking and debugging.

Holabird's photo lab is like a candy store. We're shown every piece of exotic equipment in existence. Dave Ashmore seems to love his assignment and shows us prints he's made with super long lenses and the latest cameras.

We get to play with the Minox and Steky, both considered *spy* cameras and we see examples of historic espionage cameras in matchboxes, cigarette packs, belt buckles and watches.

Ashmore proudly displays the school's *agent kit,* a fitted briefcase with a Leica IIIg camera, wide and telephoto lenses, viewfinders and a BOOWU close-up device. Each student in the Intelligence Photography class is issued one of these kits as personal equipment for the course.

For our introductory sequence, we're each given an older Leica IIIf and spend a day learning to load film, judge exposures, focus, use the controls and generally care for the camera. Then we're issued a roll of film and turned loose for a day with orders to return with 24 exposed frames by 1600 hours.

I rush to the library and find Peggy stacking and sorting books, doing the gut work of a librarian with no patrons in sight.

"Can you take a little while off?" I ask. "I've got to shoot a roll of film for the photo sequence and I need a model."

"No way, Jose. I don't take my clothes off for just any guy who comes in here with a fancy camera."

"No damn it. Leave your clothes on. I just want to shoot a couple of portraits."

"Will I get prints?"

"I don't know. Maybe. We have tomorrow in the enlarging room scheduled. I don't know if they'll let me make prints."

"Dave Ashmore's a good guy. You make a good picture, Five, and he'll let you make a print."

"Does this mean you'll pose?"

"Sure," she grinned and gave me a hug. "Just let me get into something better than this sweatshirt." She ducked into her office, then hustled into the restroom.

A minute later, she appeared in the ruffled blouse she'd worn to the St. Patrick's party. "I've been meaning to get this to the cleaner's... but I guess the sweat stains won't show up in black and white."

I shot a couple of portraits of her by the window, gazing pensively away from the camera. Then a couple more with her looking directly into the lens. Peggy seemed to enjoy posing. She unbuttoned the top three buttons of the blouse, shrugged in back a bit and gave me a lot of cleavage.

"Ashmore will definitely let you print one of these," she grinned. "If you make a copy for him."

"It would appear," I observed, "that you took your bra off."

"It might appear," she said in a husky voice, "but only for your private collection."

Peggy turned back to the window, then lowered one shoulder and there in the IIIf's viewfinder was her beautiful profile and a full breast exposed. I pushed the shutter gently and was rewarded with a click, then a quick kiss on the lips.

"Private collection only. Remember that or you're in big trouble with your model."

On the way back to the lab, I came across Desmond and Clay shooting the post's famous Sphinx statue.

"Hey Five, I got some great shots of the water tower," Clay exulted. "Did you get anything good?"

"I hope so," I replied and hurried on.

"Thirty seconds, so... agitate." Dave Ashmore is like an orchestra conductor with fifteen mariachi players. "Now bump! One time. Get those bubbles off."

We are developing our first roll of film by time and temperature. Gaffney has the stricken look of a midwife in a giraffe maternity ward. We each stand by our little silver Nikor tanks and watch the sweep-second hand of the darkroom timer.

"One minute. Agitate... and... bump."

I imagine Peggy's wonderful small breast inside the little tank, agitating and bumping bubbles off to keep spots from forming on the fixed negative.

160

"Three shakes," Ashmore intones. "Your're not mixing martinis here. Too much agitation and the film'll be overdeveloped and grainy."

The timer dings and we pour, in a studied motion, the developer into the sink, then reach for the beaker of stop bath. "One minute, no more," Ashmore instructs. "Rinse your beaker and fill it with fixer. Everyone make sure the temperature is plus or minus two degrees."

This process... so mechanical, so much a part of chemistry class which I hated... now has a fascination for me. Not since Dicky West developed the film of the OU field hockey portrait have I felt so much anticipation.

"OK, pour. Now fixer. Agitate once a minute for two minutes. Then six more minutes before the wash."

I agitate and feel agitated.

Our fixed and rinsed negatives are hung in a long drying cabinet in each darkroom. With lights on, the darkrooms seem tiny.

"Motherfuck!" the calm-spoken Gaffney roars. "What are those awful white spots?"

"Your film stuck together on the reel, Sarge," Ashmore consoles. "You didn't load the film properly."

"Mine's all clear!" someone screams. "What in hell happened."

The patient Ashmore follows the cry. "No exposure at all," he says, examining the transparent strip of film. "I don't think your film went through the camera. Are you sure the rewind knob turned when you wound the film?"

"What the fuck's the rewind knob?" Luck whines.

The next morning, we go through a step-by-step instruction on making contact prints. Cut the negatives into strips of six frames. Slide them into the printing frame. Insert the paper. As our contacts peeled off the big drum dryer, Ashmore glanced at them and made comments. "Nice water tower, Escobar. That's some sphinx, Desmond." To Gaffney, he's especially charitable. "Look Gunny, here's part of an image and on the next frame, here's part of another. You can print these together and the spots will make an artistic effect."

The perfectionist gunnery sergeant's response, "Fuck artistic."

161

Viewing my contact, Ashmore gives me a grin. "Hmmm. No watertower. No Jeep Hill. Very interesting stuff, Lowrey. The general's daughter?"

"Niece. And a good friend."

"Yeah. Hang onto these. I mean, *really,* hang on. We'll make some prints later. OK?"

"Good grief, Five! These are *good.*" Peggy looked at the three 5x7 prints I'd brought her. "Man! Look at this. I'm not even embarrassed."

"Ashmore helped me print them. I think he just wanted to see your boobs but he's a good printer."

"How did you get this so moody? My breast is there, yet it's not really."

"He did something with a cigarette pack. Took the cellophane off, crumpled it up, then lit a cigarette and burned a hole in the middle. Then he held that under the negative and did some things with his hands. Neat, uh?"

"I really like it," she smiled, clutching the print to her chest. "Is it mine to keep?"

"Yep. I've got the negatives in my locker here. You can have them if you want."

"Perhaps I'd better... knowing what kind of a place this post is. But Five? Could you paint me like this? Maybe all blues and grays and deep shadows?"

"I could. Sure I could. But I'd have to break an old rule."

"What rule is that?"

"Not to get involved with my models?"

"But we're not... *involved*... kind of," she giggled. "At least that's what I've told my brothers. Do you want to get involved?"

"Ah, your brothers. Could we get involved and I get to keep my fingers and kneecaps?"

"Five, my brothers are good guys. They'd never to anything to hurt me... and hurting you would definitely hurt me!"

34. Rules Made To Be Broken

Five of us on the streets of downtown Baltimore, with five more each in a pair of cars trailing behind. It's our first surveillance field exercise and we've just picked up our subject, one of the actors from our interrogation classes.

He's wearing slacks and a windbreaker and an Orioles ball cap, so we quickly shuffle two of the better dressed guys back to the cars in exchange for watchers in more casual clothing.

Desmond is on the point with Lindscombe trailing about fifty yards behind him. I'm on point on the opposite side of the street and Ploughman trails me. The subject crosses Pratt and suddenly I'm on point as he walks briskly up Charles. We cross Lombard and Baltimore and he keeps heading north.

Thanks to Peggy's tour of downtown, this is familiar country to me and I hang back a little. Desmond creates a minor scene by trying to cross Lombard against the light and the subject looks around at the screech of brakes and honking of horns. So do I and when I look back to the front, the subject is gone.

Immediately I look into a shop window. A store selling surgical trusses and prosthetics. Ploughman walks by me at my signal and proceeds on up Charles. As he passes a tobacco store, the subject emerges and is suddenly trailing Ploughman.

At the top of the hill, the subject strolls across the diagonal walks from Mount Vernon Place toward the Washington Monument. I see one of our *inconspicuous* government Chevrolets pull up on the far side of Charles Place and four of our team get out.

Gaffney meanders toward the monument from the other direction and takes a seat on a bench. Our subject also takes a bench, closer to me and I'm standing like a stork out in the open. I keep going and boldly walk by the subject and take myself out of the surveillance.

With agents scattered all over the park, the subject leans back and watches a pretty woman feeding hundreds of pigeons. She joins him on the bench and removes her bright red coat. As they chat, he picks up her bag and begins tossing peanuts to the pigeons.

Shortly, she gets up and says good-bye, walking off with the red coat still draped over the bench. The subject lets her walk about twenty-five yards, then yells and runs after her with the coat. He keeps the peanut bag. She walks out of the park and down Cathedral Street. I join Mennosovich and Adamich to trail her — the cutout — to Enoch Pratt Library, which she enters.

I get the nod from Adamich and follow her into the library, immediately encountering the tweedy librarian I had met with Peggy weeks ago.

"Hello there," he calls jovially. "Are you here to pick up some more books for the spook factory? Peggy didn't call."

As I try to fade into the floor, the woman turns and gives me a little smile with a fingertip wave. I am burned!

In the friendly confines of our classroom, Walt Blevins debriefed us. "All in all, not a bad exercise. You were well coordinated and handled signals and switches pretty well."

Clankus spoke up. "I'll take walking a tail any time compared to driving in that traffic."

"Walking's not such good duty," Desmond said sheepishly. "I almost became a corpse on Platt Street."

"Yes," Blevins said, "and you drew the subject's attention. But I don't think you were burned. Still, you were smart to get out of the sidewalk team.

"At one point on Charles, you guys were so well coordinated, you looked like a drill team. You need to work up on making your movements more sporadic... more natural."

"We knew who the guy is," I volunteered, "but he didn't acknowledge me when I walked past him in the park."

"The actors are playing a role. Their job isn't to embarrass you by letting you know they recognize you.

"As you can appreciate," Blevins continued, "parks are a bitch to conduct a surveillance, especially if they're not crowded. It was noon and a nice day, so you had the advantage of blending into a small crowd. But on a really cold day! Tough work."

"Mr. Blevins, you said the actors aren't supposed to recognize us," I asked, "but the girl in the library plainly burned me."

"Yeah, that was a cute stunt she pulled. You should've stayed and talked to that librarian instead of rushing out of there."

"I'll say," Adamich chimed in. "By the time I got in there, she was gone. And when she came out of the restroom with different hair and a new coat, I didn't recognize her."

"Don't forget what you've learned. She took off a wig, became a blonde, and reversed her coat."

"As far as the librarian recognizing you, Lowrey," Blevins grinned evilly, "coincidence can be a real killer in a surveillance. You're never prepared for that."

Remembering our night at Obrycki's, I thought *You just said a mouthful, Mr. B.*

Plates of crab cake sandwiches and cold beers arrived at our dark booth in the back of the Dundalk Tavern. Peggy and I went there after that night's art class where Shandra got to pose in a nearly transparent two-piece bathing suit, pleased to be displaying her outstanding body despite goose bumps the size of marbles.

"Little Sham said he watched your little parade downtown today," Peggy said. "He said you were *real cute* marching up Charles Street."

"I didn't see him," I answered with a mouth full of crab cake. "Where was he?"

"Oh, here and around. He saw you coming flying out of Enoch Pratt. What happened there?"

"Your librarian friend recognized me and struck up a loud conversation. That was the end of the exercise for me."

"Well, at least he didn't have to arrest any of you. That's happened on surveillance exercises before. The guys at the cop shop get a great kick out of it."

"Well. I'll try to stay out of your brothers' way... for more reasons than one."

"C'mon Five, I told you they wouldn't bother you. They like you. They think you're Irish." She squeezed against me and reached over to snag half of my sandwich. Munching away, she stayed snuggled against me.

"So what about our *project?*" she asked in a coy tone.

"Peg. There's no privacy at the recreation building. Can't you just see me sitting there, painting and holding up your photograph with everyone standing around watching? Besides, I'm not sure I can work from that little print."

"What? You want the negatives back to make a bigger print?" I shook my head no.

"I see, that's just an excuse to get me to take my clothes off," she giggled. "I thought you didn't want to get *involved.*"

"But I do want to get involved. Intensely involved... with you." I looked into her nearly black eyes. "Peg? Why do you want me to paint you?"

"All my life I've been a *good girl.* Go to mass, go to confession. And I've never got anything to confess but impure thoughts." Peg bit her lower lip. "Oh, I'm the dancing queen at the annual Finn's St. Paddy's booze up and all the guys try a grope.

"But Five, I've never had a *real* boyfriend. And I'm sick and tired of not having any fun. I don't want to end up like Mary Frances, get pregnant, give away the baby, become a nun." Tears were welling up. "But I do want to have some fun. Do something naughty. Give the good fathers something to really think about in confession.

"You're fun, Five. I know you won't always be here but while you are, can we have some fun together? I'll pose, you'll paint. And we'll get involved! And I'll have something to remember it by."

35. Stages Of Involvement

"Class A's after lunch," Clankus reads from his clipboard. "We'll have an hour at 1300 to shine up for a 1400 graduation parade and we're done for the weekend."

A59-1 echoes the bay with a cheer. This will be the last graduation review before our own in three weeks. It's a beautiful Friday morning and we route march off to class. We're now in an agent handling sequence: recruiting agents, turning agents, the art of defection, and how to identify a double-agent. Real spook stuff.

Lunch is a celebratory affair of big cheeseburgers with the works. Everyone passes on the onions for tonight is a big mixer with Goucher College.

Holabird reviews are colorful ceremonies, culminating in General Muldoon riding onto the parade ground standing in the back of his spit-shined jeep with white sidewalls and chrome bumpers.

For all our lack of drill in the weeks gone by, we pass in review and do a smart *eyes right* as we go by the reviewing stand. The colors precede A58-10 and everyone salutes as the graduating class passes by. Then we stand at parade rest while my buddy General Muldoon makes a short speech. And it's over.

"This is the Holabird social event of the spring," Peggy announced to the waiting troops. "These gals from Goucher are usually very pretty, a lot of fun and if you're looking for a rich woman, your chances are good tonight."

"Does that include me?" I ask with mock sincerity. Peggy threw me a scowl.

"You've already got a good woman, mister. And don't forget."

"And I'm probably as rich as I'm going to get as long as I'm in this man's Army."

Peggy smiled and gave me a surreptitious hug as the Greyhound bus rolled up to the Rec Center.

The Goucher girls disembark to the cheers of Holabird's spooks in training. Peg is indeed accurate. They are gorgeous, well dressed, ready to party and they tackle the mixer like a small-town cotillion.

It's fun to see the difference in haircuts among today's graduating class, the slightly shorter tonsures of my own class, and the skinheads just out of Basic. I stand with Peg in a darker corner, helping play chaperone. It's not a hard job, watching the young men and women bopping to the rhythms of rock and roll.

"Remember our first mixer, Five? I don't feel the need for any vodka tonight."

"Me neither, Peg. All these bouncing bodies are giving me a dry mouth, though."

"Aw. Let's see if this helps." She pulls me into the darkest part of the corner and lifts her head for a kiss.

At 2130 hours, Peggy flicks the lights. Less than thirty minutes later, the Goucher girls ride away with waving hands extended through the bus windows. The young spooks wander off in the direction of the Rathskellar and I turn to helping Peggy and Jeannie clean up the mess.

As they check the doors, I fill my painting box and grab a medium-sized canvas and sketch pad and throw them into the back of Meadowlark Lemon with my gym bag.

"You drive," she flips me the keys. "I'm pooped and... nervous."

"Nervous? Wait'll you see me drive. I haven't driven since Christmas."

"You get a weekend pass?" I nodded affirmatively and smiled. Peggy huddled in the far corner of the front seat as I pulled the Lemon through the main gate.

Her apartment was neater than my first visit, magazines piled straight and the kitchen counters bare of dirty dishes. She plugged in a coffee pot then turned, rubbing her hands on the jeans she'd changed into after the mixer. It seemed a helpless gesture. Her smile was weak.

"I fixed up a treat this morning. Hope you like Irish coffee."

"I've never even heard of Irish coffee but," spying the bottle of Jameson's she pulled from a shelf, "I'll bet it's good."

She dropped two sugar cubes each into a pair of glasses, then poured the glasses half full with whisky. "They won't be ready til the coffee's done. Make yourself comfortable and go to the john if you need to, cause I want to shower and clean up."

Making a quick latrine stop, I returned and sprawled on the couch. I tried not to show Peg that, I too, was nervous.

As she went through her bedroom door, she called "You can have a shot of the Jameson's... or there's beer or vodka... but don't touch the Irish coffee until I get back."

In a few minutes, I heard the shower running. I did pour a generous slug of Irish whisky and slouched on the couch. I chugged the whisky and before the shower stopped, I was drowsing.

The clinking of glasses woke me. Clad in a huge pair of flannel pajamas with a pattern of tumbling teddy bears, Peg was pouring coffee into each glass.

"Sugar cubes have dissolved in the Irish," she said with a brighter smile. "Now I mix the coffee in thoroughly and then comes the masterpiece step." She pulled a bowl from the refrigerator and spooned out big dollops of whipped cream on the top of each glass. Padding toward me in bare feet that just peeked from beneath the pajama legs, she offered my coffee and sat down. "Careful, it's hotter than a banshee's bunghole."

I laughed at her simile and raised my glass. "To us."

"To us," she responded, smiling with a quivering lower lip.

Irish coffee is a wonderful sweet drink with a red-hot spike hiding beneath the whipped cream. I squawked as it dribbled down my chin. She reached over and wiped my chin with the end of her long sleeve.

"I should've told you it was hot," she grinned. Tucking her legs beneath her, she reached to the side table and plucked two Pall Malls from a pack and lit them. "In the movies, they always smoke after,"

169

handing me one of the cigarettes. "But with a nice hot drink, I feel like one before."

"Peg. There doesn't *have* to be an after," I whispered earnestly. I put my finger to her lower lip.

"But I want there to be an after!" She blew a smoke ring inside a bigger one, something I could never do. "It's just that I'm so damned nervous. Scared!

"I told you I've never had a real boyfriend," she said vehemently. "I'm afraid you'll laugh at me."

Solemnly, I shook my head no and leaned over to plant a soft kiss on her lips. "Never."

She grabbed my glass and padded to the kitchen to refill our drinks. More whisky than coffee this time. Bending over to retrieve the whipped cream bowl, her trim body was silhouetted beneath the baggy PJ's by the refrigerator light.

Laugh at that figure? Not likely?

The third Irish coffee released a lot of our tensions. We snuggled and smooched and whispered little jokes. Then Peggy jumped up and walked into the bedroom.

"Be right back. Don't go anywhere."

After a couple of minutes, she emerged. Somehow I expected something different but she still had the teddy bear pajamas on. She kneeled on the far end of the couch and slowly smiled.

"So you'll really paint me, eh?" When she twisted and leaned forward, I realized she had unbuttoned the pajama top to about the same degree as the day I made her photo. "Sort of like this?" She struck the same pose.

She turned to face me straight on and slowly undid two more buttons. "Or maybe this way?" she said in a husky voice. The bottom button kept the pajama closed as she leaned forward. I gasped and felt myself hardening.

She jumped back and undid the last button, shrugging the top off with her shoulders. She smiled briefly and then her expression went to a puzzled look. I just stared with my jaw hanging.

"I'm not exactly Shandra, am I?" she asked, looking down at her gorgeous breasts as if they were something brand new to her.

"Hon! No one's exactly like Shandra. You're beautiful! Absolutely beautiful. And I'll paint you any way you wish."

"Oh, Five!" She flung herself onto my chest, clinging tightly to my shoulders. "You say exactly the right things." She nuzzled my neck and ears with her tongue. I could feel the warmth of our bodies increasing, even with her PJ bottoms and all my clothes on.

I fondled her breasts gently and she squirmed her pelvis against mine. We kissed with flickering tongues. I ran my fingers up the groove of her spine and she shuddered in response. Carefully, I did not go beneath the waistband of her pajamas.

Our embrace got tighter. "Ohhh, Five. You feel so good," she whispered, grinding into my pelvis even more.

"Mmm. You too," I answered. I massaged her back and managed to work my hand between us to caress her breast.

Peggy made little noises, grunts and squeals, and then... a huge yawn.

"Forgive me, please." she murmured. "I never knew making love could be so exciting. And I never knew I could be soooo... tired."

We got up from the couch and marched into the bedroom, arms around each other's waist. I grabbed a pillow from her bed, and pulled a blanket away.

"That's enough smooching... that's enough involvement... for one night. Your couch is terrfic and I'll sleep well. So will you. Goodnight, love."

And I kissed her and returned to the couch.

Masturbation has never been a big thing for me. But one small touch to my private parts and... boom... I was no longer the raging, swollen creature I had been.

I curled beneath the blanket, snuggled into the couch which still smelled of Peggy, and, ignoring the soaked crotch of my warmup suit, fell sound asleep.

Somewhere in the early hours, I thought I was awake but still gave over to sleep. My dream was of a soft hand, gently brushing across my forehead. I did not waken.

Gray light was seeping through the front window. Far off, I heard the flush of a commode and the sound of a shower.

I could stand it no more and tiptoed to her bedroom door. Peggy lay on her bed, curled up beneath the blankets. I tried to sneak past to the bathroom unheard.

"Why're you walking like that, Five?"

I turned my back and bent over, shuffling toward the bathroom door, which seemed at least fifty yards away. "Gotta pee," I muttered.

"Oh, Five," she said brightly, "I grew up with four brothers. Do you think I've never seen *that* before?"

Without a word, I scuttled into the bathroom.

When I came out, Peggy was lying on her back, cover pulled up to her chin. I was still acutely aware of the bulge in my warmup pants.

"This is the time I have my most erotic dreams," she said in her husky voice. "Is this one of my dreams come true?"

Lost for words, I just stood and stared at her angelic face above the covers.

"Come here and let's talk about dreams," she said. "Did you dream last night, Five?"

I staggered to the side of the bed and looked down at her. She flung the cover back, revealing the whole Peggy. Her pajamas were in a pile on the floor.

"It's time to get more involved, Five. But you've got so many clothes on!"

Peggy reached out, snagged a finger over my warmup pants and dragged them down. My tumescence sprang out.

"Oooh, look at that! I've seen my brothers but they never looked so dear. May I touch it?"

She reached out and stroked my erect penis, which wasn't, with the rest of me, ready for that touch. Involuntarily, I spurted across the bed.

"Whoop!" Peggy giggled. "Wow! So that's what it's all about?"

Immediately, the erection began to subside. "Well look at that," she said in wonder. "One shot and it's all soft and tender again. Isn't that marvelous?"

I stared at her glistening body and as she stroked my flaccid member, life resumed. Gasping, I flopped into her bed as she scooted over to make room.

172

"I'm sorry to upset you," she whispered and attached her warm body to mine. "But I've never done anything like this before. And... it's *such* fun!"

36. Getting To Know You

By noon, Peggy and I had exhausted each other and discovered other appetites. She was wearing her big terry cloth bathrobe and frying bacon. I came up behind her, slipped my arms around her waist and into the bathrobe, cupping her breasts.

"No fair," she said, "you can feel me. But I can't *feel* you." She wiggled her butt into my groin.

"Peggy! For God's sake, I'm only a human being. You Irish girls are like… rabbits!"

"And what do you know about Irish girls, besides me? Pour some coffee and sit down. We need to eat something and help you get your strength back."

The morning had been a carnival of affection. We wrestled like bear cubs, showered together, snuggled on the couch, and read one section of the Saturday paper. All interjected with romantic coupling.

After getting out of bed, Peggy looked at the small crimson spot on the sheets and said, "Is that all? I thought it would look like a crime scene. I expected Da and all the Muldoons here with guns drawn."

My privates shriveled at the thought.

"I'll bet they didn't even *realize* this morning. that little Pegeen was getting deflowered and having the time of her life! While they were fast asleep."

"Hold still! You're wiggling like a worm."

174

Peggy wriggled again and grinned. She sat on a footstool, nude, and grinning like crazy. "I didn't know you had to become a statue to pose. How many sketches are you going to do? I'm freezing."

"Almost done with this one. And then we'll be done with sketches. By the way, where are you going to put the painting? Not here in the living room?"

"Naw. I'll hang it in the bedroom. The brothers use the bathroom like they were going to confession. They never snoop in my room."

"That's a relief," I sighed, thinking about possible broken fingers.

"Hurry up, Five. Look at my nipples. I'm growing big bumps all over."

"I've been looking at your nipples. They're magnificent. Now hold still."

I smudged in some shadows with my thumb, then indicated I was done with a flourish. Peggy hopped off the footstool and ran over to me. She hugged me around the neck and I drew a charcoal cross on her breast with my finger.

"For shame, Five! That's blasphemy. Now I've got something else to confess."

She intoned, "Bless me father, for my boyfriend has drawn the holy sign on me boob. I think I'm sleeping with the devil." She chuckled madly at the thought.

"Peg! I think you're more excited about scandalizing the church. What if we have a baby?"

"Aw Five. I've read all the books. We Catholics know how to count. You can stay for nine more days. Are we done with the sketching? I'd rather make love than pose."

Dressed all in black with a scarf over her head, Peggy looked as if she'd just stepped off the boat from Ireland. "I'm off to confession," she said, "and then I'll go to afternoon mass. Be back in a couple of hours.

"Will you be OK here?" she asked.

I had the canvas set up on a tabletop easel and was lining in a charcoal cartoon from the sketch we'd selected. "Sure. I'll be able to work. What do I say if one of your family shows up?"

175

"Don't worry. They never bother me on weekends. And Alyn is working a shift today." She gave me a soft kiss on the back of the neck. "See you later."

By the time Peggy returned, I had several washes done, including a white background for her figure.

"Oooh! I like it already. I look like that faerie girl on the soda bottle."

"The White Rock nymph? Yeah, I guess it does. Do you want some little gauzy wings."

"No, but my boobs could be bigger."

"That's what they all say."

While I continued to paint, she stretched out on the couch, clad in her familiar warmup suit... something I insisted on as her new-found love for nudity was too distracting.

"Five?" she asked languidly, her bare feet crossed on the end of the couch. "How am I?"

"How are you? Peg, you're fine."

"No... I mean as a lover. Compared to Darcy?"

"Darcy was a long time ago, Peg. Besides, I don't keep records."

"Well, that's a straightforward answer. How about Andy? Culden told me you guys were quite a thing."

I turned from the easel and gazed directly into her eyes, ignoring her sly grin. "Peggy. This is God's truth. I've never slept with a woman I didn't feel love for."

"Ahh, Thompsen Lowrey, you're a lovely man." She blew me a kiss.

"I'm going to keep records," she laughed. "And you're going to be on page one."

We had pizzas at Carson's Inn and then went to a movie in Patterson Park... Marilyn Monroe, Jack Lemon and Tony Curtis in *Some Like It Hot*.

Home again and for the first time, in Peggy's bed to sleep.

It must've been about midnight when I was awakened by a noise. Light from the full moon beamed through her bedroom window. My love was curled up tightly beside me and making the most unbelievable snoring sounds. I mentally debated what to do? Finally I nudged her.

"Hmmpf. What? What's the matter?" she mumbled.

"Peg! You're snoring."

"That's the only reason I had my own room at home," she giggled. "Well, now that you've got me awake…" She threw back the covers and rolled over to look at me.

"Five? Have you read the Kinsey Report?"

"Just the good parts in the one on women," I replied.

"I think it's just fascinating. I read the whole thing at Maryland. The sisters wouldn't let us read it in high school." She ran her finger along my soft penis and instantly I began to react.

"I mean," she went on, "just look at this. You guys just can't help it, can you?" She peered intently as my member jerked from soft to attention. "This could be so embarrassing… I mean, out in public and such."

I lay there in the moonlight and watched her playing with me… probably not for long if she kept it up.

"If I get excited… why, no big deal. My nipples pop up and I can feel it but there's nothing much for anyone to see… if I've got my clothes on."

"There won't be much to see in a minute, if you keep it up" I gasped and rolled toward her. She moved as well and pulled her legs up until her knees were pointing at the ceiling.

The moon was gone but it wasn't morning. I awoke to a sharp jolt in the ribs.

"Five," she giggled. "You're snoring. Snoring something fierce."

"Peggy," I snorted. "Have you read the Kinsey Report?"

"Just the good parts," she laughed as I pulled back the cover and rubbed a soft breast.

"Do you know? If we turned the lights on and I kept this up, your chest would get all red and splotchy and your breath would become short and…"

"That's what I read," she whispered. "But I've never looked at myself in a mirror. That would be sinful."

"Almost as sinful as going the whole night without any sleep." I kissed her breast and rolled over. "Good night, Peg."

"Good night, lover."

37. Sunday In New York

I awoke to a door slamming. Peggy's side of the bed was empty and I could hear her moving around in the living room. Cautiously, I peered from the bedroom door and found her propped on the couch with a cup of coffee and a fat newspaper.

"Sunday morning treat, Five," she said, looking up as I cleared my throat. "The *New York Times* and a dozen hot glazed donuts."

"Good morning. You've been out?"

"Of course. I've been up for nearly an hour. You don't think hot donuts deliver themselves. Hurry up, or they'll either be cold or gone."

In the bathroom, I shaved and was ready to get in the shower. She cleared her throat in the doorway, grinning at me in the mirror.

"Aw, look at your poor *thing*. It's all red."

"And sore too," I replied, watching my *thing* react to her pulling off her warmup suit.

"Oh, yeah. I could barely walk. And I'm all hot and smelly. Let's take a shower."

"The donuts'll get cold."

"They'll be almost as good," she replied, climbing across the tub and pulling the shower curtain. "Now come and scrub my back."

Scrubbed and clothed, we drank coffee, ate donuts and pored through the *Times* in pure bliss and comfort.

"Here's a story about *Some Like It Hot,*" Peggy observed. "It says the movie is a big hit within the homosexual community. Did Jack Lemmon and Tony Curtis in dresses do anything for you?"

"No, but Marilyn Monroe and your hand on my thigh certainly did."

"Five!" she scolded. "Can't you think about anything but sex?" She giggled. "I can't!"

Later, she thrust the paper at me. "Here's your old girlfriend in the Style section.'

Sure enough, there was a fashion spread featuring Darcy, wearing designer swimming suits on a rocky beach. I could recognize the cliffs and distinctive cliff of Etretat, a favorite haunt of Monet's. In one photo, Darcy has crossed arms with her hands covering bare breasts.

"Rudy Gingrich's new topless bathing suit," Peggy read. "I can see me going to Dundalk Pool this summer in one of those."

Of special interest to me was the photo credit on the page: Luc Roituer.

I worked some more on Peggy's portrait while she carried a load of stuff off to the laundromat. "Evidence," she said. "There's always a first time that my paranoid cop brothers will raid the place, tear my bed apart, and shoot you for molestation of their wee, baby sister."

"Peg, I don't find that in the least funny."

Peg's portrait was well along by the time we left for the post. She had to relieve Jeannie Best while I had to resume life as a soldier. She pulled the Lemon up to the library parking spot and we got out.

"Five? Do I look different?"

"Well, you are walking kind of funny," I grinned. "And you sort of glow."

She growled her mock noise. "Are you coming over here this evening?"

"No reason why I can't. I'll try to come over and help you close up."

"Great! Well then," she held out her hand. "I'll see you later."

We shook hands, grinning like fools, and I headed for the barracks.

38. Smile For The Sphinx

Feet propped on the library coffee table, Peggy and I slumped on the couch side by side.

"Your weekend pass isn't over until reveille. You sure you don't want to come home with me?"

"Peg! Want to? Are you crazy? Can I? No way! I've got to get back to the bay and find a clean white shirt. Uniform of the day tomorrow."

"Oh!" with a slow pause. "New agents are gonna get their picture took." She paused. "When you filled out assignment preferences, what did you ask for?"

"Lordy that was a long time ago. Uh, France, Germany, I think."

"Why Europe?"

"Because I want to see all those great museums, great artwork. Plus, I've never been overseas."

"Not because you knew Andy was going to be in Europe?"

"No. Not really. But it may not matter. Colonel Stendall seems to have plans for me here."

"You mean you might stay at Holabird?" she asked excitedly.

"I guess. I'm not sure."

Peggy threw her arms around my neck and kissed me hard. "That's terrific, Five. Why didn't you tell me before?"

I pulled away and smiled at her. "Don't know. I just don't want to take anything for granted."

Just then a loud knock sounded on the locked door. We jumped apart and Peg went to the door. Two soldiers wearing white fire guard brassards were there.

"Everything all right, Miss Muldoon? We saw the light on and it's after hours."

"Everything's just fine. Just fine."

"OK! You've got a choice of three ties and find a coat the fits you," Dave Ashmore instructed. A makeshift studio was set up in the photo lab and A59-1 was getting its photos made for credentials.

He helped me select one of five identical gray suit coats and I picked a tie with a small rep pattern and tied it. I sat on a stool and Ashmore turned on the studio floods.

"Relax now. No big smile, just look moderately serious." He made a couple of exposures with the Rolleiflex. "Remember, some suspicious housewife is going to be comparing this photo with your real face."

As he dismissed me, I joked, "Three five by sevens and a dozen billfold size please. And do I get to see a proof?"

"Right! The proof'll be encased in plastic when you see it and it'll be proof that you got out of this place and got a job as a real spook!"

Our afternoon was taken up with Mrs. Klecko's last typing class. She beamed as we hammered away at our *final exam,* a seven-minute timed exercise. Her smile grew bigger as we cross checked our typing and reported the results.

We all made 35 words per minute, even Gaffney who still tapped with two fingers when Imogene wasn't watching.

"Now gentlemen. We are done. But I have a very special surprise for you today. Follow me."

We followed Imogene's swaying figure down the hall of the school building and into a conference room where several men in dark blue suits stood beside a desk and a big machine.

"This is our first look at the newest technology," Imogene trilled. "This is a photocopy machine from the company called Xerox."

The salesman type took over, extolling the virtues of electrostatic copies over the heat induced versions from 3M's Thermofax.

Then Imogene gathered us up and trolled us down the hall. "So, you rapid typists, you report writers. With the new Xerox machine, and this, the electric typewriter from IBM... you can say goodbye to carbon paper for ever."

Peggy drove me to her apartment on Wednesday night where we feasted on hamburgers from the skillet and spent the evening working on her portrait. She supervised over my shoulder as I added depth and shadow detail to the white wash of the previous weekend.

From time to time, we'd break for some smooching but I amazed myself with creative diligence. Finally, it was finished for the night and I carried the easel into her bedroom and set it on her dresser top.

"Face it the other way, Five," she directed as she pulled her sweater up. "It spooks me to see myself naked in the painting *and* in the mirror."

I did so and felt my resolve to get back to the post early vanishing as Peggy continued to disrobe.

One by one, the members of A59-1 were called out of class to the G1 office. As they returned, each guy wore a different expression. Some were jubilant. Others were extra grim. It was orders day.

Stein lit up a Pall Mall at the break and scowled. "Another six weeks in this place and lockpicking at that." His orders were to the DAME school.

Zigafoos was happy and Escobar was not about their mutual assignments to DAES school.

"Shit! I wanted to get to Panama." Escobar said glumly. "Thought sure my Spanish would be an automatic ticket to the Zone."

"I love it," Ziggy said. "I can get home on weekends and besides, I think that electronic crap is kind of fun."

We route marched back to the barracks for lunch, as our two class leaders were still at G1.

Over lunch, those with assignments discussed their futures. I kept my mouth shut since I hadn't made a visit to G1 yet. Mennosovich, Clay and Linscombe were headed for Korea. Ploughman and Adamich had orders for Germany. Everyone else had stateside assignments and especially concerned was Calvin Moon, headed for Fort Rucker, Alabama.

183

"I can just see my black ass getting rousted by rednecks down there," Moon groused.

"Hell Calvin, I've never seen a redneck bigger than you. Besides, you'll have the badge," Vlad comments.

"What about you, Five?" Escobar asks. "What did you ask for?"

"Ah, France, Germany, Europe somewhere. I don't much care."

Instead of G1, I'm escorted by Fiona into Colonel Stendall's office. I enter, salute and am put at ease, told to take a seat.

"Mister Lowrey! Well, almost a mister," Stendall smiles. "This is Warrant Officer Jack Moony." I nod to the thin man with thick glasses.

"Hello, Mister Moony." Moony smiles and whispers hello back to me.

"Mister Moony, unless you have any objections, is going to be your new boss," Stendall says. "These are your orders." The colonel hands me a stapled sheet of papers.

The first thing that hits me is the heading: *PFC Thomsen Lowrey, V, is ordered..."*

"Congratulations, PFC Lowrey," Stendall grins. "As of next week, you'll have an increase in pay and permanent assignment."

"Where? Sir?" The colonel nods to Moony.

In a high, squeaky voice he says, "Right here, Lowrey. Your assignment is to the AIC's Technical Response Unit. It's a new, very small unit but I think you'll fit right in."

Stendall takes over. "You'll be attending the Intelligence Photo School and taking some special training. But you will not be on temporary duty."

"The TRU is being set up to respond to any unit, anywhere, with special technical requirements. The team will be composed of agents with special skills... DAME, DAES, other talents, like your particular talent," Moony says.

"However," Stendall interrupts, "your permanent assignment orders have been cut, just in case you don't want to *volunteer* for the TRU." He hands them to me.

I read *Private Thomsen Lowrey, V, is hereby assigned to the 321st Combat Intelligence Support Unit, Seoul, Republic of Korea...* No doubt, I'm being extorted but what pleasant extortion it is.

39. FIGMO

A59-1 gathered at the Carson Inn for a *Fuck It, I Got My Orders* party that night. Peggy had declined my invitation to join us.

"You'll be wasted by the time I get the library closed," she groused. "Besides, I'm a little pissed that you won't tell me what your next assignment is."

"I told you… I saw orders to Korea."

"I don't believe you," she responded.

"Well… there is something else. But I've got to make a decision."

"A decision between Korea and what? I'd take a tent in Greenland before I'd willingly go to the DMZ," she nearly shouted. But in the end, she gave me a peck on the cheek and a pat on the butt to send me off to the FIGMO party.

Desmond arrived late, having successfully spent the afternoon lobbying to get assigned to the Photography school. So, six of our fifteen would stay at Holabird for a few more weeks at least.

Clankus and Gaffney bought several rounds and then ordered steak dinners for the class. They were overjoyed at their assignments to the Advanced Intelligence Analyst class, whatever that is.

"Sheeit," Stein drawled. "I'd have to take a loan to buy one steak dinner. Gunny, do you think I'll *ever* be a rich NCO?"

"Doubtful Stein, doubtful." Gaffney slugged down another shot of rye and chased it with his National Bo. "I have serious doubts you'll ever be an NCO. Period."

A59-1's final week was filled with activity. I *volunteered* for the TRU, putting the possibility of Korea behind me and establishing a future in Baltimore. Peggy's reaction seemed strange to me.

"You mean you're going to stay here? Here? At Holabird?"

"Yep," I grinned. "Now I've got to find a place to live. I get a housing allowance and a clothing allowance."

"Well, you can't live with me, that's for sure. But I've got an idea or two."

As a class, we spent two days in a mock field exercise which put the entire actor corps to work portraying German refugees as we liberated World War II Dresden. Each of us took turns interviewing the *refugees* and monitoring a huge map of the city as interviews turned up new leads.

I took delight in discovering "Donaldduckstrasse" and the "Klub Mickey Mouse" on the detailed pre-war city map of Dresden.

Broken into three-man teams, we spent a day conducting security surveys at various defense contractor installations around the city. This turned out to be a boring preview of everyday agent life, rattling locked file cabinets, checking wastebaskets for carbon paper and reviewing security logs.

Then we toured the Photo Interpretation Lab where dozens of students peered through stereo viewers at aerial photos. After talking to the student interpreters and hearing of headaches and blurred vision, we agents shared a collective sigh of relief.

On our last Friday morning, we donned Class A's and marched smartly to school for a long briefing by John Scarletti, Walt Blevins and other members of the instructional staff. Lunch was followed by a 1330 hours assembly and graduation ceremony.

As Lieutenant Glen Buckner called each name, we went forward and fired a snappy salute to General Muldoon, who awarded our USAIS *Certificates of Completion.* As the general shook my hand and passed over the parchment with the purple and gold sphinx seal on its top, he muttered congratulations and never let on that we'd once sung "I'll Take You Home Again, Kathleen" as a drunken duo.

As we exited the room, Buckner collected each certificate to be put in our 201 files.

Finally, it was time to pass in review. With the entire post on parade, Class A59-1 marched behind the colors and received salutes from the reviewing stands. It was a great pleasure to be on the receiving end of salutes.

Returning to the bay was a glum anticlimax. The nine guys shipping out were scurrying to return bedding and other issued equipment and packing their civilian clothes into already stuffed duffel bags. The six of us remaining made many trips to carry our gear to the Support Company's TDY bay. A59-1 was no more.

40. A Move To The Safe House

After graduation, we lived in the TDY bay for nearly a month, waiting for other agent classes to graduate and fill the enrollment for the tech schools. The two privates pulled KP and CQ chores and got to play *subjects* for downtown surveillance training. Clankus and Gaffney went to school.

With permanent assignment to the TRU, I reported to Mister Moony's office in the Tech Center every morning and usually got sent to the photo lab to help Dave Ashmore. Helping mostly meant playing with exotic cameras and lenses, washing the stainless steel development tanks, polishing the stainless sinks and mixing fresh chemicals in twenty-gallon containers.

It was light duty and Jack Moony turned out to be an easy boss. I spent most of my afternoons reading in the post library until Peggy told me I was becoming an attractive nuisance and declared the library off-limits until after dinner. I took on teaching another six-week painting class to help finance our social life.

We settled into a comfortable routine of low budget dates and weekend drives to Annapolis, Washington and over to Hood College once to see Culden. Usually I would spend Saturday night at her apartment and we would laze through Sunday mornings reading the paper and making love.

When the Intelligence Photography course began, our schedule became more hectic with night shooting, study sessions and darkroom work taking up much of my time. A guy named Bob "Bop" Schwalburg came down from New York to conduct a week-long Leica School for our class. My six classmates carried their briefcases full of Leica gear diligently while I went a more casual route and wore my IIIg around my neck.

Then one Wednesday evening, things began to change. Peggy and I were cleaning up after the painting class and heard a knock on the library door. It was Zigafoos.

"Hey guys, I've got news," he said with a big grin. "We're gonna be roommates again."

"How so, Zig?"

"I just accepted an assignment to the TRU as its number two DAES guy and Mr. Moony said he's found the team a house, just off Holabird Avenue."

"That's terrific, Henry," Peggy grinned. "I wonder if it's the place I told him about? If it is, you'll love it. It's a big old barn of a place just a block from Finn's. Someone got murdered there years ago and the rent is really cheap."

"Oh, great," I groaned. "Cure your hangover from Finn's by staring at the bloodstains on the carpet."

The next morning, Mr. Moony took Zig, Gunny Gaffney and me to see the 'big old barn.' Gaffney's appearance was a surprise to me but he had joined the TRU as an "agent handler" and would effectively be our top NCO.

Peggy's description of the place was true — three stories covered with red shingles. Unlike the adjoining row houses, this building sat back from the sidewalk and boasted a small front yard of smooth clay.

"Rent on this baby is only $300 a month," Moony said proudly. "It's got six bedrooms so each team member will have his own room and sharing the rent won't put a big dent in anyone's housing allowance."

"Does the rent cover utilities, Mr. Moony?" Gaffney asked.

"Everything but phone and we'll be installing an issue phone system. If you want a private line, you'll have to pay for it yourself."

I looked at Moony. "What's this I hear about a murder?"

"Intelligence Center rented the place a few years ago as a safe house," he replied. "One of the defectors living here was found dead. Garroted in his bed."

We all stared at each other. Moony continued, "Just a reminder lads, this is not a parlor game we're playing. It's serious business."

Inside was typical row house architecture. A hallway followed the left wall and stairs led to the upper floors. On the right were a bay-windowed living room, then an open dining room and a door to the kitchen.

The floor plan repeated on the second floor except the living space was broken into three smallish bedrooms and a bathroom. Stairs led to the third floor where two larger bedrooms flanked a bathroom.

"Where's the other bedroom?" Zig asked. "And which bedroom was the murder in?"

Moony replied, "In the basement. And the answer to the other question is classified, Further, I don't want any of you people seeing ghosts of a headless defector."

Headless?

After touring the rest of the house, including the basement and outbuildings, Mr. Moony told Gaffney, as the ranker, to pick his choice of bedroom. He took the largest second floor room overlooking the street. Zig opted for a third floor room and I chose the basement with its tiny makeshift bathroom and shower.

"There's a surplus furniture warehouse on post," Moony told us. "Pick up a transportation chit for a truck and go see what's there. Get serial numbers and I'll sign a furniture chit, too."

By Friday afternoon, we were nearly finished with the move to the Safe House. The furniture warehouse, filled with items left behind by people going overseas or to smaller housing somewhere, was a bonanza. We ragged on Gunny for choosing a four-poster canopy bed. I ended up with a single bed so my basement room resembled a college dorm.

With mismatched chairs, a sofa, side tables and lamps, the living room had a certain homey feel. An ornate dining table set with eight matching chairs filled the dining room, an ignoble end for someone's Korean tour souvenir. Mr. Moony looked away as he checked the box for our requisitioned bamboo bar.

On Friday evening, we were moved and ready to christen our new home. Gaffney brought in a case of cold Lowenbrau from the NCO club. Peggy showed up with a stack of pizzas from Finn's. During the evening,

190

Escobar and Desmond stuck to Mr. Moony like limpets, hoping for an assignment to the TRU.

"Well... it's certainly quaint!" Peggy shuddered as she sat on my bed and surveyed my new home. "Is that a Lucky Strike pack crumpled in the corner? I thought you smoke Pall Malls?"

"Peg! I just got moved in a couple hours ago. We'll have the place ready for the IG by Monday morning."

"We? You and me? That's not on my agenda for the weekend," she grinned. "Nor yours."

"What do you mean?"

"I've got us reservations at the Kent Manor Inn in Annapolis tomorrow night. We're going to eat some serious Eastern Shore crabs and just relax for the weekend."

"We are? That sounds like something I can't afford," I said glumly.

"It's my treat," she responded. "My special weekend."

41. Eastern Shore Leave

We prowled the Eastern Shore on a bright Saturday morning, watched crabbers sort their catch on the dock at St. Michaels, then followed a crate of the squirming blue crabs to a dockside restaurant where they were promptly steamed and served to us.

On the horizon, Skipjacks moved slowly under the white wings of their sails. Peggy described to me how the oyster fishermen used long-handled tongs to bring up their catch in this traditional fishing method.

Back in Annapolis, the bay was dotted with dinghies and larger yachts under sail. As we strolled the Naval Academy waterfront, a crew of midshipmen boarded a shell and stroked into the Severn River.

I used the Leica to photograph these scenes with an eye toward future paintings. I shot Peggy snuggled in the lap of the Tecumseh statue, his feathered headdress painted in bright colors by midshipman pranksters.

A giant four-poster bed dominated our room at Kent Manor. Later, we were snuggled drowsily in the big bed, Peggy's breath against my neck in short little gasps. Another minute and she would be snoring. A gentle tapping on the door brought us both alert.

Peggy looked at her watch and muttered, "Oh, my God, it's five o'clock already."

She bounced naked from the bed and to the closet, pulling out two big terry cloth robes. She slipped into one and threw the other to me. "Here."

At the door, she asked, "Who is it?"

"Room service, ma'am. Your order."

Tightening the belt of the robe, she opened the door for a young man who wheeled in a trolley.

"Please put it on the porch," Peggy said sweetly, rummaging in her purse. She tipped him two dollars as he pushed the empty trolley out.

"Come on, Five," she said with a sly grin, beckoning to the little porch. "Cocktails are served."

I sat in the big wicker settee as Peg lifted the dome from a large silver platter. On a bed of ice, two dozen oysters gleamed from their half shells. A pair of tall silver glasses and a pitcher gleamed with frost. Peggy handed me a glass and then plopped beside me, letting her robe fall open.

The mint julep was icy and strong with bourbon, touched just slightly by the sweetness of sugar syrup and crushed mint. We each sipped through silver straws. Peggy picked up an oyster and slurped it noisily.

"Oh, Five. This is one of my dreams. A dream I've had ever since I started having *that* kind of dream."

My condition was evident beneath the tent of my robe. With our feet on the railing, we ate oysters and sipped our juleps as the bay before us turned pink with the sunset at our backs.

Oyster juice dripped down her naked chest as Peg leaned over to give me a kiss. As our lips parted, she slipped an oyster from her mouth to mine. She slid her hand beneath my robe.

"Isn't this just absolutely the sexiest thing you've ever done, Five?"

I was at a loss for words as she gently pushed me sideways and then onto my back on the settee. She opened my robe and then slowly lowered herself onto me.

"I wonder if it's true what they say about oysters," she murmured into my neck as her body rocked slowly.

"Maybe we'll find out," I gasped.

The lights of City Dock glimmered on the water. Inside the waterfront restaurant, table candles provided flickering illumination.

Across the small table, Peg took both my hands and held them tightly. Her smile was the sweetest I'd ever seen.

"I cannot believe we did that!" she exclaimed in a low voice. "And I cannot believe I'm hungry. I think I'll have Oysters Rockefeller."

"Me too," I chuckled. "Followed by Oysters Casino and oyster stew."

We ate slowly, savoring each plump oyster. The restaurant's mint juleps were good but nowhere near the ones we'd enjoyed on our porch.

Peggy kept reaching over to grasp and hold one of my hands. Through apple pie and brandy, she kept smiling at me as if I were a new Christmas toy. Finally, the smile faded and a single tear glistened in her eye.

"Peg? What's wrong? You look like you're going to cry."

She wiped her eye and smiled again. But this time, it was a brave smile with a quivering lower lip.

"Five... I have something to tell you." Pause. "I know you'll be happy for me and understand."

I nodded affirmatively, my mind racing with possibilities. *Was I about to become a father-to-be?*

"Months ago, back in October," she started slowly, "I took the Civil Service exam and passed. With quite a good score."

Her narrative picked up speed.

"Then I applied for a job I saw posted. And this week, I got a letter saying I had been accepted."

A painful lump came into my throat. I squeezed her hands across the table.

"I'm going to be the librarian at the Army Language School in Monterey," she blurted.

"Monterey? In California?"

"Yes! I'll be in charge of a staff of nine. It's a GS-10 position. I'll nearly double my salary. And they say it's one of the most beautiful places in the world. And I'll be able to learn a new language... maybe two," she gasped out. "Are you happy for me, Five?"

"Oh, God, Peggy. Of course I'm happy for you! When does this all happen?"

Peggy pulled a frown. "I've got to be there by the first of the month."

"That's less than three weeks," I exclaimed.

"I know. And I'm going to drive out so we have even less time."

Grimly, I signaled for the check and left a twenty dollar bill on the table, more than enough to cover our oyster feast and a fat tip. Silently, we got up and left the restaurant.

Walking back to Kent Manor with our arms around each other's waist, we stopped to embrace and kiss about every fifty steps. In our room, a maid had made up and turned down the plump bed and removed the mess from the porch. Rapidly, we disrobed, embraced and staggered into our feather bed.

42. The Morning After

Quietly, we ate our room service breakfast on the porch clad in our robes. Peggy's hair was tousled and her eyes were swollen as if she hadn't slept much last night. I felt like she looked.

But coffee, rolls and cigarettes revived my flagging spirits. And as my spirits rose, Peg's seemed to rise with the tide as well.

With hesitation, I told her about the previous women in my life. Of Darcy and how she vanished into the world of fame. And Andy, how she left me, then reappeared and left me again.

Peggy grinned. "Why, listen to you, Five. You sound like a little boy whose first model airplane just crashed. I can't believe you're feeling sorry for yourself."

I returned her grin. "It's just that *all* my model airplanes seem to crash. Or at least fly over the horizon."

"Come on," she jumped up and grabbed my arm, "let's go back to bed and read the newspaper."

With me at the wheel of the Lark, we drove home that afternoon with Peggy tucked under my arm.

"How do your Da and the brothers feel about Monterey?" I asked, trying to sound casual.

"Oh, they say they're happy for me. I know they'll miss me. And I'll miss them." She gave my arm a little squeeze. "And I kind of think they're just a little bit relieved."

"Because of me?"

196

"Oh, Five. They really like you. I mean it. Da talks about you all the time." Peggy paused. "But you're being a soldier and Protestant and all... well."

"I could become a Catholic, you know. I really like your church."

"You'd convert? For what?" Peggy looked up with soulful eyes. "To marry me? To make an honest woman of me?"

Whoops! Had I stepped into something, here?

"I don't want to get married, Five. And you don't either, I know." Peggy gulped. "You won't be an agent forever. Even in the Army. I'll bet you won't re-up. You're going to become a great, a famous artist. I know."

"I *would* marry you, Peggy..."

"Hah! If you had to," she retorted. "But I'd pull a Mary Frances if I got pregnant before I'd let you marry me at the point of an Irish shotgun."

Silence engulfed the Studebaker.

"That's the last talk of marriage. OK, Five?"

"OK."

A few miles on, I broke the quiet. "Are you nervous about driving to California?"

"Oh my gosh, yes. Scared to death. Gettysburg is about the fartherest I've ever driven. But it'll be an adventure. The Muldoon boys say I've got to take at least five days to drive it. That's about what? 600 miles a day. I can do that."

Peggy counted on her fingers. "If I take five days, that means we'll have nine days together. Let's make every minute of them count."

I gulped and squeezed her tightly to me.

Peggy dropped me at the Safe House, announcing her plans to go to mass and then early to bed. In my new home, I found the Friday night mess cleaned up and several new pieces of furniture installed. On the wall at the foot of the stairs hung a telephone.

I spent the rest of the evening sweeping, dusting and mopping my basement cell and adjoining bathroom. I even swept up and enormous pile of coal dust from the furnace room at the end of the hall.

By the time my housemates came home, I was fast asleep in my new bed.

197

43. Case Number One

My plans to spend every available moment with Peggy went off the tracks pretty quickly Tuesday morning. With Photo School graduation less than a week away, I was printing as fast as I can to finish my final assignment — a photo essay on Annapolis and the Eastern Shore.

A whoosh of the light-trap door announced Dave Ashmore's entry to the printing room.

"Hey, Five. Colonel Stendall's office just called. They want you over there right away. Fiona said it's 'come as you are.'"

"OK. Do you mind giving these prints five more minutes in the fixer, then putting them into the wash?"

"No problem. But haul ass. Fiona said it was urgent."

I hung up my apron, washed fixer off my hands and put on my fatigue shirt, donned my flat-top hat and headed for AIC.

"Hey, Five! Long time, no see," Fiona chirped from her desk. "Conference room, second door on your left."

I knocked and opened the door without waiting for an 'enter' command. Colonel Stendall and John Glisson were seated at the big conference table with a fat file folder between them. I snapped to attention but Stendall beckoned me to a seat.

"Agent Lowrey," he said. "You remember Agent Glisson don't you?"

"Hello, Agent Glisson," I said, shaking his hand.

"Hi, Five. And it's John, not agent."

Stendall rekindled his pipe and began. "Lowrey, we've got a situation and John specifically requested that you be brought into it."

"It's our old friend, Captain Behrens," Glisson said. "He's been AWOL for five days. A couple of agents went to his base housing in Aberdeen and found his wife worried sick and with no idea where he could be."

"I've ordered Mr. Moony to get a kit together for you and detach you from TRU for TDY to this case," Stendall said through a cloud of blue smoke. "John here will take you home where you can pack some civvies, change and get on your way."

"We pulled Bherens' 201 file and then his records from the AIC. We've found a couple of interesting discrepancies," Glisson said. "I'll brief you in the car."

WO Moony had what looked like a medium-sized camera bag waiting for me. He also handed my credentials and badge to me. "Sign this receipt and don't lose these, Lowrey. The KGB will pay ten grand for them, remember?"

He added, "And I'll call Peggy and tell her you went off on sudden TDY."

I changed into slacks, tie and sport coat, packed a clothing change and toiletries, and rejoined them in the Safe House dining room in ten minutes. Moony was saying to Glisson "...a guy named Stein about to finish up DAME and I'm bringing him on the team. Elderson says he's a natural-born burglar. If you need him, I could pull him out of school. Let me know."

In the car, I examined the contents of the hefty bag. A brand new Nikon F camera, a wide angle and a macro lens, strobe light, a Polaroid camera, sketch pads, pens and pencils, and a baby Nagra tape recorder. Film and mini tape reels filled the pockets. I felt fairly well equipped for God knows what.

"Here's what we've got so far, Five," Glisson said as he drove us north on Route 40 toward Aberdeen. "Berhens hasn't been seen in five days. He runs a one-man shop at Aberdeen so no one near his unit missed him for three days. Then his wife called the Provost Marshall, said he hasn't been home for four nights. Today's his fifth day.

"Aberdeen Field Office sent out a pair of agents but when they went to pull his 201, they noticed an investigative flag on it and called me.

They got permission from Mrs. Behrens to search their quarters. They're waiting for us now and babysittin' her."

Glisson paused for a minute, then reached into the back seat and pulled up a leather portfolio. Fortunately, there was no traffic as his eyes were off the road and we swerved into the oncoming lane.

"Sorry 'bout that," he muttered as he regained control of the car. "Check out the file in this," handing me the portfolio.

The top document was a Xerox copy of Behrens' 201 file, his official Army record. Beneath it was a crispy sheaf of Thermofaxes of faded record forms and fingerprint cards.

"Coincidentally, my request to Army Records Center for all of Behrens' full documentation arrived today. Takes a long time because a lot of this stuff is ancient and on microfilm. Check out the DOB on his initial CIC interrogation report, the bottom sheet dated July, 1946."

I looked at the bottom photostat and saw Behrens date of birth listed as 2 June, 1908, in Graz, Austro-Hungary. I pulled the next sheet from the folder. It was title *Allied Interrogation Center — Nuremburg — September 1946.* Behrens' date of birth was listed as 10 June, 1923, and place of birth was Bad Reichenhall, Germany. The form was signed by Special Agent Sam Marchant.

"Wow! Some discrepenciess here," I commented.

"Yep. The kind of discrepancies that would turn a modern BI into a negative case," Glisson responded. "The '46 report is from a Displaced Persons camp in Fussen, Germany. At the end of the war, CIC units were all over that part of Europe working to uncover Nazi officers, possible war criminals, and generally sort out the hundreds of thousands of people on the move. Marchant was one of the agents assigned to interviews.

"Marchant's kind of a CIC legend," Glisson continued. "In France as a college boy before the war... married a French girl. They had a couple of kids, came back to the States just before Hitler invaded Poland.

"He joined the Army and with three, four languages. Then got assigned to OSS. He turned down the CIA after the war, came back to us and he was a natural to conduct post-war interrogations."

"Many of these displaced folks had no documentation of any kind. Others had papers and passports, crudely written passes, stuff you wouldn't believe. In many cases, it would be easy to pass an initial interrogation with little more than a note from the teacher."

"Sounds like an impossible task," I replied.

"It was an impossible time. According to the SPH signed by Behrens, he was put to work by the CIC as an interpreter in the Fussen DP camp in July of '46. He enlisted in August and Marchant sent him to Nuremburg to be investigated by G2. He must have done OK because he was assigned to Nuremburg as an enlisted interpreter."

"This is odd," I mentioned. "It's hard to make out from these crappy Thermofax copies but the two sets of fingerprints don't look like they match."

Glisson took the documents and peered closely. "We'd have to get an expert to look at them but you're right, Lowrey. His prints in Nuremburg have a left thumb with a big scar running across the pad."

I studied the SPH. "Says here he was commissioned in December, 1947. How could that be without his attending OCS?"

Glisson grunted. "Evidently it was Army policy back then if a person had special skills. And Behrens had 'em. Three languages. And training as an engineer before the Germans took Austria in '38.

"What's interesting to me is that Lieutenant Behrens was assigned to the States to begin an extremely sensitive Army career and never had another BI run on him," Glisson said in a stern tone. "Give me your judgment. How old would you think this man is, based on your seeing him in Baltimore?"

I thought back to the night we watched Behrens meet Luc Roituer and Darcy at Obryki's Crab House in Baltimore. "I'm not very good at ages, John… but I would guess somewhere between 35 and 42."

"Exactly. And if he was born in Austria in 1908?"

Running the figures through my head, I replied, "That would make him 51. That guy wasn't any 51! That's old!"

"Easy son! Some day it won't seem so old but I think you understand our problem."

The Behrens' quarters were in a row of Capehart houses, obviously a cut below the larger field grade homes we drove by as we entered Aberdeen. Mrs. Behrens met us at the door with Agent Keith Cowdrey looming at her shoulder.

She was short and thin, would have been cute except for the swollen eyes and lack of makeup. She invited us in with a pronounced German accent.

Glisson introduced us and I presented my credentials for the first time. She showed us into a modest living room where a bookcase sported a collection of Bavarian beer steins. The furniture was PX quality, much like the stuff we'd lugged back to the Safe House.

"Mrs. Behrens, I know Agent Cowdrey and his associate have already asked you many questions. Please be patient with me if I repeat some of them but we all are very concerned about your husband's whereabouts," Glisson said to the woman.

Glisson's interview didn't turn up any new information. No, her husband hadn't said anything about TDY, or traveling anywhere, although he often was gone one or two nights on TDY. Yes, she was an American citizen of German descent, originally from Potsdam.

Finally, Glisson got permission for us to search again through her husband's effects and papers.

In Behrens' small desk in the bedroom, we turned up nothing of interest. Their bookshelf was modest, stacked with paperback thrillers. I opened a map of the Greater Baltimore area and stumbled onto our first lead. Three areas were circled in ink and telephone numbers penned into the map's margin. In the same ink, *202* was circled in the map's top margin.

Glisson signed a receipt for the map and we left for the Aberdeen field office.

Cowdrey and I watched as Glisson dialed the numbers, getting an apartment complex each time.

"I'm trying to deliver a package to a Mr. Behrens in apartment 202," he opened with. The response: a one-story apartment complex and no tenant whose name started with B. The jackpot came with the second call, Gardner Arms in Brooklyn Park, where the manager said 202 was occupied by a Mr. Bern, not Behrens.

Leaving Cowdrey to mind the field office and keep an eye on the Behrens' quarters, Glisson and I set out for Brooklyn Park and the Gardner Arms. After 30 minutes in heavy traffic, we passed through the Harbor Tunnel and drove into Brooklyn Park.

Gardner Arms was a tidy brick apartment building of two stories in a U-shape around a grassy courtyard and parking lot. It was considerably upscale from the worn neighboring homes on the tree-shaded street.

In the foyer, we checked the boxes and found *Bern - 202*. Glisson rang the bell and got no response. He then rang the bell marked *Manager* and immediately, the door opposite the mailboxes was opened by a bald man in an undershirt.

"We got no vacancies," he said in a high-pitched voice.

Glisson reached into his shirt pocket and did a flash-and-splash presentation of his credentials. "I'm Agent Glisson with the U.S. Government and this is Agent Lowrey. We're looking for William Behrens." Glisson snapped his boxtops shut and slipped them back into the shirt pocket.

"You're the guy on the phone, aren't ya?" the manager squeaked. "We got no Behrens, here. Just Bern. And he ain't in."

I withdrew the enlargement from Behrens' ID photo and held it out. "Is this Mr. Bern?"

"Yeah, that's him. 'Cept he wears glasses."

"When did you last see him, Mister...?"

"Gandolf. Ralph Gandolf," the manager answered. "He was in... oh, four, five days ago. Left that night with his friends."

"His friends?" Glisson asked.

"Yeah. I didn't see much of 'em though. Just heard them leave. Bern and two other guys. I could hear 'em talking as they went out the door. I looked out the window to the parking lot, saw the three of 'em getting in Bern's car."

"Would you recognize these men, Mr. Gandolf?"

"Naw. Street light's bright but behind the parking lot. All I could see was their shapes. There was a tall guy and a stout guy about Bern's height. He must've been drinkin' cause they were helpin' 'im into the back seat of the car."

From his inside coat pocket, Glisson produced his badge case and flipped it open again under Gandolf's nose. "This is a very urgent matter of national security, Mr. Gandolf. Would you please allow us entry into 202?"

"Aren't you guys supposed to have a warrant or somethin'?"

"It's a federal matter, Mr. Gandolf. And, as I said, urgent and concerns national security."

"Well… I can give you the house key but it won't do not good. He's got his own deadbolt on the door. Never asked me but he's a quiet tenant and I didn't want to raise hell with him."

"May I use your phone, Mr. Gandolf?"

We watched the Orioles and New York on Gandolf's tiny television for 45 minutes. Jack Moony drove up with Ray Stein in tow. Moony wore a dark suit while Stein was dressed in khakis and a crewneck sweater. Peeking from beneath the khakis were his GI boots so he'd obviously been pulled out of class quickly.

Moony flashed his credentials at Gandolf who showed no interest in accompanying us. We went up the stairs to 202. I could tell Ray was surprised to see me but he didn't let on.

Glisson knocked on the door, then inserted the house key and turned the lock. The door didn't budge.

"OK, Private Stein. Here's your chance to show your stuff," Moony said.

Stein peered at the second lock, set flush into the door. He tapped the door. "Steel door. Double-bolt Schlage. This baby's going to be a challenge." Then he pulled out an oilcloth packet and knelt before the door.

44. Surreptitious Entry or B & E?

The challenge to Ray Stein's skills took all of 45 seconds. I marveled as he maneuvered an assortment of probes and picks, all the time pressing on a tension wrench. Then, the tension wrench slowly moved and we could hear a soft *thump* as the first bolt turned.

"One down," Stein whispered. With his left hand, he removed a probe and replaced it with another from his kit. Then another tool which I recognized as a *feeler pick* by its curved point. A second soft thump was accompanied by a sigh from all of us. Stein had a big grin.

The door opened to what had once been a nice apartment. What met us was a jumble of tossed furniture, ripped cushions, broken picture frames and scattered books.

"Holy shit," Glisson exclaimed. "The place has been tossed."

"We'd better call the police," Moony muttered.

"Ahh, yes," Glisson whistled beneath his teeth. "Four Army spooks breaking and entering without a warrant. Let's *do* call the cops, Mister Moony," he said. He walked gingerly into the room, tiptoeing around the scattered paper and books and leaving a wake of sarcasm.

He turned to Warrant Officer Moony and opened his notebook. "Jack, here's a number I want you to call from a payphone. It's the Baltimore P.D. and don't talk to anyone except Detective Sergeant Seamus Muldoon. He'll answer the phone or it won't be answered."

"What do I tell him?" Moony asked. "Tell him the whole story but go light on why we're investigating. Just a matter of national security."

We stood just inside the door, pulled shut to shield the mess from neighbors' view. After about half an hour, Little Sham showed up by himself. He gave me a nod then shook hands with Glisson. "Long time, John," he said in a low voice. "What's going on?"

Glisson explained succinctly how we'd come to discover the apartment without going into the investigative details. The two tiptoed through the apartment while the rest of us searched it with our eyes from the doorway.

When they returned, Muldoon left the room and returned shortly with another man. "This is my fingerprint guy. He'll dust the place but I doubt we'll find much. This looks like it was a glove job."

"There's an inexpensive safe in the bedroom, Stein. Pulled out of the wall but still shut. It's hanging by its security cables. Put on some gloves and see what you can do with it," Glisson ordered.

With one twirl of the dial, Ray Stein popped the little fireproof safe's door. "Not such pros," he said. "They had the combo, just didn't know to give it a last left turn."

The safe's contents were meager. A small velvet bag contained five gold coins and less than 50 dollars in American currency. A small notebook, the same kind used by the CIC, was blank except for one notation.

Mehr geld für gesamte liste.

"German," Glisson observed. "More money for, what's 'gesamte'? Liste? List?"

"I think 'gesamte' is 'all' or maybe 'whole'," Moony said.

"More money for the whole list?" Glisson's eyebrows went up. "We're going to be looking for a list?"

Little Sham Muldoon came back into the living room. "OK, Agent Glisson. I can't find any sign of homicidal activity so technically this isn't my call. You get us a set of this Behren guy's prints and we'll run what we found.

"But for the time being, you've got it as a 'matter of national security.' When you're done, give the department a call and we'll handle the rest as discretely as we can." With a wink at me, the two cops went out the door.

Our search began. Glisson and Moony went through closets and drawers. Stein started through the books on the floor and in shelves. I checked the picture frames scattered about the place, their backing cut out and glass shattered.

The remains of some good quality prints were ripped or torn. Behrens had showed good taste in his art. On the back of one frame, the corner of a torn label read,

Wolfe Gal... Pari...

"Here's something, John," I said, showing the partial label to Glisson. "I made a shot of it."

The search proved fruitless, although something niggled at my mind about the place. Just as we were ready to leave, it suddenly occurred to me.

"Wait a second. Look at these walls where the picture frames hung. The picture in the bedroom was obviously hiding the safe. But in here, he had these pictures hung for decoration... or enjoyment."

"What's your point, Five?" Moony asked.

"Why was this one," I said, pointing to a nail that had held a smaller Mondrian print, "the only one with a gallery lamp? And a gallery lamp with no electrical cord?"

Indeed, above the hanging nail perched a small brass, cylindrical gallery light designed to illuminate the hanging artwork.

With an approving nod from Glisson, I pulled a chair over and reached up to remove the gallery light. The other three watched as I examined the fixture then twisted the cap on one end, revealing an opening in the false lamp.

"Oh wow," Stein breathed out. "A hidden compartment. Oh wow."

With the tweezers from my kit, I removed a piece of tissue parchment with a hand-printed inscription:

Renard, Blaireau, Aigle, Souris... Marchant

"Fox, Badger, Eagle, Mouse," Sergeant Clankus translated. "French of course. But what's a Marchant?"

"I have a good idea," Glisson said with a nod to me, "don't you Agent Lowrey?"

"Special Agent Sam Marchant," I whispered. "Could the animals be cover names?"

"That's what I hope to find out as soon as we pull all of Marchant's agent reports," Glisson said.

45. All's Fair In Love And Espionage

"Why Five, it's so good to see you," Peggy exclaimed archly. "I heard your name mentioned just this afternoon."

"Come on, Peg. You know I have to work sometimes... and this is one of those times."

"I know. And I *am* sorry to be so bitchy. Jack did call me," she apologized. "But our weeks are becoming days and I haven't seen much of you at all."

Peggy's apartment was slowly transforming into a small warehouse with boxes stacked and other belongings piled, waiting to be packed.

"And when Little Sham said he'd seen you three days ago, I realized he'd seen more of you than I had. Where did you see him?"

My response was slow... "aaah, that's ah, classified."

"And that's total bullshit," she replied loudly. "He's a homicide detective and you don't have any business in homicide. Unless you tell me what's going on, *this* will be classified!" Peggy threw one arm across her chest, the other over her pelvis, looking like *The Birth of Venus* in a sweat suit.

Glisson, Cowdrey, Clankus, Moony and I sat at the TRU conference table attempting to piece together the collection of facts into something that might resemble a case.

209

"It'll take a few more days to pull and get copies of the Agent Reports written by Sam Marchant," Glisson reported. "Detective Muldoon's man pulled a bunch of prints from the apartment but they all match Behren's. No surprise there."

"I think we have enough material to open a case on Behrens as a double agent," Glisson says, "but a case on what? We have no evidence that any data has been compromised."

I raised my hand. "Here's one other thing. It may not be important but I looked at these prints of Behrens from the old SPH forms. The left thumb shows a distinct scar, probably from a large slice, perhaps a bad wound."

Everyone looked up at me expectantly. "But if you look at his current file, the left thumb shows no scars."

"It's a shame we can't make out the whorl details from that 1946 SPH," Clankus contributed. "These copies aren't worth shit."

He leaned back and drew deeply on his cigarette. "But consider the possibility that the Behrens Marchant cleared and the Behrens who arrived in Nuremburg were not the same guy? Consider the possibility that someone switched places on the train or whatever."

Peggy warmed up a bit after our argument about my absence, although her favors remained "classified." She looked about twelve in her jeans, tee shirt and a bandana tied around her hair like a turban. We were cleaning out her personal belongings from the library/rec center.

"My last weekend at home," she muttered. "And you want to take me out to dinner? I cannot believe Da and the brothers aren't planning a big shit kicker party."

"Honest Peg. No one has said a thing to me. I just thought a big dinner at Hausner's with me paying would be great. Then a quiet evening at home," I added with hope in my voice.

"You're sure you aren't in cahoots with Little Sham?"

"Cross my heart," I said earnestly.

Three more days went by without much progress on the Behrens case. Then, on Friday Glisson called a meeting and produced a large folder on case file copies.

"There's not much in the Stateside reports," Glisson announced. "Mostly routine BI's from Marchant's tours in St. Louis and New Haven. And we don't have anything from the DP interviews he conducted in '46."

"In 1947, Marchant refused recruitment by the CIA and became an agent handler for southern France, working out of Bordeaux and later Toulouse. His cover name was Surgeon." Glisson looked up. "This is the time period we'll start with."

We each took a stack of AR forms and began reading. The prose was just as stilted in 1948 as it was today and it was all I could do to keep my eyes open.

Less than an hour later, Cowdrey let out a small cry of triumph. "Here's one. I think we've got our Badger."

Subject Sebastian LeClerc (Blaireau) cleared to return to his pre-war home in Soulliac, Perigord, to resume occupation as auto repair mechanic. LeClerc served honorably with Armee Secrete groups and was cleared of collaboration charges with the Milice. Blaireau will organize network from Soulliac region.

"Badger. A stay-behind agent and the beginning of an asset network," Glisson exhulted.

It took two more hours before we had discovered agent reports covering Fox, Eagle and Mouse plus seven other agents with animal code names.

"Cowdrey. Call AIC Records right now and have them check the logs for these reports," Glisson ordered. "If Behrens shows up in the logs, even as a request for access, I think we have the beginning of our list.

"If this list is what I think it might be," he continued, "every foreign asset we have... and perhaps the CIA has... could be compromised. If such a list gets out, the loss of life could be awful."

46. Hail And Farewell

The movers showed up Saturday afternoon with a huge plywood shipping container. Carefully, they stacked all of Peggy's boxes into the container then built partitions to protect them from the furniture.

"Lord, Five. They even packed the cigarette butts in an ashtray I hadn't cleaned," she exclaimed.

By four o'clock, the container was filled and Peggy took one last look at her apartment. I held her while she wept on my shoulder. Then I drove her in the Lemon to her room at the Dundalk Inn.

"There is no way I'm staying with the Muldoons tonight," she stated. "They've barely paid attention to me this week and I'm pissed off about it."

"C'mon Peg. You can't be leaving home with a case of the mads for your family."

I drove to the Safe House in her Studebaker with a promise to pick her up at seven o'clock. I too was puzzled by the lack of goodbye enthusiasm on the part of the Muldoons.

Hausner's is a big, old German restaurant near the Muldoon house in Patterson Park. It's famous for its twelve-page menu and food, as well as the dozens of valuable paintings on its walls… paintings so numerous that Old Masters overlap Impressionists in their frames.

The restaurant was packed but the maitre d' acknowledged my reservation and cheerfully led us through the huge first room. Then the second room and finally, to a closed door, which he indicated we would use.

I opened the door gingerly and there was the entire Muldoon clan, all of the library and rec center staff, my TRU buddies, even the General. "Surprise!"

Peggy glared at me but I returned her look with pure bewilderment. This was as much a surprise to me as it was to her.

It was a gala dinner with many toasts and many speeches. Finally, after the candlelit presentation of a Baked Alaska, it was time to leave Hausner's.

Everyone adjourned the few blocks to the Muldoon home where a keg was iced on the porch and piles of steamed crabs occupied the pingpong table.

We sat on the big couch and listened as each person made his goodbye and contributed advice from living on the west coast to driving across country. By midnight, it was time to leave.

The Brothers Muldoon met us at the door. "We know where you're stayin' and we'll be there bright and early," Little Sham said to Peggy. "You've got to be on the road by nine if you're going to make your 600 miles tomorrow."

Our last night together was sweet and quiet. Peg nestled against my shoulder and snored softly. I lay there and listened to the early morning traffic on Holabird Avenue. Doors began to slam up and down the hallway of the Dundalk Inn, signifying early risers eager to get on the road.

I slipped out of bed and quietly put my clothes on. Then I nudged the sleeping Peg Muldoon and whispered, "reveille, reveille."

"Oh my God, I slept," Peg groaned. "What time is it, Five? And what're you doing all dressed?"

"It's ten after eight and I want to be out of here before the brothers arrive."

"Aw, they know you stayed here last night," she grinned. "But just the same, the Da' will be with 'em and let's not risk him getting upset. I'll meet you in the lobby in 45 minutes."

Steaming coffee and Pall Malls brought me back to life in the Dundalk Inn's coffee shop. I was glad to be discovered there by the four Muldoon men before Peggy appeared.

"Good mornin', Five," the Da' said cheerfully, pounding me on the back. "Here to see our Pegeen off to California?"

"Yessir," I replied. "That was a nice surprise last night."

"Surprised even you, I bet," Little Sham chimed in. "The look on your face. Hope we didn't ruin your last evening together."

Just then, Peggy walked into the coffee shop and the six of us moved to bigger table where the brothers immediately started dishing advice.

"You'll make it to Indianapolis by nightfall," Sean contributed.

"Only if she breaks the speed limit in four states," Michael chimed in.

Sean continued, "Kansas City, then Denver, then somewhere in the desert by the fourth night."

"Be careful where you stay in the desert," Little Sham said.

Peggy sipped her coffee and smiled through the storm of useful information. "Yes, Da, I'll stick to Route 40 all the way. Yes, Sham. I won't eat where the parking lot is empty. Yes, Sean. I'll call from Monterey as soon as I get there."

Then it was time to go.

Outside, four Baltimore Police Department squad cars sat at the curb. Peg brought the Lemon around and Chief Muldoon turned on his red lights and led the procession out of town, three flashing squad cars trailing us.

"Oh Lord, but this is sooo embarrassing," Peggy groaned. "As soon as I get to California, I'm going to get this damned car painted black."

"Peg! Peg, it's a procession of love," I said. "Your family is seeing you off in style."

As we neared Westfield and the Baltimore city limits, Chief Muldoon signaled to pull over. Everyone piled out of the cars for one last hug and kiss goodbye.

Tears rolled down my shoulder as Peggy and I embraced. "I'll be back soon, I promise, Five," she sobbed.

Wiping her eyes, she crawled back into Meadowlark Lemon and rolled west down Route 40.

47. A Summary Of Bits And Pieces

Little Sham indicated I should ride back with him. Tears glistened in his eyes and he started the squad car and headed back to the city.

"I'll take you back to the 'Bird' but first," he said. "I got a call on the way out. I tried to reach Glisson or Cowdrey but they're out of contact, probably down in D.C." He paused then leaned forward over the wheel.

"I think they've found your man Behrens... or at least what's left of him."

Much to my relief, Little Sham turned south toward the 'Bird' instead of heading downtown to the morgue.

As if he were reading my mind, he said, "I've already dispatched our CID liaison guy to bring in the wife for identification of the body."

"Where did they find him?"

"He was tied to a piling under an abandoned pier on Curtis Bay. His car was hidden in a collapsed shed. Some kids found the car and told their folks. They called the sheriff's office and that's all I know."

Little Sham let me out at the TRU and left for downtown. Jack Moony took one look at me and nodded toward the photo lab. I realized I had been awake for 25 hours.

"You look like crap," Five. "Hit the rack back there for as long as you can. I'll wake you when something happens."

216

I thought Moony shook me awake after a half hour of sleep until I looked at the clock. Nearly 1500 hours. I had slept for six hours.

"Glisson and Cowdrey will be here any time. He wants a meeting at 1530, so run over to the safe house and grab a quick cleanup," Moony said kindly.

"OK, let's see what we have to date," Glisson intoned. "Detective Muldoon will call with the autopsy report as soon as it's available."

"Our counterespionage case has taken a big turn," Cowdrey said, "since the subject is now deceased and his control is unknown."

Clankus reported from his assigned duties. "AIC Records reports that Behrens attempted to register to pull European case records on the four cover names on the scrap of paper. AIC security notified us and, of course, denied Behrens's access."

"That was four days before he met Roituer in Baltimore," I added, "and the other subject we can't identify."

"All four of the assets were recruited by Special Agent Sam Marchant during the period 1947 to 1949," Glisson continued, "and we can't forget Marchant was the one who cleared and ultimately hired Behrens in 1946."

"Could Marchant be culpable in this case?" Cowdrey asked aloud.

"I don't think so," I chimed in. "Remember, there were two DOB discrepancies in Behrens' background records, plus the mismatched fingerprints. Marchant probably never had a chance to compare the different SPH forms."

"Right, Five. It would indicate that the Behrens Marchant cleared and the one who showed up in Nuremberg were two different guys.

The intercom buzzed and Jack Moony's voice crackled through the speaker, "Mister Glisson, Sergeant Muldoon has just cleared the main gate."

Little Sham entered the conference room and sat wearily, plopping a manila folder on the table. I realized he had probably enjoyed as little sleep as I had.

"No autopsy report yet but here's what we've got. Mrs. Behrens identified the body as that of her husband, Captain William (Willem)

217

Behrens. Cause of death was probably strangulation by a thin ligature... probably a garrote. His throat was badly mangled."

The three CIC men shared a look. The garrote was a favorite spy weapon.

"The body was found upright, bound to a piling beneath an abandoned pier on Curtis Creek. The property is evidently an abandoned crab processing plant. High tides came to the victim's waist and his lower torso was pretty badly damaged."

Sergeant Muldoon looked at each of us in turn. "The victim's fingertips had been removed, probably with bolt cutters."

Little Sham shrugged. "His vehicle, a black 1959 Chevrolet four door, was found in the partially collapsed structure near the pier."

Glisson looked up expectantly. "Any prints, Sergeant?"

"We got one partial... a left thumb and forefinger on the sill of the rear passenger side door. The rest of the vehicle had been wiped clean.

"There are very small bloodstains in the front passenger seat and a larger one on the back upright."

The news of Behrens' death put our case into a new perspective. Simmons and Franklin were assigned from the D.C. field office and immediately plunged into old agent records from the period.

Glisson put in a request for Sam Marchant to TDY in Baltimore. To our surprise, this was quickly turned down by AIC and we found out that Special Agent Sam Marchant had not been seen in Europe for ten days.

As we tried to assemble the bits and pieces, little became clear. Behrens had been conducting espionage-like activities. We had seen him meet at *Obrycki's Olde Crab House* with Luc Roituer and Darcy Robinette but had no evidence that anything had been passed among them.

A third, unidentified stocky man joined Roituer and Darcy in the cab after the meeting.

Behrens was last seen five days after that meeting in his hideaway apartment being helped into his car by a tall man and a stocky man. According to his landlord, Behrens appeared to be drunk and was helped into the car.

A search of the hideaway revealed scant evidence: an agent notebook with a scrawled notation about a list; a list of four animal names in German, and the last name *Marchant*, and a torn label from the back of a picture frame.

AIC records indicated that Behrens request for Marchant's reports had been made four weeks before his disappearance.

"Four weeks is really pushing it," Cowdrey observed. "Without specific case numbers, those files might not be accessed over a year or more. Behrens was definitely in a hurry."

On Monday morning, the five agents and WO Moony reconvened. Glisson read the autopsy report which confirmed the cause of death: strangulation by a small ligature, possibly a parachute cord garrote. The report's only surprise was large amounts of sodium amytal in his system.

"Drugged," Glisson noted, "with a so-called truth serum."

"They wanted something from him," I said softly. "The list, perhaps?"

"And they were in a hurry for it. If he resisted, that probably accounts for the missing fingertips," Cowdrey said. "Or to keep his prints from being run again."

We spent the rest of the afternoon poring over old case files, mainly reports written by Sam Marchant. Marchant was a CIC legend, having broken two spy rings run by former Nazi stay-behinds, handling numerous defectors and persuading many of them to stay put and work for the CIC.

I was weary when I began a new interview file with a Marcel Gammard, an employee of Gallery Maeght in Paris. The report was the newest of Marchant's production, only two weeks old. Gammard had been given as a positive throwoff in an investigation of a piece of missing artwork.

Describing his previous employer, Gammard referred to him as "a turncoat, willing to serve whoever would serve him best." Gammard went on to claim the man had worked with the Nazis during the occupation, then with the Resistance. He named the man as Gregory Wolfgram, the sole proprietor of Gallerie Wolfe, 6 rue Say.

The name rang a bell with me immediately... the label fragment from Behrens' picture frame.

"Speaking of prints," Glisson said, "here's the partial the sheriff's office pulled." He handed me the card and the large scar across the thumb leaped at me. "Can we check this against the '46 prints?" I asked.

219

"I've already had Baltimore PD do that. The '46 card is so fuzzy but the print man thought it could be the same."

"And, one more piece of news," Glisson continued. "I requested Agent Marchant be sent here on TDY as soon as possible. He hasn't been seen in France for the last ten days. I think it's time we got someone over there."

48. An Innocent Goes Abroad

Four days later, I was shocked to have Moony hand me my TDY orders for France.

"But I don't speak French, Mr. Moony," I protested.

"No worries, Five. We have a field office in Paris and the Acting Agent in Charge will get you fixed up with a translator or guide."

"Do I take my credentials? What do I wear?"

"No to the credentials. Colonel Stendall and Agent Glisson decided to send you as sort of undercover... you'll use your real name and passport but as an American art student. We'll work out a simple cover story."

I penned a quick letter to Peggy in care of the Fort Ord library in response to the one postcard she'd sent me from Kansas City. And I also made a collect call home. Mom sounded excited and told me she'd always wanted to go to Paris.

Also, I drew per diem and travel allowance for 20 days and was issued my first passport with a visa for the Republic of France. The next evening, Clankus drove me to Friendship Airport where I would catch a flight to LaGuardia and a jet to France.

"Holy shit, Sarge," I exclaimed. "I can't believe I'm going to France. And on a jet! Have you ever flown in a jet before?"

"Yeah, and it beats the crap out of a prop plane," he said. "I hope you can find a few hours to see some sights over there. I really think France is a great place, especially to get laid."

The Pan Am 707 was a bulbous but sleek airplane, especially compared with the Eastern Airlines DC-3 I took to New York out of Friendship. My stomach was in my throat as we tore down the LaGuardia runway at a speed that would surely launch us into the bay ahead.

Instead, we launched into the sky and the wheels came up with an ominous thump. I peered out my window at the lights of New York and Long Island receding and found myself missing the reassuring sight of spinning propellers.

Free drinks were followed by a lavish dinner and small bottles of wine, all served by a cute young stewardess. The drone of the jet engines combined with the booze put me to sleep by nine o'clock.

Robert Theriault was very tall and thin, stooped from years of leaning forward to hear conversations. His blond hair hung over one side of his face in a long swatch that reached nearly to his jawline. *How did this guy ever pass an Army inspection?* I thought to myself.

His grip was firm and he snatched up my suitcase with the other hand. "Lowrey, I'm Bob Theriault. Welcome to Paris."

He pronounced it "Pa-ree" but I thought it best not to correct him.

"Pleased to meet you, Mister Theriault. I can't believe I'm in France."

"Well, it sounds like you may be onto something that's been really bothering us," he said. We walked out of the terminal building, across a big parking lot and into a street where automotive chaos was taking place.

"Frenchmen drive with their horns," Theriault informed me. We dodged across the street to the parking lot, Theriault seemingly oblivious to near death bearing down on us in strange little cars. He stopped at a small black car with two wheels up on the sidewalk.

"Here's my car," he said proudly. "Parking on the sidewalk is another quaint, French tradition."

"I saw a car like this in a movie not long ago," I exclaimed. "It's not a Volkswagen but…"

"It's a Citroen *deux chevaux*, a 2CV. This one's a 1938. And you're thinking of the car in *Mister Hulot's Holiday,* tall guy with a pipe, looked somewhat like me?"

"Yeah, that's it, Mister Theriault," I exclaimed as I pulled the door open on the 2CV.

"That's a Citroen, too," Theriault explained. "But it was a *cinq chevaux*, five horsepower built in the 1920's. I'd love to get my hands on one of those. And... call me Bob."

Bob reached up and released the Citroen's canvas top and with one sweep of his arm, it rolled back and we were in sort of a convertible. "Thing has two window shades," he laughed. "The top and there's another one in front of the radiator. When it gets cold, you pull it down and the heat comes into the car."

I was charmed by the tiny French car, which seemed much less substantial than the VW Beetles, which had just made their way into the States. As we motored into the city and through the Paris streets, the car shook and rattled and its body panels even skewed sideways as we turned corners. Its horn reminded me of the Schwinn bike I received for Christmas 15 years ago.

To the constant tootling of the *deux chevaux's* horn, we drove down a broad boulevard. Never lifting his finger from the horn stalk, Bob gave me a running commentary on the sights and the CIC's role in Paris.

"This is Boulevard Sebastapol. We've got avenues, boulevards and streets; *rue* is the French word for street. And this part of town is known as *rive droite. Droite's* the word for right and this is the Right Bank, mostly north of the river."

We turned right onto another street that paralleled the river. "That's the Seine and the island is where Paris began... *isle d'Cite.* Notre Dame is at the far end. And this is the Louvre coming up on the right. Then Tuileries Gardens.

"Our office here isn't quite like the other CIC field offices in Europe. Our role in France is minor since we don't have troops based in-country any longer. Assisting the Art Recovery Units... maintaining our assets from the war... and helping the French track down agents who may have a connection with our activities in the past."

"So we're not in a clandestine situation?" I asked.

"Not exactly. The French know we're here and cooperate with us. But operationally, I report to G2 USArmy Germany in Heidelburg. The military attaché here keeps an eye on us but has no direct responsibility."

"This is the *Place de la Concorde* on the right and this bridge is the *Pont de la Concorde* which takes us over to the Left Bank."

223

"Ah, the Left Bank," I exclaimed. "That's where all the artists hang out, isn't it?"

"Paris has artists, art students, everywhere. But yes, the *Ecole nationale supérieure des Beaux-Arts* is nearby. That's the major art school. And these all government ministries," he said, waving his hand at the huge buildings on all sides of us."

"I've arranged for an interpreter-guide to take care of you while you're in France," he commented. "Not an agent, I'm afraid. I only have five available in the whole country. But someone who has excellent language skills and a special interest in the case you're working on."

Bob turned onto a fashionable broad avenue lined by trees and stylish shops. "Boulevard Saint Germain and now we're onto Boulevard Raspail."

Two more quick turns and Bob pulled the *deux chevaux* up to a broad door set into the face of a building. A trio of horn beeps brought a sturdy looking older man through the Judas door. He gave us a frown and then pushed the bigger doors open. Bob drove into a small courtyard, while the doorman closed the doors behind us.

"Henri," Bob said, addressing the doorman, "this is Mister Lowrey. He'll be with us for awhile."

"Henri is the concierge. If you come on foot, just ring the bell set into the Judas door frame. And by car," he grinned, "our *secret* signal is three beeps of the horn."

49. Enter A New Marchant

We left my bags in the car. I followed Bob into the building and up a staircase. "We're on the first floor, which you'd better get used to 'cause unlike the States, first floor is always one above ground level."

He produced a key and turned it in an imposing deadbolt on a door marked simply with a numeral seven. *"Bonjour, Marthe,"* he called out. *"c'est notre nouvel homme, Monsieur Thompson Lowrey."*

"Bonjour, Monsieur Lowrey," The woman responded with a weak smile.

Mr. Lowrey does not speak French, Marthe. So please use English. Has Gigi arrived yet?

"No sir," Marthre replied. "She is still at the interview with Mister Varigny. She called and said it might be several hours more."

"Fine. Have her come right to my office when she gets here."

Bob took my elbow and led me toward a closed door. "Marthe is Henri's wife and co-concierge. They live on the ground floor. She also answers the phones and does a little filing for us here.

"Marthe's an intensive Frenchwoman… speaks some English but very grudgingly," he shrugged. "But she will understand you if you ask a question."

Robert Theriault's office was a typical mess with piles of files and folders flanking three locked security file cabinets. Again, I recited the story of the Behrens case as he held an agent report and followed along. When I finished, he leaned forward and spoke. "You've got to be crapped out after that flight. There's a cot in the other room. Catch a couple of

225

hours sleep and then we'll go ahead and brief you on some of the things you'll encounter here."

Theriault was merciful. Although I'd slept on the plane, I managed another three hours on his cot before he shook me awake. Marthe brought in a tray with coffee mugs and the crescent shaped rolls I had enjoyed on the plane.

"*Croissants et café, Monsieur. Prenez-vous du lait avec votre café?*" she asked.

"English, Marthe, please. She wants to know if you take milk with your coffee. They heat it up over here and call it *café au lait.*"

"No thank you, black is fine."

Theriault began the briefing. "Sam Marchant is our Agent in Charge and was running a routine recovery case when he encountered the throwoff that led him to the interview with Marcel Gammard, a former associate of Wolfgram's. You must understand that Sam is an old-timer and has run his own agents and worked intensively in art recovery following the war."

"When Gammard gave up the name of Gregor Wolfgram, it rang a bell with Sam. He came back here, requested some old case files from Holabird, and made an appointment to interview Wolfgram. He left that afternoon and that's the last we saw of him. This was ten days ago."

"Two days after he vanished, we got a report that Sam had been seen in Strasbourg. Then, two days later, our field office in Lyon reported that an asset had thought he's seen Sam there… in the street. But he never checked in, never sent a report."

A knock on the door interrupted us. "Come in," Theriault called.

The door opened and a young woman dressed in gray and black stood in the doorway. She gave me a once-over look, then stalked into Bob' office. Her hair was strawberry blonde and curled over her shoulders. A gray wool cape concealed her figure but I could see she was gorgeous.

When she removed her glasses, I could see a sprinkle of freckles across the bridge of her pert nose. Her lower lip showed a slight pout, a look I'd come to associate with Frenchwomen thanks to Bridget Bardot movies.

"Mister Lowrey, this is Mlle. Genevieve Guinivere Marchant."

"I'm pleased to meet you, 'Madam-oselle,'" I stammered. "Marchant?"

"Yes. I'm Special Agent Marchant's daughter," she answered coolly, then turned to Theriault and shrieked, *"Qu'est-ce que c'est, Robert? J'ai demandé de l'aide. Et que m'envoie-t-on? Ce bébé!"*

"Facile, Gigi. Il a le même âge que vous. Et il a quelques perspicacités spéciales dans le cas de votre père."

Bob turned to me and shrugged apologetically. "This is the woman I arranged for as your guide-interpreter. I'm sure she'll find her manners as soon as she gets over the shock of your youth. I think she expected AIC to send an agent who was Sam's age."

"Damned right, I did," she blurted in English. To me, "Bob says you've got some new facts that might pertain to my Dad's disappearance?"

"Hold it, hold it just a minute," Bob raised his hands placatingly. "Let's get some of the ground rules straightened out here, Gigi. Have a seat."

Gigi Marchant settled into Robert's other chair, crossed her magnificent legs and frowned at me.

"First of all, Thompson Lowrey is a Special Agent of the CIC, perhaps with less experience by far than your *père* but certainly as well trained. In addition, he brings some special skills to this case."

Then to me, "Mlle. Marchant is a French citizen. She works for the French Sureté as an agent on the Art Recovery Team and is our liaison with the Sureté."

"That's the French security agency, isn't it?" I asked.

She nodded and reached into her purse, producing a warrant card. The photo showed a blonde woman with a much more pleasant expression.

"I'm sorry if I seemed rude. I did have a bad interview with one of Robert's informants and I'm afraid I took it out on you."

"S'all right," I murmured. "I hope I'm not going to be an imposition on you, though."

"No! Anything that will help me find out where my Dad is... or what happened to him..." She shook her head and looked into her lap.

Robert drove us in the *deau chevaux* to a safe house on rue Racine. "It's not fancy by any means," he commented, "but it's a real Paris garret. The ideal place for an art student to live, if only for a week or so."

The atmosphere following our initial meeting had improved and Bob outlined where I would live, how we would work together. Genevieve Guinivere introduced me to, Madame Boneau, the concierge at 21 rue Racine and followed as Bob led us up four flights of stairs.

"I've never been up here before, Bob," she observed. "How many more safe houses do you have tucked away in Paris?"

"Classified, Gigi."

I put my suitcase on a narrow bed tucked into a corner beneath a steeply sloping roof. The only light in the room came in through a rain spattered dormer window that overlooked rooftops and a tiny glimpse of the street below.

"No cooking, Lowrey," Bob warned. "You'll burn the place down."

Genevieve Guinivere walked back into the room. "At least you don't have to share a bathroom. It's not *en suite* but it's all yours." She grinned and led me past the stairs and around a brick chimney. "Alors!" A tiny pair of commodes sat in a dark nook beneath the sloping roof. One had a seat. She saw my puzzlement and smiled, "A bidet. Perhaps you'll learn how to use it. And there's the tub," she exclaimed triumphantly, pointing to a greenish copper appliance on the other side of the room.

I hesitatingly turned the faucet and a thin trickle of water poured out. "We'll have a word with Madame about when hot water will be available," Bob said. "I'm going back to the office. Gigi, why don't you talk with the concierge about water and other arrangements and we'll let Mister Lowrey get settled.

"OK," she said. "I'll meet you downstairs, Agent Lowrey, and we'll try to get to know one another better."

We walked a couple of blocks and settled into sidewalk seats at a small café. The narrow street was packed with young people, laughing and talking. "This is the Latin Quarter," Genevieve Guinivere told me, "where most of the universities are located. In the old days, all academics spoke Latin, hence its name."

"Speaking of names, how long do I keep calling you Genevieve Guinivere?"

"Oh, that's thanks to my mom and dad. She was French and I was named for her. Dad is English and loved Sir Walter Scott, so they tagged me with Guinivere. My warrant card reads 'G.G.' but everyone has called me Gigi since I was a little girl."

"Oh, I thought it was maybe from the movie."

"Ah, that wretched movie. I don't mind the nickname but now everyone expects me to look like Leslie Caron. And in ten years, I'll be one of a million Frenchwomen with the same name."

"Well," I said slowly, "I've been saddled with an unusual name also… since I was a little kid."

Her eyebrows arched up in question.

"My name is Thomsen Lowrey V, and everyone calls me Five. I've found it very difficult to answer to Mister Lowrey or even Tom."

"Mon dieu, cinq générations!" Gigi gave me a wry smile. "You're as bad as French royalty."

We continued to exchange background stuff and I found this austere girl more charming as she loosened up and talked.

"I was born in '35 in a town called Sarlat de Canada… in southern France. But when I was three, we moved to the States and Dad joined the Army. He returned to France in late '43, worked with the OSS and Resistance, then was reassigned to CIC after D-Day.

"My brother Jean-Marc and I went to high school in the states. When the family returned to France in 1950, I finished high school in the states and attended Hood in western Maryland for two years. Then I came back and was accepted at the Fine Arts school in Paris."

"That's amazing," I exclaimed. "I have a friend who teaches art at Hood now. It's a really pretty school."

"After graduation from the *Ecole Beaux Arts,* I volunteered for the Allied Art Recovery Unit, mostly because my Dad worked with it and it seems like a worthy cause. The pay was awful but the hours were very loose." Gigi paused.

"After a year, the Sureté recruited me… again, probably because of Dad. But the warrant card gives me extra influence with some of the shady characters in the art recovery world."

The time seemed to fly as Gigi and I exchanged background stories. Then, she brushed her blonde forelock back and stood. "It's time I must go. I have a date this weekend. I'll walk you to the Metro and we'll get you fixed up for dinner."

True to her word, Gigi introduced me to a waiter at Bistro Pingo, just a square away from my Metro stop and new flat. She also gave me directions and instructions to get around on the Metro. "I think Bob will be in the office in the morning. He usually is. If you want to walk over there, it'll be quicker than the Metro.

"Try the Croque Monsieur," she advised. "It's just a ham sandwich with cheese on a toasted piece of bread. Monsieur Gregory will bring you the correct wine and he does have a few words of English so you should be OK. I'll pick you up Monday morning." And with that, she was gone from the Bistro Pingo.

Monsieur Gregory had more than a few words of English and worked with me through the bistro's menu.

After dinner, I wandered the streets of the Latin Quarter as dusk settled in. I came to the Seine and crossed a bridge that had a nice view of Notre Dame. I stood at the rail and sketched the cathedral and the colorful buildings on the islands.

At loose ends, I climbed down the stairs of the ornate *Cite* Metro station and doled out my francs for a ticket. Entering the next train, I rode to the end of the line then caught a train back to *Odeon.* Emerging from the Metro, I realized that I was somewhat lost and wandered the narrow streets until I found the familiar lights of Bistro Pingo.

My waiter was gone for the night but I successfully ordered a glass of beer and smoked and drank until I was ready for home. I crawled into bed with my feet beneath the narrow part of the roofline. Out the window, the chimney pots were silhouetted against the glow of Paris at night.

Saturday dawned bright and clear. I had *café a lait* and a *croissant* on the sidewalk table at Gammard, feeling very much the Parisian sophisticate. Then I walked through Luxembourg Gardens to rue St. Placide and found the CIC doorway. I pulled the bell cord and Marthe responded a minute later, opening the Judas door.

"Monsieur Theriault is in his office. He said for me to send you up, if you came at all," Marthe muttered in accented English.

"Good morning, Five. How did you survive your first night in Paris? Hung over?" Theriault seemed pretty chipper.

"Morning, Bob. Some wine with a ham sandwich and a bedtime glass of beer at the bistro. I wandered around, seeing the sights. What a great city!"

"And how did you get along with Gigi? I'm sorry she was so rude yesterday but she's very aggressive and frustrated... and very worried."

"Ahh, we had coffee and smokes at a café and exchanged backgrounds. But I got the feeling she wasn't telling me everything about herself."

"Well, there's a lot to tell," he said, "and frankly, she's got a lot on her mind."

"You mean her missing father?"

"There's that, and her boyfriend."

I answered, "Yeah, she mentioned a date for the weekend. Her boyfriend doesn't live in Paris?"

"Charles Bleriot, works in the Ministry of Defense. Comes from an old family with links to the French royalty. They have a villa in the country. He's been badgering Gigi to marry him for nearly a year."

"And why doesn't she?"

"Well, he's a typical Frenchman," Bob continued. "I think he's on mistress number two since Gigi has been dating him. Also, I suspect he's after her only for her money."

"Her money?"

"Gigi's a relatively wealthy young woman, thanks to her parents and their travails. And as I said, she's aggressive and usually gets what she goes after... including men." Bob was obviously winding into a story."

"Sam Marchant met Genevieve Emperitain in the early thirties just after he'd graduated from college. Her parents were big landowners in the Perigord and they approved of Sam because of his charm and his skills with the French language. They were married in 1933 and settled in a small farmhouse on the property.

"When Genevieve gave birth to Jean-Marc, then Gigi, they decided to move to the States."

Bob went to the outer office and poured us each a cup of coffee. It was a vile brew, obviously not concocted by Marthe.

"War came and France fell to the Nazis in short order. With the occupation, the Emperitains found themselves citizens of Vichy France and opposed to the government's collaboration with Germany. They took part in the Resistance, were turned in by collabos and disappeared in late 1943."

"Executed?" I asked.

"Not immediately," Bob replied. "Sam Marchant was back in France at the time, an OSS agent trying to organize the Resistance groups. Many of the Resistance groups were Communists and de Gaulle's effort to unite them was not succeeding. There was a lot of jealousy and treachery between the Gaullists and the Communists and much of it was used to settle old scores from before the war.

"Sam's assignment was to recruit operatives and organize routes to remove Allied escapees from France. But he always felt a responsibility for not getting the Emperitains out of the country."

"The Melice, the Vichy government's secret police, had the Emperitains transported to Dachau. They died there in early 1944."

Bob and I ate lunch at a brasserie near his office. Then we walked the narrow streets over to the Parc Champ d' Mars.

"It's hard to believe that the swastika flew from the Eiffel Tower less than twenty years ago," he commented as we strolled across the broad lawn toward the tower. "There was a rumor in 1942 of a Resistance plot to blow the tower down but nothing ever came of it.

"Resistance cells in Paris were active but not so large and organized as in the unoccupied part of the country. And it was always hard for Resistance operatives to appear to collaborate with the Nazis because of so much gossip throughout the city. An agent could mistakenly end up hanged by another Resistance group."

From the *Tour d' Eiffel,* Bob pointed out the sites and landmarks of the city. The basilica of Montmartre gleamed from its hilltop, while Notre Dame hunkered on its island in the Seine.

"Paris is a city for walkers," Bob opined. "Oh, the Metro lets you get around quickly but if you want to get to know the place, on foot is the best way."

In the *Palace d' Invalides,* we looked down at Napoleon's Tomb, then entered the Military Museum. "This used to be a barracks, then a hospital for veterans," Theriault pointed out as we strolled among cabinets exhibiting uniforms and weaponry from France's military past.

A narrow set of stairs led to the third floor, in reality the attic, a long gloomy room beneath the eaves of the pitched roof. Small pools of light broke the darkness and illuminated showcases with models of old French fortifications.

"This is a great place for a quiet meeting," Bob whispered. "I've rarely seen anyone in this room except those I was scheduled to meet."

Late in the afternoon, I left Bob and ambled into the Luxembourg Gardens. My sketchbook was barely touched since the night before and I was determined to do some work.

Bob had suggested a visit to the Louvre for the next day and perhaps Montmartre. The contents of my sketchbook were notes from his many suggestions.

I drew young children sailing their toy boats on the reflecting pool, nannies and mommies pushing prams along the smooth graveled paths. I refrained from staring at the many couples entwined in kissing embraces but drew one or two from memory.

Footsore and weary, I staggered back to the Bistro Pingo and was happy to find my English-speaking waiter.

"Monsieur Gregory bonsoir. Comment allez-vous?" I assayed my one bit of Theriault-taught French.

"Ah, Monsieur, your French is very good tonight," he grinned. "Would you care for an aperitif?"

I shrugged, "Can you suggest something? Surprise me."

He returned in a few minutes with a small glass of tan liquid and a side glass of water. "A Ricard," he announced, "a brand of Pernod. And after dinner, I can introduce you to a *digestif*, perhaps a Calvados?"

Monsieur Gregory also guided me to a *crepe de poulet*, a tasty thin pancake filled with chunks of chicken and an incredible sauce. And the Calvados was a warming brandy, which I took an instant liking to.

Later, I wandered the Latin Quarter, stopping at cafes for a Calvados and a sketch session. At one café, I encountered a couple of American students and we talked until midnight.

50. The Curse Of Calvados

Horns! Whistles! Shouts from the street! An insistent thudding! All of these sounds penetrated my pillow and into my Calvados infused brain. Slowly, I realized the thudding was coming from my door.

Staggering to the tiny sink, I soaked my parched mouth then tottered toward the door where the knocking was getting louder.

Without thinking, I opened the door and discovered Gigi, her fist raised for another knock. An expression of surprise swept her face as she saw I was standing in my underwear.

"My God, Five, You look terrible," she exclaimed. "Do you have a *putain* in there with you?"

I turned away quickly, muttering "what's a putain? All I have in here is an outrageous hangover." I pulled on my wrinkled pants from the previous evening.

"I thought you were going to be away for the weekend? This *is* Sunday, isn't it?"

Gigi frowned and shrugged simultaneously. "Well, I'm back. And if you'll get cleaned up and dressed, I can guide you to wherever you want to go for the entire day. I'll be at the bistro." And she spun on her heel and clopped down the stairs.

With a raised eyebrow, Gigi had the waiter scurry forward with a large cup of black coffee as I approached the sidewalk tables.

"You look some better but I'll bet you don't feel it," she commented, scanning me up and down. I was dressed in khaki trousers, a

234

rusting black crewneck sweater with holes scattered around its surface, and scuffed dirty tennis shoes. "Very beatnik," she appraised. "Perfect cover. The young American art student abroad."

Her attire was a shortish wool skirt, beneath which her legs were encased in black tights. A sweater and her cape from the previous day completed the ensemble.

I sipped at the coffee in silence and tugged the crumpled remains of my last pack of Pall Malls from my pants pocket. Gigi produced from her small shoulder bag a pack of Galouise, the French brand that everyone seemed to smoke. I took one and lit it, instantly bursting into a fit of coughing. She giggled.

"So, why are you back in Paris instead of at your boyfriend's?" I gasped.

"I came back last night. That asshole had the nerve to bring his new mistress to the country! He met me with a big embrace, reeking of her," she growled. "Obviously, bathing isn't one of her talents."

Gigi glared at me, "and how did you know I was at my *ex*-boyfriend's?"

"I spent the day with Bob, yesterday. He briefed me on a number of things... including your love life and all."

Some recovered by coffee and Galouises, I walked with Gigi across what she called the "Pont Neuf" and onto the Ile St. Louis, one of the two islands in the Seine. Below us on the quai by the river, a small crowd had gathered around a photographer and his technicians.

"It's a fashion shoot," Gigi exclaimed. "Let's go down and watch."

We descended the steps from the bridge to the quai and stood on the edge of the small group of onlookers. A photographer danced around a model who kept striking poses with the river and Notre Dame in the background. After a few minutes, he dismissed her with a flurry of French and a Gallic wave of his arm. She scurried to a canvas pavilion to escape the chill air.

Assistants changed film in his camera backs and he lit a cigarette, glancing at the sky and checking his wristwatch.

"It's Gleb Derujinsky," Gigi exclaimed. "He's a famous fashion photographer, at least over here."

Suddenly, a murmur swept through the crowd as a new model appeared from the pavilion. Clad in a simple white dress with a flowing

235

skirt, white heels and a string of white beads around her neck, the model shimmered as the strode across the quai.

"Darcy!" I murmured, not even knowing I was speaking.

"Darcy," Gigi echoed. "She's famous over here also."

I could scarcely breath as we watched Darcy strut and twirl gracefully across the stone cobbles of the quai. Her skirt billowed behind her. Her dark hair was long and piled in an elaborate bouffant. Her smile and her eyes controlled the camera.

She seemed grown up and sophisticated, yet her eyes and smile were the same saucy kid who captivated me at the Begorra Burger in Athens, Ohio.

Moving quickly through the ranks of watchers, I wasn't aware of the minor disturbance I was causing as I jostled my way to the front. Suddenly, Darcy's composure vanished and her hand flew to her mouth as she recognized me.

"Merde!" Durujinsky screamed, whirling around to glare at me as Darcy ran to the tent. He quickly followed Darcy into the pavilion.

"Five! What on earth?" Gigi exclaimed. "What did you do?"

"I think maybe we'd better take off," I said uneasily. Just then, a girl ran from the tent and grabbed my arm.

"Darcy asks that you please stay. She'll only be a moment."

Gigi stared at me in wonderment. I didn't try to explain. Onlookers also stared at the scruffy looking boob who had destroyed their Sunday morning entertainment.

More than a moment passed. Then Darcy emerged from the pavilion clad in jeans and a sweatshirt which made her elaborate hairdo seem ludicrous. She ran to me and threw her arms around my neck. Off balance, I tottered and she swung around me with a shrill squeal.

"Five! Five, my god, it's you. I knew it was you! Oh my god."

Gigi's mouth dropped open as she watched me embrace and kiss one of the world's great fashion models. Tears were in Darcy's eyes as she leaned back in my arms and peered into my face.

"You haven't changed a bit," she whispered. "I explained to Gleb and he's given me an hour. Oh Five, I'm so excited."

Words finally came to me. "Darce, it's so good to see you. I didn't know if I'd ever see you again." I turned to Gigi. "Darcy Robinette, this is my associate Gigi Marchant. Gigi, this is Darcy."

Torn between discretion and curiosity, Gigi reluctantly accompanied us to a café in the Ile St. Louis when Darcy insisted she not leave. We sat inside to escape the gawkers who trailed behind us. I could almost feel the hands of the clock moving as our hour went by.

"It's a shoot for *Harper's Bazaar*," Darcy explained. "This is our last day and tomorrow, we move on to Rome. Gleb's a dear to work with although he was pretty shook when you appeared."

I explained my presence in Paris and Gigi's role, skirting the details.

"Sissy told me in one of her letters that you were a spy for the Army," Darcy said. "I saw you that night in Baltimore," she said in a low voice. "I wondered what was going on."

"Darcy, can you tell me what happened that night?"

"Not much. Luc just asked me to have dinner with him. We met that Mister Bering, was that his name, and made small talk while we ate crabs. God, those crabs were delicious!"

"A man got into the cab with you as you left the crab house. Who was he?"

"I don't know. I thought he was just someone Luc offered to share the cab with, although that's not a bit like Luc. He's a mean sonofabitch. But he spoke French with the guy... like he knew him."

I paused, believing her story. "And Luc. Where is he?"

"I don't know that either. I was in Paris two weeks ago to shoot a layout for French Vogue. He was supposed to be the photographer but he disappeared a few days before we arrived. Everyone was in an uproar about it. I heard he had gone back to Hungary but I don't know for sure..."

"Luc Roituer," I explained to Gigi. She raised an eyebrow in recognition of the name.

"He's famous over here as well," she said. "Or at least he was."

I persisted in finding out more. "While I was being investigated for a clearance, your name came up several times. Demonstrations? SDS?"

"Oh that stuff," Darcy said lightly. "When I was first in New York, I met this guy Jerome Dukas. He's a director." Gigi and I nodded in recognition. "He wanted me to take some acting lessons and I went to his Riverside Acting Guild a couple of times."

"There were lots of college kids and it was more of a political club than an acting class. I didn't go back. Haven't seen him since."

Too soon, the hour was over. We strolled back through the narrow streets. Darcy and Gigi chatted, heads together like schoolgirls. "I can't cry," she said aloud to anyone who listened. "Gleb has been patient with me and my makeup artist is a real dipshit. He'll have a fit if my eyes are all red."

On the quai, the tent was struck and only a Peugeot van remained. The girl who had asked us to wait sat on the running board. One of the photographer's assistants was behind the wheel of the van.

"Am I late?" Darcy asked. The young woman shook her head no. "They just went ahead. Gleb said for you to come as soon as you can."

Darcy's eyes glistened as she and I exchanged one last, lingering kiss. "Adieu, Five. We'll meet again, I know."

"Goodbye, Darce. And good luck."

51. Walking Among The Masters

"Five, I'm just astounded. And I won't go another step until you explain everything," Gigi said. On a bench overlooking the Seine, I told Gigi an abbreviated history of Darcy and me. "Do you still love her?"

"Until today, I wasn't sure. She's certainly grown up in four years and we're not the same people any more. When I first saw her, I felt a pang in my gut but I'm pretty sure it's not love." As I talked, my pencil skittered across the pad as I unconsciously put my last impression of Darcy's face to paper.

"Why did you ask her about Roituer?" Gigi asked. I recalled the night surveillance at Obryki's and Darcy's unexpected appearance.

"You know, the Sureté has more than a passing interest in Roituer. He's posed as a Frenchman these past five or six years and became nearly as famous as Robert Doisneau. But he *is* Hungarian and some think he's involved in more than photography.

"I've encountered his name in several art recovery cases," she added. "And he tried to pick me up at a cocktail party once. He's an arrogant bastard and I think Darcy is right. He's probably a mean bastard too."

Beyond the entrance to the Louvre, a set of broad stairs led to the landing where the *Winged Victory of Samothrace* overlooked each visitor to the museum... that is, overlooked if she had a head. I was spellbound by this ancient masterpiece of Greek sculpture. I would remain spellbound for the next seven hours as we strolled from gallery to gallery, each filled with the work of masters.

239

"How did these people work on canvases so huge and still maintain their perspective?" I asked as we stood before Delacroix' *Liberty Leading The People.*

The works of the Impressionists were equally marvelous as the Old Masters, although they seemed jumbled in their narrow gallery. "There's a movement to obtain a separate home for the works from the last two centuries," Gigi commented. "It's hard to believe the Impressionists weren't taken seriously until a few years ago and many experts still express their doubts."

She drew me to a window that looked out on the Seine. "Over there, on the other side, is the *Gare d'Orsay,* an abandoned train station. It used to be the main terminal for the south. Some want it to be the new home for the Impressionists. Others want it razed. We'll see."

Gigi examined my sketch of Darcy's face, then leafed her way back through my sketchbook. As she viewed my sketches, she made small sounds in her throat that I hoped were of approval.

"And you do paint, Five?" I nodded yes. "We'll have to get you to paint something, if there's time. And..." she paused at the unfinished lines of the mysterious cab passenger in Baltimore, "what's this?"

"Ah, it's just a quick sketch of the man I glimpsed that night in Baltimore. I didn't see much of him but got these lines down as a reminder."

"It looks vaguely familiar," she said. "Perhaps the shape of the head, like he was on his back a lot as a baby. Here I thought the sketchpad was just part of your cover, if you needed one. So that's the special skill Bob mentioned."

"Well, not quite," I tried to say modestly. "Pick a single person at a table behind me. Just tell me which table."

Gigi looked over my shoulder for a second. "All right. Three tables down the sidewalk, one in."

I turned and found her chosen table, staring at the young man reading a paper for about ten seconds. Then I turned and began sketching. Less than a minute later, I turned my pad toward Gigi to see the results.

"Mon dieu!" she exclaimed. "That's incredible. And fast. Yes, you really do have a special skill."

That night, Gigi insisted that we go to dinner in the Latin Quarter. She chose a tiny restaurant called *le Coupe Chou*. As we were seated, she told me the story of the restaurant.

"It means "the chopped cabbage" and the building was a barbershop in the last century. The story goes that it was very easy to pay the barber to cut an occasional throat to provide a cadaver for medical students." She added, "but the food is terrific."

Over salmon and oysters poached in Calvados, our conversation became serious.

"Bob told me about the Occupation and your grandparents," I mentioned. "How is your mother taking your father's absence?"

Gigi's lower lip disappeared behind her teeth and she shook her head. "My mother's dead, Five."

I half expected her to cry but she looked up at me with dry eyes. "When the Gestapo transported my grandparents, the Vichy government seized their estate and sold it to loyal party members at a *very* good price. In 1945, my mother returned from the States to reclaim the estate. My father was there, of course, and helped in the tribunal."

She paused then continued, "They won, of course, although the present 'owners' hadn't been found to be actual collaborators. A few days later my mother drove over to Sarlat to visit friends. While she was there, a bomb exploded and destroyed the house, killed her friends and seriously wounded my mother. She died the next day."

"God, how awful for your father... and you," I exclaimed.

"Less than an hour later, a car went off the winding road between Carsac and Châteaux Montfort and exploded with a terrible impact. Windows were blown out for several miles," Gigi continued. "The occupants were two of the three former 'landowners' of my grandparents' estate. The gendarmes matched tire treads from that car to tracks found in the mud outside the Sarlat house.

Catching her breath, Gigi went on. "The third *owner* tried to flee but was arrested and tried for murder. In 1946, he went to the guillotine. All three were former Resistance fighters and Communists."

"Couldn't they have been arrested for being Communists?" I asked.

"Five, it's not against the law to be a Communist in the Republic of France."

241

We ate in silence for a few minutes, then Gigi picked up the story. "After about a year, the title to the estate was totally clear and my father sold much of it."

"How big was the estate?"

"There was a smallish Château and nearly 300 hectares, much of it across the Dordogne River and very good farming land. He sold the Château and kept one of the best farms and about 25 hectares. My brother and his wife live there now."

"And a hectare is… how big? As big as an acre?"

"A hectare equals about two and a half, not quite, acres."

"Lord, you mean your family was screwed out of almost 800 acres… and a castle? And the cost was your grandparents' and your mother's lives?"

"And my father's peace of mind. He's a very bitter, very determined man," she replied sadly.

"Gigi, do you believe your father is alive?"

"It's all I can believe, Five. We've no evidence that he is not and until some is produced, I can continue to hope and search."

As we walked the streets of the Latin Quarter, Gigi's mood became mellower. "If you'll escort me home I'll show you that not all young people in Paris live in rooftop garrets."

"Where exactly is your brother's farm?" I asked.

"Oh, it's still my father's but it's located near St. Cyprian on a bend in the Dordogne River. The Dordogne runs westerly to Bordeaux."

"That's very far south, isn't it? Is it what they call Provence?"

"No, it's in the Perigord and that's north and west of Provence. More people are calling the country either Perigord or the Dordogne. It's kind of backward country, sort of like West Virginia in the states… but it's beautiful and filled with historic towns and castles."

We walked across the Seine on the Pont de Sully and into the Right Bank neighborhood Gigi said is called The Marais. She led me to a large ancient building overlooking *rue Saint Antoine*, a busy thoroughfare.

"I don't have any Calvados but I can offer you a Marc and a look at my apartment," she said as she applied a large key to the doorway. I followed her into a lobby with a couple of antique chairs and an ornate birdcage elevator. "I would live here just for the fun of riding the lift," Gigi said with a grin.

The gilded car gave a lurch and then ascended through its glassed in channel upward. At the fifth floor, it lurched again and Gigi gave the door bar a shove. "This is hard to do with arms full of groceries," she grunted.

Another key opened a door at the end of the hall and we entered Gigi's flat. It wasn't large but it was spectacular with high ceilings and floor to ceiling windows on two walls. French doors opened to a corner balcony with views of Sacrè Cour and Montmartre to the north and the Tour Eiffel to the west. In between were many huge buildings I couldn't identify and the same landscape of chimney pots that I enjoyed.

"Do you like it?" she asked with a note of pride in her voice.

"Like it? Gigi, will you marry me right now? I could live here forever."

"Don't rush it, Five," she laughed. "Don't forget I've already turned down one proposal this weekend. Now, let me get you a Marc."

Marc turned out to be another popskull brandy like Calvados but after a couple of sips, it became very smooth. We listened to an Edith Piaf album and watched the last glow of sunset. Then it was time to go.

At the door, Gigi put a finger to my cheek. "This has been a very nice day after all. It could have been total *merde* but you've helped make it much better. I'll see you at the office tomorrow."

And with a brush of the finger, she pulled the door to, leaving me to wonder what 'merde' is.

52. Walking Back Le Chien

On Monday morning, Bob Theriault took me to a bank and we exchanged my travel dollars for francs. "That's 25 dollars a day," he commented as he thumbed over huge 1,000 franc notes. "Twenty six days makes 13,000 francs. Don't forget you'll have to pay back any days you aren't on TDY so don't go spending this in some casino," he laughed.

Gigi burst into the office, throwing a small briefcase on a desk. "Can you believe that dickhead?"

"And what dickhead is that?" Bob said calmly.

"Charles fuckin' Bleriot, that's who!" she screamed. "He spends *my* country weekend fucking his *putain,* asks me to marry him, and then calls at the crack of dawn to ask me if I'm angry with him." She exhales loudly. "Hi, Five."

"One more time, what's a putain?" I ask, hoping to bring the pressure down some.

"A whore... and I told him one more time. We are through. *Fini.* Done. Come on Five, there's work to be done."

Our first task was to talk to Sam's last throwoff lead. We went to Gallery Maeght in the Seventh Arrondisment to interview Marcel Gammard. I was awed by the fabulous collection on the walls of the bright gallery — Braque, Kandinsky, Miro, Leger — all familiar from Art Appreciation class. "The Maeght brothers befriended many of the Impressionists and Modernists when they were just struggling. This collection was built on friendship and trust."

244

After talking with Gammard for a few minutes, then to the gallery manager, Gigi led the three of us down the sidewalk to a nearby café. I was beginning to believe all business in Paris is done in cafes. Gammard turned out to be a fawning little man with thick spectacles and a thin swatch of hair combed over his high forehead.

Gigi didn't explain my presence except to say she was my associate and translator. Did this make me an honorary member of the Sureté?

Gammard opened up right to my first question in rapid, breathless French. "How long did I know Monsieur Wolfgram?

"For nine years as Wolfgram. Seven as Wolfe. Two during the Occupation as Longmont, when he was in Vichy. Nearly two in Paris under the Germans as Wolf Gunter. And dog's years before the war when he was Gregor Karz. It seems as if I've known the bastard all my life."

"When did you first meet him?" I asked, watching as Gigi scribbled notes.

"In Budapest, '36 or so," he replied in the same breathless tone. "I was at a second rate art school as he was. We both got out of town two years later when Hitler declared his *anschluss* in Austria. We came to Paris and stayed.

"He worked in a gallery on rue du Faubourg and I ran errands for him, mostly to the studio of Herrolt. Herrolt was a marvelous painter whose talent was devoted to creating fakes.

"Karz would remove a small painting from the gallery for reframing, I would deliver it to Herrolt and a week later, two would come back. The fake would go back to the gallery and he would hide the original. In 1940, Karz got new papers and became Wolf Gunter. By June, he was ready for the Nazis with a stock of very good pictures.

"That racket lasted until '42. Then the Gestapo showed up one morning and he was gone. Later I heard Herrolt had been detained then shot. For some reason, I wasn't picked up and remained to work with the Paris Resistance cells."

Gammard removed a filthy handkerchief and wiped his brow. Gigi looked at me with an arched eyebrow.

"I heard through the grapevine that he was in the south of France, going under the name Longmont and working with the Gaullist Resistance. These groups were intent on training new fighters, helping Allied airmen escape and the like. They got a lot of help from SOE and OSS," he said.

"Then in early '44, he was back in Paris and opened the Wolfe Gallery. It was then I realized that Wolfe, this was his name then, wasn't so much dealing in art as in information. He hired me to work in the gallery and we sold lots of small paintings to departing German officers."

"Then came Liberation and the gallery name remained but his name changed again to Wolfgram. He hob-knobbed with French and Allied officials and escaped all notice of those who were searching out collabos."

Gigi ordered another round of coffees and Gammard pulled out a pocket watch and glanced at it. "It's all right, Monsieur Gammard. We have plenty of time," she said.

"We did a lot of matting and framing after the war. I always thought it was slight of hand stuff to hide a painting with dubious provenance. Wolfgram continued to paint — mostly landscapes from the south — but he became a true master framer and often spent more time on the frames than the art.

"He drank a lot more as he got older. He was always a talky bastard and now he regaled me with tales of his heroism in the Perigord, working under the noses of the Gestapo and Melice. Than the next week, it would be a drunken story about working as a Melice informant.

"I left him two years ago when the Maeght brothers opened the new gallery and needed an assistant manager. God but it's good to be working with legitimate dealers. I haven't seen him since then but I've heard he took the gallery in the direction of photography and sold off his painting inventory.

"And," he said with a loud exhalation, "that is all I can tell you."

"He's either an awful blowhard or a great novelist," I said, "consulting Gigi's notebook. How much truth is in this stuff, d'ya think?"

"Much of it rang true, especially with what I could find in the Sureté files. Wolfgram and his aliases had near-perfect papers, which meant he either was a master forger or had connections with the actual agencies that issued them," she said.

"I find it hard to believe he escaped the postwar hunt for callabos, though. Even my mother was accused of being a collaborator when she returned in 1945. There was so much accusation and reprisal but Wolfgram seemed to come through unsoiled."

Gigi left me at the Olympus typewriter beside Marthe's desk to type my report on the interview. Bob Theriault's door was open and I could see him talking on the phone. When he hung up, I walked in and gave him a synopsis of Gammard's rambling account.

"Do you think Gigi got an accurate translation?" he asked.

"I've no way of knowing but she kept right up with Gammard, almost simultaneous."

"OK, finish writing it up. By the way, I've got to run over to the embassy. I'll be back in an hour or so."

I finished the AR, frustrated that Gammard could name no acquaintances or contacts from the years he knew Wolfgram. The few he mentioned were customers and most of them were dead. AIC didn't really like to get AR's which contained no throwoff leads.

53. Wolfgram And The Dark One

After a couple of train changes, we exited the Metro at Anvers and went in search of rue Say. It turned out to be a shabby, narrow street hunkered beneath the shadow of Sacrè Cour between two high schools. Number 7 had no sign, just some yellowing framed photos and a peeling outline of the Wolfe logo in the window.

We peered in the window and seeing no one, tried the door handle and found it would turn. "We go in and you find out where Wolfgram has gone to?" I asked.

"Right. And whoever's in there is going to tell us the truth?" she responded sarcastically.

"Let's go see."

The filthy door opened and from the rear of the small shop a bell tinkled. *"Un moment, s'il vous plait,"* called a voice from the rear. I examined some photos in a bin. Some were poorly matted and exhibited hypo stains from improper washing.

"Gigi, do you think this is authentic?" I asked her, holding up a print of a speeding racecar with egg-shaped wheels.

Just then, a young woman in a black sleeveless jumper came through the curtained door. Tufts of hair sprouted from her armpits. Her black hair was a mass of uncombed curls.

"Bonjour madame, monsieur. Comment est-ce que je peux vous aider?" she asked.

"Bonjour, mademoiselle" Gigi responded. *"Parlez-vous anglais?"*

"A bit," the girl responded. "But slowly."

Gigi introduced us, again as Sureté agents as she waved her warrant card vaguely in the air. "And you are?"

"I am Anna Stansbury," she answered, "and this is *my* gallery."

"Stansbury's English... or American?" I queried.

"My father was a G.I. I kept his name even though I never met him."

"And is this the Wolfe Gallery?" Gigi asked.

"I guess it still is," the girl yawned, "although Monsieur Wolfgram left me ownership papers when he left."

"Please tell us about him leaving," I asked.

"Ah, you'd best come back and sit down. You'll want to hear about the dark one.

"The dark one, Anna, what do you mean?" Gigi asked.

"I've lived here since 1956 when my mother died. Monsieur Wolfgram took me in, let me sleep in the back and then started giving me odd jobs. He was kind of like a father until he started trying to get into my knickers and feel my titties.

"Monsieur Wolfgram would tell me stories about his adventures. At first I didn't believe him but when the dark one first came, he was so frightened that he had to be telling the truth," the girl wrapped her arms around herself and mock-shivered.

"When was this?" Anna, "I asked gently.

"About six months ago," she replied. "Monsieur Wolfgram had been working on what he called his 'freedom plan,' selling off the few good paintings, buying and selling photos whenever he could, and working on his list."

"His list? What was the list?" Gigi asked.

"His stories were all about spying and espionage. He claimed he had recruited spies for the Nazis, for France, for America... and, he was putting them all down on a list. And when the list was complete, he was going to sell it to the highest bidder and retire to a beach in Goa," Anna giggled.

"Where did he keep the list?" Gigi pressed. "Don't forget, I am an agent of the Republic of France and espionage can mean the guillotine." I found it hard to take Gigi's threatening tone seriously, coming from this gorgeous agent of France.

"Ahhh," Anna smiled. "He said he entrusted it to his brother. But I'm sure he has no brother."

"The dark one frightened him, you say," I interjected. "How was he frightened? And do you know who the dark one is?"

"Luc Roituer, the photographer. Monsieur Wolfgram had pestered him to sell some photos but said that Roituer thought he was too good to deal with a gallery like ours.

"He always wore black and a long black coat. That's why I called him the dark one.

"He came for Monsieur Wolfgram one day and they left for America very quickly. He was gone about 15 days and returned in a terrible rage. He ranted about betrayal after all these years."

"Two days later, an American showed up. He spoke excellent French but I could tell he was American, sort of like you," she said, shrugging in my direction. "They talked for a little while mostly about caves and castles then left for a café. I'm not sure what they talked about there but Monsieur Wolfgram returned in a highly agitated manner. The talk of caves made me think the American might be a wine merchant."

"He spent the next morning at an advocate's office, returned with the papers for me. Although I never let him screw me, I gave him a couple of blowjobs out of gratitude," she smiled. "When I awoke the next morning, he was gone. All that remained was a note telling me to sell off the photographs and close the place down.

"On the following day, Roituer came asking for Monsieur Wolfgram. He was insistent that I tell him where he'd gone, although I had no idea. He slapped me and knocked me down. He tore the place apart and hit me with his fist. I remembered one small thing but by that time, I wouldn't let him lick my ass. Something about bugs.

"And..." she hesitated, "Monsieur Wolfgram gave me this." Anna produced from her cleavage a small scrap of material. "He cut it out of one of his paintings and told me to keep it for safekeeping or to give it to the American if he returned."

The scrap was irregular in shape and the obvious corner of a painting. But it was too small to determine the nature of the painting. "May we keep this?" Gigi asked. "The American was my father and now he's gone missing. It may be helpful in finding him."

Anna nodded her assent. "One more thing," she added, "I thought I saw Roituer at Sacré Couer this morning. So be careful."

Anna Stansbury was obliging about letting us search the dusty shop. The back room had once been a part of the gallery but was now a living quarters with a partition for a bathroom and a small sleeping space for Anna.

Gigi continued to question the cooperative Anna but the information fountain had seemed to run dry.

"Yes, the photographs are authentic," she said to me as I browsed the bins. "It may seem little enough return for a few blowjobs and a grope or two, but someday they may be quite valuable. I would like to someday be able to open a shop in St. Germain de Pres," she nodded to Gigi.

"How much for this one?" I held up the racecar print.

"Oh, that's a Lartigue. It's titled *"Papa at 80km Per Hour."* With the stain and all, I'd say... for you..." she hesitated as if trying to weigh my wallet, "...300 francs."

"My god, that's twenty dollars," I exclaimed loudly.

Anna seemed shocked. "Well, I could go 250 francs, but no lower."

I counted out 300 francs into her palm quickly. "I can't rob you, Anna. Do you have more photos?"

"Oh yes, I have a couple by Brassai, some by Kertesz, a wonderful print by Robert Doisneau taken in 1942, one more Lartigue. Would you be interested?"

We scoured the collection. On the wall hung a framed triptych of prints of a black woman, posing nearly nude. Her large breasts and bulging eyes fought to be the focal point of each photo, although her only clothing was a brief skirt made of bananas.

"Who's this?" I inquired of Anna.

Gigi interrupted. "My God, it's Josephine Baker! Don't you recognize her, Five?"

"She's a movie star... or something," I guessed. "A stripper?"

"She's one of France's most famous entertainers. She's a wonderful singer and dancer," Gigi exclaimed.

"Those are the last of Monsieur Wolfgram's personal photos. He always claimed to be present when the photographer made that series. He said he worked with Mlle Baker in the Resistance," Anna contributed. "I don't think I wish to sell those."

Gigi and I left the Wolfe Gallery with a bulging portfolio of photos. An investment of much of my per diem money netted me a Brassai and a Kerstez as well as the Lartigue. Gigi spent more than 12,000 francs but owned a fine collection of nighttime Paris scenes by Brassai, some marvelous portraits by Lartigue and Doisneau's "The Fallen Horse," taken in Paris in 1942.

"I'm going to come back and help that girl get to St. Germain de Pres," she said firmly. "She's too smart about photographers and their work to waste away in a Montmartre alley."

"Well, we know a whole lot more about Wolfgram, especially that he's flown the coop. It's not my job to analyze but my report will certainly show that Wolfgram and Roituer are culpable in the murder of Behrens," I said.

"And Roituer's last visit to the gallery coincides with his disappearance from Paris. Do you suppose he's on the hunt for Wolfgram?" Gigi asked.

54. To The Perigord And Rainbow Village

"You two are beginning to build a pretty good case," Bob commented as he read my AR. "It sounds as if Wolfgram has left the City of Light. Any ideas where?"

"A couple of things that Anna mentioned. If Wolfgram did indeed work with Josephine Baker, it could've been in the Perigord. She owns a big Château on the Dordogne, not too far from our place," Gigi said. "She calls it her Rainbow Village."

"So you want to go home?" Bob grinned. "I should authorize Five's travel down there just on your hunch?"

"It's more than a hunch. If the American who visited Wolfgram was my Dad, and I'm sure it was, they talked about caves and castles Anna told us. She thought he might be a wine merchant because of the caves. But the Perigord is full of caves, caverns, grottoes, hundreds of them. They've discovered dozens with prehistoric paintings on the walls."

Bob walked over to a huge map of France on the wall. "Can you get there by train?" he asked, tracing his finger southwesterly from Paris.

"Through Limoges on the main Bordeaux line to Perigeaux, then to le Bouisson on the pufferbilly," Gigi grinned. "Jean-Marc can meet us there."

"And will the Sureté let you go?"

"But of course. This is in pursuit of a possible murderer, an art thief, a spy. My only problem will keep them from sending a big team down there."

"Maybe a big team is what's needed," he commented.

"Five and I can handle it," she responded firmly.

He turned to me. "You'll be out of contact with me or anyone else. We have an agent in Lyon, another in Marseille, but no real support. And I won't want you mailing AR's. The French *Poste* is very good but keep the classified stuff in your head until it's over."

"Does this mean we're going?" Gigi asked. Theriault nodded yes.

55. Adventure On Le Chemin de Fer

It took the rest of the afternoon to make arrangements. I went to the safe house and packed. Then Bob picked me up and we drove to Gigi's apartment for her.

"Here's a little fatherly advice, Five," he said. "Gigi likes her men so if you've got a girlfriend or fiancé at home… well, watch your step."

Gigi was on the sidewalk when we arrived in The Marais.

"I was able to get a second class sleeper compartment," she said, "on the 1830 train. That means we'll probably share the compartment with someone else."

Bob drove us to the sprawling Gare Montparnasse with a constant stream of instructions and advice. On the platform, he shook my hand firmly, then turned on his heel and walked back into the station.

"Well," I said, "here we go."

Gigi led me down the platform past several cars until she found the right one. Ahead, I could see a steam locomotive backing slowly onto our track.

Gigi was dressed in tan slacks and a sweater with an anorak pulled around her shoulders. Unlike my Gladstone and suitcase, her belongings fit into a bulging backpack and a string bag. We climbed onto the carriage and made our way down the aisle until she found our compartment.

Inside the empty compartment, two bench seats faced each other.

255

"If we're lucky, it'll stay this way. Our tickets are for the upper and lower but we'll make them up later." She sniffed, "if we're unlucky, we'll get some fat salesman in here who'll smoke cigars all the way to Limoges.

At half past six, the locomotive's calliope whistle shrieked and slack clanked and jerked as the train eased out of the station. The other seat in our compartment was still empty. I peered out the window and watched the wide maze of tracks narrow through switches to a pair of main lines heading south.

Gigi pulled down the string bag from the overhead and produced a pair of demi-baguettes. "We'll eat early," she announced, "in case someone else comes along who doesn't have food. I always feel guilty when that happens on a train."

As we rattled out of Paris, Gigi constructed a pair of sandwiches of sausage and cheese, slathered with rich mayonnaise. At 1900 hours, the train slowed and hissed to a halt at a smaller station. The station sign read "Etamps."

"This'll be the first of four stops," Gigi said. "We'll go through Orleans, another town, then Limoges, and arrive in Perigeaux about 0600."

"Perigeaux sounds like Perigord. Is there a relation?"

"Hmm, I'm not sure. Perigeaux is the principal city of the region but the *real* Perigord is to the southeast. It's rugged country with caves and cliffs and lots of Châteaux. The 100 Years War was fought along the Dordogne and many of the castles are still there."

"Will I see them?"

"Hah! Will you see them? I'll say. If Dad hadn't sold off the estate, you'd have been living in one while you're there."

Darkness fell and the *chemin de fer* or "iron road" through France seemed vastly different from railroads in the states. There weren't as many lighted towns and very few blinking, ringing grade crossings. Several times the train took a siding to await an approaching train and often we crept over some really rough trackage, a leftover from the war, Gigi said.

Finally, she stifled a yawn and dug into her backpack for a nightgown. "Pull the shade, Five, and turn out the lights while I change. And do not look," she warned. She kicked off her shoes.

I did as she ordered, asking "isn't there a restroom?"

"There is but at this time of night, there'll be a line of both sexes waiting to change. If you need to pee, check out the little cubicle between this and the next compartment."

In the dim compartment, I could see Gigi pull the gown over her head, then wriggle out of the sweater beneath the nightgown. No brassiere followed. Then she shimmied out of her slacks and hung the clothes from a hook.

"Help me pull down the upper," she asked. "I'll sleep up there and use the lower as a ladder."

The sleeping bunk eased down from its hidden compartment, at the pull of a small lever. Then a similar lever collapsed the seat we'd been using and a sort of bed slid out.

I gave Gigi a boost and she vaulted into the upper bed. Then I pulled down the sheets and stripped to my underwear and crawled into bed.

"Can't we lock the compartment?" I asked.

"Nope! That's another of the problems of riding a second-class carriage. Good night, Five."

56. In The Rubble Of
The 100 Years War

Something soft brushed my forehead. My eyes snapped open to the view of a trim ankle leading to a shapely calf, not two inches from my nose. Gigi's bare leg was joined by another as she climbed down from the upper bunk. Then the view was obscured by the falling hem of her nightgown.

The train was slowing and I watched as she pulled down the window and leaned out. The early morning light revealed the shape of her body through the thin nightgown. A nice body.

Once we were stopped, Gigi dug into her purse and in a minute, produced two large cups of steaming coffee and a paper twist with sweet rolls from a vendor on the platform.

"Breakfast in bed, Five," she exclaimed. I pulled my legs up and she perched on the end of my bed on top of my blanket. "We're in Limoges, less than two hours from Perigueux."

A noise in the hallway was followed by the hiss of our compartment door opening. Two middle-aged nuns entered the compartment, dragging their portmanteaus behind them.

Gigi primly pulled down the hem of her nightgown and said, *"Bonjour, soeurs. Voyagez-vous à Perigueux?"*

"Non, vers le Bordeaux," one of the nuns replied as they settled into the bench seat across the compartment.

Gigi and I continued to drink our coffee. "How am I going to get dressed, Gigi?" I asked. "I slept in my underwear and my pants are on that hook."

"We'll ask them to close their eyes, just as you did last night... I hope," she replied with a wink.

To my astonishment, Gigi pulled the shades on the compartment windows and doors and, with her back to me, whipped the nightgown over her head and quickly stepped into her slacks and sweater.

"Don't be shocked, Five," she said, "these sisters have seen a woman's body before. Now, it's your turn."

The nuns seemed to oblige me by holding their breviaries high while I slipped into my pants, then limped down the corridor to the water closet, hands over my crotch to conceal my obvious erectile condition. Perhaps they peeked over the covers of their breviaries.

A cold-water shave and wash up was all I accomplished for the moment. A reminder of basic training days. As the morning wore on, the train labored more as we entered hilly, then mountainous country. Finally, we pulled into the medium size Perigueux station and gathered our bags.

As we left the compartment, one nun flashed us a shy smile while the other arched her eyebrows in a glare that might have been the evil eye.

We had to wait for our Bordeaux-bound train to pull out before we could cross the platform for the connecting line. Much to my surprise, it was a narrow gauge railroad and Gigi's description of the train as a "pufferbilly" was spot on. The tiny tank engine was glossy black with red driving wheels and chromed siderods. It looked to be World War I vintage.

Three tiny freight cars — two boxes and a flat — were coupled ahead of a small four-wheeled passenger car with open platforms.

"Gigi, this is a joke, right?" I asked skeptically.

"It's no joke and it's become a very popular railroad. People from all over the world are coming to ride the Perigord Line, from here to le Buisson. It's one of the last working narrow gauge lines in France."

We boarded the passenger car and I stood on the front platform to watch four workmen use a small crane to load a *deux chevaux* truck onto a flat car. The crane was powered by a hand crank and it took three men to pivot the truck into place.

More people climbed onto the little coach until all the seats were full. With another shrill toot of its calliope-like whistle, the pufferbilly departed Perigueux.

The railroad paralleled a major road for about 45 minutes then plunged off into the hills.

"Now we're getting into the *Perigord Noir*," Gigi said with a nudge. "It's kind of like Germany's Black Forest. The trees are thicker, the cliffs steeper and higher. And the ground is filled with black truffles and holes leading to prehistoric caverns."

"Here's the River Manaurie," Gigi exclaimed as we clattered across a bridge and paralleled a small stream. "Troglodytes still live in those caves across the river."

I could see a long narrow cave entrance in the side of the steep cliff.

"And in some of them, signs of man's habitation go back to the Neanderthal Man," she continued. "He was discovered just a few miles up the Vezere valley. And now we're coming to les Eyzies, the capital of prehistory."

It was easy to share Gigi's enthusiasm for the Perigord. The country was beautiful and les Eyzies was as charming a village as any I'd seen in France. After a brief stop, we wound our way out of town and across a larger river.

"This is the Vezere. We'll follow it a few miles to the Dordogne," Gigi instructed, "and le Bouisson. That's where the Perigord line meets the regular Bordeaux railroad to the east. And that's were we'll meet my dear brother, Jean-Marc."

Jean-Marc hugged Gigi and swung her feet off the ground. He was muscular, a couple of inches taller than Gigi, and his hair was darker than her strawberry blonde. A pretty young woman hung back with a bulging abdomen and a big smile on her face.

Gigi hugged her and cried, "Silvie! You're going to have a baby? Why didn't you guys tell me?"

Silvie rattled something in French and the three of them hugged and danced in a small circle.

"Who's this?" Jean-Marc asked, looking my way. "You said you were bringing a man but I naturally guessed that Bleriot person."

"That horse's butt is history," Gigi growled. "Jean-Marc, meet Thomsen Lowrey V, a CIC agent who's trying to help us locate Dad. He answers to Five, though." Jean-Marc's handshake was firm and his palm was callused with the signs of hard work. "And this is my sister-in-law, Silvia Marchant. She answers to Silvie and soon… to *maman*."

We piled our luggage into the bed of a small Renault truck and Gigi hopped into the back. "Ride with me here Five. We've got to keep *maman* comfortable. Also, you can see more."

We drove along a major road with the Dordogne to our left, then crossed a bridge and turned into a broader valley. "Here's the beginning of the old Emperitain estate," she exclaimed, pointing to the broad bottomland. "In a minute you'll see the towers of the Château, over in the trees there."

Indeed, two round towers with conical roofs appeared. "It was called *Château Corneille* when grandpa and grandma lived there. Corneille means 'crow' in French and when the corn was ripe in the bottom, the land was filled with them."

"Who lives there now?" I asked.

"Jean Tremblay, a wealthy builder from Paris. They're rarely at home."

57. La Tour de Gigi

Jean-Marc slowed the truck and we turned left onto a narrow graveled lane through groves of bushy trees. "Walnuts," Gigi explained. "They'll be ripe in another couple of months. It's one of the crops of the farm."

The tidy walnut groves gave way to an untamed woodland with heavy oaks but very little undergrowth. Then we were in a broad meadow, which swept up to a yellow stone farmhouse, barn and outbuildings.

"La ferme de Marchant," Gigi declared. "The Marchant farm. Now, if we can only get Dad back here, everything will be perfect."

"Welcome to *au pays de truffes et noisettes,"* Jean-Marc said. "We'll have a glass of wine before we get you settled. I opened the tower last night, Gigi. Is that all right? I lit the boiler so you'll have hot water but if you want electric, you'll have to run the generator."

"Of course," she laughed. "Five and I have only known each other for a few days but we'll all appreciate the privacy."

I gave her a puzzled look as we entered into the cool living room of the farmhouse. The place smelled of pine and a stronger, pleasant odor I couldn't identify.

"Truffles. Truffle oil." Gigi explained. "It's the main cash crop and why Jean-Marc calls the place 'the truffle and nut.' He has nearly 15 hectares of prime truffle forest. In season, this place is like the 100 Years War all over again with him installing his alarms and potting away at poachers with his shotgun."

262

"I'm afraid I don't know much about truffles," I answered.

"It's kind of like a mushroom," Jean-Marc explained. "Grows under the earth beneath the oak trees. Truffle hunters use trained dogs... or even pigs... to locate the truffles. I'm a dog man, myself."

"A good truffle can bring up to 300 francs per gram," Gigi said. "It's a very profitable business and gets Jean-Marc out in the woods with his dog and his gun."

The wine and a bowl of shelled walnuts made a good mid-morning snack. I sat back as the Marchants brought each other up to date.

"Still no positive trace of Dad," Gigi lamented, "but I'm convinced he's still alive and down here somewhere. Five and I have uncovered some leads, though. Wouldn't it be something if he *were* right here in the Dordogne?"

"The last time I talked with him, two months ago" Jean-Marc said, "he was in Lyon and probably going to come down here. He was pursuing some lead and I just figured it was another missing artwork."

"Do you know if Madame Josephine Baker is at les Millandes," Gigi asked.

"I don't know," Silvie replied, "but I saw her at the market in St. Cyprien just a week ago. She had a new child, a darling little boy wearing a yarmulka. I believe she's got more than 10 now."

"Josephine has adopted orphan and refugee children from all over the world," Jean-Marc explained. "She calls them her 'Rainbow Tribe.' Why do you want to know if she's home, Gigi?"

"She may be a key to a lead we're following," Gigi responded. "I'll call and see if she's home."

"You can just 'drive over' to visit a movie star?" I asked.

"Wait until you meet Josephine," Silvie said. "She's a terrific person and you'll never know she's famous to talk to her."

After a quick tour of the house and courtyard, Gigi said it was time to make the last lap of our journey. I looked at her quizzically.

"You don't think we're going to stay here do you, Five? When we have a castle to live in?"

She took me by the elbow and led me to the end of the courtyard. "See! Up there. *La Tour de Gigi.*"

Indeed, high on a cliff above the end of the meadow, a round tower with a cone roof rose out of the trees.

"A castle?" I exclaimed. "You have a Château and Jean-Marc lives here in the farmhouse."

They all laughed.

"You'll see," Gigi said. "When Dad sold the estate, this was the richest land and he kept it for the farm. Under French law, Jean-Marc is the heir so Dad sold me five hectares and *Le Château de Pouce*. It meant Castle Thumb and you'll see why."

"It was originally a 14th century watchtower, built to protect this side of the valley," Jean-Marc said. "Now we call it *La Tour de Gigi.*"

"Is my *deaux cheveaux* running, Jean-Marc?" Gigi asked.

"Running and gassed up. You owe me for petrol, don't forget."

We put our bags in the rear of a battered 2CV, in worse shape than Bob Theriault's Parisian model, and Gigi drove through the courtyard.

"We'll see you for dinner," Silvie called, "won't we?"

Gigi never got the little Citroen out of low gear as we followed a narrow, twisting lane through the trees and up a steep grade. At one point, the farm appeared below us and I felt a flutter of vertigo as I looked down a sheer cliff.

We rounded a curve and Gigi stopped the car. Above us, I could see nearly all of Gigi's tower with three courses of windows and built right out of the cliff. Then a steep roof showed to the right where another building obviously sat.

"This is the first glimpse. In a minute, you'll see why it was called Castle Thumb," she said.

We continued up the grade and around another sharp curve. Now the cliff had become a chasm and I could hear the sound of a waterfall. Ahead of us, the little castle sat on the pinnacle of its rock foundation and at the edge of a deep gorge. Much like the thumb of a mitten.

A swinging footbridge crossed the gorge to the building. Gigi drove another half kilometer and pulled the Citroen into a small clearing close to the bridge.

"We're here Five. Grab the bags."

I obeyed orders and followed her along a graveled path to the edge of the gorge. A waist-high wall abutted either side of the footbridge. "Gigi, do I have to walk across that thing?" I said in a tremulous tone.

"Unless you want to sleep in the woods, you do," she answered.

The bridge swayed as she stepped onto it. Then the uneven rhythm of our footsteps on the board walkway made the structure hop up and down, ever so slightly. The gorge dropped deeply into shadow and at the bottom, a small cascade bounced its way down the mountain. My stomach did flip-flops.

Then we were across and stood in a small courtyard, surrounded by a similar waist-high wall of yellow stone. To the right, a small stone house extended from the ancient tower. Gigi produced a large key and unlocked the door that led into the tower.

"Welcome to my Château," she sang, performing a pirouette in the large, circular room. "This is the main hall and Eleanor of Aquitaine may have once sat in this very room."

"Once it was a complete demi-Château. As Jean-Marc said, it was a watchtower to guard this side of the valley for *Château Corneille*. The story goes, during some battle, they think perhaps around 1590, the English attacked the place and attempted to mine the drawbridge and portcullis."

"The blast was so powerful that the entire living portion of the Château was blown away and the rock foundation split and fell down the mountain. The result was the gorge and my little tower, sticking up like a sore thumb," she laughed.

"It's wonderful," I said enthusiastically. "Absolutely all I'd ever want in a Château."

"Well, it was a ruin for about 350 years. The Resistance is alleged to have used the tower but the place was just a shambles. When my parents were married, my Dad had the idea of building the little house onto the hogback ridge but then the war came and…" her face fell.

"Then, he decided to finish the project and it was done in 1955," she said. "Come on and I'll show you the rest."

We walked through another door and into the newer building. "A small guest room or study to the right, then a bathroom… has a septic tank, too… then the kitchen and back gallery." She led me up some stairs. "This is my bedroom and another W.C."

We descended the stairs. "Out this door is a small deck, tucked in between the tower and a big rock. It's a great place to sunbathe when the air is cold and there's a shower for the summer."

Entering the tower room again, Gigi climbed a staircase that circled around the inside tower wall. "This is the top floor. You can sleep here, if you want, but the WC's down the stairs and hall." She paused. Shafts of light came through the three windows in the tower room, painting the floor in golden stripes. Gigi opened a door and stepped outside. "Here's a little balcony. Used to be called a hoarding in the old days. This is where you poured boiling oil on the bad guys."

I expressed my approval of the 500-year-old room and followed her back down the stairs. Gigi opened another door, which led to a downward staircase in the same circular pattern.

And this is the *donjon,"* she described in a sinister voice. "Actually, it was my Dad's idea for an office or library but he's never been able to use it much."

"And this… is my pride," she said. She pushed a rock in the mantelpiece and a narrow door slid open with the same sound that I'd grown up with in horror movies. "My secret passage. It goes straight up to the top of the tower but this one," and she unlatched the bar on a second door, "goes down." She opened the door and the sound of crashing water was loud.

"It used go down to the real dungeon of the original castle, I would guess. But now, it just opens onto the gorge face about eight meters above the cascade. Carefully, we walked down the narrow staircase. As the light faded from above, Gigi produced a battle lantern and illuminated the steps.

We reached another wooden door and when it opened, a 20 meter gap in the chasm was revealed. On the other side, I could see the same rock striations that were visible on our side. Gigi closed the door and barred it and we made our way back up the winding passage.

"Going up is really more fun," she giggled. We stopped at about the sixteenth stair and she slid open a tiny door, revealing a peephole. "See! We can spy on anyone in the main chamber." On up the stairs to the top of the tower. Another peephole revealed my bed, stacked with suitcase and Gladstone.

"And I can check up on any of my guests, so be careful what you do tonight."

Sitting on the sundeck, I continued to explore Gigi's background and her life in the Dordogne and Paris. "How did your Dad get all this stuff up here?" I asked. "All the stone didn't get carried across that little footbridge."

"We came up the fast road," she said. "A longer, less steep grade goes up the mountain for about three kilometers, crosses the stream at a shallow ford, then works its way back up the ridge to the back porch. That's how we get food, supplies, all that sort of stuff, up here. It takes nearly a half hour more."

"Was your Dad going to live here?"

"I really don't know. Certainly, if Mom had lived. Although he loved the idea of farming. If we find him, he'll be more than welcome to live here even though it technically belongs to me."

"What's your plan for tracking down Wolfgram?" I asked, changing the subject to the work at hand.

"If he really were at the photo session where Josephine Baker posed, I hope she can shed some light on him. And if he really did work with the Resistance down here, she should certainly be able to help."

"Why? Was she involved with the Resistance?"

"Oh yes, she smuggled secret messages in her sheet music and helped escaping Allies along their way out of the country. And she entertained the troops in Algeria," Gigi enthused. "She won the Legion of Honor and some other medals for her effort."

"Is she originally from Algeria?"

"Oh no," Gigi sounded surprised. "She was born in St. Louis... in America."

We walked along the back road through the woods along the ridge. The drop-off on each side was steep but ancient trees would catch and crush a runaway car rather than let it plunge to the bottom of the gorge. Gigi had a string bag and occasionally stooped to pick a mushroom from the forest floor.

As the sun lowered in the western sky, the forest turned reddish gold, matching Gigi's hair. I had her stop and sit on a stump while I made a quick sketch and color notes.

"We won't need to change for dinner," she said once we'd returned to the house, "but put some clean clothes on anyway and I'll wash our dirty stuff at the farm."

267

"Can't we take it to a laundry?" My question brought out a huge gale of laughter.

"Jean-Marc and Sylvie have a washing machine," she hooted, "and the nearest laundry is named Genevieve... or in Sarlat. I'll start the generator so we'll have lights to return to."

As she locked the front door, I stared at the swinging bridge. A breeze had come up and the flimsy structure swayed perilously across the threatening chasm.

"Can't we take the back road from now on?" I whined. "I really don't do well with heights."

"Well Five, you've come to the wrong country. Everything is high in the Dordogne. Do you want me to hold your hand?" she simpered.

The drive down the winding cliff road didn't seem quite as harrowing, even when I opened my eyes. At the farm, Jean-Marc took me on another tour as Silvie cleaned the mushrooms and Gigi tended our dirty clothes in an old-fashioned washing machine with a wringer.

Dinner was a festive affair. A salad of greens in walnut oil and vinegar was followed by crispy fried potatoes and sautéed fois gras with mushrooms. "This is great," I exclaimed. "Exactly what *is* fois gras? I know it's expensive in the states."

Silvie responded. "It's a kind of sausage made from the livers of the goose. The finest fois gras in the world comes from the Dordogne."

"We grow corn here for feeding the geese," Jean-Marc added. "My partner, Hebard, runs the goose farm in the bottomland across the river."

"Thank goodness," Silvie sighed. "They're noisy birds, especially when a thousand of them decide to talk at one time."

"Bonsoir. Mlle Baker est là? Est-ce que je peux parler avec elle, s'il vous plaît?" Gigi spoke into the phone. *"Ahh. Vendredi. Voudriez-vous lui dire que Mlle Marchant a téléphoné? Fille de Genevieve Emperitain. Mon numero est 15 75 13 14."*

"She's in Nice," Gigi explained. "Won't be back until next Friday. So? We've got a whole day. If no one objects, I thought I could take Five on a little trip to see the castles."

The Citroen's headlights pierced the wooded darkness like two bright, thin spears. The glowing eyes of animals stared at us from the forest. Steering around a curve, Gigi slid the car to a sudden stop.

"What's the matter?" I asked.

"Look at the track on the edge of the road," she said. "The *deaux cheveau* didn't make that."

Indeed, a deep gouge in the red dirt at the edge showed where a vehicle had left the road and churned up the earth. We stared at the track for another moment or so. "There's only one," I commented, "so perhaps it was a motorcycle. Do you know anyone who rides a 'cycle?" She shook her head no.

We proceeded more slowly up the hill, although the grinding of the 2CV would have warned anyone of our approach. At the top, the parking area was empty.

We crossed the footbridge and paused before opening the door. Inside the tower room, we stopped again, hearing only the chirp of crickets. Then a clank came from the back of the house. Startled, Gigi reached into her shoulder bag and produced a small black automatic pistol. She moved quickly to the fireplace and pushed the stone for the secret passage.

We stepped into the stairway before the door rumbled full open. Gigi tugged it closed and we climbed the steps to the first peephole.

Footsteps echoed on the tile of the new house, then the tower room door was swung open and a tall figure entered below us. Only his shape was visible but the long coat made me think 'the dark one.' He turned on a flashlight and swung it around the walls.

"I can't get the gun through the peephole and see to shoot," Gigi whispered. "Go down to the secret door and be ready to push it open," she instructed.

I climbed down the staircase and stood by the slab of stone. I heard Gigi's voice echo through the chamber.

"Arrêt! Mis vers le haut vos mains et ne vous déplacez pas."

I shoved the door but it opened slowly. The figure burst through the front door and into the night. Gigi clattered down the passage and we followed.

Stepping onto the footbridge, Gigi spun and stared into the woods as the harsh cough of a motorcyle's startup echoed through the trees.

Suddenly, the bike burst from the bushes and careened down the roadway, its rider a black outline against the glow of its headlight.

We ran back to the car. "Should we follow?" I cried.

"No! There's no way we could catch it before the bottom of the hill. Perhaps Jean-Marc'll hear him coming." She shrugged. "We don't get many prowlers or vandals in this country... but a few."

We went back into the house. Pistol in hand, Gigi cautiously made her way to a small room and revealed the generator. I lit a candle and held the automatic while she started the machine.

Thanks to the generator, we were able to turn on the lights although their illumination wasn't much better than candles or kerosene lamps. I followed Gigi as she did a thorough search of the place, pistol at the ready.

She lit several oil lamps and then shut off the generator, which wasn't very noisy in the first place. The only sound was the low roar of the cascade and crickets chirping in the woods. Gigi found a small flashlight and her battle lantern, then rummaged in a chest until she came up with a wicked looking tool.

"This is a climbing hammer. Be careful 'cause it's got two sharp ends and a point on the handle. But it'll do the job if you need to hit someone with it. Let's check out the woods."

We crossed the bridge again with lights extinguished. She checked to make sure the car doors were locked... although a determined person could get into a 2CV with a penknife. Then we walked slowly toward the bushes and Gigi suddenly turned on the battle lantern. Its wide beam illuminated the bushes.

Inside a tiny clearing, tracks were clearly visible where the cyclist had peeled out. A crumpled cigarette butt lay in the grass. "Galouise," Gigi growled as she sniffed the butt. "Fat lot of good this'll do us. Could've been half of France."

Every door in Gigi's Tower had a heavy bar, as did the shutters on all the windows. We secured the ground floor and settled on the couch in the main hall. Gigi produced a bottle of marc and poured us each a healthy portion.

"Do you think that was Roiteur?" I asked. "All I could see was tall, thin and a long dark coat. If it were him, how did he get here so fast?"

"He could have been watching Gallerie Wolfe," Gigi responded. "When he saw us with Anna, he decided to follow us. Remember, I've met him several times and he knows I'm the daughter of a CIC agent." Then with a big yawn, she said, "I'm too tired to think about it any more. *Bonne nuit,* Five."

58. Truffles And Bugs

I had spent a restless night, listening to the far-off murmur of the cascade, to every different sound from the forest, the cry of birds and as the sun rose, I heard a cuckoo clock chime 14 times. That was when I realized it was a real cuckoo.

A different sound of water splashing alarmed my swollen bladder. I went to the window and looked out to behold Gigi, naked as the day she was born, beneath the shower on the deck below. Before she could look up, I ducked away from the window and pulled on my pants... with difficulty.

The main floor water closet was welcome and as I finished, I heard her footsteps in the hall. I flushed and opened the door.

"Bonjour, Five! Did you sleep well," I heard as her nude butt vanished up the steps. "There's warm water in the shower if you'd like," she called down.

Later, we checked the far side of the footbridge again. Instead of looking for tracks and evidence on the ground, I examined the trees and discovered the small box wired into a fork. Smeared with dirt, it sat about seven feet above ground and had a six inch-long rod pointing toward the house.

I put my finger to Gigi's lips and pointed to the device. Then we walked back across the bridge and looked for more signs of intrusion. What I found was a small wire protruding from one of the closed shutters. The shutter covered the window to the water closet.

At the farm, Jean-Marc reported that he'd heard the motorcycle the night before. "He must've taken the back lane to the main road, though, because he didn't come through here. I'll activate my motion detectors so we'll have some warning from now on."

I raised my eyebrows in question. "Motion detectors?"

Gigi told me, "Jean-Marc was in the *paras,* was wounded and evacuated from Dien Bien-Phu just before the end."

"I use every bit of wartime stuff I can to protect my truffles," he added. "Poachers and thieves are quite common when it comes to truffles."

"And I'll get a dead-bolt installed on the main door today. It's my fault he got in the house." He paused, grinning ruefully.

He and Silvie thought the idea of the tower's bathroom being bugged was hilarious. "Just don't *pet* too much in there or they'll be able to blackmail you." Silvie explained that 'pet' was the slang term for passing gas.

"Are you sure you didn't find any more bugs?" Gigi asked me.

"Yes. That's a simple receiver-wire recorder in the tree," I replied, trying to recall my horrible days in DAES class. "The sound-activated mic-transmitter picks up the vibrations sounds cause on the window glass. The receiver couldn't handle more than one signal."

Gigi again. "Are the devices French... or American?"

"I'm not sure they're either so but I'd want to have an expert to make that determination."

Jean-Marc chimed in. "Why don't you remove the bug, Five?"

"The wire machine can't hold more than a couple of hours worth of recording. Then it'll have to be serviced, one reel replacing another. Since all they're going to hear is the commode flushing and a few natural noises, the bug won't do any harm and we'll have more chance catching someone."

I looked at Jean-Marc. "You're right about the dead-bolt. Anyone with a stiff identity card could have slipped the single-bolt lock that's on that door."

Breakfast was a huge affair with home-baked biscuits and jellies and honey, scrambled eggs, plus lots of hot coffee. "Jean-Marc loves American breakfasts," Silvie said in mock complaint. "I had to learn to make perfect bis-kweets and it took me nearly two years. I'll take a good *brioche* any time."

"The eggs are delicious," I enthused. "What are the black things?"

"In your honor, Cinq," Silvie said, "the master allowed me to shave one of his best truffles."

"That's a 500 franc egg you're eating there, mister," Gigi joked.

Silvie turned down our offer to visit the market at St. Cyprien, saying she'd go herself. "The big market is Samedi, how do you say, Saturday morning, in Sarlat."

And so, we left the farm and drove east through St. Cyprien and its busy market. "Many of these vendors are at each market," Gigi explained as she tootled her horn at people carrying string baskets and long loaves of bread. "Each village and town has its own day, so you can always get fresh produce and bread without having to travel too far."

"Frankly though, I think the best bread comes from the *boulangerie* in St. Cyprien and the best meats come from the *boucherie* in Beynac. Jean-Marc and Silvie will have a stand at the Sarlat market on Saturday, selling walnut oil and Silvie's pate fois-gras."

"And truffles?" I added.

"Oh god, no. Truffles are something special. Jean-Marc will take his truffles to a secret market where no one says a word. They examine each truffle and then a deal is struck with hand signals beneath a cloth." She laughed. "There's nothing more secretive than a truffle market."

As we drove along the river bottom, I could see another large Château, about the same size as *Château Corneille*. "Another Château, Gigi! Are there many of them?"

"That's *Les Milandes,* Josephine Baker's Château. And yes, there are a lot of Châteaux, especially residences like that."

The road swung very close to the river and in the distance I saw a huge castle on a cliff top. "My god, what's that one? It's more than a residence."

"That's Beynac! The village below and the Château with a capital C," she responded. "It was a French fort during the 100 Years War, then was turned over to the English for eight years, then the occupiers went to the French side again. That's the story of most of the castles along this stretch of the Dordogne."

"There are more?"

"Oh my yes. Wait 'til you see."

We continued along the road, now flanked by the steep village of Beynac on the left and a sheer wall down to the Dordogne on the right. "Look up to your right, Five," Gigi urged as we swung around a curve. Another tall castle crowned a steep hill on the other side of the Dordogne, about two miles away.

"That's Castelnaud. It was English, then French, then English again during the 100 Years War. But it was really a well-defended place and never conquered except by treachery. And this smaller one coming up over there is Château Fayac, more a residence. And over there... Marqueyssac."

The road now clung to the cliffside. The next village resembled an American cliff dwelling, its steep streets lined with steps. The sign said 'la Roque Gageac'. I gawked at the houses stacked hundreds of meters above, even a few built into caves in the cliff.

"This one is really neat," I said. "But I'd be afraid the cliff will fall down."

"Someday it might," said the mistress of Château Thumb.

Soon, we turned right and crossed the river on a stone bridge. Above us, a fortified wall clung to the top of the mountain. "This is Domme," Gigi said as she steered the 2CV up narrow streets and through a big gate in the wall. "It's a *bastide,* one of the fortified towns instead of just a castle or residence. We can take a break here and let you see the view. It's magnificent."

From the edge of the precipice, the view was magnificent above a giant curve in the Dordogne and the Château Beynac far down the river. We took seats in a restaurant where the tables perched beside the cliff wall and ordered crepes and coffee. Mine came with a huge slab of butter and covered with Gran Marnier.

"You know Gigi, I think this is more fun that sitting in a Paris sidewalk café," I observed.

Following the mid-morning snack, Gigi left Domme by a back road and we wound our way down through forests and farms until we paralleled the river again, this time on our left side. "I have just one more castle to show you," Gigi said.

We turned up a hillside road at the village of Ste. Mondane. The road got narrower and more twisting with some hairpin curves that appeared to have been set into the courtyards of farmhouses. We crested a small hill and there, on the other side on a hill of its own sat a magnificent castle.

"Château Fenelon," Gigi said as we pulled to the side of the road. "It's my favorite Château 'cause it looks so mysterious."

Indeed, Fenelon *did* look shrouded in mystery with a light fog bank lingering in the late morning sunshine. Two rows of trees flanked a dirt road that led up the hill to its main gate. Unlike the other Châteaux we'd seen, Fenelon sat atop a gentle hillside of pastures. Its sloping walls were imposing but not impassible.

"It's named for a famous French cleric and author who was born here in the mid-17th century. And that's all I know."

"Does anyone live here? Can we visit inside?"

"It's not open to the public and I don't know for sure who owns it. Someone does live there, though, probably a vampire," she giggled.

59. It's A Big Dordogne

On the way home, we detoured to visit Sarlat-la-Canada, the central town of the Perigord Noir. The old town sat within a city wall that sloped down a hillside. Gigi pulled up beside a sporting goods store where she bought two cartons of .32 caliber ammunition.

"You do fire a weapon, don't you Five?" she asked. "Because I have little Smith and Wesson Airlite that belongs to my Dad. It's a .32 like mine so we can share ammunition if you want to use it."

"I'm more comfortable with a sketch pad but yeah, I qualified on the range."

Gigi led me through the heart of old town Sarlat with stops at a bakery, butcher shop, a wine store and shop selling general groceries. We also stopped at a *tabac* where I bought a carton of Galouises.

"This may look like a sleepy place right now," she commented, "but wait 'til you see Saturday morning's market."

At the farm, Jean-Marc set up a pair of targets against the hillside. Gigi handed me the tiny S&W snub-nose, which I checked for loads, clean barrel and cylinders. Then we loaded up and each took five shots at our respective targets. Gigi's showed a tight pattern around the bull's-eye, which amazed me, considering the small size of her automatic French pistol.

My pattern was in an upper corner of the target so I shot a second set, concentrating on correcting my aim. It was better but I figured that a

277

range of more than two meters would be a distinct handicap with the two-inch barrel.

Jean-Marc potted away with a .410 shotgun after we had finished and declared himself ready to stand off any motorcyclist invaders.

We returned to the Tower and flushed the commode several times, then inspected the house and surrounding grounds. The wire recorder box looked untouched but to be safe, I placed a twig on its top where it couldn't be seen from the ground. Anyone trying to open the box would probably dislodge the twig.

Later, I was sitting on the sun deck sketching the valley below. Gigi came out of the house with two glasses of lemonade. "Isn't this a gorgeous afternoon?" she said, handing me a glass. "I wish we could see the sun like this more in Paris."

I was astounded as she sat in the lounge chair, reached down and pulled her jersey over her head, exposing her wonderful bare brown breasts.

"Gigi!" I gasped. "Put your shirt back on."

"Why? It's a beautiful day and I'm losing my tan."

"Because you make... make me *uncomfortable.*"

"Americans," she pouted. "Take your shirt off too. You're as pale as an oyster."

"It's not the same," I whined.

"Why not?" Gigi gave me a sly grin. "You have two nipples, just like I do. Perhaps a little more hair."

I noticed that *her* two nipples seemed to be growing. I gathered up my glass and sketchbook and staggered into the house. As I closed the door, I could hear her chuckling softly.

Time came for us to go down the hill to the Marchant farm for dinner. Gigi had on the same jumper but now I was very aware that she didn't wear anything beneath it... perhaps didn't even own anything to wear beneath it.

"Don't be angry with me, Five," she said softly, steering the 2CV down the rocky rollercoaster of a road. "I'm enough American to understand how you feel. But you've just got to get used to Europeans.

There's nothing to be ashamed of about one's body, even an American body covered for years by this weird sense of modesty."

"I understand what you're saying," I answered, "but it's just not something I can get used to overnight. I mean, we've only known each other for what... five days?"

"You'll get used to it, I'm sure," she said.

Silvie served us all a Ricard with water on the side and we sat in the setting sun beneath the Marchant's grape arbor. In the distance, a horn tooted.

"That must be the *poste,*" Jean-Marc commented. "He's very late today. I'll see to it."

He wheeled a rusting bicycle out of a shed and peddled down the lane toward the highway. In a few minutes, he labored up the grade, a small bundle of mail in one hand.

The two of them took turns ripping open envelopes, growling over bills and exclaiming about notes of good news. Suddenly, Silvie said, "I don't think this one's for me. It's marked 'Mlle. Marchant," and that's not me."

Gigi took the torn envelope and withdrew a small folded sheet of notepaper. She stared at it then read aloud.

"Rempart de Castelnaud. 18h.30. Jeudi. Nous avons les mêmes buts."

"What's it say," I asked. "Battlement of Castelnaud. 1830 hours. Thursday. We have the same goals."

"No signature?" Jean-Marc inquired.

"Just this," Gigi said, handing me the note which had a crudely drawn version of the three-line Wolf logo.

Again, the four of us played dominoes until the day had turned to darkness. Then Gigi and I began our drive back to the Rock. Shadows played across the meadows and a pair of deer looked up from the edge of the woods.

"Why would Wolfgram want to meet with us?" I asked. "We have the same goals. What does that mean?"

"And why Castelnaud? On the battlements, especially. That could be anywhere."

279

"Do you think it's a trap?" I asked. "Is someone, perhaps Roituer, trying to get at us?"

"We won't know until tomorrow night," she answered grimly.

We carefully checked the wire recorder box and examined the ground for signs of disturbance. Across the bridge, Gigi wielded a straw broom and swept the gravel of the little courtyard into a smooth pattern that would show any footprints.

Inside, we battened down all the shutters and lit the oil lamps. Then we retired to the deck for an aperitif of marc, our feet up on the stone rail. The last rays of the setting sun painted the sky. The smoke from our Galouises drifted across the valley below.

"Gigi, this is really a peaceful spot," I said softly. "Hard to believe that people have been beating up on each other … killing each other… along this river for centuries."

"And it hasn't really changed," she answered.

Later, she leaned over and gave me a soft kiss on the cheek. "Good night, Five. Sweet dreams."

It must have been two in the morning when I awoke with a full bladder. Rather than stumble down the steps and through the darkened hall to the water closet, I opened the door and stood on the moonlit balcony, admiring the stream I cast to the woods hundreds of meters below.

Through the wisps of fog skimming the valley below, I saw a single headlight and heard the faint noise of a two-cycle engine. It slowed, then turned off and disappeared in the woods at the edge of the Marchant farm. The engine noise shut down.

I ran from the tower room to the main floor and up the stairs to Gigi's room, pounding softly on the doorframe. "Gigi, wake up. Someone's coming on a motorcycle. I saw them from the balcony."

"Mmmf, I'll be right there in a second."

I ran back to my room and stepped onto the balcony. The only sounds were the song of a nightingale in the distance and the noise of Gigi's bare feet slapping up the stone steps. She came onto the balcony, rubbing sleep from her eyes. She wore a long man's dress shirt and carried her small automatic.

"This better not be some trick to lure me up here to your room," she muttered. "Cause it worked and I'm really sleepy."

"No. I was out here… ah, watering the lawn down there… and I heard a motorcycle then saw its headlight turn into the road over there. Then he turned it off."

We stood at the railing and watched the woods below. The waxing moon gave enough light that we could make out individual trees along the lane and the buildings of the farm below. Gigi shivered and crossed her arms across her chest. I put my arm around her shoulder and she snuggled against me.

"It's chilly up here, even in late summer," she said as she scooted around me allowing both of my arms to encircle her. On my bare legs, I could feel the skin of her naked bottom beneath the shirt. I felt my natural reaction beginning.

"I'll keep watch if you want to go get some more clothes on," I volunteered.

"You keep trying to dress me up! Why is that, Five?" she simpered. She dropped her folded arms to her side, letting my arms slide down over her chest. For some reason, I felt bold enough to cup her breasts through the shirt.

Just then, a faint crack of light appeared from the farmhouse below as Jean-Marc slid out the back door. We watched as he stalked across the barnyard. There was just enough moonlight to follow his progress to the edge of the meadow. Then he raised his weapon and fired two quick shots.

The shotgun blasts echoed across the valley, followed quickly by the cough of the motorcycle starting. We watched its taillight as it vanished up the highway toward Sarlat.

As he marched back to the farmhouse, Jean-Marc aimed a red flashlight at the tower.

"Dash, dash, dash. Dash, dot, dash," Gigi said aloud.

"Morse for OK," I said. We both applauded and in the moonlight, Jean-Marc mimed a broad bow.

"Show must be over," Gigi whispered. "I'm going back to bed."

She put her arms around my neck and gave me a long kiss. I probed with my tongue and felt hers as well. She broke out of my embrace and walked into the room, flopping on my bed and pulling off her shirt. "Are you coming, Five?"

281

60. A Rainy Thursday

We finally drifted off to the sound of rain falling on the slate roof of the tower. Gigi proved to be a marvelous lover and we both seemed exhausted. Thin light pierced the eastern windows of the tower. I raised on one elbow and stared raptly at the beautiful French girl who had suddenly graced my bed and my life.

We hadn't even shared a serious kiss until her brother flashed the OK sign.

Rain spraying through the open balcony door had soaked the shirt Gigi wore earlier. I dug in my Gladstone and pulled out a Johns Hopkins sweatshirt and draped it over her sleeping form. Then, without another thought, I padded bareass downstairs to start the coffee pot and perform my morning ablutions.

As I waited for the coffee to boil, I heard the commode flush and then the slap of bare feet on the tile floor.

"Hah, you're not such a modest American after all," Gigi chortled as she cupped her hands softly over my buttocks. The sweatshirt afforded her about the same degree of modesty, barely covering her pelvis.

Leaning over my shoulder, she whispered in my ear, *"Et maintenant tu penses que je ne suis qu'une putaine bon marché, eh?"*

"Parley Anglais, silvu-play," I responded.

"And now you think I'm just a cheap French whore, eh?" she said.

"It sounded more romantic in French and no, I think I'm a very fortunate American."

Her arms sneaked around to my front and I pulled the coffee pot off the burner. "This time in my bed," she whispered.

Later, I ran my finger from her breasts and traced a fine line of nearly invisible hair down her body. "How do I say 'you are beautiful' in French?"

"Tu es belle."

"And that sounds more romantic in English," I countered.

"Et toi, tu es trés beau. Un amoureux merveilleux," she responded. "Don't forget, French is the language of love."

We finally got to drink our coffee, staring at the drizzle and the soaking woods beyond the swinging bridge. Gigi blew very perfect smoke rings and laughed as mine came out as figure eights and lopsided football shapes.

"We must put our minds to business," she said with a grin. "Silvie will suspect we've been up to something if we don't show up for breakfast." I shrugged reluctantly.

"But first, we must attend to our hygiene. The boiler should be hot so we'll take a shower now."

The rain seemed icy but the hot water stung our skin as we cavorted under the outdoor shower. We soaped each other slowly, exploring the other's body in smooth sensations.

"Ah Five, but no more," she panted. "We *must* attend to business. There is work to be done."

Silvie met us at the kitchen door with a sly grin and I was sure that our night of lovemaking was apparent on our faces.

"Jean-Marc, that was a magnificent battle last night. Although the enemy got away," Gigi joked.

"I didn't shoot to kill," he responded. "And the .410 wouldn't carry that far anyway. But my motion detectors did work. Do you suppose he was going to change the wire in the recorder?"

"Who knows?" I said. "But it was good work, just the same." I felt coffee-laden after my second cup with Silvie's homemade brioches.

"What are you going to do today," Jean-Marc asked.

"Well," Gigi said, "I must check in with my director and Five should probably do the same with Robert Theriault. May we use your phone to call Paris?"

Gigi returned from her call and announced, "Michel is not unhappy with our progress. And he said I have enough holiday time to stay as long as I wish, so long as I find a missing painting or two in the process."

She then took me into the sitting room and called the CIC office in Paris for me. Marthe answered and put me directly through to Bob. I explained the events to date and our progress.

"Don't take any chances with the bug and recorder, Five," he ordered. "Pull the damn thing right now and bring it back with you. I can't imagine anyone so stupid as to bug a bathroom window but don't underestimate these guys."

"I figured they just didn't know the layout and figured that was one of the living room windows," I responded. "but we'll go back up right now and get it down."

The three Marchants were having even another cup of coffee, this time with cigarettes. I joined them with a smoke and listened to their family chatter in French. A big round of laughter made me wonder if I were the subject of conversation.

In borrowed slickers and barnyard Wellingtons, Gigi and I drove back up the rain-slicked lane to the Rock. The soggy twig was still on the top of the recorder box. I carefully unwired the harness that fixed it to the tree and we put it into a string bag.

Opening the shutter, I tried to pull the bug out by its antenna with no luck. Then I poked it from the other side with a pencil and it popped out of its hole. The tiny mic/transmitter looked like a three-inch section of pencil. A serial number along its barrel didn't tell me anything except that the device wasn't American since the zeros had slashes through them.

As we locked up I extracted several straws from a broom and wedged them into the cracks between the bridge's floorboards. Anyone crossing the bridge would make the gaps wider and the straws would fall out.

We returned to the farm and Jean-Marc carefully wrapped the listening devices in a burlap bag. "I'll put them in the root cellar," he said, "it's very dry and should be a safe place. Now, what are you going to do the rest of the day?"

Gigi gazed out the window at the steady rain. "It's certainly a good day to stay inside, so we'll stay inside. Josephine can't see us today and we don't have to be to Castelnaud until this evening. I thought we'd drive up to les Eyzies and show Five some cave paintings."

"I studied the paintings of Lascaux in art class," I said. "But didn't you say there were many caves with artwork?" I asked Gigi.

"Gigi, they're working to restore the electricity in Rouffignac," Jean-Marc said, "but the guides still push the train by hand."

"Grotte de Rouffignac will be perfect," Gigi said with great enthusiasm. "You'll love it, Five. Wonderful paintings and a tiny railroad that runs into the cave for four kilometers."

By the time we reached les Eyzies, the rain had turned to a light mist with shifting banks of fog rising from the warmer rivers. We left the main road shortly then kept branching off on ever-smaller roads. The last lane ran directly between the house and outbuildings of several farms and folks standing in the damp doorways nodded at our passing.

Down a steep hill and into a thick forest, the road finally ended at a low, wide rocky ledge. A tiny wooden sign nailed into the rock read 'Grotte de Rouffignac — Admission 20 Francs.' The cave entrance was barely seven feet tall but quickly enlarged to a bigger room.

Three people sat at a deal table beneath a pool of light from an acetylene lamp. Gigi paid the 40-franc fee and we followed a young woman with a battle lantern illuminating our way. A young man trailed us with a smaller flashlight.

Gigi translated as Veronica, the young guide told us about the cave. "Before the War, the train was powered by huge battery cells," she said. "But the Nazis destroyed those because they thought the Resistance was hiding in the cave." She held the light below her chin and gave us a ghoulish smile. "They were."

"Now we are working to restore the electricity so the train can carry more visitors. It's all Louis can do to push one car with me and four passengers."

We climbed into a tiny car that resembled something from the mine in *Snow White*. Veronica sat on a higher seat behind us and Louis began pushing from the rear. The faint light from his helmet gave us slight illumination in the stygian cave.

"The carvings and drawings you will see date back 13,000 years, but first, we shall see a true wonder." She turned on the battle lantern and swept it across a broad room, dimpled with moonlike craters. "These are the dens of bears. Not one family of bears, mind you, but prehistoric cave bears who curled up here for tens of thousands of years."

We continued to roll through the darkness until Louis pulled the brake lever and brought us to a stop. Veronica stepped out of the car and shown her light obliquely on the wall. The outline of a wooly mammoth jumped out at us, a round flint nodule appearing to be his eye.

"This engraving is called 'The First Mammoth." Veronica recited. "Rouffignac was 'discovered' by four cave explorers just five years ago and this was the first artwork they beheld.

"But in reality, people have been coming to this cave since the mid-1500's and much damage has been done to the prehistoric engravings and paintings by them, including a bishop of the church who frescoed his name over a painting with candle smoke."

Louis pushed us through a cavern of wonders. Rouffignac's walls sported mammoths, horses, ibex, rhinos and other animals etched from the soft chalk. Deeper in the cave, the prehistoric artists switched their media to pigments and the paintings were magnificent, ending in a giant ceiling frieze of many animals.

Outside, we shared sandwiches and cider with the staff of the cave and chatted about the wonderful artwork. "Oh no, Lascaux isn't closed," Veronica stated, "but they're doing measurements on the amount of calcite buildup. There are rumors that it's going to be closed to the public very soon."

Lascaux was a Technicolor wonder compared to the monochromatic Rouffignac. It also had images engraved into the chalk walls. The colors in the Painted Gallery were still vivid, making the bulls and bison, which marched across the walls, seem almost alive.

"You should have seen it when the cave was first discovered in 1940," a guide told us. "The colors were much brighter. It's a shame but so many people have visited Lascaux and their breath has damaged the environment. We're working on an exact duplicate of the major galleries which should be ready in two years."

Bright sunshine greeted us on the way home, mixed with thick black clouds in the west. It was nearly four o'clock when we reached the

Tower. Gigi and I stretched out for a nap, which quickly changed to lovemaking and by the time we showered again, it was nearing six.

We changed into dark clothing. I wore a pair of black trousers borrowed from Jean-Marc and my tattered crew neck sweater. Gigi donned a similar dark outfit and twisted her hair into a knot to fit under a knitted watch cap. We each checked our weapon and ensured they were on safety. My little revolver tucked into a pocket in the trousers. Gigi's automatic slipped into her anorak.

The drive to Castelnaud was a matter of 15 minutes. Beyond Beynac, we crossed the Dordogne and drove up the winding road through the village.

"Lord, you'd have to be a goat to live here," I commented. No two streets seemed on the same level. Above it all loomed the Châteaux itself, its steep walls and turrets forbidding in the waning sunlight. "And where is everyone? This is like a ghost town."

"This is one of the poorer villages in the Dordogne," Gigi responded. "If the Château ever gets restored, the economy may come back. But for now," she paused, "many of these houses are as empty as the castle itself."

Thunder rumbled in the west. We made our way to the edge of the Château's grounds. A path led up the hill then switched back toward a gate where a tiny watchman's shack perched. Gigi left the path and began to climb the hillside away from the gate.

Moonlight suddenly appeared from clouds scudding across the sky then vanished just as quickly. "How do we get in?" I whispered.

"Any number of ways," she whispered back. "The walls are riddled with holes and cracks."

We found a broken place in the outer wall and crossed a grassy area and a filled in moat. At the corner of the castle itself, two narrow doorways gaped open and we were inside Castelnaud. It was truly gloomy in the fading light. Gigi led the way to a curving staircase and we proceeded up by the light of her small flashlight.

Landing after landing led to each of the many levels of the huge pile as we climbed the staircase. Finally, we reached the top and emerged upon a narrow battlement walkway overlooking the village. The battlement walls surrounded a courtyard 30 meters below and led to the huge square tower. We followed the walkway until we were on the wall overlooking the river. This passage was more narrow and led to the base of the castle's central tower.

I peeked over the edge and was swept by a wave of vertigo. It seemed like an endless drop to the cliff below. Gigi took my hand and we edged toward a smaller tower with a doorway.

The old wooden door was ajar and we cautiously slipped through onto an even narrower rampart. The door behind us creaked and slowly closed with a distinct click.

"My god, Five. See if it opens," she said in an alarmed whisper. I tried the handle but it wouldn't budge. The newest passage had a wooden floor and we quickly recognized it was a small drawbridge, which trembled as we crossed it.

"This way Mlle Marchant," a hollow voice instructed, "toward the donjon." We found ourselves facing a door in the tower wall with a small barred window. As we stepped off the drawbridge, it suddenly began to rise behind us, leaving us on a narrow walkway about five feet long and a drop-off where the bridge had been.

Gigi drew her pistol and approached the door. She turned the handle but the door wouldn't open.

"I am Wolfgram," the voice said in a flat tone. "We share the same goals. But I have not invited you in. So listen carefully. My daughter told me of your kindness to her. She said she thought I could trust you."

"Your daughter?" Gigi queried.

"Anna Stansbury. I have treated her like a daughter since her mother died seven years ago."

"Yeah," I growled, "she told us."

Thunder continued to rumble and flashes of lightning down the valley broke the evening darkness.

"To the point. I have information that leads me to believe your father is alive," Wolfgram said. "For that information, you must perform some tasks for me. I *must* retrieve the list."

"What list?" Gigi asked with an air of innocence.

"You know what list because your friend here knows. Isn't that right, Monsieur American? I remember you from one night in the city of Baltimore."

"All right, but why can't you get the list? You hid it, didn't you?" I asked.

"Because of the Dark One... Roituer. You must beware of him. He's an animal who delights in doing the bloody work of his Russian masters. He wants the list without paying me. And he's furious because I've taken measures to hide it.

"Anna is also sure that he followed you from the gallery," he added.

"So how do we go about getting your list?" Gigi asked.

"Anna has already given you a key. You will understand when you see the rest."

"You mean this," I asked, holding the corner scrap of painting.

"Yes, that is the key. It was supposed to go to Monsieur Marchant. I believe the Americans would have paid. But you will do, mademoiselle, as you are his daughter."

A nearby bolt of lightning was followed by a rapid crash of thunder. We both instinctively ducked as the first sheets of rain swept in.

"All right," I said. "but isn't this a pretty flimsy way to retrieve the list? I'm beginning to have my doubts about the importance of this list."

"Oh, you'll discover how important. In the wrong hands, every allied agent in Europe could be exposed and killed," he said calmly.

Gigi asked, "How do we contact you?"

"I will contact you and," his voice seemed fainter, "don't forget, beware of the Dark One if you wish to live."

"He's gone and the damned door is still locked," Gigi screamed. "We're getting soaked. What do we do now?"

I pulled her down into the corner of the doorway and wall and we huddled from the driving rain. Lightning and thunder were constant now. It felt like we were inside a kettledrum.

With the flashlight, I studied the door. Only a wrought-iron handle protruded. "We could try to shoot this handle away but I don't think our caliber is heavy enough," I mused.

"I'll bet he made the drawbridge go up. Probably just to delay us so he could get away," I walked back to the edge of the drop off and scanned the light at the drawbridge. A single length of rope dangled from its lip, seductively out of reach.

"I'm freezing," Gigi's teeth chattered. She clung closely and pulled the anorak over both of us, then thrust icy hands under my sweater. I did likewise and slowly our bodies warmed a little, but not in the way that would help us survive. Rain kept falling heavily but the electrical part of the storm moved on up the river slowly.

"If we can get the watchman's attention he can come up and let us out," I said.

"If there is a watchman. He's probably at home in front of a fireplace, drinking a warm cider. We were so dumb not to have Jean-Marc follow us."

The rain abated a little and I stood at the railing to look down. No houses below, just the cliff and the river beyond. The village was all on the other side of the Château. I pulled out the Smith & Wesson and fired three rounds into the air.

Twenty minutes went by and we had no response to the international distress signal of three shots. I had two rounds left. Gigi fired three more shots then tried blinking an SOS with her little flashlight. It got darker and colder and the minutes ticked by.

We huddled and shivered as the village clock tolled ten, then eleven o'clock. Gigi's body was wracked with shivering and I rubbed her vigorously. "I'm not sure we can last until morning," she chattered. "What's the word in English for *hypothermie?* I wish I had brought a rope.*"

"To hang ourselves with?"

"No *imbecile,* to climb with. I could rappel out of here in a minute," she said.

"You're a mountain climber, Gige?"

"Not exactly, but a rock climber. Many French women love to climb and we're as good as the men in many cases." She looked up at the sloping timbers which braced the hoarding parapet maybe ten feet above us. "Five, I have an idea."

"No way, if it involves me dangling from a rope."

"I'm not sure I can do it in these soaking clothes." Already, Gigi was up and stripping off her sweater. She had a simple jersey underneath. She removed her shoes and socks, then her slacks, shivering in panties and the jersey.

"Get down on your hands and knees," she ordered, "facing the wall." She rubbed her hands together vigorously. I followed orders. "Now, I'm going to stand on your back and pick my way up the wall. When I tell you, slowly... slowly, come up to a crouch. Then as I get higher, you can try to get in a full standing position."

"What if I stumble or slip?"

"Don't! And don't think about it. But I should be able to hold my grip, even if you slip."

I assumed a hands and knees position and Gigi crawled onto my back. I felt her weight lessen as she found her first handgrip in the joints of the wall. Slowly, she made her way up the wall and with great care, I raised beneath her until she was standing on my shoulders.

"I can just reach it, Five, with a little jump. When you feel me jump, move out of the way toward the door. If I don't make it, I'll drop back to the parapet but I can't drop back onto your shoulders."

"For God's sake, Gigi, please be careful."

When her weight left my shoulders, I moved quickly away and looked up. She dangled by one hand from one of the diagonal timbers. Then she got a toe into one of the cracks and gripped the timber with both hands.

"Now I'm going to move to the left, away from the catwalk. I see an opening in the hoarding over there and I should be able to get through it."

With more fear than I ever felt at a circus, I watched Gigi as she effortlessly hand-over-handed her way across the face of the tower. She now hung at least 70 meters above the stony courtyard below. "S'not bad, Five," she grunted. "The wood is smooth with age... no splinters." She kept a running commentary, to reassure herself as much as me. "Arms are getting tired but almost there."

"I'm there. Now a toe-hold. Ahh. One good pull-up and if the door isn't locked..."

In an extraordinary move, Gigi lifted her body up until her head touched the floorboard, then kept going as the door slowly raised from her effort.

"I'll be down to get you as soon as I can find the way, Five. Damn but it's dark up here.

In less than 15 minutes, Gigi called through the windowed door, then appeared in the open doorway. We hugged in triumph. She quickly jumped back into her clothes and picked up the little flashlight. "Let's get the hell out of here," she muttered.

"Gigi, that was wonderful. I've never seen a girl do anything like that, except in a circus."

"I can't say it was nothing," she said, "look at my hands." The light showed scraped calluses and peeling skin. "We might have survived the night but I'll tell you, that old bastard is going to pay for these hands."

With weapons drawn, we inched our way down the spiral staircase. This time we headed for the main gate and left Castelnaud by the path, past a closed watchman's shack.

"Damn! We could have fired all night and no one would've heard us," I observed.

At the 2CV, Gigi raised the hood and pulled on a small ring. The radiator screen rolled down. Almost instantly, the little engine began to throw heat into the car.

"I'm starving. We'll stop by the farmhouse," she said, "cause I know they'll be worried. Silvie can find some eggs and sausage."

Silvie and Jean-Marc appeared in the lighted farmhouse door as soon as we drove into the courtyard. They both looked alarmed as we dragged ourselves out of the Citroen.

"What happened to you?" Silvie cried. "We were worried sick."

We took turns telling the story of our Castelnaud adventure. I thoroughly enjoyed telling the part about Gigi clambering across the wet tower wall and saving us.

"She's part ape, that one," Jean-Marc commented. "I've seen her hang by one hand 200 meters up on a sheer cliff. What kicks she gets from climbing are all hers. I want no part of it."

61. The Rainbow Village

Thursday's storm was erased by Friday morning sunshine. Gigi was gone from the bed when I awoke and I found her in the kitchen, frying eggs and slicing sausage.

"Bonjour, Five. You slept like a cadaver," she said.

"Thanks a lot. And we could've been cadavers if it weren't for your ape-like skills," I grinned.

"Actually, I like to think of myself as a chamois, tiny and sleek, hopping from ledge to ledge." She inhaled a cloud of Galouise and with a kiss, blew it into me. "Are you ready for breakfast?"

Later, we drove up the hill to les Millandes and parked in the curving drive. A group of kids scattered and ran around the house as we approached.

As we walked toward the entrance, a lithe brown woman came trotting around the corner of the Château. I recognized her instantly from the photos I'd seen, taken 20 years before.

"Bonjour, Mlle Baker. Comment alle-vous?" Gigi called.

"Bonjour!" she trilled then switched to English. "And you must be Miss Marchant? You're as beautiful as your mother was."

"Thank you for speaking English," Gigi asked. "My friend here, Monsieur Five Lowrey, doesn't speak much French."

"But of course," Josephine answered. "Please join me on the terrace for some tea or coffee."

293

The broad terrace overlooked the rooftops of the village of les Millandes and the river beyond. Josephine motioned for us to sit in some canvas sling chairs then sent one of the older children into the Château for tea.

"You are English? Mr. Lowrey," she questioned.

"No ma'am, American."

"Ah American. My ex-country 'tis of thee," Josephine intoned. "and my cross to bear. My husband and my so-called friends are advising me to go back again. I'm not sure I could."

"Why not?" I inquired.

"Oh, it's a long and torturous story," she said. "I went back in 1936, expecting to be treated like a big star... as I was here in Europe. What a disaster. Audiences shunned me. Critics were cruel. My entourage and I were forced to go into our hotel — the Waldorf-Astoria, no less — through the kitchen and ride a freight elevator."

"No country should treat a Negro person in that manner or a person of any color," she stated vigorously. "If I do return, it will be under different circumstances."

As the morning drew on, Gigi and I adored Josephine Baker more and more. Here she was, a big star, visiting with us as if we were next-door neighbors. One by one, her ten children of the Rainbow Tribe came out and accepted their polite introductions.

Josephine took us into the Château and led us through each room, including the dining room where we had a lunch of cold truffled potato soup and American bacon, lettuce and tomato sandwiches.

Finally, I said, "Miss Baker..."

"Josephine, please Five!"

"Josephine. This has been a wonderful morning but we're also here to ask your help, if you can."

Gigi added, "You may have heard from Silvie that my father has gone missing in the course of an investigation. We've been given reason to think he may be in the Dordogne."

"And how can I help?" Josephine asked.

"During the war, when you worked with the Resistance, did you know the identity of any other agents?"

Josephine frowned. "Oh, but that would still be classified, I'm sure. But why do you ask?"

"There's a man who is our only lead to where my Dad might be and we know he's in the Dordogne," Gigi said. She went on to give Josephine a brief synopsis of our adventure at Castelnaud.

"When he was in Vichy, we're told he went under the name 'Longmont'." Josephine's huge eyes got even bigger and she inhaled a shudder.

"Longmont, that bastard," she muttered. "Oh yes, I recall him. He came from Paris and was a big cog in the evacuation chain. Helped transport escapees from Rouffignac to his station in le Bugue."

Gigi gave me a sharp look. "Anna mentioned 'bugs' but *le Bugue* never occurred to me."

"Where is it?" I asked.

"Not far from here, about 30 kilometers... near les Ezyies," Josephine answered. "The filthy bastard. So he's back?"

"Why is he a bastard?" Gigi asked. "I mean, we know he is but what's your reason?"

"It was in late 1942 when he arrived. Had good recommendations from a cell in Paris. Of course, they were Communists," she noted. "I worked for the Free French and there was rivalry but... we all worked together most of the time."

"Everything went smoothly for more than a year. The traffic in downed airmen, and returning OSS and SOE agents was increasing every month. Longmont was established in a little house in le Bugue and the next step on the escape route was a boat down the river to a town called Lalinde."

"That was about all the distance that could be traveled at night on the river," she said. Josephine's narration was expansive with much eye rolling and waving of hands. "So long as the Melice was the policing authority, the route worked beautifully. We lost only one in that period and he drowned after falling overboard."

"Then the Nazis came and the Gestapo started *assisting* the Melice in rounding up Jews for transportation and generally terrorizing the Dordogne. They came to my home, right here, and took the place apart.

"In a few weeks, we lost two Allied agents in the woods near Rouffignac. Then the Gestapo totally destroyed the nearby village of Rouffignac," tears were forming in Josephine's eyes.

295

"One night three agents were put on a boat from Longmont's home in le Bugue but when the boat pulled away, it wasn't our Resistance fighters on board but Gestapo. All three agents were taken into custody and executed in the square at le Bugue the next day."

"Longmont disappeared that same night," she wept softly, "and we left for Algiers two days later."

"Do you remember the house in le Bugue?" Gigi asked softly. "Could he have returned to it?"

Josephine answered, "I believe the slime paid for it when he arrived. There's a chance... even after all these years... that he could still own it. I know he was never brought to justice for his betrayals."

"It's an ancient stone house on rue Dordogne, the street that runs along the river. The house sits on the river bank and has a landing in its lower level." She stopped and thought for a minute. "As I recall, it was five houses down from the fountain in the little square of rue Dordogne. Or perhaps six."

"You can recognize it by the stone lintel over the door. It's a 'plague carving' and depicts a skull and one bone, plus the date. I believe it was 1540 but can't remember exactly."

With a promise to visit Josephine again and tell her of our progress, we left les Millandes bound for les Bugue. The road from St. Cyprien went overland to the Vezere valley so we stopped at the farm and told Jean-Marc of our plans. We also picked up our pistols.

Le Bugue was a picturesque small town with graceful willows hanging over the fast-moving river. Gigi found rue Dordogne easily and we parked the car near the fountain described by Josephine.

"I've never been here before," she commented. "It's a cute little town." We walked along the cobbled street, checking each house on the river side. "I'm glad Josephine didn't just say 'it's a very old house' because all of these places are ancient."

The sixth house was more ancient looking than its neighbors. A pitted stone façade was pierced by a thick wooden door and one heavily shuttered window. Over the door, a faint outline of a skull with a long bone emerging from its jawless mouth was carved into the lintel. Barely visible was the date: 1541.

We walked past and conferred. "What now?" I asked. "Just go knock on the door?"

"I can't think of anything better," Gigi answered and we walked back to the doorway. Gigi pounded firmly on the door, which didn't even tremble. The street was empty at mid-afternoon so she withdrew her automatic and used its butt to hammer on the door again. This was followed by the faint sound of a latch being turned and the locking bar sliding open.

"*Oui?* What is it? Who is it?" a quiet but familiar voice asked as the door opened a crack. Gigi thrust the barrel of her pistol into the crack.

"Who are you expecting, Monsieur Wolfgram?" she asked. "And now... you'll let us in or I'll shoot."

The door opened slowly and we got our first look at Wolfgram, our prey and our nemesis. An unimpressive look. He was shaggy and unshaven. Workman's trousers and a tattered shirt covered his corpulent body. His feet were in shaggy terrycloth slippers. Wire rimmed gold spectacles sat on his fat little nose. He looked like a ratty old man, not the evil personage who might have killed us the night before.

Gigi motioned him back into the room with her pistol. Then pushed the door violently open to trap anyone who might be hiding behind it. The door hit the old wall with a terrific bang and Wolfgram jumped. With my S&W in hand, I jumped into the room and made a quick circuit with my eyes. Wolfgram limped across the room and sat heavily in a sagging chair.

"No one is here," he said tremulously. "Were you followed?"

"Hmpff, I never gave it a thought," Gigi answered. The look of fright on Wolfgram's face increased. "Who would follow us?"

"Why Roituer, of course. You're the only way he can find me," he cried out. "You fools. You've probably led him to this street. Bar the door! Quickly!"

I stuck my head out the door and surveyed the empty street. Then I closed the door and slid the heavy medieval beam across its brackets.

62. Wolfgram's Story

"For more than 35 years, I have served espionage masters in Hungary, Austria, France, Nazi Germany, Russia, even America. And in all those years, I have compiled a secret list... the legend names and real identities of agents, sleepers, stay-behinds, whatever they're called."

"As you appreciate, it is a list that could cause great havoc throughout Europe and America. Informants, agents, assets, could be eliminated wholesale. Nations could fall."

"I was determined to live a decent life in my final years, if I survived to see them, by selling this list to the best bidder. Two years ago, I put out the word that the list *would* be available. Everyone paid some interest but it was the Germans... or the Russians behind them... who really responded."

"How so?" I asked. "Didn't you establish rules for bidding? Dates?"

"And why would the Russians or their East German toads pay any attention to rules?" he responded. "They immediately sent Luc Roituer to Paris under the legend of a young, soon-to-be famous photographer. And he was a damned good photographer," Wolfgram added. "But his name means roughly *Killer of Kings*. He's perhaps a Bulgarian but certainly KGB."

"He has one job and that is assassination. Just his presence in Paris was enough to frighten me, the famed agent controller. But he became *my* controller. And I lost control of my list and my plan."

Gigi wanted information on her Dad but allowed me to take Wolfgram back to the meeting in Baltimore.

"The Russians knew I had contacts in the U.S. Army and other branches of American intelligence. Roituer insisted that we include American operatives in the list, although I only knew a few cover names.

"The man you knew as Willi Behrens had been supplying me with excellent information... technical and weapons stuff... since I recruited him in 1945. Roituer insisted that we force him to search the Army Intelligence files for identities to go with the cover names we had.

"I was reluctant to expose Behrens to such compromise but after a session with Roituer... he broke three of my toes... I agreed to accompany him to the States and meet with Behrens.

"He wangled an assignment from a magazine and I met him in Baltimore after a few days."

I interrupted. "That was the meeting we had the surveillance on... the meeting where I glimpsed you getting into the cab?"

"That's right," he answered. "Roituer wanted to meet Behrens alone. He took the girl along as cover and passed a message that demanded Behrens obtain the names of four agents."

"Fox, Badger, Eagle, Mouse," I intoned. "All recruited here in the Dordogne by Sam Marchant."

"That's correct," Wolfgram answered. "Several nights later, Behrens notified us to meet him in an apartment in the outskirts of Baltimore. It was then the fool told us he *could* get the names but he would want a huge increase in payment for the list.

"Roituer lost his temper and insisted Behrens already had the names. He was wrong as it turned out. He beat Behrens, then injected him with something, but Behrens wouldn't talk or he couldn't tell us anything, as he maintained the whole time."

"We searched the apartment thoroughly... really tore it up... even the picture frames I'd used to convey secret messages. I was very proud of those frames." Wolfgram rubbed his hand across his eyes. The wide white track of an old scar on his left thumb caught my attention.

"Then we dragged him out to his car," he continued. "Roituer drove and I followed in our rental. We took him to an old shack and pier where Roituer proceeded to lop off a fingertip every five minutes until Behrens talked. He never talked. Finally, we tied him to a piling and Roituer garroted him."

"Why the fingertips?" I asked. "to obliterate his real identity? Or just plain torture? I mean, you *are* the person Sam Marchant interviewed in Fussen, Germany, in 1946, right? I've seen the original fingerprint card and it matches that big scar on your left thumb. The mismatched fingerprint cards are what put us on to you in the first place."

Wolfgram jumped and stared down at his thumb as if it had just sprouted. "For Roituer, I think the sheer joy of hurting someone substitutes for information. He was ecstatic when he garroted Behrens. I was sad since Willi was my nephew. I slipped him on the train to Nuremberg to escape the Nazi hunters. I never thought about the fingerprint cards… so long ago."

"And my father?" Gigi said. "How did he come to find you again?"

"When we got back from the States, Roituer went on a rampage. He's a big man and it was easy for him to push me around, beat on me… and Anna as well. I determined to hide the list from him and get protection from the strongest bidder."

"Then one day, Sam came into the gallery. At first I thought he didn't recognize me but he was investigating the death of one of his stay-behinds. Badger was an auto mechanic in Souillac and somehow Roituer found him, obviously got no information, and garroted him."

"I thought Marchant knew about the list and said some things that aroused his interest. My big mistake. I was so flustered that I forgot my tradecraft. Sam obviously followed me when I went to my advocate and then when I bought tickets for Sarlat."

"Two days later, I spotted him in Sarlat. I contacted my old Resistance cell and had him kidnapped."

"You what?" Gigi screeched. She raised her pistol threateningly.

"Had him kidnapped. How could I get on with my project with Marchant following me all the way."

"So where is he?" she screeched again. "Tell me you bastard… or you won't live out the hour."

"Tomorrow is market day in Sarlat. One of my associates has been instructed to cooperate with you when… should I say if?… you approach him with the key." Wolfgram paused, seeming more confident as he outlined his scheme. "You will understand when you see it."

"My brother Auguste has been entrusted with the list. I am confident you'll find him and… when you do, show him the key and tell him you are sent by Longmont. Bring me the list and I'll have your father freed. Fail to bring me the list... and I'll have your father killed."

Suddenly a loud explosion rattled the windows of the rue Dordogne. I opened a shutter and peered through the window. People were staring out their windows and doors at the flames and cloud of black smoke from the area of the fountain.

"Gigi, I think your car has been blown up!" I shouted. She came running to the window. Neither of us noticed as Wolfgram scuttled through the room's other door, slamming it behind him. I turned and we heard the click of a key turning in its lock.

Gigi grabbed her warrant card and pistol in hand, ran out the door and up the street toward the blazing hulk of the 2CV. I went to the other door and tried its handle. Locked. From somewhere else, I could hear sounds... grunting, a muffled yell. I pulled the S&W and fired a round right into the lock.

The door shivered but didn't open until I fired a second round. Then, I shouldered the door aside and entered the next room. It was a small den that led to a kitchen. Both overlooked the river. To the left, a door stood ajar and revealed a set of steep steps leading down.

63. The Killer Of Kings

The stairs ended at a passageway that led off to a shadowed room. I slowly inched my way down the steps, my back to the rocky wall, my revolver at the ready. A couple of thumps and a final gurgling scream came from the room around the corner.

I leaped four steps to the bottom landing and crouched with my gun aimed into the room, suddenly filled with light as a door crashed open. I just glimpsed Roituer's tall figure leaping out the door. Wolfgram was lying in a pool of blood in the doorway.

Leaping over his body, I jumped onto a narrow landing stage by the river. By this time, Roituer was two houses away and disappearing up a set of steps. I fired one shot but obviously missed as he vanished around a corner.

The cough and crank of a motorcycle added to the sounds of sirens and claxons in the le Bugue afternoon. As I watched, Roituer sped across the bridge, his black leathers and helmet gleaming over a very dark motorcycle.

Back in the house, I found Wolfgram still alive but barely, an awful gash in his throat spurting blood into a growing pool. It was dripping through the cracks between the stones and down into the river below. His eyes were glazing over as he stared up at me.

"Gallery…" he gasped. "Place d'Peyrou…" and he died with the garrote still twisted around his neck.

Footsteps and crashing of doors upstairs caused me to be more alert, even though I had only two rounds in my revolver. Then Gigi called down the staircase, "Five, Five! Are you OK?"

"I'm OK Gigi, but Roituer got away." She appeared in the doorway, pistol raised toward the ceiling and behind her stood a very confused gendarme.

"My car is gone," Gigi lamented. "And our lead is gone. And... so is Roituer." Her eyes were blurring with tears.

"I think blowing up your car was a distraction which worked. And Wolfgram reacted just as Roituer knew he would, trying to make an escape. He escaped right into a garrote," I said grimly.

Gigi and the gendarme were on good terms, having first examined her burning car, then rushing back down the street toward the sound of gunfire.

Shortly, a small man entered and identified himself as Detective Inspector Laval. After a cursory inspection of Wolfgram's body, he turned on me and began a rattling interrogation in French. Gigi interrupted, "he is my associate Monsieur Laval and please speak English. I know you do."

His suspicions about my role in this grim scene allayed, Detective Laval began questioning Gigi about our being with Wolfgram.

"It's a Sureté case, I assure you," she said, "and a matter of the highest security of the Republic. I can't tell you any more until I've talked with my superiors."

I described Roituer and his motorcycle but all I knew was that he tore across the bridge. From there he could've gone to Bordeaux or Sarlat. Gigi watched as Laval and the patrolman carefully searched Wolfgram's body. She requested a set of fingerprints when the medical examiner did his autopsy.

Then we were free to go, to call Jean-Marc and ask him to come to le Bugue to pick us up.

64. Sarlat Market Day

We stood by the dripping, blackened hulk of the 2CV. Le Bugue's fire department had responded rapidly but the little car was a total loss. The crowd of onlookers had dwindled to a few curious kids and the admiring gendarme who alternated his stares between the burned car and Gigi's legs. Gigi had telephoned Jean-Marc who said he'd be there as quickly as possible.

"Wolfgram said a few words just before he died," I whispered to her. "My god, I've never seen anyone die before. Especially with his throat cut."

"What did he say?" Gigi asked.

"I'm not quite sure. His voice was weak and he was kind of... gurgling. But it sounded like Gallery... and then... Plas Payroo?"

"Could it have been Place d' Peyrou?" she asked. *Her French pronunciation sounded to me exactly like what I'd just said.*

"I think that was it. Does that make any sense?"

"Place d' Peyrou is a little square in Sarlat's old town, very near the cathedral." She glanced at her wristwatch. "We'll have to check it out in the morning... market day."

Just then, a small boy ran up to us holding an object in his hand. "Look lady, what I found." The gendarme moved quickly to us but not before we could examine the scorched and broken fragment of a radio detonator. Roituer had set the bomb off while he was already in Wolfgram's house.

Jean-Marc picked us up in le Bugue in a shiny powder blue Renault Dauphine which I hadn't seen before. After a cursory dinner of bread, cheese and pate, the four of us burned the midnight oil in Sam's old office in the Tower. Jean-Marc went off to recruit the goose farmer Pierre Hebard and his cousins to guard the farm.

Hebard, another ex-para from Indochina, showed up with a wicked looking little submachine gun. The cousins carried shotguns of various ages.

"If he exploded the car by remote," I surmised, "Roituer could have had a bug in the house and heard everything Wolfgram told us. Can you have the detective search for listening devices, Gigi?"

"My guess," she replied, "is that he followed us to le Bugue, planted the bomb and followed us to Wolfgram's house. I'll bet he was in the house the whole time."

"You don't think he intended to murder you?" Jean-Marc asked.

"No," I replied. "We think the bomb was a diversion. A diversion that worked. And if he overheard our conversation, then he wants us alive to lead him to the list."

"What's this key?" Silvie asked. "How will it work with Wolfgram dead?"

"Best you don't know," Gigi replied. "I just hope it's enough to lead us to the list... and to Dad!"

Jean-Marc and Silvie drove down the hill in the truck, leaving Silvie's new Dauphine with us to drive in the morning. Silvie's last words were, "please don't let my precious machine be blown up."

Gigi set an old fashioned alarm clock for five a.m. and we crashed into bed and fell asleep immediately. My inner alarm woke me seconds before the raucous clanging of the wind-up clock. I leaped from the bed and tried to shut it off before Gigi awoke but by the time I hit the lever, she was staring at me, the sheet falling to her bare waist.

"God, is it morning already?" she moaned. "Five hours sleep isn't enough."

I went down the stairs and turned the burner on beneath the coffee pot, then jumped beneath the outdoor shower. Pre-dawn light was showing in the east but the lukewarm shower encouraged me not to linger. Gigi hopped under the spray just as I was finished.

"No fooling around, Gigi. There's work to be done today," I chanted her now familiar mantra.

By 5:30, we were at the farmhouse for sliced bread, coffee and a tiny glass of marc "for luck and stamina," Jean-Marc said. "Market days are exhausting."

By six o'clock, the Citroen truck was loaded with cartons of walnut oil, bags of unshelled nuts, a small crate of Hebard's pate fois gras, plus some other items to sell in Sarlat. Hebard and one of the cousins showed up to guard the farm and we left for Sarlat.

The old town of Sarlat de Canada, surrounded by the remnants of its medieval wall, was a bustling place when we arrived. We followed Jean-Marc's truck through an old gate and down a steep street to the Place de la Liberté, the town's biggest square. Jean-Marc backed the truck into his space so that its bed faced the open square.

He erected a canopy over the truck while Silvie set up a counter on two sawhorses and they were ready for business by 7 a.m. All around us, market stalls displayed fruits and vegetables, mushrooms, cheeses, wines, breads and other products of the Perigord.

"Let's look for the gallery," Gigi said, "although it probably won't be open for another hour. But shopkeepers do open early on market day. The streets will be filled with shoppers by eight."

We walked about four blocks toward an imposing cathedral and came to another square, not so large as the market square. "This is Place d' Peyrou," Gigi said. The cathedral and a large palace occupied one side of the square. The other was lined with old buildings whose ground floors were occupied by small shops and stores.

As we walked around the square and into its narrow adjoining streets — alleys really — we spotted four storefronts that proclaimed themselves galleries. One window was occupied by souvenir items. The other three displayed small paintings and drawings on tiny easels. All were closed.

We returned through an arcade beneath a 16th Century building and into a maze of narrow streets. Rounding one corner, we came upon a space occupied by about a dozen motorcycles. Nearly all were postwar Peugeots with their distinctive straight handlebars. Six were black or very dark colors.

We both glanced around the square, just now growing lighter as the sun moved higher in the sky. Gigi slipped her hand into her shoulder bag and said, "I only wish the le Bugue cops hadn't confiscated Dad's revolver. He'll be upset if I don't get it back."

"I'll be upset if I get shot at and can't defend myself." We examined each motorcycle but none displayed any clues that might lead us to Roituer. "I think we'll just have to assume he's here," I commented, "and he heard everything Wolfgram told us."

"If that's the case, the only thing he doesn't know is the key... what it is... who has it," she answered.

When we got back to the market square, it was filled with shoppers and their net bags and the cries of vendors proclaiming the superiority of their products. The Marchant's table was already half empty and Silvie was digging into the back of the truck for more walnut oil and fois gras. To kill time until the shops opened, Gigi and I strolled the square always keeping an eye out for Roituer.

At one stall, Gigi urged me to buy a small Opinel folding knife with a walnut handle. "It's not an Airlite Special," she said, "but it's a thing of beauty and will give you some protection."

We split up and wandered the different sides of the square. I doubled back several times trying to spot a tail if Roituer should be there. Once I glimpsed a tall figure ducking between two trucks but by the time I got there, he was gone.

As the clock struck ten, we were at the edge of the Place d' Peyrou. I watched from the shadow of the Cathedral as Gigi sauntered by the first of the galleries then nodded for me to join her. I casually strolled across the square and peered into the gallery.

"See anything," she asked.

"Nope. But how about the next place?" We walked a few steps further and turned into an alley that led to a tiny courtyard where two more galleries faced each other. In the window of the Gallery Estep, the display had been changed and now a small painting about the size of a magazine sat on an easel.

Gigi gasped. "Rocamadour!" she whispered, "of course." The painting depicted a sheer cliff topped by a Château, then dropping to a shelf covered with buildings, and finally a village at the bottom. The lower right corner of the painting was missing, revealing its white mount board.

307

"It's one of the most famous places in all France. That's why he couldn't just use the painting to tell where the list is hidden. Anyone could have recognized it," Gigi exclaimed.

I reached for the door handle but Gigi grabbed my arm. "Wait. What if Roituer's watching? I'll go in and you enter the other gallery. Wait a few minutes and we'll meet in the street outside, pretend to argue. Put on a show."

Inside the Gallery Estep, Gigi talked animatedly to the clerk, then looked at several paintings on the wall. I went into Gallery Fouche and pretended interest in the prints the owner had on display. Some were quite well done but all featured the motif of geese. I waited a few minutes after Gigi left her gallery, then walked through the passageway to the Place d' Peyrou.

We mimed an argument while Gigi told me, "The owner is Georges Estep. When I mentioned Longmont, he showed mild interest but denied anything without seeing the key. I asked him if the Rocamadour painting is for sale, and he said only with the owner's authorization. So you have to go back with the scrap. He does speak a little English."

Gigi spun on her heel and huffed down the street toward the main plaza. I went back to the Gallery Estep. Our painting had been replaced by another in the window. A bell tinkled as I pushed opened the door. A burly man in a shirt with sleeve garters eyed me suspiciously.

"Good morning," I said in English. "Monsieur Estep?" He nodded yes.

"Monsieur Longmont has sent me. I wish to buy his painting." I leaned over the counter and produced the scrap of canvas in the palm of my hand. He studied it for a second, then reached behind the counter and produced the painting.

"There is no charge," he said in a low voice, extending his hand. *"Bon chance, mon ami."* We shook and he carefully wrapped the painting in brown paper then tied it with a string.

Again, I sauntered casually back toward the market square, scanning the crowd of shoppers carefully. As I got to the Marchant's stand, Jean-Marc beckoned and handed me a paper bag, one of the few I'd seen in France. I almost dropped it, surprised at the weight.

"Something for your trip," he said. "Walk up the hill and wait by the fountain with the statue of geese. Gigi will pick you up in the Dauphine. I know you're going to Rocamadour so call if you run into trouble. We'll be home by 1400 hours."

As I walked away, Silvie hissed, "don't let Gigi get my precious Dauphine blown up."

65. Amadour's Rock

Gigi alternated between fast and slow as she wound aimlessly through the streets of Sarlat. I peered through my side mirror in search of a tail. In the paper bag, I discovered an oilcloth bag. In it was a huge .38 caliber pistol with a half moon grip and saddle-shaped hammer.

"A Webley," Gigi commented. "I know Jean-Marc brought home some souvenirs from Indochina but I've never seen that before. Still... it may come in handy."

She accelerated the Renault to a roundabout and made three circuits of the circular roadway. "Get ready, Five, cause here we go." With a jerk of the wheel, she skidded the little car into a turnoff at the last second and we sped down a tree-lined lane. "If we haven't lost him, we never will," she muttered.

While I cut bread and cheese with my new Opinel, Gigi briefed me on Rocamadour. "It's an ancient religious town. People come from all over France... all over Europe... to worship at the religious sites. The painting's really not very good but it's definitely Rocamadour."

We drove along with the Dordogne to our right and entered Souillac, the home of the murdered agent Badger. Then we turned south on a tiny road and eventually crossed the river and into some mountainous country.

"This was really Resistance country," Gigi commented as we drove up and down hill, around hairpin curves and over and under sheer cliffs. "Can you imagine the Nazis trying to drive a column of armored cars down this road?"

310

At an intersection, Gigi took a left and said, "Oh merde, Five. We've got company." I looked in the mirror and saw the black-clad figure of a motorcyclist climb on his bike and kick the starter. As he grew smaller in the mirror, he kicked again and again."

"I don't think he can get it started, Gigi! Does this road only go to Rocamadour?"

"I'll look for a turnoff," she muttered as the Renault roared through the tight curves with squealing tires. I watched the mirrors, finally turned around in the seat to watch the road. "Hold on," she cried and we went into a skid and left the road for a gravel track nearly covered with bushes. A real moonshiner's turn!

"I hope the dust settles before he gets here," she cried. She drove slowly across a tiny stream, then up a slope and parked under the shelter of a cliff. Gigi killed the engine and we sat in silence. Her automatic was in hand and I fingered the weight of the Webley nervously.

Minutes went by and then we heard the whine of a motorcycle. Roituer flashed around a curve up the hill, then disappeared, reappearing quickly on the next curve. He took the curves almost horizontally in classic racing form, whizzing by our turnoff lane down the hill. We waited and watched as he kept reappearing on the curving road to Rocamadour.

We got out of the car and stretched in the shade of the rocky overhang. The small road wound around the cliff and out of sight. Sooner or later, Roituer would make enough speed to realize he had lost us. Gigi reached into the glove box and pulled out a Michelin map.

We spread the map, about the size of a poncho, across the trunk of the car and she traced the route from Sarlat. "Here's the intersection back there," she said, "Cales. So here's our turnoff," she poked at a tiny white road that wound southwest of Rocamadour. "We can stay on this and then come into the town from the south."

"Are you sure the map is that accurate?" I questioned.

"Five! Michelin maps are the best in the world. See this village? Couzou? See the two little black blocks on each side of the road?" I nodded yes. "I can guarantee you that Couzou will

311

have two blocks of built-up houses, probably a boulangerie and a tabac."

We got back in the Dauphine and I tucked the Webley into my waistband where it dug at my stomach. Gigi set us off for Couzou, barely making five kilometers per hour on the rough, graveled road. "I don't want to raise any dust and I don't want to get there too early."

"Come to think of it," she added, "we'd probably throw Roituer off the track if we didn't show up in Rocamadour today at all." We slowed to a halt and she rested her forehead on the wheel. "Tomorrow is Sunday and it'll be a big pilgrimage day. The town will be crowded. That will work to our advantage and maybe Roituer will believe he's lost us… or we weren't going to Rocamadour in the first place."

An hour later we entered Couzou with its boulangerie and tabac as well as the predicted two built-up blocks of homes. "Is this where we stay?" I asked.

"I don't think so," she commented. "According to the map, we're only about two miles south of Rocamadour so if Roituer wants to, he could scour the countryside on that Peugeot and spot our Dauphine easily." Pause. "I sure wish I still had my little beat up *dueux cheveau,* there are millions of them."

We drove across the main road to Rocamadour and continued on a tiny country lane. About a half mile out of Couzou, Gigi pulled into a rutted farm lane and drove several meters. Branches and weeds slapped at the side of the car.

I sat amazed as she stripped off her jersey. "Give me your shirt, Five. It won't fool anyone but he'll be looking for me in the black shirt instead of your green one." I removed my forest greet shirt and handed to her, admiring her exposed breasts in the process.

Opening the trunk of the Dauphine, she found an empty picnic basket, a blanket, and produced a brown cloth napkin, which she tied over her head like a scarf. Then she swung the picnic basket on her arm and gave me a wave. "Stick right here. If he comes, use the Webley without question. I'll explain it away to the cops later."

And she strode off down the lane toward Couzou, a little peasant girl on her way to market.

Bare chested, I crawled up an embankment, spread the blanket and sat in a bushy clearing looking down at the Renault, the Webley in my lap. The afternoon sun dappled the floor of the clearing and the warmth of the day made me quite sleepy.

The lane was absolutely free of traffic until an ancient tractor with cleated iron wheels came by from the village, a wagon of hay in tow. As the tractor passed our farm lane, Gigi hopped out of the hay wagon and gave the farmer a cheerful wave.

She approached the car carefully, one hand in the picnic basket where I knew her automatic was. "Five?" she called out softly. I watched from the shadows of the woods then gave her a low whistle. She looked up the embankment and I arose from my hide in the bushes.

"That was smart. You're really quite bright," she said with a grin as she climbed up the bank. "I could barely see the car from the road but if he'd come, you would've had an ambush." Gigi stood before me and offered the picnic basket. "And what a beautiful spot for an ambush."

"The bread's half a day old, stale by French standards. But there are two bottles of *vin de pays,* wine of the land, and some homemade cheese. So, we won't starve tonight."

"Where are we staying, here?"

"No, as pleasant as this is, I'd just as soon have a roof over my head. That was Monsieur Poudurac driving me back. He has a farm just up the road. He was a really nice man and offered us his barn. We can hide the Renault in the barn and as you could see, he has a load of fresh hay."

"I called Jean-Marc and told him where we are. He said that someone beat the gallery owner, Georges Estep, unconscious this morning and wrecked his gallery. That could be how Roituer knew where to intercept us."

With my new Opinel, Gigi cut slices of bread and smeared the soft, pungent cheese on it. The corks were sticking out of the necks of the wine bottles and she removed one of these with her teeth. "Ordinary wine," she commented. "They use the bottles over and over."

As the afternoon sun chased the spots of light across our clearing, I lay back and closed my eyes. I felt Gigi's head settle upon my chest. Opening my eyes, I found my shirt and her skirt hanging primly from a nearby limb. Our eyes met as she ran her lips up my chest.

"This *is* a most beautiful place, Five. I feel just like Eve," she whispered.

"You look just like Eve," I gulped as she reached down to unbuckle my trousers.

"We shouldn't waste this beauty."

Her body glistening with perspiration, Gigi tucked her legs beneath her and leaned back on her arms. My pencil flew across the sketchpad as I attempted to capture the artless, but desirable pose.

"We are well suited for making love, aren't we Five?" she smiled. "My body fits yours just perfectly." Pause. "Or is it the other way around?

"If you make a painting, can you capture these little spots of light?" she asked, nodding at the dapple patterns on her breasts. "It's the most fantastic light... and it must be paradise because there are no bugs."

As dusk settled, we reluctantly put our clothes on, gathered up the blanket and went back to the Dauphine. Once during the afternoon, we heard the whine of a motorcycle moving at high speed through Couzou. But now, the only sound was the beginning chirp of crickets and the far off lowing of a cow.

Gigi turned the car around carefully while I, brandishing the Webley, walked down the lane to the bigger road. Seeing nothing in either direction, I motioned her on and climbed in the Renault as she pulled onto the road.

"Monsieur Poudurac said it was just 400 meters to the left. He was so nice, offered to sleep in the barn with his wife, but I wouldn't hear of it." She gave me a sly smile. "I've always wanted to sleep in a haystack, just like Van Gogh's peasants."

314

We turned into a nearly hidden lane and up a small hill. To the right, a thick forest marched up the hill. Monsieur Poudurac stood in the farmyard and motioned Gigi to steer the car into a stone barn. He shut the door behind us and stood in the evening gloom.

In French he told Gigi, "I'll have some food down for you after awhile. And you should be safe here. I'll drive the tractor down to the main road and back to obscure any tracks you made."

Later, he brought us a pot of beef stew, 'cassoulet' Gigi called it, and some bowls. Combined with our *stale* bread, it was a delicious dinner. Poudurac lit a gnarled pipe and sat on a milking stool while we ate.

I listened while he earnestly talked with Gigi. She nodded several times and smiled.

"Monsieur Poudurac has an idea for getting us into Rocamadour without drawing Roituer's attention. The town is built along a river valley with the religious sites and the Château climbing up the cliff behind. He says we should drive his farm truck into town and park it at a place in the valley, then walk up to the town. On Sunday, he's sure we'll be able to get lost in the crowd."

Poudurac talked some more and pantomimed driving, making engine noises with his mouth. "He will drive our Renault by a round-about route and park it at the top of the hill, behind the Château. It's not likely Roituer will see it there. We hide the keys in each vehicle and can leave when we need to."

"It sounds like a good plan to me," I commented. "Are you sure it isn't a slick farmer's scheme to trade a crappy old truck for a new Dauphine?" I joked.

"I promised him 500 francs, left in his truck," she replied seriously.

They discussed the plan some more. Poudurac said he would bring some clothes of his grown children for us to try on in the morning. He advised us to not arrive too early, before the pilgrims started to fill the town. Then, he bid us good night and we pulled the bar lock behind him.

We climbed into the hayloft and we prepared a nest for the night near a small window. I found a soft cloth faintly redolent of some animal and spread it across the hay. Scudding clouds created flickering moonlight through the window, allowing me to admire Gigi's body once more as she removed her clothing.

Together, we entwined naked into the soft bed of hay, kissing and stroking. "Hmmm. This is better than in Van Gogh," she commented. "His peasant lady still had her skirt on."

The first soft rumble of thunder occurred minutes later. Lightning flashes became more frequent, as did the echoes of thunder. "It reminds me of Castelnaud," I commented, "but this is more comfortable." Gigi pulled our picnic blanket over us and we snuggled to listen to the approaching storm.

By the time the first raindrops rattled off the barn's roof, she was snoring softly.

It was still raining when morning came, heralded by faint gray light through the window and cracks in the loft's siding. In the barnyard, sounds of daytime activity rose up. I tried to get up without disturbing Gigi and when I did, she rolled into the depression my body had made with a sleepy snort.

Below, Monsieur Poudurac was dumping something into a trough where squealing pigs awaited breakfast. Perhaps sensing my presence, he looked up and gave me a small wave, which I returned. I climbed down the loft ladder and eased the door latch open, then walked into the muddy barnyard. The rain had turned to a foggy mist.

"Bonjour monsieur," I called to our host. He returned my greeting and indicated an outhouse when I pantomimed my need. When I returned, he stepped to an outside pump and worked the handle. I ducked my head and washed the straw out of my hair under the icy stream.

Then I followed Poudurac to the house. He indicated I should sit at a table under the porch eaves. Shortly, he brought a steaming cup of black coffee and a small jug of thick cream. Gigi's whistle drew my attention to the barn window. She waved, now wearing her black jersey from the day before. I indicated my coffee cup and she disappeared immediately.

316

She too went to the outhouse and I pumped while she washed her hands and arms. Straw clung to her jersey and skirt. "You look like Van Gogh's peasant woman today... just after a healthy roll in the hay," I joked.

"I itch," she said simply. Soon she was seated at the porch table with her own cup of coffee. "We can't go into the Poudurac's house with muddy feet like this." She indicated Monsieur Poudurac's yellow rubber Wellington boots by the door. "French farmers all wear boots or clogs to work outside."

Monsieur Poudurac came out and spoke to Gigi. "He says he'll bring some clothing for us to try. But we should take off our shoes and come in barefoot."

In the warm kitchen, we met Mme. Poudurac for the first time. She looked to be 20 years younger than her husband but still had a work-weary face. She stirred some scrambled eggs in a skillet of sausage grease and told us to sit.

Later, the Pouduracs produced a pile of worn clothing. Gigi held up a black shirt with a high collar and white piping. "I think this'll fit." She also chose a medium length skirt with tiny black and white checks, giving an overall gray appearance. A worn coat and gray scarf for her head completed the outfit.

My choices were narrower. A pair of brown trousers with a patch on one knee came closest to fitting me. A brown turtleneck sweater covered me up to my chin and I rolled up the sleeves. An old corduroy coat seemed too large but at Gigi's urging, I accepted it. "You have to look dressed up," she said, "even for a poor farmer. It's Sunday." It was topped off with a tweed soft cap which made me look vaguely like a Prohibition gangster.

The biggest problem was my faded and worn white tennis shoes which no one in France seemed to wear. None of the young Pouduracs had feet as big as mine. Finally, Monsieur Poudurac produced a pair of scuffed brogans. "His own," Gigi said. "I'll offer him some money."

We took our bundles of clothing back to the barn. Gigi stripped to her panties and marched back to the pump. I followed and manned the handle while she washed her hair and body as best she could with no soap. Mme. Poudurac appeared with a big smile and a huge threadbare towel.

In our new clothes, we looked the part of simple country folk into town on a weekend. Gigi carefully tucked her pistol and Sureté warrant card in the pocket of her coat. We put the Wolfgram painting in the string bag. We decided to leave the Webley in the Renault as it could be embarrassing if I dropped such a huge weapon in the midst of religious pilgrims. So my only armament was my Opinel knife.

At 10 a.m., we cranked up Monsieur Poudurac's farm truck, an even older 2CV than Jean-Marc's, and I drove carefully back through Couzou and north toward Rocamadour. In just a few minutes, we arrived at the bank of the River Alzou and parked near the footbridge. Since the truck couldn't be locked, Gigi tucked the key and an envelope of francs beneath the tattered floor mat.

From the footbridge, Rocamadour reared up like a sheer wall. The old village sloped up toward a main street which ran along the foot of the cliff. Gigi pointed out the *Cite Religieuse,* a hodgepodge of churches and spires clinging to a narrow shelf halfway up the cliff. Above that loomed the Château with a tall clock tower and ramparts that ran to the edge.

On the town side of the footbridge, we entered a parking area packed with buses and joined crowds of pilgrims making their way toward the town. Many of them fingered rosaries and marched with heads bowed, lips moving in prayer.

We marched with the crowd beneath a medieval gate at the lower end of the main street. I was amazed at the throngs. Guides thrusting flags and umbrellas skyward. Pilgrims everywhere. Even the shops were open on a Sunday morning, a rarity in France.

It began to drizzle again and we ducked into a creperie, ordered two coffees and split a hazelnut crepe. Gigi posed the question of the day, "now how do we find Auguste Wolfgram or Auguste Longmont or whatever his name may be?"

Gigi motioned for the waiter and asked him if he knew a man named Auguste. He responded with a Gallic, negative shrug. After a few more words, he went to the cash register and asked an older woman. She also responded negatively with a shake of her head.

After Galouises, we went back into the street and walked beneath a second old gate. I was amazed at what I saw next. Dozens of pilgrims were ascending a set of steep stairs on their knees. The crowd of penitents was thick and the uniform chant of 'Hail Mary full of grace...' gave the procession an eerie feeling.

A narrow space on the left side of the stairway was kept open for those who wished to walk up. Men in brown cassocks lined the stairs, offering assistance to pilgrims who faltered.

"Five, here's a thought," Gigi said. "What if brother Auguste isn't a relative? What if he's a monk?" We ducked into a shop selling religious medals, icons, rosaries and souvenirs.

"Excuse me?" Gigi asked the young salesgirl. "Do you know of a Brother Auguste?"

"Ahh, no. I'm not Catholic," she responded. "But there is only one order and any of the monks on the Pilgrim Stairs could perhaps help you."

We stood in line at the bottom of the stairs, awaiting our chance to walk up... not on our knees. As the stairs curved around a first landing, we approached a monk whose face was hidden in his deep hood from the rain.

"Excuse me, brother? Do you know of a Brother Auguste?" Gigi asked in French.

"But of course, my child," he responded pleasantly. "And if you wish to see him, you're in luck. He returned just last night."

"And where can we find him?"

"Why in the Museum of Religious Art and History. He's the director."

We continued up the 216 steps to a small plaza, *le Parvis des Eglises,* where staircases led up and down to at least six churches and chapels. Pilgrims were kneeling on every available level space and the amplified sounds of mass echoed throughout the plaza.

We followed a sign that read 'Musee' and came to a doorway in one of the newer looking buildings. Past the doorway, a long open hall was lined with paintings and tapestries. A small counter and turnstile prevented us from entering. A bell rang somewhere in the back and a short, fat monk with bottle-thick glasses hurried toward us. *"Bonjour mes ami,"* he said with a smile.

"Good morning brother," Gigi responded. "Do you speak English?"

"A little but slowly, please."

I spoke up. "We are looking for Brother Auguste. Is he available?"

"But I am Brother Auguste. How may I help you?"

Gigi reached into her coat pocket as I slowly withdrew the paper-wrapped painting from the string bag. The monk looked at me suspiciously.

"We are here on behalf of Monsieur Longmont," I said quietly, unwrapping the painting and sliding it over the counter. Then, from my pocket, I produced the star-shaped key. "We have come for the list."

Brother Auguste gasped. His eyes bulged, even bigger behind the magnification of his spectacles. "Monsieur Longmont, of course," he choked out. "The list. Of course. I must get it."

"We'll come along if you don't mind," Gigi said in a neutral voice.

"That will be 20 francs each," Auguste said. "Otherwise, the turnstile won't open." I deposited four 10-franc coins in the slot and we slipped through the turnstile.

We followed the squat friar as he hurried through the exhibition hall. Beams of pale light came into the hall from tall narrow windows in the outside wall. He paused at a door and extracted a ring of keys from his cassock. "I regret but you cannot come farther."

"You don't understand," Gigi said more threateningly. "We will come with you." She gestured with her hand in the coat pocket. He unlocked the door and we entered a narrow tunnel about 20 meters long. A second door was unlocked to reveal a large room of bookshelves, stacked high with publications bound in shades of white to buff.

"The secrets of Rocamadour," he murmured. "Our library holds documents from the Fourteenth Century. These are all bound in vellum... real vellum," he added, "the skin of unborn lambs."

"It's very interesting Brother Auguste but we are in a hurry and want this list. Right now!" I said vehemently.

Another smaller key from his ring opened a drawer in a small cabinet and he withdrew an oilcloth envelope. "Please, let's leave the library and go to my office," he asked. "We can talk there." We followed him back through the tunnel and waited while he locked each door. Then we entered an office with a desk and two chairs. I stood in the doorway while Gigi sat.

Auguste undid a string tie around the envelope and produced a small book, also bound in *real* vellum. It was about a half inch thick and roughly four by five inches. The covers were held together by a thin strip of the same vellum. He handed it to Gigi and said, "open it."

The pages were of a rough texture and the manuscript was tiny and in brown ink. "An Ordnance For The Behavior Of Women In The Church," she read. "The author is Francois Fenelon, Cambrai, 1683." She stared at Auguste who stood with a very pleased expression on his face.

I looked over Gigi's shoulder. "It's an old book, a very old book. But this isn't the list. What are you trying to pull, Brother Auguste?"

He took the book and held it up for us to see, the pages spread. "Our friend Longmont, or Wolfgram as many of us know him, is a very talented artist and even more skilled forger. The cover and outside eight pages are authentic."

"But the inside eight pages," he riffled them gently, "are the work of Longmont." We could see no difference from a distance of three feet in the manuscript as he riffled the pages. "Look more closely now." He handed the book back to Gigi who examined the inside pages.

"It is a list, written line after line, in the same hand as Fenelon's. It's amazing," she exclaimed.

"It is *the* list," Auguste said firmly. "And after you deliver it to Longmont, he will notify me and we'll proceed."

"You have a prisoner," Gigi stated. "We want him freed... now!"

"Sorry," the monk said smugly, "but only after Monsieur Longmont says to do so."

"That will be impossible," I growled. "Longmont is dead."

Auguste's eyes again grew huge behind his glasses. *"Morte!"* he exclaimed. "How can that be?"

"He was killed by an assassin named Roituer yesterday afternoon after he gave us the instructions to use the key. He promised that if we got him the list, he would have my father released," Gigi intoned.

"Your father? I don't understand."

Gigi produced her warrant card in one hand and revealed the pistol with her other. "Perhaps you'll want to study my warrant card. Sam Marchant, the man you kidnapped, is my father."

"Sam Marchant! Mother of God, I didn't kidnap him. I know where he's held... but I swear, I didn't kidnap him. I wouldn't have abducted him even if Longmont ordered it. I worked with Sam in the Resistance. I am Mouse."

"Then tell us if you know where he is," Gigi hissed. "Or I'll have you arrested for treason, espionage against the Republic. I'll see you... a man of God... go to the guillotine."

"Please," Auguste pleaded. He put his finger to his lips and looked around as if the walls were full of listening devices. Then he took Gigi's hand and opened the List book to the first page. Slowly he ran her finger across the word 'Fenelon'.

I slipped the list book back into its cover and then into the breast pocket of my jacket.

66. A Flight Of Escape

Wringing his hands, Auguste explained how the Château Fenelon had been used by his Resistance cell during the war. It is now owned by the family Maleville but is in the care of his old Resistance mates, Pierre Chirac and Georges Rostang, members of Longmont's stay-behind cell. "When Longmont brought me the list book, he said he might have some more entries for it but he never returned.

"Then he sent me a note saying a dangerous man had been abducted and would be held at Fenelon until someone claimed the list book in a proper manner," Auguste whined. "If I had known the 'dangerous man' was Sam Marchant, I would have called the authorities immediately.

"Your father saved my life several times."

He then instructed us on the best way to get through the pilgrim crowds and up to the top of the cliff where our Renault awaited. We hoped. Gigi reassured him that if we freed her father, she would tell him of Auguste's help.

Then blessing us with a sign of the cross, Auguste let us out a small door in the rear of the exhibition hall. Worshipers were kneeling everywhere as the priest's voice intoned the Mass over a loudspeaker. Gigi and I made our way down a staircase and across a crowded courtyard, then up another staircase.

I followed several steps behind her, constantly scanning the crowd for Roituer among the worshipers... anywhere. She entered a tunnel-like passage that led to a terrace and the Way of the Cross.

323

Suddenly, an arm shot out of a darkened doorway and grabbed Gigi by the hair. She staggered and the tall figure of a man in a long coat stepped into the passageway, reaching for her.

"Where is it, bitch?" he growled, swinging one end of a garrote around her throat. He didn't hear me running at him and with both feet, I landed between his shoulder blades. Gigi was up in an instant and running down the passageway.

People screamed and a small crowd formed around us. Roituer rolled over and looked up at me with pain and hatred. I hauled off and kicked him squarely in the groin, then took off after Gigi down the path.

"Here's the Way of the Cross," she panted as I caught up to her. The pathway serpentined up the hillside, each curve marked by a Station of the Cross. "Where's Roituer? What did you do?"

"I kicked him in the nuts," I grunted as we started up the path. "He's bigger and I didn't want to try to wrestle with him. I wish I'd had a gun. We could have ended it all right there."

At the seventh Station, a smaller path led off to the left, straight up the hill toward the Château. Nearly exhausted, we took the path and then plunged into a thicket of rhododendron to catch our breath. Shortly, we heard the crunch of gravel as Roituer hobbled up the path, one hand clutching his groin.

He kept going to the right, following the Stations of the Cross. With her automatic in hand, Gigi led me up the steep path to a small door in the very bottom of the Château wall. It squeaked as we opened it. We followed a set of steps upward and emerged in a tunneled portcullis, obviously the main gate to the Château.

"I think I see the Dauphine," I said. "Over there by those trees."

"You're right. Let's go," she said and started through the gate. Then the far gateway was filled with the outline of Roituer in his long leather coat.

Gigi spun and we both ran into the Château. "Up these stairs, quick Five," she grunted. We mounted a set of narrow stairs that led to the first level of ramparts. Looking back, Roituer was nowhere to be seen. "This way. If we can get into the Château, perhaps we can get out another way."

We ascended a second set of metal stairs, this one narrow and quivering with our weight. On the right, the wall of the Château dropped away two stories to the parking lot below where the blue Renault sat invitingly. We tried two doors jutting out of the sloping roof of the castle but both were locked.

Another rampart, even more narrow, turned left and led along the roof ridge of another building. It ended in a small square tower, much like the one at Castelnaud.

"I'll bet there's a staircase in that tower, Gige," I said. "You take the list book and wait for my signal."

I walked softly to the doorway in the square tower. Before entering, I opened my Opinel and held it up by my jaw as I would a revolver, the blade edge pointing out.

As I stepped through the doorway the force of Roituer's attack knocked me to my knees. The cord of the garrote dug into the cloth of the turtleneck. I twisted the blade of the Opinel as we staggered through the little tower room and onto a slightly wider rampart.

Roituer was wringing the garrote with all his strength as I sawed the blade of the Opinel against the nylon cord. Suddenly the pressure was gone as I severed the garrote and we tumbled over each other to the railing of the rampart.

I jabbed with the knife... another jab... as the giant tried to get his hands around my neck. My third thrust encountered flesh and he screeched and lurched away. The Opinel fell to the floor. I scooted back and tried for another kick in the groin. He jumped back at me with blood gushing from his thigh.

Roituer's move surprised me and suddenly my back was against the railing with him pushing at my throat. He screamed again as Gigi plunged my knife into his back just above the buttocks. As Roituer lost his grip and staggered away, I grabbed the collar of his leather coat and pulled it over his head, then dropped to my back and pushed against his body with my feet. Gigi shoved from behind and the assassin catapulted over the rampart railing into space. His scream faded quickly as he fell 450 feet to the courtyard of the Ecclesiastical City below.

We leaned on the iron railing and stared down at the spread-eagled figure lying face up below us. "Why didn't you shoot him, Gigi?" I moaned.

"I lost my gun, Five. Somewhere on these damn steps. I couldn't shoot him. All I knew to do was stab him as hard as I could. Thank heavens you had that knife." She put her head on my shoulder and cried. "That could have just as easily been you."

People in the courtyard were looking up and pointing. But no one else seemed to be injured by the falling assassin.

"Thank heavens," Gigi intoned, "the Mass is ended. Come on Five, there's work to be done."

67. Shots Fired In Anger

Once again, Gigi's Sureté warrant card kept me out of a French jail. Several people witnessed Roituer's assault on Gigi in the passageway, which confirmed our story of self-defense. No mention was made of the list or Brother Auguste's role in the affair.

Roituer's body yielded no identification other than a *Paris Match* press card. If the fall from the parapet hadn't killed him, landing with my Opinel still in his lower back would have.

The Rocamadour gendarmes promised they would search for Gigi's automatic. Gigi prevailed upon them to let her make a couple of telephone calls then we were free to go with promises to return for an inquest.

Monsieur Poudurac had done a good job of parking the Renault with the keys and my Webley hidden beneath the front bumper. We headed for the farm to return their clothing and thank the Pouduracs once more for their help. Leaving the farm, Gigi parked the car at the little lane where we'd spent the afternoon and we walked hand-in-hand to our sun-dappled copse.

"I'll always want to remember this place," I told her. "And I'll try to help us both remember by painting you in this scene."

We headed west by a different winding road to Payrac then entered a maze of tiny roads and lanes that marched northwest toward the Dordogne. It was nearly five o'clock when we entered the hamlet of Masclet and saw Jean-Marc's familiar farm truck.

327

We alighted and hugged and shook hands with Jean-Marc and his army, Hebard the goose farmer and the two cousins. All carried weapons, Jean-Marc's being a tiny machine pistol.

He handed Gigi the faithful .410 shotgun and made sure I still had the Webley revolver. Then we spread out the Michelin map and over Galouises, planned our strategy to rescue Sam from Château Fenelon.

"The Château is circled by two roads," Jean-Marc advised. "The main one goes in front and then down the hill into the woods. The other climbs the slope behind the castle and circles some pastures before joining the main road again."

"I was in the Château once as a small boy," one of the cousins added. "As I recall, there is the outer wall and then in some places, two smaller inner walls. It's a well-fortified place, even better than some of the Châteaux on the tall rocks."

"If you'll give us at least twenty minutes," Gigi's brother continued, "we'll go by the back road and use our hooks and ropes to scale that section of wall. It didn't look too steep when we drove over."

"Then Five and I go to the front gate and demand entry," Gigi said. "And we'll have some convincing reasons to be admitted," she said, nodding at my Webley and her shotgun.

By 1830 hours, we had driven to Fenelon and up its tree-lined lane to the imposing main gate. The late afternoon sun cast long shadows across the grassy slope that ran down from the castle walls. The gate consisted of two giant doors with a Judas door inset in one.

Not seeing a knocker, I picked up a big rock and pounded on the door, chipping away the dark red paint. I knocked several times before footsteps could be heard on the other side.

"Yes, what is it?" a voice called in French.

"Monsieur Chirac?" Gigi responded, "we have a message from the Monsieur Maleville from Telegraphiqe Francais in Sarlat. Your telephone seems to be broken."

"Nonsense," he replied. "I just used the telephone not 20 minutes ago." The little window in the Judas door slid open and Gigi poked the barrels of the shotgun through it.

"This is our message. Open up," she ordered. A bar was thrown and the door creaked slightly ajar. Gigi nodded at me and then pushed the door open with her foot. As she stepped through, a man on the other side scuttled back and aimed a pistol at her.

I jumped through the door and fired the Webley. It kicked and gave a giant report which echoed throughout the Château. The man's pistol vanished in a cloud of blood and smoke, along with several of his fingers. He dropped to the ground in pain, clutching the stumps of his hand against his chest.

"Are you Chirac?" Gigi asked.

"No, I'm Georges Rostang," he moaned through gritted teeth. "Who in hell are you?"

Gigi flashed her warrant card and pronounced, "Georges Rostang, you are under arrest for assault on a Sureté officer, abduction, unlawful imprisonment, espionage, and treason against the Republic of France. Where is Chirac?"

"You're too late, bitch," he hissed. "Chirac should be with him by now. You've already ensured that Marchant will die."

Another sound echoed through the Château walls, this time the stutter of submachine guns. Rostang's eyes grew big. Gigi ordered him to stand and we marched him into the Château through gates in a second, then third defense wall. We headed toward the sounds of gunfire… single shots punctuated by bursts of automatic fire.

Rostang resisted leading us so Gigi applied the shotgun barrel under his chin and informed him that as Marchant's daughter, she was very ready to pull the triggers.

"In the chapter room," he grunted, "down those stairs." He nodded to a long hallway with a set of stairs at the end. "For God's sake, give me something for my hand, please?"

I ripped a small tapestry from the wall and wrapped it around his bleeding hand. Then I used the hanging cord to tie his arms behind him. He screamed in pain. More shots rang out from below. I wrapped the cord around Rostang mummy-style, then kicked him in the groin and left him writhing beneath an ornate couch.

"That's probably a Fifteenth Century tapestry," Gigi said. "I wouldn't have wasted it on him."

Cautiously, we descended the stairs, weapons at the ready. A long hallway led off to the right and Gigi flipped a switch, causing electric lights in wall sconces to illuminate the passage. At the end of the hall a man whirled at the sudden light and fired at us with a pistol.

"Chirac," Gigi said as we ducked behind a large wooden chest. Splinters from his shots showered down upon us. Another round of automatic fire came from a slightly different direction and then we heard steps running toward us.

I peered around the chest at floor level. "Here he comes," I shouted as Chirac ran down the passageway, a machine pistol flapping from its shoulder strap. I jumped up and aimed the Webley, "stop there, Chirac. Don't move."

He grabbed for the machine pistol as I pulled the Webley's trigger. The roar from my shot was matched by a simultaneous blast from Gigi's shotgun. Chirac bounced into the wall, staggered back two steps then fell heavily.

A voice echoed down the passageway. "Gigi, Five, are you all right?"

"Ca va, Jean-Marc," Gigi yelled. "Chirac is down. I don't think there's anyone else."

Our four compatriots moved cautiously around the corner and up to the recumbent Chirac. One of the cousins prodded him with a shotgun barrel.

"He's done for I think," Hebard pronounced.

"We wounded another one by the second wall," Jean-Marc said. "But he wouldn't tell us where they are keeping Dad. Hebard wasn't very nice to him but I think he'll walk someday with crutches."

"Rostang is upstairs," Gigi said. "We've got him trussed up and willing to talk, I think. He told us Dad's in the Chapter Room, wherever that is."

Leaving the cousins to guard the hallway, we returned to the room where Rostang lay in a larger pool of his own blood. "It's over, Rostang," Gigi informed him. "Chirac is dead and you're on the way to the guillotine. Where is the Chapter Room?"

I unwound some of the binding so his legs would work and Rostang shuffled back down the steps, leading us into the passageway. He glanced at Chirac's body and shuddered. At the door where we first saw Chirac, a narrow set of stairs led further down.

"The chapel's down there. Move the big chest and you'll see the doorway to the Chapter Room," he said with a grimace and led us down the stairs.

The chapel was a simple room with one deep-set window that cast a long beam of the day's last sunlight. Beneath the window, a huge chest sat. Jean-Marc poked his machine pistol into Rostang's ear. "Are there any booby traps? Anything at all?" The bloodied Rostang nodded no.

Hebard put his shoulder to the chest and shoved, surprised when it slid easily away from the window. Another passage led steeply down six steps, revealing a head-high door in the wall.

"Where's the key?" Jean-Marc asked.

"Chirac had it. The only key to the Chapter Room."

Jean-Marc put his head to the door and called loudly, "Dad! Dad, it's Jean-Marc. Can you hear me?"

A faint voice answered but we couldn't make out the words.

"Stand away from the door, Dad. Get away." He waited a few moments, fired a burst into the keyhole, then kicked the door open just like in the movies.

The Chapter Room was long, with a row of benches on each side leading to an altar. Beneath the altar, a long glass case displayed the skeleton remains of some ancient. From behind the case in the darkened, smoke-filled Chapter Room, a grinning Special Agent Sam Marchant rose slowly.

68. There's Work To Be Done

The Marchant reunion was joyful with hugs and kisses, much backslapping and more hugs, the three of them dancing in circles. Sam looked remarkably fit for a prisoner in filthy clothes and short gray beard.

Gigi and Jean-Marc each introduced me and I shook hands with the CIC legend. We returned to the chapel and everyone took a knee at the altar, even Rostang who was prodded by my Webley. Each Marchant said a short prayer of thanksgiving. Most of them made the sign of the Cross then we arose and walked up the stairs.

Gigi used the Fenelon phone to call the police and while we waited, our stories were told and woven into one coherent explanation. I found some dishtowels in a kitchen and applied a makeshift dressing to Rostang's finger stumps.

"Lord, I never thought I'd see my children shooting up a castle like this," Sam grinned. "But I'm grateful, you don't know how grateful. I've known these three clowns since the war, worked with them even though they were Communists. Right here in this very Château. I never thought they'd carry through with killing me until today... when they suddenly moved me down to the Chapter Room."

"Do you suppose Brother Auguste called Chirac?" I asked of Gigi. She shrugged. "I didn't think he'd dare."

"Auguste?" Sam asked. "The Mouse? He had a role in this? The sneaky fat bastard would betray his best friend... even the Pope."

Gigi and I explained that Wolfgram-Longmont had ordered Sam's abduction in order to protect his plan for the list and how Auguste had maintained he knew nothing of Sam's identity. "Perhaps I'd better have him picked up," Gigi said.

"I feel so stupid," Sam said vehemently. "This whole episode started with a routine interview on some missing paintings. When Wolfgram said a couple of things that made me suspicious, I thought I'd keep tabs on him, especially if he were coming down here."

"So you're following Wolfgram, hoping he'd lead you to some missing artwork," I asked, "and he's thinking you're after the list?"

"Hell, I didn't even know about a list. Then I run into these old Commie Resistance types, the next thing I know they've stuck me with a needle and I'm in a dungeon." Sam paused.

"So our whole adventure has been two divergent cases slowly coming together," Gigi added. "And Wolfgram kind of outsmarted himself with the elaborate charade about the list."

The gendarmes arrived from Souillac and questioned us thoroughly. Gigi took credit for Chirac's shooting to keep me out of more French legality. I took credit for blasting away Rostang's hand. The cops expressed doubts about the legality of our entry method but Gigi pointed out that she, the Sureté agent, was operating with knowledge that a foreigner was held prisoner and crimes were being committed.

Finally, it was over for the night. We piled into our vehicles and headed downriver for St. Cyprien and the farm. When we arrived, Silvie and Hebard's wife had a huge feast prepared but the majority of our party stuck with wine and marc.

One by one, the cousins, then the Hebards, drifted off. The Marchant clan sat around the fireplace and continued to catch up. Finally, after a chorus of yawns we drove Sam up the hill to Gigi's Tower. It seemed to me we'd been gone forever, rather than just a single night.

"Please Dad, take my room," Gigi said. "The bed's nice and fresh and you can sleep as late as you need to. Five's been sleeping in the tower room and I'll use the couch... or something."

333

Sam Marchant gave his daughter a wise look and a wink. "Or something? Well Gigi, I can certainly approve of your 'or something' more that fop in Paris when we last saw each other. I assume he's ancient history?"

Gigi nodded and put her arms around his neck. She kissed his grizzled cheek, then turned away and winked at me.

"Come on Five, there's work to be done."

THE END

L'Envoi

With hearings and inquests to attend, I received ten extra days of TDY from Bob Theriault and all the leave time I had coming, which turned out to be twenty more days. Gigi's boss, Michel Tossier, came down from Paris and eased our way through the inquests. Gigi was awarded a promotion and a certificate for her role in recovering the list and taking Roituer off the French streets.

Sam Marchant took my agent reports with him and traveled back to Paris to write his own. Then Gigi and I spent a glorious two weeks traveling the Dordogne and Perigord in her new Peugeot convertible. I drew and painted and after much work, even achieved a fine nude study of her in the sun-dappled glade.

We revisited Josephine Baker at les Millandes time and again, spending wonderful afternoons with her and even watching her sing and dance for her adopted children.

Finally, it was time to bid adieu to Jean-Marc and Silvie, and sadly, to Gigi's Tower. We climbed into the red Peugeot and headed north for Paris.

Anna Stansbury beams as she surveys the small storefront on rue St. Germain near the University of Paris. The sign above the door reads *'Galleries Stansbury-Marchant – Art et Photographie Fins'*. Anna looks as shiny and clean as the new gallery and she grins at us unabashedly.

In less than a week, Gigi has located the property and turned loose a small army of workmen to convert it from a defunct tabac to a gallery. Anna's collection of Wolfgram's photos have been re-matted, framed and catalogued. Seven of my paintings have received the same treatment, although small 'not for sale' or 'sold' stickers grace their frames.

It's hard for me to believe that in less than two months, I've helped solve a case and found a Paris gallery for my work.

We move from the sidewalk to the gallery's interior where the framed works sit in stacks upon the floor.

Gigi gives me a kiss on the cheek and a big hug. Then she says, "Come on Five. There's *work* to be done."

James Patterson
September 2, 2003

About the Author

James Patterson served as a special agent in the Army's Counterintelligence Corps in the early 60's. He has called upon his experience at the CIC's training school in Fort Holabird, Maryland, and in the field to create *Sphinxes.*

Patterson is a writer, photographer and retired graphic designer. He is a contributing photojournalist for *Mac Design, Photoshop User, Nikon Capture,* and *SBS Digital Graphics* magazines. He specializes in covering digital cameras, digital photography and imaging, and inkjet printing.

He is a well-published freelance travel writer. Patterson is a 1958 graduate of Ohio University in Athens, Ohio. He and his wife Betty live in Largo, Florida.